CLARE LITTLEMORE

Quell

This book was professionally typeset on Reedsy.
Find out more at reedsy.com

Contents

Dedication

To Daniel and Amy.

Brit Alert!

If you are reading this book and not from the UK, a brief warning that I am a British author and use British spellings throughout the book. In The Beck, characters wear overalls of different 'colours' (not 'colors'), might run towards (not toward) each other and may even, on occasion, have to apologise (rather than apologize).

Happy reading!

Chapter One

I sat in the darkness, shivering. All around me the silence hung like a heavy shawl draped around my shoulders. I should have felt comforted by it, but instead it seemed to press down on my shoulders, suffocating me. All night I'd felt like something was wrong. I had tried to dismiss my fears, telling myself it was nothing, but they continued to plague me.

The courtyard was deserted. Everyone who wasn't on duty was fast asleep. Guarding the main buildings of The Crags community was one of the lighter tasks we could be assigned. It didn't require a lengthy walk, and I had easy access to the rest of the citizens here, should assistance be required. Plus, the shift was almost over.

Still, I felt on edge.

It had been seven days since we had received the devastating news. The sickness, which had already torn through our new community, had been transferred to The Beck. And we were the ones responsible.

In an attempt to collect vital meds to save Barnes, we had unintentionally infected our old home. Despite efforts to make contact with the Beck Resistance, we'd heard nothing since. Knowing so many of the citizens were suffering and being powerless to help was horrible, not to mention the guilt I felt.

We had stolen from them to save our own people, leaving their stores of meds severely depleted. And while The Beck did not generally dispense medical care to the citizens in its Lower Sectors, it did produce drugs for those citizens in the more privileged sectors, and for emergency purposes. They were stored in Governance, for use in situations like the one the community was facing now. The loss of countless Beck citizens would be devastating. And without sufficient meds to combat it, we were all frightened for them.

The one thing I was certain of was that Cam had it. Anders' original message had been clear about that. Now, the lack of new information was driving me mad. No matter how many times I was reassured that The Beck would be prioritising the citizens in the Upper Beck, I couldn't rest easy that Cam was ok. When I did sleep, my dreams were haunted by distorted images of Cam's face twisting in pain, the way I had witnessed Barnes' in the days before his death.

Shaking my head, I tried to rid myself of the haunting thoughts, and focused on the space around me. I knew Harper would arrive soon. She was never late, and we often sat and talked when she replaced me on a shift. I enjoyed these chats, which occurred without interruption, a rarity now that Harper and Walker were often attached at the hip. Seeing them so happy together was painful for me, knowing how far away Cam was and being so unsure of his condition.

While I was disturbed by the idea of Cam being gravely ill, there was something else lurking in my mind, an uneasiness that refused to leave me. Yet the space around me seemed peaceful and undisturbed. I decided that I'd been standing still for too long. A final turn around the buildings would calm my mind and pass the final moments before Harper arrived to take over.

I stretched, easing the stiffness in my tired limbs, snapped on my flashlight, and cast it around the courtyard once more. There was no one in sight. I wandered to the building's main entrance, which was in darkness, as it usually was during the night. Continuing on, I rounded the corner of the building, passing under the windows of the dining room. As I did, a faint light caught my eye. I positioned myself to the right of the frame and peered inside.

The light was coming from the kitchen area at the rear of the dining room. I was certain that Baker, the only person I would usually find close to the stoves after hours, was in bed. I had seen her pass me, trademark grouchy expression on her face, several hours ago. And it would be very unlike her to leave a light on. I wondered if someone else had been in there after her.

The glass was dirty, which made it difficult to see inside, but the glow of a light was definitely there. I thought back to my earlier patrols: had I missed it? Had the light been on all along, simply forgotten by some careless citizen who had gone back to retrieve something once their shift was over? The explanation was reasonable, but I still couldn't shake my earlier doubts. Concerned, I hurried back to the courtyard. In my haste, I slammed into a body coming in the opposite direction. Startled, I backed away, my hand going instinctively to the knife at my belt.

"Woah!" The voice was definitely familiar. "You ok, Quin?"

Hearing my friend's familiar voice, I relinquished my hold

3

on the weapon.

"Sorry, Har. Don't know what's wrong with me tonight. I'm so jumpy."

Her face clouded with concern. "Still worried about..."

"I'm fine." I brushed her concern aside and moved past her. "Taking over?"

"Yes." She followed me back into the courtyard. "Get yourself off to bed, won't you? You look like you could use the rest."

"In a minute." I knew I couldn't leave without investigating. "There's a light on inside. Need to check it out."

"Someone probably just left it on." She frowned. "I hope no one sneaked in after hours. They'll be in for it if Baker catches them!"

"I'm not so sure." I frowned. "I want to check it out."

She looked surprised, but then moved closer. "Ok then. Let's take a look together, if it'll make you feel better."

I walked to the door of the main building again. There was still no light showing from this direction, and I eased it open slowly, wincing at the creak that it made. Flicking my flashlight on again, I made my way towards the door of the dining room, Harper on my heels.

Uncharacteristically, it was open. Peering inside, I could see nothing. Nodding to Harper to check the other rooms leading off the hallway, I slid through the door and into the space beyond. The tables were standing where they always did, empty for now of plates and cups. The benches on either side were all neatly stowed beneath them, ready for use the next morning. The light in the kitchen at the other end of the room was still blazing.

Working my way towards it, I could hear nothing. Deciding

4

that someone had simply forgotten to switch it off, I abandoned my caution and strode through the room, intending to turn it off and return to Harper. At the door though, the hairs on the back of my neck stood on end. One of the cupboards at the far end of the room was open, its contents having been emptied into a box which stood on the floor beside it.

A light left on by someone's carelessness was one thing, but a box filled with provisions, left in the centre of the room, in the middle of the night, was no accident. Something was wrong.

I raced back to the door of the dining room, stopping to check the hallway before I stepped into it. It appeared to be empty, for now. I had given Harper what I assumed was the easy job. With the light being on in the kitchen, I had decided to check that area myself, but now I had no idea where my friend was and who else might be in the building. There was really only one suspect and I knew before I set off down the hallway who it was.

Thomas.

The week since our trip to The Beck had been one of great difficulty. Although we were concerned about our friends back in The Beck, we also had problems here at The Crags which couldn't be ignored. Many of our citizens, myself included, had survived the sickness, but it had taken us some time to recover our strength. We had to hold a funeral and were still grieving. But worst of all, three of our small group had committed the ultimate betrayal by abandoning the rest of us at the worst possible moment.

Thomas, who had long made his disapproval of our community's leadership and their decisions abundantly clear to anyone who would listen, had literally run away from the area where we had been sheltering those who were sick, taking Allen and Johnson, two of his fellow Patrol trainees, with him. In a desperate attempt to avoid getting ill themselves, they had gone up into the hills and had been living in the caves ever since.

As a group, we had discussed going up there to try and speak to them about returning, but did not really have the manpower to spare since the illness had hit us hard. Rogers and Green, the citizens most of us looked to as our leaders, had considered it at length, and the decision had been made to leave the traitors until their eventual lack of supplies forced them to return. In the meantime, we were guarding our stores as best we could with the people we had left.

It appeared that, rather than face us, they were simply attempting to steal from our stores. And with our workforce still depleted, we couldn't afford to have them taking food we needed ourselves. Not without working as part of the team who gathered and produced it. A white-hot anger seized me as I gazed along the darkened hallway, wondering where they might be and how I might stop them.

At the far end of the corridor, one of the doors was slightly ajar. I edged towards it, hearing muffled sounds of movement. While I was trying to decide on the best course of action, the door opened further. A figure emerged, carrying a box loaded with additional supplies. He stopped abruptly as he saw me, panic emblazoned on his face.

It was not Thomas, but Allen. And he clearly hadn't realised anyone was wise to his presence. My hand went to the gun I had tucked in my belt. I disliked having to carry one, but knew that the situation I was faced with might require its use, at least as a threat. Sliding it out and bringing it in front of me, I pointed it in his direction, hoping against hope that he wouldn't be able to see how much my hands were shaking. We stood for several moments, suspended in time. He didn't look like he would attack me; in fact, the expression on his face had morphed from shock, to fear, and then to guilt in the time I'd been standing there.

"Sent you to steal from us, has he?" My voice was hard, bitter.

He flushed. "I... We..." He dropped his head. "We're hungry."

"And we're not?" I snorted. "How dare you sneak down here at night and steal from us?"

He remained silent, his eyes fixed on me, as though trying to gauge what to say next.

"Do you even know what's going on down here? You think we're so weakened you can just walk in here at night? That we won't have anyone on watch?"

Allen seemed to resent the insult to the sense of their plan. "We knew you were on guard. That's why we came in through the back. Through the window."

"And what exactly did you think would happen when we woke in the morning and didn't have any food to eat ourselves?" I spat the words at him. "You realise how selfish you're being?"

He opened his mouth to reply and then seemed to think better of it, allowing me instead to continue to rant.

"Barnes is dead. Did you know that?" I watched his face fall. "You didn't. We held a ceremony for him a few days ago, not that you'd care. But the rest of us? We survived. And we're getting stronger every day. Did you hope to come back and find us all dead, so that you could move back down here?

Just the three of you?"

Allen's gaze shifted. Until now, he had at least had the decency to meet my gaze, but at my final accusing question, his eyes shifted. I presumed for a moment that his shame had caused him to break the eye contact, but the voice which came from behind me sent a chill through my body, and suddenly I knew what he was looking at.

"Hello, Quin."

It was Thomas. And while I had a gun pointed at Allen, he was behind me, which made my own position far more vulnerable. We knew they had a single gun between them, and as Allen had no visible weapon, I presumed that Thomas did. A sinister click as he primed the gun left me in no doubt. I froze, wondering if he would actually shoot me.

"We don't want to hurt you." His next words were reassuring, but I still shook with anger at the thought of them walking out of here with provisions we badly needed and disappearing into the hills again. "All we want is to leave with the items in these boxes. We need them."

"We need them too." Still, I didn't turn. "We need them more than you. There are more of us."

"But we're starving. We haven't been able to catch much in the way of game: we don't have the weapons. All we're doing here is making sure we survive."

"But at our expense, Thomas. At the cost of others." I paused for a moment, wondering if I could shoot Allen in the leg and duck before Thomas managed to pull the trigger. "Look, I don't want to hurt anyone either, but I'm not prepared to let you go with supplies we badly need."

He sighed sadly. "I don't think you have a choice, Quin."

I turned slowly to face him, knowing before I did that I was

8

beaten. When I faced him, I could see that I was in no danger from his bullets. He had primed the gun, it was true, but it was not pointed in my direction.

Huddled close to his side, with Thomas' arm wrapped tightly around her neck, the barrel of his gun resting against her temple, was Harper.

Chapter Two

"Drop it." The command was brief, but indisputable.

Very slowly, I bent down and placed the gun on the ground in front of me. Then, raising my hands in surrender, I stepped away from it.

"We need to go." The command was aimed at Allen, who had not moved since Thomas began speaking. "Someone else could arrive at any moment."

Allen moved through the door, easing the box out through the narrow space. As he passed, he shot me a look which seemed to convey some kind of apology. I seethed quietly as he continued down the hall in the opposite direction.

Harper, who had been still until now, shifted slightly in Thomas' arms. He grunted, tightening his grip on her.

"What happens next?" I blurted out, afraid he would hurt my friend.

"What happens is Allen collects the other box from the kitchen, then we leave," he paused, as though gauging my reaction, "taking your friend here with us."

My stomach dropped away sharply, "If you hurt her—"

"I told you, it's not about that." He even managed to sound offended. "I don't want to hurt anyone."

As we contemplated one another in silent fury, Allen

returned empty handed and hurried back into the dining room again.

"She's just... *insurance*, shall we say," Thomas continued, "to make sure we get away safely. You can understand that, can't you?"

"No. I can't." My voice was small and tight. "Not when my friend's life is at risk. Not when there will be people waking up here tomorrow who'll have to go without breakfast because of you."

There was a momentary silence until Allen came back with the second box. As he passed Thomas, he leaned closer and whispered something in his ear. Thomas nodded, and Allen headed for the rear of the building again, his boots thudding against the wooden floor. I felt a cool breeze as he eased open the back door.

Thomas turned his attention back to me. "Don't follow us."

"But Harper—"

"Harper will be fine as long as you do what I tell you." He glanced down at her, as if making certain of something, and then moved his gaze back to my own. "Look, we'll hike up the hill a little. Once we're far enough away, and sure that no one is following, we'll send her back."

I stared at him. "And you think I'm going to be happy letting her go with you?"

Thomas raised an eyebrow. "As I said earlier, I don't think you have much of a choice."

"All good here, Thomas." Allen's voice drifted down the corridor.

I was running out of time. Thomas began backing away down the hall. I took a step after him, but he stopped, pressing the gun harder against Harper's temple. She cried out, a look of fear flashing in her eyes. I stopped, desperately trying to let her know that I wouldn't abandon her. As he reached the doorway, Thomas turned to Harper.

"Pick that up."

He waved his gun at the box Allen had left on the ground. Reluctantly, she stooped and lifted the clearly heavy box. Thomas turned back to me.

"Stay where you are, Quin. I know you don't want to, but it's the only thing you can do to protect your friend." He gestured to the gun and raised his eyebrows. "Look, wait here for twenty minutes. After that you can come out and raise the alarm. But by then Harper will be on her way back to you. As long as you follow my instructions."

I fought to control my breathing as I watched them leave. There was a small squeal from Harper as Thomas thrust her through the door and she caught her arm on the frame, but otherwise there was barely any noise at all. I counted to twenty, very slowly, then crept after them.

Peering into the night, I could just make out their shadows retreating into the distance. I stepped away from the door in case they decided to glance back.

My mind racing, I considered my options. Thomas had promised to return Harper safely, as long as no one followed them. But I wasn't sure he could be trusted. Plus, my blood still boiled from letting them escape with our much-needed supplies.

But if I attempted to shadow them, would I make things worse?

This was Harper we were talking about. One of my oldest friends. She had been through too much for me to risk her life to a selfish troublemaker now.

I made my decision.

Sighing, I grabbed the walkie-talkie from my belt, bringing it to my lips as I followed them.

"Rogers!"

There was no immediate reply. Frustrated, knowing that every second I waited they would be harder to catch, but also aware that if I got close to them and the walkie went off, they would know they were being tailed, I hung back and tried again.

"Rogers! Green! Come in!"

This time the walkie crackled. Once, twice, as if it too was waking up from a deep sleep. Eventually, a clearer signal came through.

"Who's this?"

Relief surged through me. "It's Quin. We have a problem. Thomas and Allen were in the main building. Stealing supplies. They've taken off, and they have Harper."

This time the message snapped through immediately. "Where are you?"

"At the back door of the centre."

"We're coming. Stay where you are."

"I'm going to—"

"No, Quin. Wait. We'll be there in a second."

I was standing in the grass behind the building now, not knowing how far the two men had managed to get. Surely with a hostage in tow they would be slower? Reducing the volume on the walkie-talkie to a minimum, I ignored our unofficial leader's instructions and began to run, powering across the field and out onto the rough path which snaked up the hillside ahead of me.

I made sure I kept to the side of the path, in the shadows of the scrubby bushes which gave me at least a little cover. I had been right about their speed: with the heavy box and Harper, they hadn't gotten very far, and it didn't take me too long to catch up to them. Several metres behind them, I contemplated my options. Now that they were away from the centre, Thomas had Harper walking ahead of him, his gun still pointed in her general direction, but this left his back unprotected.

I fingered the gun in my hand. I wasn't at all confident that my shot was good enough: in The Beck we had been trained with knives, and guns were only awarded to Shadow Patrol and Supers. If my shot went wide, I would give my presence away, and I was terrified of hitting Harper by accident. The idea of shooting and possibly killing Thomas, even as I seethed with anger at his actions, was also one I didn't relish. But I wasn't sure how else I could free Harper.

Perhaps if I simply followed them, made sure that they made good on their promise to let her go, that would suffice. If not, I could attack. It seemed like the more sensible plan: I would not be abandoning Harper altogether, but my actions wouldn't be totally rash. Deciding this was the option I was happiest with, I continued to creep along in the darkness. Thomas glanced back once or twice, but I managed to anticipate this, and ducked behind some bushes before he spotted me. A few minutes later they reached a point where the path became less defined.

There was a small crop of trees ahead, where I well-remembered gathering mushrooms just over a week ago. My heart was pounding, and I wondered when Thomas was going to release Harper, or whether he had been lying about his intentions all along. As the trio disappeared into the foliage I sped up, determined not to lose them amongst the shadows of the woods.

It proved to be my downfall. As my speed increased and I kept my eyes fixed on the trees ahead, I stumbled over a stray branch which lay in front of me and pitched sideways, thrusting my hands out instinctively to save myself. I knew as I hit the ground that they had heard me. Thundering footsteps returned from the woods and before I could push myself to a standing position, Thomas was towering over me.

"I told you not to follow us."

I groaned, reaching for the gun which I had lost hold of as I fell. He placed a foot on the barrel and held it there, just out of reach.

"I told you to stay put."

"You weren't letting her go. You said you would."

"You're right. But now I'm not sure I will." He paused, glancing down the path in the direction that we had come from and cursing under his breath. "Who did you tell?"

I glared at him mutinously. "Did you think no one would find out?"

"No." He looked desperate as he stared over my shoulder.

Following his gaze, I saw what he was frightened of: the approaching lights in the distance, clearly Rogers coming after us.

"I just wanted to get away without..." he faltered slightly, "without having to..."

"Thomas! Come on!" Allen's voice came from the shadows of the woods. "We have to go."

"Start walking. I'll be right behind you," Thomas called back over his shoulder before glancing down at me, a strange expression on his face. "This is on you, Quin. I told you how this should have worked. You just made it worse."

I stared at him, wondering what he would do next. His eyes flickered desperately between the woods, the path behind me, and my face. He looked frightened, and dangerous.

"Get up."

For a moment I stayed where I was, unsure of the wisest course of action. Thomas leaned down to retrieve the gun from beneath his foot, tucking it into his pocket.

"I said, get up." This time his tone brooked no argument.

Slowly, I pushed myself up from the ground, until I was standing in front of him. He stepped towards me, and for a moment I was paralysed by fear. When he was close enough for me to feel his sour breath on my face, he leaned down and thrust a hand into my pocket and I understood what he was doing. Within seconds, having emptied my pockets of the few extra bullets I had, he straightened up and stepped away.

"You have ten seconds before I start firing."

"What?"

"You heard me."

He raised the gun again, bringing it close to my temple this time. I could feel my legs shaking beneath me. Knowing I could do nothing more for Harper right now, I backed away slowly, my eyes fixed on the weapon in Thomas' hands. When I was a few metres away, his hands jerked sharply, and I couldn't stop a cry from escaping my lips.

A shot rang out, echoing through the darkness around me. I could hear voices lower down the path increase in volume, panic in their tones, and footsteps began to race up the hillside towards us. But Thomas had aimed well above my head. Now he refocused, centring the gun's sights on me again, and the look in his eyes said he had given me all the chances I was going to get. Knowing if my friends got much closer that Thomas would shoot again, I turned and fled down the path, tripping on stones as I went, straining to reach them before he had the chance. But there were no more shots.

When I finally turned back, the path above me was empty.

Chapter Three

Once I had reassured myself that Thomas was truly gone, I headed straight for the small group of people who were advancing up the path. Unsurprisingly, Rogers was at the helm, a furious expression on his face.

"I told you not to–"

I slowed to a stop and panted, catching my breath. When I looked up at him again, he was gazing up into the distant woods, trying to work out what had happened. As yet on The Crags, we had no elected leader, though that had been our original plan. Rogers and Green, as two of the oldest and most experienced citizens, currently ran most of our meetings, but tried to allow us all to have a fair and equal say in matters. When it came to acting without the agreement of the whole community though, both of them took a dim view.

I attempted to explain myself. "I know. And I'm sorry. But I–"

"You just can't resist when one of your friends is in danger." He sighed heavily. "We know."

A figure pushed past Rogers: Walker, his face the colour of a vivid sunset. My heart sank.

"Where is she?"

I couldn't meet his gaze. "They... they took her."

"They what?" He lunged past me, heading onwards up the path.

With a sigh, Rogers took off after him, grasping his arm firmly and standing in front of him so Walker physically couldn't go any further without knocking him out of the way.

"Let me go."

"No."

"You can't stop me."

"I can and I will."

For a moment, Walker looked like he might punch Rogers in the face, but eventually he allowed our unofficial leader to walk him a few paces off the path, where he leaned closer and began talking calmly into his ear.

Walker and Harper were almost inseparable. When Thomas had first left, he had ambushed Walker as he returned to base from a hunting shift, attacking him and stealing the game he had caught. And now the same man had taken Harper. I could understand his frustration. For now, I was just glad that his anger wasn't directed my way. Taking a deep breath, I glanced at Baker, the other person who made up the group.

She had so far remained silent, leaving the negotiation to Rogers, but now she stepped forward and focused her attention on me.

"What happened?"

Not one to waste words, Baker was a formidable force in The Crags. Though not especially good with people, when it counted, she was extremely reliable. Green had been left in charge whilst Rogers was over in The Beck during the sickness, but when she had fallen victim too, Baker had risen to the challenge and taken over, dealing with a difficult situation with an admirable cool. Whilst she wasn't always well-liked, she was capable of making tough decisions, and it was mostly because of her that things hadn't fallen apart when more than half the camp had gotten sick.

I found her difficult to talk to at the best of times. Definitely more so when we were alone. But I knew I owed the group who had come after me some kind of explanation of what had happened tonight. I took a deep breath.

"I was on guard duty, doing my last round before Harper took over. I noticed a light on in the kitchen and went to investigate just as she turned up." I heard her sharp intake of breath at the news that her beloved kitchen had been invaded. "Turned out to be Thomas and Allen, stealing supplies."

I paused, seeing if she would react, but she simply nodded at me to continue and waited patiently.

"Well I had my gun trained on Allen, but Thomas had been elsewhere in the building and, by the time I realised, he had captured Harper and put a gun to her head." I paused, trying to control the sob that threatened to escape my throat as I considered the events of the evening.

"Well?" Baker's tone was urgent. She wasn't one to wait for information, nor a person who would easily show sympathy for others.

I swallowed hard. "Well there wasn't much I could do without risking Harper's life so I... well I put my gun down and let them go." I hung my head. "He took it with him, and my spare ammo. So, I guess they have an extra weapon now."

"How did you end up here though? Did you follow?"

I nodded. "Rogers told me not to... but... well it's Harper. I had to, you know?"

I risked a quick glance up at Baker and found myself looking into eyes which were not particularly empathetic. Trying again to make her understand, I continued.

"I couldn't leave her. Abandon her to that... that..."

She surprised me by laying a hand on my arm. "He's a piece of work, I know. But to come up here alone, without backup?"

"I wasn't going to tackle them." I paused. "I was just going to watch, check they let her go like he said they would, but..."

"Thomas spotted you?"

I sighed. "Yes. And that just made it worse. He got angry, and sent Allen off with Harper, and that's when he started shooting."

She frowned at me. "Did he hit you?"

"No. He didn't even aim at me. Think he was just trying to frighten me off so they could escape."

"And you think he was planning to let her go?"

"Yes. Well, maybe." I thought about it. "Allen didn't seem very comfortable with taking Harper anyway."

Baker sighed, turning to face Rogers and Walker as they rejoined us.

"Think we'd better leave it for now. Go back to base, but plan to come back up when it's light and we have more weapons." Rogers looked resigned, but I could see Walker's fists clenched by his sides and I knew he was fighting to prevent himself from racing up the hill after Harper. "I promise you we're better going up there prepared."

"He's right." This was Baker, her usual no-nonsense tone cutting through the night air.

Walker didn't look like he agreed, but he allowed himself to be ushered back down the path.

"We'll regroup," Rogers soothed. "Gather a larger force, then he'll have to admit he's beaten."

"We've left it until now, but it's been too long." Baker

sounded angry. "We have to go up there and confront him. Starving him out just isn't working, especially now he has more food. And that's food *we* need."

Her words made me realise that Thomas had stopped being one of us. He was an enemy now. We were all angry with him, but none more than Walker.

Attempting comfort, I fell in step next to him. "I don't think he means to hurt her. He was just... just trying to get away without being caught."

"First, he attacks me to steal food from the mouths of his fellow citizens." His fists clenched, he stared at the ground as he spoke. "Now he resorts to kidnapping Harper and firing at you."

"He didn't actually fire–" I started to correct Walker, but tailed off as he glared at me.

"We have to do something."

"Agreed." Rogers continued to pacify, reaching across to pat Walker's shoulder. "We'll be up there at first light. Approaching now, in darkness, puts them at an advantage and might make things worse. But I promise you Walker, we'll be up there just after dawn, and we won't leave until he lets Harper go."

Pain etched on his face, Walker shrugged off his hand and strode off down the path alone. The three of us exchanged concerned glances before following in his wake, hoping against hope that daylight would come quickly and we would be able to resolve the conflict without further issue.

***

The next morning, we were back on the same path, marching up the hillside in ragged formation. There were eight of us in total: myself, Walker, Baker, Tyler, Rogers, Nelson, and

Cass, plus Green, who had insisted on coming, despite still being fairly weak from her recent sickness. She had promised she would remain at the rear, and merely lend our group an extra body. Between us, we had enough guns to put on a show, which we hoped would make Thomas come to his senses.

As we reached the caves, the sun had risen and was casting a faint light across their entrance. Thomas or Allen had moved a number of decent-sized rocks to partially block the entrance, making it difficult to get close enough to the cave to see what was happening inside. There was no outward sign of life, and we paused before fanning out into an arc which covered the yawning mouth of the cave. Rogers stepped a little in front of the rest of us.

"Thomas!"

The silence continued. He paused, glanced around the group as though confirming that he had the backup he required, should he need it.

"Thomas! Get out here."

Still nothing. I wondered for a moment whether the three outcasts might have moved their camp elsewhere, but doubted this. There was nowhere else which offered the same kind of shelter, aside from the buildings we inhabited down at the centre, where they would hardly be welcome.

"Thomas, I'm warning you. Get out here and talk to us, or we're coming in. And we won't just be talking."

For a moment, there was no response, but then we heard a stirring from inside, followed by a familiar voice.

"Go away, Rogers."

I could see Rogers biting back his frustration. "No chance. You need to get out of there. There are far more of us than there are of you. And we won't wait any longer."

"Leave." Thomas sounded angry. "Leave now, or we'll start firing."

"And just how much ammo do you have, Thomas?" Rogers' tone was scathing. "Enough to see us all off?"

"Well we've at least eight bullets, put it that way." He could clearly see us and had taken account of how many we were.

"You little–"

"Don't you–"

Both Walker and Rogers lunged forward, ready to attack. Green came from the back, placing a calming hand on her partner's arm. For a moment there was a silent struggle as Rogers attempted to keep Green back, but she glared at him and eventually he let her pass. Stepping past him, she took over.

"You'd really shoot us all?" Her tone was far calmer than that of her partner. "Honestly, Thomas? I don't think you want to."

There was another lengthy pause before Thomas continued. "I don't." His voice sounded strained. "Just leave us alone, and I won't have to."

"We're not going anywhere Thomas, just so you know." Rogers had regained control. "Not without bringing you all out."

Green tried again. "Why don't you just let Harper go, for starters? That way we'll know you don't want to hurt anyone."

There was a silence, as we all held our breath, waiting for his response. Seconds later, our hopes were dashed.

"Go." Thomas' tone was flat. "Just go, won't you? I have a mine filled with lead here, and a ton of boxes filled with bullets to tear through if I need to."

"If we go, then what?" Green stepped even closer, ignoring Rogers' desperate efforts to hold her back. She stopped when she got within a few feet of the cave mouth. "You can't stay here indefinitely."

"Watch me."

"You can't. What do you do the next time you run out of food? You can't believe we'll allow you to steal from us again?" She paused. "And we need access to those mines, Thomas. You know that."

"You do. And if you want access, you're going to have to go through me." As he finished his sentence, there was a loud crack and a bullet zipped through the air, thunking into the ground just behind us.

Green motioned to Rogers, who signaled for us to retreat. Once we had hurried back to an outcrop of rocks which sheltered us, we crouched in a tight circle.

"He's trying to use the mine access as a bargaining tool," Rogers snorted. "How long does he think that's going to work? As soon as he lets us in, we'll take them all prisoner."

"You're right, but for now we need to focus on getting in without anyone getting hurt." Green was the voice of reason as usual. "And remember: he has Harper in there."

"If he hurts her, I'll—" Walker broke off, his face pained.

"We know, Walker." Green exchanged glances with Rogers, gauging his reaction, but it was Tyler who spoke, her voice charged with emotion.

"We've all lost too much recently. We need to resolve this without more damage." There was a murmur of agreement.

"Ok. We need to get them out." Rogers seemed to take a deep breath to calm himself. "But if we storm in, he might well hurt Harper, or one of us."

Baker spoke for the first time. "We need to let him think he's in charge."

Green looked interested. "What do you mean?"

"Agree to some of his demands." Her voice was harsh. "Once he's out of there, we don't have to go through with any of it."

"You think he'll fall for that?" Walker barked out a humourless laugh. "He's many things, but he's not stupid."

"He's desperate though. I mean, how much longer can they last in there?" This was from Cass. "Without coming out, I mean."

Nelson grimaced. "A while, I should think. They've everything they need in there, until they run out of food. Mason knows the caves better than anyone, and he was telling me there's an underground spring for water, and even a basic latrine. These were places of work back in the old times. The miners spent long hours down there. But you're right, he's desperate. That makes him dangerous."

"We can't wait them out, now he has a hostage." Walker stood up. "We have to do something."

Before anyone could stop him, he sprang to his feet, his gun aimed directly at the cave mouth. "Thomas. Get out here. Now."

"I said no." There was no pause this time.

Tyler eased herself into a standing position next to Walker, clearly attempting to keep the situation calm.

"We're not your enemy, Thomas." She paused, glancing around at Rogers and Green before continuing. "Come out and speak to us. We can make a deal."

There was a snort of laughter. "Do you think I'm stupid? You're not prepared to make a deal. Just take a look at

Walker's face." Thomas could clearly see us from wherever he was concealed. "He's furious. He's not going to forgive me for a long time."

"Ever." Walker spat the word. "When I next see you, you're a dead man."

"Maybe he isn't willing to forgive." Tyler deliberately positioned herself in front of Walker and motioned to the rest of us. One by one, we followed her lead, until we were all standing together, facing the caves. "But we can offer you protection, if you show some mercy and reason right now."

"Tyler, I know you're trying to keep this thing peaceful, but I think you should know I'm aiming directly at your little group. Don't think I'm afraid to shoot."

She didn't move, but kept her voice gentle. "Actually, Thomas, I think that's exactly what you are."

Until now, we had seen no sign of movement from the cave. But suddenly, as Tyler stopped talking, a figure thrust its head out from behind the rocks arranged around the entrance.

The eight of us raised our guns in unison, cocking them ready to fire.

"Stop!"

The shout tore from my throat before I was aware that I had even opened my mouth. Because the head which was in the sight of every gun trained on the cave mouth was not Thomas', but Harper's.

Chapter Four

We paused, suspended in attack mode. For several seconds, no one moved. As we watched, Harper's face crumpled. She did not cry out, but tears streamed down it as she caught sight of us. Her gaze roamed the group until she found Walker. I could feel every muscle in his body taut as he fought to resist the impulse to race forward and take hold of her. Once her gaze was fixed on him, her expression changed, and I could hear his sharp intake of breath as she began to speak, the words tumbling rapidly from her mouth.

"He only has a few more bullets. After that he's—"

Her words were cut off as Thomas raised his gun and cracked it down on her head. She collapsed immediately, disappearing from view, and all hell broke loose.

Walker raced to the cave mouth and disappeared. Tyler was quick to follow, but stopped abruptly, bending over something just inside the cave entrance. It took the rest of the group a few additional seconds, but in less than a minute, all six of us had leapt the rocks which sheltered the cave opening and plunged into the darkness beyond.

I was somewhere in the midst of the scrum, almost knocked over by a panicked Rogers and Cass, who was seething with frustration. Inside, it took a moment for my eyes to adjust.

When they did, I could see Walker and Thomas, wrestling on the rocky ground, their arms and legs flailing as they both pounded their fists and kicked their feet in an attempt to overcome the other. A gun lay to the side of them, presumably knocked out of Thomas' hand, and Walker had opted not to use his own weapon, but his bare hands, to take out his fury on his adversary.

Rogers and Nelson dived in to stop the fight, dodging the flying fists as they attempted to separate the pair. Glancing around, I could see Allen standing to one side. He had a gun in his hand but it hung limply at his side, as though he had given up the idea that he might put it to any kind of use. Baker headed immediately for him, removing the weapon from his hand. He offered no resistance, only looking slightly relieved as Cass joined Baker and secured his hands with a length of rope. There was no sign of Johnson, but as my gaze travelled around the remaining space inside the cave, I spotted the reason for Tyler's pause at the cave entrance.

She had been tending to Harper, dragging her body out of harm's way as the rest of us had dived into the cave. My friend now lay to one side of the space, flat out on the ground, one arm flung out sideways. I couldn't see her head, as Tyler bent over her, studying her still form closely. I raced across, figuring there was no more danger now that Thomas' fight was three against one and Allen, too, had been taken care of. Reaching her side, I threw myself to my knees in front of her, lurching forward in my eagerness to check on her. Her eyes were closed, and although she breathed, blood oozed from a wound high up on her temple.

"Is she... Will she be..." I stumbled over the words.

"I don't know." Tyler sat back on her heels as we were

joined by Green.

She leaned in close to Harper and there was a moment's pause before she spoke. "She's breathing ok, which is a good sign. But he hit her pretty hard."

I bit my lip, leaning forward to stroke a hand across Harper's cheek.

"We'll have to wait 'til she wakes up I guess." Tyler tore a strip off the thin vest she wore underneath her overalls, pressing it tightly to the wound. "See how she is then."

Feeling helpless, I slipped off my jacket and slid it gently underneath my friend's head.

"She's stronger than she looks these days." Green squeezed my hand. "I'm sure she—"

"Stay there." Rogers' commanding voice cut across her before she could finish. "Don't move."

I turned to see him securing Thomas in a similar way to the way Cass had with Allen, but with far less care. Thomas' face was bleeding and he scowled but, for now at least, was silent. Walker knelt a few paces away, a dazed look on his face. His eyes were turned in our direction, but he seemed reluctant to come over. A small sound from beneath made me look back at Harper, whose eyelids were fluttering.

"Wha... I... what...?" she muttered.

I bent close to her, a smile breaking over my face. "Hey, you. Are you ok?"

Her eyes opened fully now, and she blinked several times, trying to focus. Green laid a warning hand on her shoulder.

"Don't try to get up just yet, Harper. You had a nasty bang on the head." She directed a poisonous look at Thomas, whose scowl deepened.

Walker was still frozen in place. I stretched a hand out to

him. "She's waking up."

He walked slowly towards us, like a ghost. All the fight of a few moments ago had deserted him. Reaching us, he knelt down and peered closely at Harper's face, pain flashing in his eyes. Seeing him, she managed a weak smile.

"M'ok."

"What?"

"I'm. Ok." She forced herself to form the words clearly.

He let out a hissed sigh of relief, tangling a hand in her hair and bending over her, raising her head until he could cradle it between his hands and whispering things into her ear. Embarrassed, I backed away and straightened up. Tyler and Green followed suit.

Looking around, the situation now seemed to be under control. Allen had given in without any kind of fight, which seemed to reflect his earlier attitude during their raid on the centre. Thomas still scowled, but I was thankful that he had chosen not to shoot Harper, and he now seemed resigned to his captured state. Rogers and Nelson had guns trained on both of the fugitives, but neither one looked like they would become an issue. The rest of us awaited further instruction.

A noise from the tunnel which led out of the rear of the cave into the mines startled us all. Baker was closest, and whipped her gun around to face whatever was headed our way.

"Who's there?"

A dark figure shuffled out into the cave. Hands out-stretched, clearly displaying a lack of weapon, Johnson came into view. Her face was stricken, and she was visibly shaking.

"Don't hurt me," she whispered, "I'm not armed."

Baker, wary of a trap, waved her into the centre of the cave with the gun. Johnson followed the non-verbal command, walking steadily into the middle of the space and raising her hands even higher, turning in a slow circle so we could see she wasn't a threat.

"I'm sorry. I'm not going to try and run. I promise."

I wasn't surprised to see Johnson giving herself up. She was a quiet girl, who had never made any close friends among the group which had fled from The Beck. I didn't know her well, but what I did know told me that she was a follower. If Thomas had targeted her to join his desperate dash for the hills during the outbreak, it wouldn't have taken much to persuade her to join him.

Equally, I wasn't surprised that she had since regretted her rash actions. Looking at her now, so clearly terrified, surrendering without any kind of struggle, I could see she was almost glad to be removed from the situation.

"Lower your gun, Baker." The instruction came from Green. "She's clearly not a threat. Just tie her wrists and she can be brought back with the other two."

Baker did as she was bidden without a word, making sure that the rope was knotted tightly around Johnson's arms before backing off and scowling at her.

I glanced back at Harper, whose head was now cradled entirely in Walker's lap. She was smiling faintly at something he had said, and thankfully had more colour in her cheeks now.

"Think we should get going, Rogers," Baker snapped. "Plenty to do today other than restrain these fools."

Rogers nodded. "You're right. Let's take them back down to the centre and then we can decide what we're going to do with them."

The reactions to his comment were instant. Johnson

dissolved into silent tears, Allen's face visibly blanched, and Thomas drew in a sharp breath. He looked as though he was going to say something, but Rogers held up a hand to stop him.

"Not now, Thomas. I don't think anyone wants to hear what you have to say at this precise moment. Wait 'til later, ok?"

Thomas closed his mouth again and glowered at the rocks underneath his feet.

"Is she capable of moving?" Tyler nodded at Harper and looked for Green's reply.

"She's weak, but she's coming round now, so hopefully she'll be ok to–"

"I can carry her." Walker's suggestion was not surprising.

"All that way?" Green sounded doubtful. "No, you can't."

"I can!"

Green seemed about to argue, but was interrupted by Rogers, who shot her a warning look. "Let him. He'll manage. And if he can't, we'll help him."

Shrugging, Green backed off and beckoned the rest of us to follow her outside the cave. Baker took hold of Johnson, and Tyler prodded Allen before her. When I came out into the fresh air, I had to blink several times at the brightness of the outdoors after being in the dark space. It felt good to be outside again: the bleakness of the cave had made me feel restricted, a fact I hadn't realised fully until I was free from its shadow.

We waited a moment for Rogers to bring a reluctant Thomas out of the cave, and finally, Walker emerged with Harper in his arms. Nelson tagged alongside him, ready to take over should he be needed, and we all began to trudge back down the hillside. Baker and Nelson's captives gave them no trouble, but Rogers had to keep constant hold of Thomas' arm, thrusting him ahead as we made slow progress back to the centre.

When we eventually reached it, a small knot of people were gathered. As they spotted us, they hurried over, concern clear in every eye. At the front of the group were Price and Marley, close friends of Harper.

"Is she−"

"Did you−"

I held up a hand to reassure them. "She's ok. Took a bit of a blow to the head, but she was alert when we set off back down here."

"A blow to−" Marley's eyes flashed. "Thomas again?"

I nodded, not trusting myself to speak.

Their eyes raked the group behind me, glaring briefly at the man in question, but skating past him for now and settling on Walker, who had refused all offers from others to take their turn carrying Harper and was still shouldering the burden. Her friends hurried past me, eager to see the state she was in, despite my soothing words.

Hot on their heels were Mason and Jackson. Mason had suffered the worst from the recent sickness, aside from Barnes, whom we had lost. Mason was now much stronger, but was still relying on support from Jackson, who rarely left his side. At the moment, he looked furious.

"You got them out then?" He called over my shoulder to Thomas, "Coward. Let's see what happens to you now you've nowhere to hide!"

Thomas glared at him, but remained silent. Rogers skirted the edge of the group, keeping a firm hold on Thomas, and headed for the main building. A few of the others started forward, angry looks on their faces. For the first time, I saw something resembling fear in Thomas' eyes. Only for a second, but it was definitely there. Then he dropped his head and allowed Rogers to lead him away. They were followed by Nelson, who accompanied a fairly compliant Allen, and Johnson, who trotted alongside him.

Green stepped up to the group as a whole, peacemaking as usual. "We understand everyone's frustration with the situation, and with the citizens who left us recently but have now returned."

There were angry murmurs all around me, and much shuffling of feet, but most of the people in the group respected Green's status and stayed where they were.

Nodding, clearly satisfied that they weren't going to race forward and tackle the traitors themselves, she continued. "I know there is a lot of bad feeling towards Thomas and his friends and, rest assured, they will be made to pay for what they have done. But we need to consider our options rationally, and decide on an appropriate sanction, rather than rushing in on the attack. Otherwise we act in as rash a manner as they did. I hope you can see the sense in that."

She waited for those standing in front of her to calm, meeting the gaze of everyone in the circle of people around her, as though she were personally ensuring that none of them would betray her.

"We will meet to discuss this later today or tomorrow. For now, there are more urgent concerns. Let's get on with our day, prioritising the actions which are most pressing to ensure our continuing survival and prosperity here on The Crags. Baker, can you give out responsibilities as you see fit, please?"

After receiving a nod from her older colleague, she hurried off after Rogers and the others. Baker stepped forward.

"Jackson, will you relieve Shaw from guarding the boat? Cass, you take the cliff post. I think its Collins up there. Mason, are you up for a walk today?"

He nodded, his face brightening considerably.

"Hike up to the caves. I want you to check out what state they're in. Collect any equipment or food which they had hidden up there. We brought most of it, but might have missed something. Take a look at any damage they might have done to the mine tunnels and see if we can get a team in to start looking at mining the lead as soon as we can spare the bodies."

She paused, and looked around. "Price and Tyler, head down and prepare the canoes. I think fish is our best chance of swelling our depleted food stores at the moment so I'd rather have lots of you on that duty. I'll send Nelson down in a few minutes too. Marley, you'll be in the fields today. Take Blythe as well, she can bring Perry with her. I'll man the kitchen alone until Green is finished and can help me out. I know it leaves every team a little short, but once we've made temporary arrangements for the prisoners, I'll allocate Rogers and the others to join you."

"Walker, take Harper inside. Quin, grab the first aid kit and go with them. Clean up Harper's wounds and make sure she has everything she needs. Walker, I'm sorry, but I need you to go out and hunt as well. Rogers should be done soon, and I'll send him out too."

Having finished her speech, she looked around at us all expectantly. "Well get going then!"

People started at the sharpness of her tone. Most of them jumped to attention and set off for their various posts with a new purpose.

Walker ducked past everyone and headed for the first dorm. I started for the office inside the main building where the first aid kit was kept, but was stopped by a voice to my left.

"Patch her up and keep talking to her." As usual, Baker sounded cool and efficient. "Make sure she's not dizzy or sick. When you're done, come across to the kitchen and let me know how she is. I can keep popping over to check on her." She peered closer and for a second, I thought I could detect a hint of concern in her eyes. "Did you sleep at all last night?"

I shrugged. "Not much."

"Then you should get some rest." She frowned. "You're no use to anyone if you're exhausted."

"I'll try." I paused before moving. Seeming to anticipate that I had more to say, Baker waited. "Does being dizzy and sick mean anything?" I asked.

She shook her head impatiently. "We just need to check that the injury to her head isn't anything serious. Between us, we'll watch her closely for a few hours." She gestured after Walker, who was disappearing through the door of the dorm. "Now go."

Heading to fetch the first aid kit before following him, I fought to control my worry. I hadn't dared to ask Baker what would happen if Harper's head injury was serious. For now, I could only hope that it wasn't.

Chapter Five

As I slipped inside the doorway of the dorm with the first aid kit in my hands, I could hear muffled voices coming from the first of the private rooms just inside the door. It was usually used by Rogers and Green, but I could see that settling Harper in a room with more peace and quiet would be a good idea. The door was standing slightly open, but I paused as I reached it, unsure of whether to interrupt.

Walker had laid Harper gently down on the bed and was kneeling down beside her. Their murmurs were low, and distinctly private, and I did not want to intrude, so I hung back for a moment, trying to decide how to announce my arrival to a pair who were clearly in a world of their own.

"...can't believe he..." Walker was saying. "...if you'd been seriously hurt, I'd..."

"But I wasn't." Harper's voice was soothing. "I promise, I'm ok."

"I hate him." Walker's voice rose in volume. "He deserves to–"

"Sssshh. I know. But you heard Green. They'll punish him."

He took her face in between his hands, staring deep into her eyes. "Not enough, though."

She smiled and leaned closer, until their foreheads were touching. He relinquished his hold on her face and wrapped his arms around her gently. As he pulled her to him, she rested her head on his shoulder and shifted closer, until their bodies fit together from the hip upwards. They sat like that for several moments, just resting against one another, seeming to draw on each other's strength.

Cast out by The Beck leaders, Harper and Walker's relationship had been forged in Clearance. I shuddered when I thought back to my own brief experience of the place, which was filled with cruelty and hopelessness. I knew what had gotten Harper through it was the people she had met there. Her refusal to leave them behind when we fled to The Crags showed how important they were to her, and no one more than Walker. While still gentle, Harper was not the frail young woman she had once been. She had gained an inner strength in Clearance, a core of toughness, which I truly admired.

In many ways, Harper and Walker reminded me of myself and Cam. Our time together had always been troubled, filled with stressful and challenging moments, but I knew I felt the same way about him that Harper felt about Walker.

Now the fear of the encounter with Thomas had abated and my mind was more at liberty to wander, my thoughts returned to my last meeting with Cam. Remembering the fierce touch of his lips on mine, I shivered. After waiting so long to be near him again, his kiss had been intoxicating. All intentions of remaining detached and completing the mission had flown out the window as I pressed my body close to his and returned his embrace. The consequences of being caught by Shadow Patrol had momentarily seemed less severe than being separated from him. I knew how empty

39

I would feel when we were parted again, and his reaction to me suggested he shared my feelings.

Eventually we had been forced to let go of one another, and continue with the quest. That part was painful to recall. I hated myself for the way we had left things, and it had been my fault. Furious at his refusal to let me continue with the mission and insulted by his constant insistence on protecting me, when he had tried to hug me good-bye, I had pushed him away. Hurt and angry, I had let him go thinking that I hated him.

Now, only a week later, I know only that he had been infected with the same sickness our camp had suffered, yet nothing more. When I considered the potential consequences of the illness for him, I was struck by a terror which consumed me. Shaking, I forced myself to draw several deep breaths before focusing on the task Baker had given me. Staying busy was the only thing that might take my mind off Cam's plight.

The couple inside the room remained silent, and I still had no desire to interrupt them, but knew that I had to. Making sure my boots thumped loudly on the wooden floor as I approached the room again, when I got to the door I was relieved to find that they had separated. Walker still looked concerned, but was definitely calmer than before. Harper tended to have that effect on people. He stared at me as I entered, and I wondered if he blamed me at all for what had happened to Harper. I stood on the threshold, waiting for some sign that they would welcome me in.

"Hey, Quin." Harper smiled, tiredly. "Come to play nurse?"

"Sure. It's one of my favourite jobs," I joked.

Walker did not look amused. "Guess I have to go hunting

then."

"You do." Harper patted his arm. "Don't worry, I'll be here when you get back."

He leaned in to plant a swift kiss on her lips before getting to his feet, still retaining a tight hold on one of her hands. "Keep a close eye on her, Quin."

"Stop fussing, Walker." Harper squeezed his hand and extricated herself.

He glared at her. "Someone needs to watch you, or–"

"We'll keep a close eye on her." I interrupted him, determined to reassure him she was in safe hands. "Between us, Baker and I will check on her regularly."

"You'd better." Reluctantly, he turned and headed for the door. "Tell Rogers I'm heading up to the area by the turbines."

"I will."

Harper stifled a yawn as he disappeared outside. We waited until the door banged behind him before we spoke.

"He's so over-protective," Harper sighed.

"It's not a bad thing." I swallowed hard. "I wish I had someone looking out for me like that."

Her gaze darted from the door to my face, flooded with concern. "Oh Quin. You do. He just isn't here right now."

"And we have no idea if he's even–"

"Don't say that." Her tone was firm. "He'll be fine, just you see."

Desperate not to show how despairing I was, I turned my attention to the cut on her head, peeling away the cloth which Green had fixed over it up at the caves. She winced.

"Sorry. How does it feel?"

"Sore." She shrugged. "My head aches. But I'm alright."

"Baker wants me to clean up the wound and put a fresh bandage on it. You ok with that?"

She nodded. I took out one of the strips of cloth we used to cover more serious wounds and laid it to one side before reaching for a salt solution Baker prepared and kept in a small bottle in the kit.

"Feel sick or dizzy?"

"No."

"Lightheaded at all? Like you might faint?"

"I'm fine," she reassured me. "It was just a bump on the head."

"A pretty hard one, though." I cautioned, "Don't just brush it off."

I washed the cut with the saltwater solution, being as gentle as I could. She winced a little, but was otherwise a fairly good patient. When I was finished with the solution, I dried off the cut and began to secure a fresh sheet of material over it. Thinking back to the final negotiation with Thomas, I remembered how she had shouted to warn us.

"You were very brave back there." I looked at her admiringly.

"I was?"

"Telling us Thomas was almost out of bullets."

She shrugged. "It just felt like a standoff which might never end. And I had the information to stop it. He honestly had only a few bullets which fit his gun. I heard him telling Allen in the night. He thought I was asleep."

"Well, what you did certainly helped to resolve things. You put yourself in danger though."

She brushed away my concern. "We might still be up there if I hadn't."

42

I grinned at her. "You seem to be recovering well."

"I'm fine. Nothing a little rest won't fix." She patted my arm. "Get to bed yourself. You must be exhausted."

I was. Having satisfied myself that Harper wasn't feeling sick, I headed back to the kitchen to find Baker slicing up an enormous pile of peeled potatoes. Clearly, she had been working hard since I'd last seen her. She was still alone, and barely looked up from her task as I came in.

"Harper seems ok." There was no reply, so I ploughed ahead. "I cleaned and dressed the wound, and she says she doesn't feel dizzy or nauseous."

"Did Walker go out hunting?" Her question was punctuated by the rhythmic sound of her knife hitting the chopping board.

"Yes."

"Good." She sounded satisfied. "I was afraid he would try to stay with her."

I attempted to defend Walker, knowing it would be useless. "He was just concerned."

"We're all concerned." Her tone was as sharp as her knife. "But we'll be a lot more than that unless we get back into a routine around here. We don't have the luxury of sitting around doing nothing. Everyone getting sick, well, it depleted our stores. We need to make sure we're sourcing food regularly again."

"He knows that. And he left around ten minutes ago."

"Did he say where he was going?"

"Up to the woods by the wind turbines."

She nodded in satisfaction. "Rogers should be able to catch him then."

I glanced around the kitchen and dining room. The building

seemed almost deserted, and I was curious what had happened to the prisoners.

"Where are Rogers and Green?" I paused, waiting for a response which didn't arrive for several seconds.

"In the storage room at the back." She stopped chopping suddenly. "They're trying to fit it out so that they can lock Thomas and his friends up where they can't try and escape."

I thought back to the previous night, and the ease with which they had managed to sneak in without my knowledge.

"Do they need any help?"

"No." For the first time, Baker peered at me over the pile of potatoes. "Go get some rest."

"But if they need me–"

"They don't. They'll clear the room of anything the prisoners could use to break out, then lock them in. They must be almost done by now. When they get back, I'll let Rogers know where Walker went."

"If you're sure."

She looked down at the potatoes again. I hovered in the doorway, unsure whether I was dismissed or not. Baker slid the pile of diced potatoes into one of the huge saucepans which she lifted onto the stove. It looked heavy, and not for the first time I admired her strength.

"Going to bed then?" Again, she didn't look at me.

I could never work out whether Baker genuinely cared about others, or whether her heart, which had long ago been broken, was capable of such concern. Green had told me how much she had suffered when, after being selected for Birthing in The Beck, she had been sent back to Patrol and denied any further contact with her baby. This was standard practice in The Beck, but some women coped with it better than others, and Baker had found the separation extremely difficult. The hard-hearted outlook she had today seemed to have been forged from the damage inflicted by the separation.

Looking at her now, I had no idea whether or not her insistence on my going to bed was more to do with concern for my welfare, or simply wanting to be rid of me.

"I am." I turned to go.

"Make sure you go straight to bed, Quin." I glanced back to find her gaze resting on me, now that I wasn't facing her. "Don't get involved with anything else on the way. You're of no use to us if you're exhausted."

I tried a smile. "You're right. And I will. Thanks, Baker."

She looked away again, and I knew I had been dismissed.

As I left the room, I could hear her take up the knife again and begin to slice through the rest of the potatoes, readying the meal as always. Despite her gruff exterior, Baker could always be relied upon to provide for everyone.

I half expected to come across Rogers or Green in the hallway, but met no one. Crossing the courtyard, I felt another pang of longing for Cam, followed by the familiar stab of fear as I remembered his situation. I picked up the pace, taking the steps to the dorm quickly before hauling open the door. Passing Harper with a rapid wave, I walked down the dorm to my own bed and, throwing my overall jacket underneath it, I collapsed onto the blankets.

I had been awake for almost twenty-four hours straight. Despite my concern for Harper, nagging guilt over my treatment of Cam and fears about his health, as I lay down, a wave of total exhaustion washed over me.

It didn't take me long to drop into a deep and, thankfully, dreamless sleep.

Chapter Six

I slept right through until the evening meal, when Tyler came and woke me, concerned that I needed sustenance as much as I needed rest. After a small, satisfying meal, I felt a little more alive. The conversation in the canteen was muted tonight, hushed whispers conveying the worries that people had concerning the events of the morning. Eventually, Rogers and Green stood up and silence fell over the group.

"We wanted to start by saying thank you for how hard you have worked today," Green began, smiling gently at the people sitting at the tables around her. "We know we had a difficult start to the day, in fact we've had a pretty hard time altogether of late, but everyone worked hard today and now that we have most people back in action, we feel like we're on the road to rebuilding our food stores and making The Crags into a functioning community. The mines seem undamaged, we have recovered the food that was stolen by Thomas and Allen last night, and the crops in the fields are coming along well, despite being a little neglected of late."

Rogers took over. "Both the fishing and hunting teams managed a fairly good catch today, and with a little luck and lots of hard work, we should be able to get back on track now." He paused, sighing as he glanced around at the group.

"But I know you're all eager to discuss the punishment we need to inflict on the three members of our community who abandoned us recently. Before we do, let me reassure you that they are all being held securely in one of the storage rooms inside this building. It has a constant guard."

"A guard we can't afford to spare." The muttered comment came from Mason.

"For now, we felt a guard was appropriate, and would make people feel more secure. Nelson is outside the door as we speak. But you're right, Mason. We could do without the three prisoners making more work for us as a group, and also taking us away from other, more pressing duties." Green glanced around. "But we said we would operate as a fair and equal society, so we wanted to take other people's opinions into account. If you have something to say on the matter, please raise your hand and we will hear you."

For a moment there was silence, and nobody moved. It seemed like everyone was waiting for someone else to speak first. After a few moments, Walker raised his hand and Rogers nodded at him.

"Look, they stole food, attacked me, attacked Harper, threatened to kill her." He paused, and I could see him fighting to keep his tone even. "Whatever the consequence, it has to be severe."

"Ok," Green acknowledged him, "what did you have in mind?"

"I say a whipping or a beating of some kind, make them feel the pain that they put us through."

A murmur of agreement rippled throughout the room. Tyler, who had until now been sitting quietly beside me, leapt to her feet.

47

"That would put us in the same realm as The Beck." She gazed around, meeting every eye. "We know how harsh their punishments are. We chose to leave because of it."

"That's different." Baker's eyes flashed as she joined the debate, reflecting her hatred of those who had treated us so badly. "The Beck punishments are inflicted for far lesser crimes than Thomas'!"

Tyler looked like she was going to reply, but she was silenced by Rogers, who held up a hand. "That's exactly it though. We are talking about punishing three people, who all played a very different part in what happened. We need to judge them on their individual crimes."

Jackson raised her arm. "You're right. A physical punishment is harsh, but it might be necessary. And we definitely need to consider who was guilty of what."

"Johnson only ran with the other two. She didn't hurt anyone, or threaten us," Green countered. "And she came quietly when we went up to confront them."

"Not to mention the fact that she is an able-bodied citizen who we could put to work." Jackson spoke again.

"She's right," Tyler chimed in. "Not only does the three of them being imprisoned take people away from our workforce to guard them, it also means we are wasting people who could be working alongside us, making our tasks lighter."

"You think we can *trust* them again?" Walker scoffed.

"I've spoken to Johnson since we returned." Green's voice was reassuring. "She regrets what she did and would do anything to be an accepted member of our society again. I believe that she'll work hard to make up for it."

There was a pause, as we digested all that had been said so far.

"First decision then." Rogers raised his eyebrows as he looked around the room. "Do we all feel that Johnson is the least at fault for what happened?"

The murmurs around the room this time were less hostile.

"Raise your hand if you feel that Johnson should be given a lighter punishment, and then assigned to a team for work duty where someone will keep a close eye on her." Green's expression was hopeful.

Slowly, hands were raised around the room, until only a few remained reluctant.

"So, by a majority vote, we agree." Rogers seemed satisfied. "What about Allen then? He chose to go with Thomas, helped him to steal from us, but did not commit violent acts of any kind. He also came back without any protest."

"Are we ranking them?" Baker sounded a little incredulous.

"I suppose so," Green mused. "It does seem odd, but surely we need to consider a fitting sanction for their individual role in what happened."

Baker fell silent, but looked a little sceptical.

"Allen is therefore more guilty than Johnson, but less than Thomas," Rogers continued. "Thomas was the one who masterminded the whole plan, and also the one who was willing to stoop to violence to evade capture. Agreed?"

This time, every hand in the room was raised.

"We need to make a decision on punishments then." Green was hesitant. "Any other suggestions than physical ones?"

I raised my hand. "We could apportion them less food? I mean, I know there isn't a lot to go around at the moment anyway, but once we build our stores up, they could be given less than the rest of us, for a set period of time maybe?"

Green considered this. "Meagre food portions still seems a

little like The Beck. We would need to make sure they weren't starving."

"True," Rogers mused. "But if they were given survival rations only until they, say, proved their loyalty again, would that seem fair?"

Walker snorted. "Depends what you consider to be *survival* rations. I'd like to see Thomas manage on the paltry portions we got in Clearance, if that's what you mean."

Marley spoke up. "What about keeping them separate from the others, for a set period of time? In addition to giving them slightly less food?"

"That might work." Tyler built on the idea. "We already have them locked up. But that would require a guard, surely." She glanced at Mason, who shrugged.

"I guess if this is an agreed punishment, and it's only for a set period of time, it's ok."

Tyler looked relieved. "Then perhaps keeping them imprisoned is the way to go. Are most of us in agreement?"

The room buzzed with conversation as people discussed the suggestion. Rogers allowed it to continue for a minute or two, before holding up a hand for silence.

"So, imprisonment seems to be an option most of us are comfortable with?" There were no objections. "And we set a specific length of time for the punishment: the least for Johnson, a little more for Allen, and the longest period for Thomas. Agreed?"

"It's probably a good idea to keep them separated when they are allowed to return to work." This was Jackson again. "That way they won't be able to forge any further plans or alliances."

"Good idea. Though I'm not sure it will be necessary, for

Johnson at least." Green nodded. "We can place her with the field team, and split Allen and Thomas up, put them to work foraging or cleaning, at least for now."

"And I don't think they can be left on guard at any point," Baker reasoned.

"Definitely not." Walker's response was instant.

"No," Rogers agreed. "But if we make sure that within each work detail someone is assigned to keep a close eye on them while they work, they shouldn't have much of a chance to act out again. We separate them, assign them lower food rations for a set period of time, and make sure that we keep Thomas under the longest duration of sanction and the closest eye. Is everyone in agreement with that?"

There were still a few murmurs of discontent, so Green held up a hand. "Let's vote. Raise your hands if you are in general agreement with what Rogers has suggested, after discussion with the group as a whole."

Slowly, hands were elevated throughout the room. The majority of the citizens seem satisfied with the suggested punishment, though I noted that Walker, Baker, and Mason remained silent and still.

"It's agreed then. I suggest we imprison them for at least another day entirely, while we decide on the lengths of each individual's punishment, the amount of food they will be allotted, and the citizens who will be assigned to guard them." Green looked around, seeming relieved to have the matter sorted out. "Ok?"

There was no further argument.

"Let's deliver the news then." Rogers turned and strode purposefully out of the room.

A silence fell over those of us who remained. Various

citizens exchanged glances with their closest allies, seeming to reflect the degree to which they were satisfied with the decisions that had been made so far. There was the sound of a door being unlocked in the distance, and muffled voices as the three prisoners were summoned. A few moments later, all eyes were fixed on the door as footsteps shuffled in the direction of the canteen. Allen was first, his head down, moving ahead of Johnson, whose eyes flitted nervously around the room as she walked to the front. They seemed to need no supervision, and Nelson merely ushered them to Green's side with a small motion of his hand.

Behind them came Thomas, thrust abruptly through the doorway by Rogers, who had tight hold of him by the ropes which still tethered his hands together. He stared around, his eyes searching the room until he found Walker and scowled. I could feel the other man's body tense as he noted the direct glare of his enemy. I sent a silent thanks that Harper was still resting in bed, because I knew that with her present, Walker's reaction might have been more extreme.

Thomas required more persuasion than the other two, but was eventually positioned at the front of the room alongside Allen and Johnson. He refused to drop his gaze, glaring around at anyone who would meet his eye, and I feared what he might do when Green revealed his punishment.

"We have discussed the situation and decided as a group that we need to punish you all in some way," Green began, "but we want to make sure that your sanctions are fair."

Thomas snorted, and I noticed Allen shooting him a dark look. It seemed Green's assumption that the bonds between them were severed was correct. I wondered what the conversation had been like while they were imprisoned together.

Green ignored him and continued. "We feel very strongly that you, Thomas, are the most at fault. You abandoned your fellow citizens in a time of great need, stole valuable resources, but most of all, you threatened members of our community with violence and even death." She turned to Allen and Johnson. "Allen, you were complicit in stealing from us, but you were not violent in any way. Johnson, you don't seem guilty of anything except running away and consuming food which was stolen from our camp. Do any of you have anything to say?"

Thomas and Allen remained quiet, but Johnson took a small step forward, a look of terror on her face.

"Everything you said just then is correct. I wanted to say that I am very sorry for my part in this. I acted in a panic and have regretted my actions ever since." Her voice wavered, and I believed the ring of truth in it. "I will happily pay the price for my actions, and hope that I can be accepted back into the community, eventually."

Green seemed to approve of her little speech. "Thank you, Johnson."

The other two remained silent, Allen seemingly lost in thought and Thomas maintaining his mutinous glare.

"Alright then." Green nodded at Rogers. "The punishments will include smaller food rations than the rest of us, and separation from the other members of the community: you will not be permitted to live in the dorms with the other citizens, for now at least. You will all be detained in the store room for a set period of time. The length of your punishment will reflect the severity of your crime."

"We hope to see a change in your behaviour, and that you will show us in time that you regret your actions." Rogers' voice was stern. "I want you to know that we did discuss sanctions which were more severe, but rejected them in favour of these punishments, which will hopefully send a message while still allowing you to be a part of the community and earn our trust again. We hope that we don't have to resort to more serious punishments in the future."

Rogers jerked the hand which still held on to the ropes at Thomas' wrists, and pushed him in the direction of the door. There was another silence while all three prisoners were escorted from the room. When Rogers returned, the room had begun buzzing with conversation once more.

Back at the front, Rogers managed a tired smile. "Anything else anyone wants to bring up before people go to bed?"

I stood up and stepped forward, noting the look of irritation on some of the faces around me.

"Yes, Quin?"

"I wanted to talk about the situation at The Beck." I waited a second, trying to gather my thoughts before I went on. "I know we're all tired, and that a lot has happened lately, but the last we heard from The Beck, they had the same sickness we experienced here, and..." I struggled for the right words. "I know that we left, but we all have people back there, and we haven't heard anything since, so shouldn't we be... be..."

"I know you're concerned Quin, we all are." Green's voice was characteristically gentle. "But what do you think we can do?"

I sighed. "I don't know. We've proved we can get there by boat. Could we go over again... try to rescue some of them? Take some of our leftover meds with us? We know they're short. That's our fault."

"But they'll definitely be waiting for us this time." Rogers' voice registered his annoyance with me for my repeated concerns over the state of affairs in our old home. "You're right – we've proved we can get there by boat, and get away again. More than once now. Adams won't just let us sneak in again. He'll have the place even more closely guarded."

"Any action we take with regards to The Beck needs to be extremely cautious," Baker butted in. "The last trip was rash to say the least, and whilst it did save the majority of our citizens," she shot an uncharacteristically sympathetic look at Blythe, "it spread the sickness and caused a larger issue in the long run. We cannot afford to repeat the same mistake."

"Agreed." Green's words agreed with Baker, but when her gaze returned to me, it was understanding. "Quin, we'll discuss what can be done with regards to helping the people in The Beck, but for now what we need to do is rebuild and strengthen our own community. What help would we be to Beck citizens at the moment?"

"She's right." I felt a hand on my arm and turned to see Jackson by my side. Her voice kind, she continued. "They have some meds, which we have to presume they're using. I'm sure Adams doesn't want the entire community decimated. And yes, we're all afraid that people might die, like Barnes, but I don't see how us rushing over there right now would help them."

"We need to wait," Tyler added, "think carefully before going over there again, prepare properly. We've worked with The Ridge once now, and with success. I feel we need to look at working alongside them from now on, seeing how we can help one another."

"Agreed." This was from Rogers. "It makes sense to work with them and increase our numbers. We've heard from

Hughes again and he's keen to meet with us. We've been putting him off until..." he glanced across at Green, "but perhaps now is the time to meet with him and discuss what we have to offer one another."

"Would you all be happy with Rogers and I travelling to The Ridge to speak to Hughes?" Green sounded cautious. "We're aware we have yet to be elected as your leaders, but we'd be happy to go, that is... if you'd trust us to represent you all."

"Why don't we have another vote?" Tyler spoke up, clearly pleased Rogers and Green approved of her plan. "All those in favour?"

The majority of the hands around the room were raised almost immediately.

"Thank you everyone." Green looked humbled. "We're so happy that you feel you can trust us." She turned to me. "I really feel like this could work, Quin. But only with time and careful planning, can we make a real difference."

Her words rang true, and I knew she was right. I was surrounded by friends who understood my concerns but were gently trying to show me the recklessness of my plan. Sighing, I gave up.

"That's agreed then." Green seemed pleased that our community was acting as one. "We'll make plans to visit The Ridge as soon as possible. Now get some rest. Great work today."

Her concerned eyes lingered on me as the group began to make its way out of the dining hall. I attempted a smile as I left the room. I knew that their arguments made sense. A second heroic dash to The Beck was not the answer.

But as I headed off after the others with Jackson's comforting hand in mine, I couldn't prevent visions of a deathly-pale

Barnes from mingling with images of Cam's warm, chestnut eyes.

Chapter Seven

The next morning, I found myself assigned to work with the small group on fishing detail. Checking on Harper before I left and extracting a promise that she would not go up to the fields unless she was feeling fully recovered, I joined Nelson, Shaw, and Tyler to walk down the cliff path towards the small cove where we kept our two canoes moored. Nelson was whistling a tune under his breath as he strode down the hill. Tyler and I were a little less enthusiastic about spending the day by the water.

It didn't take us long to reach the shoreline, where Nelson quickly allocated our tasks. He and Shaw would fish from the canoes, whereas Tyler and I were to remain on shore with the fixed lines. It was a sensible arrangement, as Shaw and Nelson were more proficient with the canoes than both Tyler and I. The two men wasted no time, quickly gathering their equipment from the small storage box which Nelson had built to hold all the fishing equipment between shifts. Once they had set off, taking a canoe each, I began hauling out the rods we needed and checking they were in good working order, while Tyler set about baiting the hooks and setting them up along the shoreline.

We worked quietly for several moments, both lost in

thought. I wondered who was guarding the prisoners this morning, and when they were likely to be allowed back into the general community. I had strongly agreed with the suggestion that Johnson was not guilty of much more than running away in fear, and felt that she could be trusted to work alongside us fairly soon. Allen, I was less certain of. And I wasn't sure if I could ever trust Thomas again.

We set the rods in place, propping them into the purpose-built stands which were ranged along the shoreline at intervals. After that, there was nothing to do but wait for something to bite. We sat on some rocks close by, where we could keep an eye on the lines. I was grateful that the weather looked fine, with only a few clouds scudding across the horizon and the sun managing to peep out and warm our faces every few minutes. I closed my eyes for a second and breathed deeply. It was nice to enjoy the momentary peace, despite my worries.

Beside me, Tyler sighed.

"You ok?" I shot her a quizzical look.

"I was just thinking about The Ridge."

I waited, knowing there was more.

"I mean. I'm glad that Rogers has been in touch with Hughes... that he and Green will see him soon, but..." she trailed off.

I had never known Tyler to be so uncertain about anything. Since I had met her, she had always been decisive, a fair leader, a calm presence. But today she seemed agitated.

"Were you hoping you might get to see Hughes again?" I tried, cautiously, not wanting to make her clam up.

"Well yes. I mean–" She shot me a sharp glance, but then her face fell. "Not just to see him. He has the file of papers, remember?"

I did remember. Tyler had been assigned as Hughes' guide around The Beck on our previous visit there. On our return, she had seemed more friendly with him than Rogers perhaps had liked. She had also confessed to me that she had been given a file of papers of some kind by Harris, another member of the Resistance from the Governance Sector of The Beck. She had stowed them away in a backpack which had been placed in one of the lockers on the Resistance's boat on the return journey. We had come under heavy fire as we left our old home and struggled to escape without injury, so no one had paid much attention to which pack went where, and when we had reached The Crags again and unloaded, we hadn't noticed that one pack was missing. The pack with the all-important notes. Since then, Tyler had been concerned that potentially sensitive information had been left with people we didn't know especially well.

"You want them back."

"I'm worried." She stared out at the distant canoes, where Nelson and Shaw were now casting lines into the water. "What if the information they contain is sensitive? We have to retrieve them."

"You're right," I shot a sideways glance at her and risked another dig, "and it'd be nice to see Hughes again too, wouldn't it?"

She went to jab an elbow into my ribs, but I was on my feet and dodging away from her before she could reach me. Wandering down to the shore, I made a show of checking that the rods were still baited before turning back to Tyler. Her face was flushed and she was now staring determinedly at her feet. Feeling a wave of affection for the new, vulnerable

Tyler, I returned to her side and sat down next to her again.

After a moment, she turned to me awkwardly.

"I do want to see Hughes again."

Her comment was abrupt. I got the impression that she didn't often confide in others, and certainly not me. Unsure of the response she was waiting for, I busied myself checking the rods unnecessarily, and when I glanced back at her she was staring out over the water.

I attempted a reply. "When you were walking round The Beck, was he... did you...?"

She turned her gaze on me. "He's just... just an interesting guy."

"I'm sure he is." I tried again. "Did he... what did he want to know about The Beck?"

"Everything!" She smiled suddenly. "He never stopped asking questions, at least when it was just us. He was quiet when we were passing other Beck citizens and mixing with people where we might have been in danger. But he was fascinated with the way the society was run."

"Did he tell you about The Ridge?"

"A little. They are very interested in The Beck. I think it has resources which they're lacking. If we have an interest in returning, I'm pretty certain they'll want to be involved, and that could be good for all of us."

"I agree."

"I'll admit I'm interested in going over to The Ridge to have a look myself. I think things over there are pretty different."

"Hopefully once Rogers and Green have met with him, there'll be a chance for others to go."

"Well now that we're starting work in the mines, we'll have lead to trade with them. And if we're serious about planning to save The Beck, however far into the future, we'll need their help. So yes, I'm hopeful to hear the outcome of these discussions, now that the situation with Thomas is resolved."

I shook my head. "I'm so glad that it's over."

"I think everyone is." She stood up and moved to attend to a jerking rod "The sooner we have the sanctions sorted out the better. Then everyone will feel like justice is being done."

She busied herself with reeling in the line and securing the fish, an ugly, greyish creature. Depositing it in the bucket at her feet, she began to rebait the hook. As she did so, a second rod began twitching, and I got up to bring our second catch of the day to shore.

The rest of the morning passed by with regular tugs on the lines, and when Nelson and Shaw arrived back to shore, we were pleased with the catch. They too had been successful, and we helped them unload the fish from their boats feeling the satisfaction that we had swelled the food stores in The Crags with our day's work.

As we were wrapping the catch in sections of material and packing it into the backpacks, we all heard a low humming noise, distant at first, but heading closer all the time. The three of us stiffened, and turned to its source: a familiar motorboat growing larger as it cut through the water towards us. We exchanged glances, all unsure how to react. The last few times The Ridge had sent its motorboats over here we had been armed and ready for a potential battle, but now we were on more friendly terms with them, we all seemed uncertain of what our reaction should be.

Nelson had just raised his walkie-talkie to his lips when rapid footsteps sounded from behind us. We turned to see Rogers and Green heading down from the path, packs on their backs. They reached us before the motorboat, both slightly out of breath.

"Is this..." Nelson looked slightly panicked. "Is this ok?"

Rogers slapped an arm on his friend's shoulder. "Yes. It's fine. After the discussion last night, I got in touch with Hughes this morning, suggested a meeting. He wants to discuss a few things with us. Said he'd bring back that file we're missing." He shot a look at Tyler, who blushed.

"I've said I'm sorry."

Green chuckled. "It's fine. And we think him being honest about having the file goes a long way towards our knowing that we can trust him. Though I'm not sure that everyone here would be willing to allow him up to the centre as yet."

Nelson nodded. "I agree."

"But I think him offering to bring the file here is a good thing. He suggested that he come and collect a couple of us, take us over to The Ridge with him." Green saw the panic on my face and put out a hand to reassure me. "Just for a day. To discuss potential trades we might set up, like we said. And to take a look around."

"And you're both going?" Tyler looked surprised.

"Yes. We're both going." Green glanced across at Rogers, smiling gently. "We've left Baker in charge. And there is a constant guard on the prisoners. None of them will be allowed out before we get back."

I remembered my concerns for the two of them after Green had been struck by the sickness. Rogers had looked like he never wanted to leave her side again, and I had been frightened for what it meant for us, and whether we would lose their leadership. It seemed that their compromise was to do things, where possible, together. While we were all aware this would leave us without their strong influence when they were absent, Baker had recently proved herself up to the challenge of leading our community and Tyler was also widely respected by everyone on The Crags. Rogers and Green seemed satisfied that things would not fall apart without them, and I trusted that they knew what they were doing.

"It'll be fine. We're not going for long," Rogers continued, raising his voice over the roar of the motorboat as it closed in on the beach. "I want to see their smelting works. Figure out how we can get them up and running, start making some more ammo."

"Yeah, now Mason has access to the mines I don't think it will be long before we have some lead to trade, and in terms of us considering The Beck's problems, that can't be a bad thing, can it?" Nelson dropped his volume as the boat's engine cut out.

We all turned to see Hughes striding through the shallow waters close to the shore. He had left the only other citizen, one I didn't recognise, in the boat. His confidence and trust in us was unquestionable. As he got closer, he was beaming.

"Hey all. Good to finally see you again." I noticed his gaze travelled around all five of us, but lingered a little longer on Tyler, who was now staring at the ground again. "How are things?"

Rogers smiled. "Well the sickness seems to have left us now, and we've resolved a difficult issue, so all things considered, better than the last time we saw you."

"I'm glad." Hughes swung the backpack off his shoulders and knelt down to open it. Rummaging around inside it, he continued. "We've been eager to meet with you again. I know you're not so keen on letting us look over The Crags just yet, but I thought a show of faith... you know letting a couple of you folks see The Ridge, might go some way towards extending the trust, as well as, well..." his eyes lit up as his hand closed around something in the pack which he had clearly been searching for. "This!"

He brandished a file of papers in the air. With a small cry, Tyler flung herself forward and snatched it from his grasp. A second later she seemed to realise how rude her actions had seemed, and her face flushed again.

Hughes merely looked amused. "I see this was pretty important to you all."

Green shot a look at Tyler and smoothed things over. "Yes. It was."

"Well I won't lie and tell you I haven't opened it." Hughes shrugged as Rogers' stiffened. "You want to build trust, I'd like to be honest. Wouldn't you have done the same, given the chance?"

"You're right, I suppose." Rogers relaxed as Green placed a gentle hand on his arm.

Hughes continued. "Look, I couldn't really make any sense of it. It's mostly figures... names which don't mean a lot to me. I guess you'll have more success interpreting its contents."

"We appreciate your honesty, Hughes." Green motioned to the packs at hers and Rogers' feet. "We're not staying with you for long, right? We didn't bring much."

A brief shadow crossed Hughes' face. "It's just the two of you coming?"

Rogers looked puzzled, "That's ok, right?"

"Of course." The Ridge leader quickly resettled his face into a smile, waving a hand around the small group. "No problem at all."

He studiously avoided Tyler's eye at this point, and I could tell his disappointment was linked to her remaining on The Crags rather than joining him aboard the boat. Her eyes were busy scanning the first few sheets of paper contained within the folder she still had clutched within her hands, and she seemed to have forgotten her previous discomfort in his presence in her eagerness to view the contents.

"We're ready when you are." Rogers motioned to the boat, which was still bobbing a little way from the shore. "Shall we get going?"

Hughes nodded. "By all means." He nodded at our group and smiled once again before pulling his backpack on and heading for the water.

As he went out of earshot, Rogers leaned towards Tyler. "You make sure you pour over the contents of that file while we're away, ok? The new schedule of the guards for Thomas and crew is with Baker. Until we get back, just keep the usual work shifts running and make sure none of the prisoners leave the storeroom, ok?"

Tyler looked up from the file and nodded, casting a quick glance over at Hughes before stowing the file in one of the packs which did not contain fish.

"We'll be back tomorrow." Green smiled. "And we have a walkie-talkie with us in case you need to get in contact."

"Be safe." I leaned in to give Green a brief hug, which she returned.

"We'll be fine, Quin."

She and Rogers collected their packs and headed after Hughes. We watched them go until they were safely on the boat, and continued to pack away the catch. By the time we were done, the roar of the boat had become a hum in the distance, and then the cove was quiet again.

"I hope they're ok." Nelson shut the lid on the tackle box.

"I'm sure they will be." I tried, hoping for a reassuring tone.

I glanced over at Tyler, hoping for her to echo my sentiments and increase my confidence that two of the most important people to our community would be kept safe. Her eyes, however, were not focused on us at all, but at a point in the distance where a small moving dot receded in the direction of The Ridge.

Chapter Eight

Back up in the centre's kitchen, we spent some time unloading the fish. Baker was nowhere to be seen, but Collins was on duty, and her eyes lit up when she saw the size of the catch we had managed to secure.

"We can cook some of this up for dinner, but there's enough for us to start drying some out and storing it, I think." She beamed. "That means we're on the way to getting a back-up stock of food ready again."

I moved back from the counter, where I had been placing the fish on the chopping boards Collins had laid out already. "That's good."

"It is." She gathered up a tray which held some hunks of bread and a jug of water. "I'm just—"

There were more footsteps from the hallway and Walker came in, several squirrel carcasses looped over his shoulder.

Collins frowned. "Quin, d'you mind taking the tray to the prisoners while I deal with this?"

I grasped her meaning and knew she'd be better off dealing with the game that Walker had brought back than I would. Stepping forward, I took the tray from her arms.

"No problem. They still in the same storage room?"

She nodded, already selecting a knife to start skinning the

catch as Walker laid it on the kitchen floor.

I headed back out to the hallway and in the opposite direction to the entrance. As I walked down the quiet corridor, I couldn't help but remember the last time I had gone this way, at night, and found Thomas and Allen stealing from us. Repressing my anger, I continued down the hall with the tray to where Price sat outside the makeshift cell door.

"Hey," she smiled tiredly at my approach, "you come to take over?"

"Nope. Sorry." I shook my head. "Just delivering food."

"Thought it was a little early," she commented, standing up to pull the key from her pocket.

"All quiet in there?" I added with trepidation.

"Sure. They seem to have all fallen out with one another, so they're not even speaking." She handed me the key and picked up her gun. "Their hands and feet are tied but the bindings have enough reach that they're able to lift food into their mouths. Put the tray down while you unlock it. Tell them what you're doing. Then slide in the tray."

"Will do."

"As long as they see me with the gun, I don't think they'll be any trouble." She shrugged. "I think Thomas is the only one with any fight left in him anyway."

Placing the tray on the chair which Price had been sitting on, I slid the key into the lock. As I turned it, I heard the click, accompanied by the shifting of bodies in the space behind.

"I'm coming in," I called loudly. "Just bringing some food."

More sounds of shifting, and a creak as the door swung open. Inside, the three prisoners stared at me with very different eyes. Johnson was closest to the door, her expression

69

baleful, her head bowed. Allen was to my right, his eyes displaying hunger and nothing more. At the rear of the space was Thomas, his eyes glittering with intensity.

"I have some food for you," I began, taking a cautious step inside the door. "Bread, and some water. Smaller rations, as discussed yesterday."

"Thank you!" Johnson's instant and grateful reply was unsurprising. She took the bread from me gently, but began to gnaw away on it with more fervour once she had removed it from my grip.

Allen also took the bread from me with care. His eyes were solemn as he managed a low, "Thanks."

Finally, I turned to Thomas. His eyes glared at me, as though he wanted to burn holes into my face. I set his share of the food in front of him and backed away, fighting not to speak to him any more than I had to.

"Barely enough to feed a child."

The words were spoken in a low mutter, but loudly enough that I could hear them. I turned to Thomas, staring openly at him now.

"We discussed that your rations would be smaller. It's part of the punishment."

"If you want us to die of starvation." The tone of Thomas' voice was as cutting as ever.

"It's more than you deserve, in some people's opinion."

"Barbaric's what it is." Thomas sounded like he might build up to one of his famous rants. "You can't expect—"

"Shut up!" Johnson's voice was strident, and growing in volume. "Just shut up! They've been more than fair, considering what you did... what we did to them!"

I had been ready with my own comeback, to get angry with

him myself, but I could see that it wasn't necessary. Johnson was clearly furious with Thomas, and from the look on his face he was hating being confined in a cell with her. That was probably enough of an extra punishment for now. He had stopped arguing anyway, and angled his body slightly away from the rest of the room.

For a moment, I worried that things in the room might get out of hand, but then I realised that all three prisoners were securely fastened by their ankles to the shelving around them, which was in turn fixed into the ground. And they weren't close enough to be able to get at one another physically.

"Ok. Meal time now, be quiet," I muttered at them, and backed away.

Outside, Price grinned at me. "Not happy, are they? None of 'em."

"Nope. But I suppose that's the point, isn't it?" I nodded at her and made my way to the centre's exit.

Tyler had gone back to the dorms with the file on our return and I knew she would be pouring over the contents. I had to admit I was curious as to what all the names and figures might reveal to us about The Beck. I had barely reached the courtyard when Mason and his small crew appeared from the path from the caves and the mine. He smiled tiredly as he saw me, dismissing the other two citizens with a nod.

"Hey, how are you?" I hurried over and relieved him of his backpack, placing it on the ground.

"I'm ok." He ran a tired hand over his scalp. "It's been a long day, that's all."

"You haven't worked since your illness," I scolded. "Make sure you're not overdoing it, at least to begin with."

"Never mind that." He brushed off my concern. "Wait 'til

you see."

He bent to the backpack and opened it, reaching in to pull out a lump of black rock. He proffered it for my attention. Taking it from him, I turned it over in my hands, examining it with my fingers. Upon closer inspection, the black was flecked with shiny, silvery sections which glinted in the weak sunlight.

"Um, it's pretty?" I tried.

"Better than that. It's lead." Mason's tiredness had temporarily evaporated and he was smiling with pride. "The sort of stuff you can make bullets with."

I looked closer at the lump of metal. "Wow. Doesn't look much like a bullet right now."

"But it will." He took the rock away from me and replaced it in his pack. "I'm going to show someone who'll appreciate it."

I laughed, and backed away while he picked up the pack again and headed for the main building. I had yet to see Jackson tonight and knew she would want to know that Mason was back from the mine. Hurrying back to the dorms, I swung open the door and looked around. It was empty, aside from Tyler, who was huddled on her bed at the far end of the room, her head bent over something, clearly the information from the file.

I stopped as I passed the door to the room where Harper had been staying because of her head injury. She smiled up from the bed, where she was fully dressed.

"Hey, you feeling better?"

"Much. Thanks." She smiled broadly. "I was waiting for Walker."

"He just got back," I pointed over to the centre. "He was

in the kitchen."

She was on her feet in an instant.

"Woah there!" I held out a hand which she did not take. "Careful, you've been injured."

"I honestly feel fine now." She swatted my hand away. "Baker said she thinks I can go back to light work duties as of tomorrow." I made a face. "Plus, I'm hungry."

"Well that has to be a good sign." I smiled. "Wait up, I'll go with you. Just let me grab Tyler."

I walked to the far end of the dorm. As I approached, Tyler's face was so intent on the papers in front of her that she hardly noticed me.

"Coming to dinner?"

She looked up. "Hey, Quin. I'm just..." She paused, gesturing to the sheet in front of her. "I'll follow you in a minute, ok?"

"Alright. I'll see you in there."

She nodded absentmindedly. Shrugging, I turned back to Harper who was waiting for me in the doorway. When I looked back, her eyes had already returned to devouring the words in front of her.

***

By the time I had eaten a satisfactory dinner, made mostly out of the fish we had caught that morning, there was still no sign of Tyler. Not wanting her to go hungry, I made her a plate of food and headed back to the dorm earlier than the others. When I reached it, she was sitting exactly where I had left her.

Shrugging off my overall jacket, I placed the food on the bedside table and went to sit on the bed adjacent to hers, not wanting to disturb her when she was in the middle of something important. Despite all that we had gone through together, I was still very much aware of the Tyler who had been my trainer when I had first moved up to Patrol. The Tyler who was my superior, and who I admired greatly. The Tyler who, until very recently, had been far more interested in Cam than he had been in her.

I knew she had strong feelings for him, and that, while she was a close friend, he did not feel at all romantically about her. This hadn't stopped me feeling jealous of the easy friendship between them, borne of knowing one another for a long time and of having gone through a lot together. Tyler was a formidable woman: intelligent, strong, excellent at defence, yet she had a sense of justice which made her a truly wonderful person to be around. Over the time we had known one another though, I had also begun to see a softer side to her, a vulnerability which she rarely let show.

Her reaction to Hughes was intriguing, and I was hoping it might turn into something more for her, and help her to move on from Cam. I knew it would make things less awkward between us, and I genuinely wanted her to be happy. But there lay a gulf of water between the two of them, not to mention their very different backgrounds. I watched her closely as she studied the pages in front of her.

"Here," she muttered eventually, so low that I wasn't sure she was talking to me. "There's a lot of documents here."

"What are they all?"

"Reports, mostly." She sighed. "Lists of names, with codes next to them. I've started looking at the first few, but there are so many. I'm not sure what to make of them, and I've no idea what Harris expected us to do with the information."

"Can I see?" I hesitated before holding out a hand. "I

might be able to make a bit more sense of them, I've looked at similar reports once before. Harris showed some to me after a Resistance meeting, a couple of days before we escaped."

She handed the folder to me. "Go ahead."

I gestured to the plate I had brought for her. "You must be hungry."

I ran my eye down the list of names on the first page while she began to eat her meal. "So... usually the codes refer to the different outcomes for the different citizens, right? Those who will be promoted have the code for the Sector they'll be moved to, and those who fail the assessments have the Clearance code."

"Well that's nothing new." Tyler spoke through a mouthful of stew, her brow furrowed as she puzzled it out. "Why would Harris collect this specific information and pass it to us? It must have some kind of significance."

"Some of these look different though, not like the ones Harris showed me." I leafed through a few more pages, fighting the feeling of nausea as I remembered those I had previously seen. They had revealed Adams' plan to inject the new Patrol recruits with drugs against their will to make them more aggressive. It had been the reason many of them had been so willing to board the Clearance boat without much information about our escape. The report had also delivered the devastating news that Harper had been assigned to the next drowning. I couldn't shake the growing feeling of horror as I ran my finger down page after page of figures. "Wait. I recognize most of the codes on the first couple of sheets, but these are new." Tyler put her plate down and moved across to sit on the bed next to me. "Look," I pointed, "there's a whole column—"

She grabbed the papers from my hand and rifled through a couple more. "You're right. There are several pages of people, all who have an X code. It's definitely new."

"What do you think it means?"

"Not sure." Her frown deepened and she looked up from the page and met my gaze. "There are literally hundreds of citizens with an X by their name"

"I don't like this, Tyler."

"Me neither. I'm not sure what it's about, but we have to do something." She stood up suddenly, startling me.

"What are you–?" I stared at her in confusion.

"We'll tell Baker. Another pair of eyes on this might just help us work it out."

"Baker?" I knew I looked doubtful.

"Well Rogers and Green aren't here right now. And I want to know what this means. Don't you?" She jerked her head in the direction of the door. "Come on. Baker's clever. She might see something we haven't."

Before I could respond, she had disappeared, leaving me with no choice but to follow.

Chapter Nine

A minute later, I joined Tyler and Baker in the kitchen. The older woman was busy clearing up after the evening meal, and looked annoyed by our interruption.

"Need to speak to you about something," Tyler began. "Now."

Baker continued ferrying piles of plates from the counter to the cupboard where they belonged. "What is it?"

Tyler dumped her plate on the counter and shook the papers in her other hand at Baker. "The documents which Hughes brought over from The Beck. There's something odd about them."

"Go on." Baker abandoned her chores and gazed at us, her attention piqued by Tyler's words.

"Well the file is filled with lists, you see... lists which have all sorts of codes and numbers we don't understand. But there's something odd about them... a new code, X, which... only appeared recently..." Tyler shrugged helplessly. "We were hoping you might make more sense of it than we could."

"Pass them here." Baker held out a hand impatiently.

Tyler spread the contents of the file on the counter and we stood back as Baker scanned over them. For a long time she said nothing, sifting through the papers in silence, her face impassive. Finally, she looked up, her gaze intense.

"You're right. It's strange." She peered at the figures again. "It looks like the citizens with an X code are the ones whose assessment results have been declining."

"But that's nothing new," I blurted out. "We know he weeds out the ones who are failing. That's what Clearance is for."

She shook her head. "Look at this. The figure here states the mark that citizens had to achieve to be safe." She indicated a different sheet. "Looks like Adams is raising the pass mark. Citizens would have to score above this..." she jabbed a finger at a number which was alarmingly higher than the previous one, "...in order to avoid Clearance."

"So, you think..." I stumbled over the words, "...you think he's trying to get rid of larger numbers? But why?"

"Who knows?" Her tone was deeply bitter. "He's always controlled The Beck population. What's to stop him changing his mind about what makes a good citizen?"

I sifted through the rest of the papers, unwilling to believe Baker's words. There were several other sheets we hadn't looked at, but my attention was drawn to two which I hadn't seen before, but which seemed similar. They were filled with columns, but instead of names, they seemed to be divided into categories.

"What are these?"

I felt the two women either side of me lean closer.

Tyler was the first to speak. "Those look like... ranges."

"Ranges?"

"See here? Next to the assessment results column on this first sheet it has the numbers 150 and 200." She looked at Baker. "So, if the results of the assessment fall within that range..."

"...the citizen is considered to have passed." I finished. "So?"

"So, this one is different." Baker pulled out the second sheet. "Here, the range is below 150. Those citizens would fail. And that's a pretty steep pass mark." She grabbed the sheet and studied it more closely. "Look! There are ranges for every category here: height, weight, bloodline, performance scores..." she ran her finger to the bottom of the page, "X! People who fall within these parameters are given the X code."

Baker's face was flushed, but I didn't understand why. "How is that different than what's always happened?"

Tyler rifled through the papers we had looked through earlier. When she found what she wanted, she laid it on top of the others. "Adams is raising the bar. This is the old pass mark, and citizens were judged on the Assessments alone."

"Now, it seems, he's looking at everything." Baker sighed. "He's trying to eliminate anyone who doesn't fit."

I stared at her. "Categorising citizens?" I glanced down at the sheet again. "Judging them by these characteristics? The assessment pass mark's so high now! And he's looking at other things too. People can't control their height. And the bloodline must mean..."

"They're tracking the mothers who produce each citizen." Baker grimaced. "Probably linking citizens to the past performance of the parent..."

"And if citizens don't meet these criteria, they're out?"

"I guess so." Tyler hesitated. "But this is a huge number to send to Clearance. Surely, they couldn't... drown these numbers all at once? It's not practical."

"Unless he plans to find some other way to... get rid of them. I mean–"

Baker's words were cut off as her walkie-talkie crackled, and Green's voice came through.

"Come in. This is Green." A pause. "Baker, are you there?"

Baker snatched up the walkie-talkie from the counter. "I'm here."

The crackling continued, but Green sounded far clearer than Anders had the last time I had heard his message. "Are you alone?"

Clearly, she was using one of the private channels to speak to Baker, rather than the central one we used for more day-to-day communication. I exchanged glances with Tyler, wondering if we would be asked to leave.

"I'm with Tyler. And Quin."

There was another pause, but then Green continued. "That's alright."

"Go ahead," Baker replied, an impatient look on her face.

"Wanted to let you know that Rogers and I are alright... that we reached The Ridge safely... Hughes is treating us well."

Even though the radio channel made Green's voice sound crackly and distant, we could all tell something wasn't right.

Baker frowned and held up her own walkie-talkie. "Green, what's wrong?"

There was a pause before Green spoke again. "Nothing... just checking in."

"Just checking in!" Baker glared at the walkie-talkie as though it were Green in the flesh. Pressing the button sharply, she continued in a gentler tone. "Can't fool me, Green. Spit it out."

"It's just..."

For a moment, the walkie-talkie cut out, and we waited impatiently for Green's voice to come through again.

"...we've received another radio message from Anders."

"Let's have it then," Baker coaxed. "You won't rest 'til you've shared it."

Another pause, but eventually Green continued, and this time the flow of her conversation didn't stop. "Oh, Baker. It's not good. Anders' message was... was far clearer and more detailed than last time... seemed to have the time to deliver it without interruption."

She seemed almost reluctant to share the information, and I dreaded the news she had to deliver. Even through the walkie-talkie, the fear in her voice was unmistakable.

"The situation in The Beck is pretty grave. The sickness... affected large numbers of the population, particularly in the Lower Beck... citizens working more closely with one another..."

"We knew that already," Baker interjected. "What's new?"

There was a silence while Green presumably considered her reply. We waited for the radio to crackle into life again. "The way Adams is dealing with the situation... we were right, he isn't offering meds of any kind to the Lower Beck citizens... leaving them in a quarantine, which he has sealed off from the rest of The Beck, to see which of them survive... he doesn't seem to care how many die."

Tyler and I exchanged worried glances as Green continued.

"...the sickness hasn't gone as far as Clearance, yet. He's forbidden any contact between there and the rest of The Beck. Seems like he's trying to keep that area disease-free."

"But why?" Baker thought aloud as the radio went quiet for a moment. "He's never cared about the citizens over there

81

before."

Next to me, Tyler leaned closer. "Do you think that the sickness is playing into his hands? I mean... if he wants to get rid of large numbers of citizens..."

I finished her thought, "...this would be a very convenient way to do it."

Baker shot us a look as the radio crackled to life again. For a moment I stopped listening, trying desperately to ignore the nagging voice in my head. I needed to know if Cam was one of the ones locked away in the quarantine. He wasn't a Lower Beck citizen, but I already knew that he was ill, so there were no guarantees that he would have been given meds or prioritised, particularly if Adams didn't feel he was worth saving.

"...we know that meds have been distributed to those in Upper Beck Sectors, but not whether they have been successful in reducing the severity of the sickness," Green continued. "...can only assume they've had a similar effect as here, if they were administered in enough time. According to Anders, many are already dead... but there's no way of us knowing which citizens are still alive... Anders said Adams isn't all that interested in saving people unless they're from Meds, Minors, or the Upper Beck... he says the Resistance citizens are increasingly concerned about Adams... acting irrationally... making even more extreme decisions... expanding Shadow Patrol numbers...

"Keep this to yourselves for now please. We know people will want to help, but like we said yesterday, there's little we can do. Anders says the one Sector Adams is making sure he protects is Shadow Patrol... recent visit made him very nervous... to risk going over there again without significant firepower would be suicide." I could almost see the frustration on Green's face as her voice crackled in and out. "On the bright side, The Ridge are proving very helpful, and we're going to stay a little longer to discuss matters with Hughes and his team... really feel if we wait, prepare, we stand a realistic chance of attacking The Beck successfully, and can get back over there and make a difference at some point fairly soon."

There was a pause and I wondered if Baker would confide our own discovery to Green. Eventually, she lifted the walkie-talkie to her mouth. "When should we expect you back?"

"Tomorrow definitely. But probably later on. Evening maybe." There was a pause and then one last message. "Thank you, Baker."

"No problem. Thanks for keeping us informed. See you then." Baker placed the walkie-talkie back on the counter and turned to face us. "No point in worrying her further when she can't do anything about it. They'll be back tomorrow. We can tell them then."

"Do you think..." Tyler began, "... I mean, this quarantine for the sick... is he?"

"Leaving them to die? Very possibly. Those who succumb to sickness hardly fit his ideal citizen." She rubbed her forehead with a tired hand. "You know, he's controlled the population for years, but I never thought he'd go this far."

There was silence, as the three of us digested all the information. Eventually, Tyler gestured to the paper.

"There are more documents we haven't looked at yet. We should probably take a look through them."

"You're right. There might be more useful information." Baker turned back to the plates she had abandoned. "Are you two happy to look over the rest of them? I still need to finish up here."

Tyler made for the door immediately. "Sure. The more we learn, the better. It would be great if we had all the information ready for when Rogers and Green get back. Then we can really start to make plans." She paused, realising that I hadn't followed her. "Coming, Quin?"

"Think I'll stay and help in here," I found myself replying. "I'm sure Baker can do with an extra hand."

The older woman looked surprised, and held out a hand in protest, but I didn't let her speak.

"It's late. The work will be done far quicker with two of us." I stopped, unsure what had driven me to want to help out the often-gruff woman. "And I could do with taking my mind off other things."

Shrugging, Tyler continued out the door, calling back over her shoulder, "Ok, see you later."

Baker pointed at a second pile of dishes and jerked her head at the cupboards. Then she went into the smaller room beyond the kitchen. I heard running water, and a moment later she returned with a bucket of water and began to mop the floor. We worked in companionable silence for a while, both lost in our thoughts. The clattering of plates and swishing sound of the water on the floors was soothing to begin with, but eventually I was unable to prevent images of a sick and feeble Cam from invading my head.

Baker seemed to sense this somehow. "Look, there's nothing we can do right now." Her tone was not as sharp as usual. "I know you're thinking of people over there... I can hear your mind whirring." She sighed. "Look, believe me, I am too. Once everyone knows, we'll all have someone we fear

84

for. But you must see that we can't do anything right now. It's torture, knowing we have friends and allies who might be suffering or even..." she stopped short, aware for once of the hurt her words might cause, "...but preparation is the only way we stand any chance of helping them. In the end."

I knew she was right. Our most recent trip to The Beck had been risky, and had resulted in us infecting the citizens still living in our old home. And though the meds had saved the majority of the citizens here, they had not been enough to save Barnes. The sickness was not something to be trifled with, and we had to take it seriously. Our own community was just recovering from it, and was still weakened, plus we had limited amounts of weapons and ammo at the moment. Even I was beginning to see that with limited resources, we stood little or no chance of helping The Beck citizens.

My only hope lay with the fact that Green had sounded positive about The Ridge. Perhaps, with a second force on board, and with proper planning, more ammunition, we could change things at The Beck for the long term. As Baker and I finished up the chores in the kitchen, I tried to focus my thoughts on how we could prepare to successfully invade The Beck in the future.

But my heart sank even as I thought this, fearing that, by the time we were ready, it would be too late for many citizens.

Including Cam.

Chapter Ten

When I rose the next morning, I still felt anxious, and the need to act, or at least *plan* to act, burned in my stomach. I had returned to the dorm the previous evening to find Tyler slumped over the remaining papers, her breathing heavy. Sliding them out from her grip, I had placed them back into the file and left them on her bedside. Now there was nothing to do but wait. Rogers and Green would not be back from The Ridge until later. There was no point planning until they were back with more information.

When she woke, Tyler had shrugged, seeming embarrassed that she had not been able to discover much more from the papers before passing out for the night, so I had left her alone. She told me that she would head out for the day with a work detail like the rest of us, and take a look at the remaining papers later on. There was nothing more to be learned for now, so I left it alone.

Breakfast was a quiet affair. People were still readjusting after the sickness, and we had a significant number of citizens missing if we counted the three prisoners, plus their guard, and Rogers and Green. The few of us who remained ate swiftly and quietly, aside from Perry, Blythe's daughter, who seemed oblivious to the tension swirling within the room. She sat on her mother's knee, happily gurgling and waving a small spoon in the air as Marley shovelled mashed up vegetables into her mouth.

There had been a time when Blythe had been extremely concerned about Perry's appetite, when she had not taken well to eating solid food, but things in that area seemed to have improved lately. She certainly seemed to be enjoying whatever it was she was being fed this morning. Marley was seated with Walker, who was making silly faces at Perry over her shoulder, and the distraction seemed to be what was needed to make the small girl happy and encourage her to both eat and communicate with the others around her.

It was nice to see Walker smiling for a change. I had spoken to Harper as I left the dorm that morning. She was feeling much better, she said, but Baker had insisted on her taking it easy for a little longer and she had therefore stayed in her room to eat her breakfast. She was eager to get out and help with the efforts to rebuild the food supply though, and said she hoped that Baker would allow her out later today to do a few light chores and prove that she was feeling better. Walker's happiness was certainly linked to Harper's recovery, and the harsh worry lines that had creased his handsome face lately were absent this morning.

Blythe was less happy. She supported the wriggling bundle on her knee with no issue at all, but stared off into the middle distance and did not seem to be present in the moment, nor aware of the playful child in her arms. Her face was pale, and although she had recovered well from the illness, having not been particularly strongly affected by it in the first place, she was now suffering mentally from the loss of Barnes, her close friend and partner.

Although a tough, arrogant man, he had softened immeasurably when Blythe had returned from Meds, and when Tyler had rescued her child to bring over to The Crags, he seemed to understand their necessity to be together and stepped into the role of father with surprising ease. His loss was felt all the more by Blythe because his death was directly linked to his love for Perry and his desire to protect her. We had to hope that the presence of a baby who needed her would help to get her through her grief.

There was no need for announcements at the end of the meal. Everyone was aware of the necessity of getting on with their chores, and Baker, who had taken to chalking up a list of the day's schedule on a board to one side of the dining hall, had made sure it was updated the previous evening before we retired to bed. One by one, people got up, cleared their plates and checked their assignments for the day before leaving to begin them.

I myself was part of the small group who were hunting today, as Rogers was absent. I didn't mind. I needed more practice with the weaponry, and relished the idea of being more active than I would have been on guard duty. I'd had enough of fishing the previous day, and those assigned to the hunting team were people I liked. I was looking forward to spending the day with Jackson, whose time was almost always spent with Mason now that they had been reunited, and, because Walker was an excellent shot with a bow and a rifle, I was hoping I could ask him for more training with both. Plus, as the partner of a good friend, I still felt like I didn't know him very well and wanted to remedy the situation.

The hunting areas were rotated between the different wooded sections on The Crags. There was far less woodland here than over on The Beck, and our success with the hunting was variable. Fishing provided us with a far more consistent source of food, but the variety provided in our diet by the squirrels and rabbits found in the woods was worth the effort. Today's hunting spot was a lengthy hike away, past the caves and over to the other side of The Crags island. It was a place I was unfamiliar with, but I enjoyed the walk there, observing Jackson's returning strength after her time in Clearance and Walker's much-improved mood now that Harper was recovering.

The first job was to check the traps, which were unfortunately empty. After the initial disappointment, Walker set about resetting them with fresh bait while Jackson and I found several quiet spots where we could conceal ourselves and wait for unsuspecting prey to appear. As we settled down behind a screen provided by some dense bushes, she leaned close, so that Walker couldn't hear.

"What's up? You seem very far away today."

I had forgotten how well she knew me. "It's good to have you back."

She smiled, waiting for me to continue.

Wondering how much of the information I should reveal when not even Rogers or Green knew it yet, I considered what to tell her. I knew she would be angered by the news of Adams' plans, but felt also that she deserved to know.

"I'm worried about Cam. But also about all the Beck citizens. We've had... some information. About The Beck and what Adams is trying to do over there."

Beside me, I felt her body tense.

"We're not sure what it all means yet, but he seems to be acting to reduce the population. More than he has done in

89

the past."

Her eyes flashed with anger. "But why?"

I shrugged. "That's what we're trying to work out. We aren't sure yet. Still working on the information."

"We'll help them, right?" Her voice was calm and low, but had undertones of steely resolve. "I mean, not right away, but we don't intend to leave them all over there and do nothing?"

I shook my head. "No. Once Rogers and Green get back, we can discuss what to do. You heard them the other night. They want to act. But they're right, there's no point going over there without backup, weapons, a plan which stands a chance of working."

"And Rogers wants that too?"

"More than anything. You have to remember he was the one who risked coming back originally." I stared at her, knowing what the fight meant to her. "We won't abandon them forever. We just can't help them right now."

Footsteps sounded as Walker approached, a finger to his lips to silence us.

Indicating we should move further apart and conceal ourselves in separate areas of the woods, he moved to a sturdy tree and hoisted himself up into it. Jackson backed away and moved to the other side of the clearing and we all checked our weapons and readied ourselves for a lengthy wait.

Several hours later we had managed to catch some rabbits and a couple of small ground birds. Satisfied that we had something for the evening meal, as well as meat which could be dried and stored to add to our reserves, we headed back to camp. The sun was low in the sky and, as we descended the path down the hillside, we could see a motorboat in the distance.

"That'll be Rogers and Green on their way back." Walker sounded relieved.

"You were worried for them?" Jackson said.

He rubbed a hand against his stubbled chin. "We don't know Hughes that well. We sent two of our key citizens over there. Anything could have happened."

"Hughes seemed like a pretty good guy when we went to The Beck," I mused. "Tyler trusts him, and she's a pretty good judge of character, in my experience at least."

He shrugged. "We'll see." Picking up the pace, he strode ahead of us down the hill, clearly eager to see Harper.

When we reached the centre, Walker took our catch into the kitchen and Jackson and I joined Mason at a table in the dining hall. Their reunion was a warm one, and I turned away and seated myself next to Shaw, who Mason was sitting with, embarrassed by their closeness.

He chuckled. "Don't think I'll ever get used to that being so public."

I glanced over at the couple, who had separated only slightly and had slid on to the bench next to one another. They grinned at us ruefully, but didn't seem sorry. Their time apart when Jackson had been left behind in The Beck had been difficult, and they were making up for lost time now.

"I know," I muttered at Shaw, attempting to roll my eyes and make light of it whilst fighting the surge of jealousy inside as I considered how long my own separation from Cam had been.

He stared at me for a little too long, and I wondered if he had not been fooled by my act. Eventually, he glanced away, the grin reappearing as he spotted Collins heading out of the kitchen doors.

"When's food ready?" he called playfully.

She threw him a dark glance. "Not for a while yet. Been on my own all afternoon. Baker decided to head out to check the progress we've made in the gardens earlier on. She isn't back yet."

"Want a hand?" he offered.

Her face softened. "But you've been mining all day."

He pushed himself into a standing position. "S'fine. I just need to go wash up a little."

Nodding at me, he headed towards the door, passing Rogers and Green with a smile as he headed out. Seeing the two returned, a number of the citizens in the room called out greetings. Interest in their trip to The Ridge was keen and there wasn't a single person on The Crags who wasn't desperate for a glimpse into the new place, which had the potential to be our ally. It wasn't long before the two were surrounded by excited faces, all waiting to pose questions.

Rogers waved a tired hand. "Look, I know you're all curious, but could you wait until we've had a moment to sit down?"

Green patted his arm. "He's right. We have a lot to tell you all, but just give us a few minutes, alright?"

The door behind them banged open again and the field team came in, headed up by Baker. Harper was with them, which surprised me for a moment, but then I considered Baker's insistence on visiting the gardens today and wondered if her giving permission to Harper to return to some kind of shift was partly the reason she had gone up there. Harper looked tired, but also invigorated, as she always did when she had been working with the plants. Her smile only widened when she saw that Rogers and Green had returned.

Typically, Baker did not smile. But when I watched her

greet her old friends, I could see the relief in her eyes and knew that she had been concerned about them while they were away. After she had spoken briefly to them, she hurried off towards the kitchen and disappeared inside. I suspected that our meal would not be long in the making, now that she was back and everyone was eager for news.

After a few moments, Rogers and Green shook off their followers and headed into the kitchen after her. Glancing around, I saw no sign of Tyler and felt like one of us should participate in the discussion about the papers from The Beck, so I slid off the bench I was on and went after them. Inside the kitchen, Baker was bent over a large pan of stew while Collins busied herself ferrying plates and silverware back and forth. Rogers and Green stood to one side of Baker, and glanced over at me as I entered.

"Will you fill these two in on the new information, Quin?" Baker jerked her head towards the smaller storage room at the rear of the kitchen.

Surprised that she didn't want to be involved in the conversation, I followed Rogers and Green inside and shut the door behind us. When I turned to face them, their eyes burned with curiosity.

"Well?" Green prompted.

I took a deep breath and dived in. "The papers from Hughes. We haven't managed to check them all out yet, but they seem to imply that Adams has something big planned. That he wants to... well he wants some kind of cull. He's trying to reduce the population, but pretty drastically."

"Why would he do that?" Rogers' voice was cold.

"We're not sure..."

"I mean," Rogers paused for a second, his eyes blazing,

"How can he sustain production of food, livestock, defences, maintain buildings, and so on... without a large workforce?"

"He's right," Green chimed in, "we struggle to do that here, and he has such an organised set up at The Beck... not one we feel is fair, of course... but it's effective."

"We're not entirely sure as yet. But he seems to have some kind of ideal in mind." I struggled to explain. "Like a 'perfect' citizen... who has all the qualities he feels are desirable, but he wants all citizens to fit that stereotype."

There was a silence, the two of them considering my words.

Rogers turned to Green. "Do you think... that's what Anders meant?"

"About Adams acting more irrationally?" She frowned. "Could be."

They turned back to me. "The message from Anders is that Adams is only taking certain measures to stop the sickness. Only in Upper Beck citizens..."

I took a deep breath. "So... it makes sense. He didn't expect the sickness, but he's happy to let it get rid of the population he considers surplus. Those who don't fit."

Rogers slammed a hand into the shelf behind him, making it shake. "He won't need such a large workforce if he doesn't have as many mouths to feed."

"No, he won't." Green removed his hand from the shelf, seemingly concerned he might hurt himself or break something. "Some clever reshuffling and he'll be able to maintain smaller numbers of livestock, cultivate a smaller number of fields, and so on. At least for the time being."

He scowled. "But there's still nothing we can do. Not yet, anyway."

She stepped closer to him. "That's what we agreed. For

now. But after our Ridge visit, there are things we can be doing. Small things, but preparing to act in the near future."

He sighed deeply. "Not soon enough for some though."

"No." She shook her head. "But we can't focus on that, can we?"

She turned back to me. "Thanks for filling us in. The meeting with Hughes was really useful, and the Ridge visit was truly eye-opening for us." Her gaze took on a more positive shine. "Their lives are so different."

"In a good way?"

"Yes, mostly. We could learn so much from them." She let go of Rogers' hand, seemingly certain that he had calmed enough not to hit anything. "Come on. We should go and say hello to everyone, reassure them. After dinner, we'll talk to them properly. There's a lot of news to share.

Realising that Tyler had yet to appear, I headed outside and walked over to the dorm, hoping to find her. I knew she wouldn't want to miss a big meeting. When I reached the door though, she was just exiting.

"Hey, where were you?" I smiled. "You need to come over for dinner. Sounds like Rogers and Green have big news." I stared more closely at her, noticing for the first time how pale she looked. "You ok?"

"I need to show you something."

"Show me later. We might miss the meeting."

"Quin." Something in her tone stopped me. "This can't wait."

For the first time, I saw the papers she clutched in her hand. I felt a chill down my spine. "What is it?"

"I've been reading more of the information from the file and... well, let's just say there's something you need to see."

"Ok." I sucked in a deep breath. "What is it?"

"Not here." She took hold of my arm and led me away from the dorm, across the courtyard and down the path a little way.

When we were almost out of sight of the buildings, she guided me over to a low rock. My heart was pounding, and I wondered what she had discovered. Something about Cam? About one of the others I knew, still trapped back in The Beck?

Once seated, she turned to me, brandishing the paper in one hand. "Look, Quin, it took me a while to work it out, but the records at the base of the pile relate to Meds. I've never seen them before, and I guess that Harris included them because of Adams' plans to impose even stricter control over the Birthing process."

"Ok." I hesitated. "What did you find?"

She paused, and a look of concern shadowed her features for a moment before she shook it off. "There are some recent ones, which suggest that they've started to restrict the women selected for Birthing to the Upper Beck only."

It made sense. "That works, if Adams is focusing his efforts on those citizens who fit with his ideal. He's clearly further limiting the pool he draws the parents from, making sure that the only ones able to have babies are those he's directly approved."

"That's right." Tyler glanced away from me, a strange expression on her face. "But... Harris included some older records in there too. Maybe to give us some idea of how Adams ran the Birthing programme in the past. To compare, if you like."

"And are there major differences?"

"Well some. But that's not what I need to tell you. The fact is..." she stopped talking for a moment, almost as if she couldn't find the words, "...the fact is that although the pool of citizens used for Birthing has been wider, for years Adams has been tracking those citizens selected for it, looking at how well they cope, how it affects their productivity afterwards, and so on. To decide whether or not a citizen should be used for Birthing more than once, and how they readjust afterwards."

"Right." I still wasn't sure where Tyler was going with this, and was keen to tell her the news from Green and Rogers. Shifting slightly on the rock, I tried to hurry her. "So, did you learn anything useful?"

"*Useful*? Perhaps."

"What?"

Finally, she thrust a paper in front of me. "See these names here? They're the names of the women selected for Birthing, and their Sector. Some of them go back more than twenty years. And here? Scores about how well they coped, how healthy they were during pregnancy, how easy the birth was for them."

I scanned the page, nodding as I took in the columns of information as she continued.

"This is the name of the baby that they gave birth to. And in the last column, the name they were given as they left Meds and were transferred to Minors."

Every child born in The Beck was given a name at birth, and a second one when they moved Sectors. This was done purposefully so that it was almost impossible for a mother to track down her child later in life. It was another harsh fact of Adams' cruel system, and Tyler's expression betrayed how she felt about the injustice.

"Mostly, it's a mystery who the mothers are. No one ever

sees these documents; they're locked away in Governance. We know from past experience," I knew she was thinking of Blythe, "how difficult some of the women find it to be separated from their baby and sent back to work. And how long the average life of a Beck citizen is."

I was well aware that our life expectancy was not long. There were few Beck citizens who were older, and those who did exist were novelties.

"Most of the mothers on this list are long dead, so the names in this column are quite unknown to me, even if the children aren't, but..." She trailed off, and I found my eyes scanning the page faster and faster, searching for a name that was familiar.

And then I spotted it. Around halfway down the page, in the final column, was my name. And as I followed the row of information across the page, my eyes lighted on the name of the woman who had Birthed me. The name of my mother.

Baker.

Chapter Eleven

As I read the words, the world seemed to stop for a moment. I heard a rushing sound in my ears, and found I was breathing faster than I should have been. I felt Tyler's hand on my arm and realised that I had jumped to my feet. The next thing I knew, she was stroking a hand down my arm and guiding me back onto the rock.

"You ok?" I couldn't meet her concerned gaze. "Quin?"

Taking a shuddering breath, I tried to find some words.

"Look, it's a shock, I get it—"

But she didn't get any further.

"Hey Ty, Quin!" The voice came from the direction of the courtyard. We looked up to see Mason staring across at us. "Dinner's ready. And Rogers wants to have a meeting. You comin'?"

He waved a hand and disappeared through the door towards the canteen. I felt Tyler's hand on my arm once more, but this time I shook it off. When I stood, my legs felt shaky, but I forced myself to put one foot in front of the other and began making my way after Mason. After a second, Tyler followed, her reassuring presence helping me to quicken my step and act like everything was normal.

Inside, we went about filling our plates with stew and

potatoes on autopilot, and I had just slid into a seat next to Cass when I spotted Baker across the room. She was just exiting the kitchen, bringing a second pan of stew out to the table where others were waiting hungrily. I watched as she exchanged a brief comment with Harper, before taking a portion for herself and retreating to a table at the rear of the room.

Tyler shot me a look of sympathy and I dropped my head, attempting to eat despite the fact that my stomach was churning. The rest of the meal passed in a blur, as those around me debated what news Rogers and Green had to discuss while I wondered how on Earth I would break the news to Baker, and how she might react.

After the meal was over, Green stood up at the front of the room.

"We have news," she began, "lots of news. Some of which can wait for discussion at a later time. For now, we need to let you know a couple of things. And, if you're in agreement, as we hope you will be, there are things we need to put in place in the coming days which will hopefully set us on the path to returning to The Beck to help our friends."

The mood in the room around us brightened further, and I found myself feeling curious, despite my distraction. Rogers held out a hand to quell the excitement. "Not all of our news is positive. And we must prepare for more trying times ahead. But we do have a plan."

"A workable plan," added Green. "Which we feel we can put into practice very soon, and which should, all things going well, mean we are able to return to The Beck with a realistic chance of stopping Adams in the not too distant future."

All eyes were fixed on the two as they stood together at the front of the hall. They held the respect of the group, despite never being elected as our leaders. I remembered a time when Thomas had questioned their command and demanded some kind of vote which would establish them as chosen rather than self-appointed. That time had yet to arrive, as things at The Crags had rarely been settled enough for us to hold such an election properly. But at the moment, I couldn't imagine that many among our number would argue with their leadership, especially now that Thomas was locked up and had little say in the matter.

"We have heard again from The Beck," Green began. "Anders tells us that many of the citizens over there are sick, and that Adams is doing little to support the Lower Beck. Sadly, some are already dead. And more may follow."

The enthusiasm on the faces surrounding us faded at the news, but the eyes remained attentive. Green continued. "We don't know why, but Adams seems bent on reducing the population on The Beck, and doesn't seem too fussy about how he achieves this. Disturbingly, he also seems to be building the number of Shadow Patrol guards, and experimenting with the effect of drugs on them, probably the ones he was about to deliver to those of you in the group who escaped with Rogers here."

Green nodded at Cass and the other Patrol recruits as Rogers took over. "Look, the sickness is clearly going to have a devastating effect on the community over there, and the larger numbers of Shadow Officers is worrying, but while we understand this, we stand by our previous statement that there is very little we can do about it at the moment."

There was a growl from the crowd, and I could see how difficult most of us found it. To know that their friends were dying and we couldn't help was agony.

Rogers interrupted the general reaction. "We do not have the resources: weapons, ammunition, manpower, to mount an attack that would be successful. The mission would be doomed if we went over there right now. However..." he paused, ensuring that everyone was paying attention before he continued. "...if we are prepared to stand with The Ridge, we feel we will, in the very near future, be in a strong enough position to fight back."

This time the noise was more hopeful. Hushed whispers began circulating, people beginning to pass comment on the hope Rogers offered. Most people seemed to find themselves encouraged by it.

Rogers continued. "We've had detailed discussions with Hughes and the other leaders on The Ridge. Despite our shaky beginnings, which were bred from their fears about the threat that we posed, they continue to prove themselves helpful. They have greater numbers than we have here, though not as many as we first believed, plus a large supply of weapons. They value their freedom, and their previous habit of firing at any passing craft stemmed from a paranoia that the island they had worked so hard to turn into a sustainable home might be taken from them."

"Like us, they try hard to demonstrate to outsiders that their community is larger than it actually is." Green smiled at the irony. "And they do this well. We believed that their community was potentially as large as The Beck, but in fact it's not. They have a lot more people than we do, but, previously at least, they have kept a close control on their population. Their leader before Hughes was very strict and had to grant permission for children to be conceived.

Now that they have new leadership, Hughes is in favour of expanding the community further, but he wants to ensure that they build up greater food stocks and other resources before they do. The Beck would allow them to do this."

"The current issue," Rogers finished, "is their lack of ammunition, as we know, but they have a smelting plant, and we have a lead mine. We would be able to trade lead for them to create bullets, and this will allow them to build their stores of ammo up again, and strengthen their defences, make their community stronger, and—"

"We don't fear that they wish to *take over* The Beck," Green interjected hurriedly, seeing the doubtful looks on the faces around her, "but they're very interested in having access to some of the resources there. Particularly their medicines, which they only have a very basic knowledge of on The Ridge." She paused, glancing at the sea of faces, seeking to reassure our community that working with Hughes was a positive step. "They're interested in working together with us, and they're prepared to provide us with additional manpower as we try to stop Adams and free The Beck."

"What do they get in return?" Walker's voice sounded strident above the silence in the room.

"For a start they'll get a regular supply of lead," Green said, "which they're prepared to assist us with by sending a few workers over to speed up the extraction."

"After that, looking ahead," Rogers continued, "they would like to have access to The Beck. Not that they would take it over, but that they would like to set up a working relationship between our communities, so that, wherever we live, we can have the benefits provided by the other islands."

"All of this would be agreed upon as we move forward,"

Green was quick to add. "And we have a long way to go with working it all out. Clearly we can't agree on any kind of working relationship with The Beck until Adams is removed—"

"You think that's even possible?" Price's expression was doubtful.

Green paused and looked directly at her. "I'm not sure. Before our discussions today, I would have said no. But wait until you see what The Ridge can offer us. As long as they show we can continue to trust them, we feel like we stand the best chance we ever had of standing up to Adams and winning."

Total silence greeted her final words, and I could see a range of expressions on the faces of those around me. Hope sprang anew in some, while others still looked mistrustful. But in all, there was something new. A sense of purpose. A sense that we were, for once, not useless, and that achieving our goal was an actual possibility. Even I felt it, though the shock of Tyler's news was still uppermost in my mind. Green had won the majority of the people over, and on the whole, they seemed to accept the sense of bonding with The Ridge to become a greater force.

But there was a long way to go yet.

"Look," Rogers sounded tired. "There's a lot to organise. The main idea we discussed with Hughes was the distribution of our combined workforce. We discussed hosting some Ridge citizens over here, to work in the mines, while at the same time, we plan to send some of our stronger citizens over there to begin training with their guards."

"*Live* over there?" Nelson's voice was incredulous.

"The additional weapons and ammo will only get us so far," Green soothed, sensing the shock at her partner's suggestion.

"Without trained soldiers to use them, we don't stand a chance."

"We have a number of ex-Patrol staff here who are excellent with weapons," Rogers continued. "On The Ridge they also have their specialists, those assigned to guard duties and defence. But we can't be naïve. We'll need large numbers of soldiers to win this fight. Without greater numbers, we won't stand a chance against Shadow Patrol who, by the way, are among the first citizens that Adams is protecting. If we put our experienced guards in charge of a larger, less-practised group, they can train them so that they're all able to use weapons effectively and therefore participate in a potential battle with The Beck."

"But that means splitting up our society," Green said, wanting to make it clear. "Temporarily, of course. But a necessary measure. We have to make some difficult decisions. Like who will stay here and man the usual posts, mine the lead..."

"...and which of us are capable of, and willing to, take on the role of soldier," Rogers continued. "We will, of course, attempt to take your feelings into account. We won't force people to fight. But we do need numbers, significant numbers, who will move to The Ridge and train, with a view to participating in the fight when the time comes."

"Think of it as your way of helping all those citizens in The Beck at the moment, who have been abandoned by their leader." Green always seemed to know what she should say to ease people's minds. "Even if you can't help them *specifically*, you'll be helping people *like* them to survive this. Enabling the beginnings of a new Beck. One where citizens won't have to live like this in the future."

Looking around at the tired faces in front of her, she turned to Rogers. "I think maybe we should..."

He nodded. "You're right. That's probably enough for now. Look, all we ask is that you think about what we've said. Tomorrow is the time for making decisions. We'll suggest the people we feel are appropriate choices to go to The Ridge and begin training. There won't be too many surprises I don't think: if you were Patrol or a trainee in Patrol, chances are we'll think you're a good bet. But before that, consider how you feel about it, whether you're prepared to go and fight."

"And remember it won't be forever." Again, Green provided comfort. "The goal is to be reunited with our closest friends and live in a fairer society. We just have some way to go before we get there."

All around me, people sensed our dismissal and began to leave. Those who were not present would want to know about the plans, and I suspected that many of the crowd would not go straight to bed, but would scatter to the various guard posts around The Crags and let those who weren't present in on the news. From the corner of my eye, I peered at Baker. She had remained silent throughout the meeting, presumably because Rogers and Green had told her the news beforehand.

Now she seemed thoughtful, and I found myself wondering whether she approved of the plans to liaise with The Ridge so closely. As I watched, she got up and walked to the central table. Lifting the large stew pan, she carried it across the room to the kitchen. Without planning it, I rose from my seat and followed suit, clearing our table and following her with the stack of plates.

Once the door had closed behind us, the sound of voices from beyond was muted. Baker nodded a quick thanks for my assistance and began spooning the leftover stew into a dish to save for later. I placed the plates on the counter next to the sink, and lingered in the room while others came in and out, clearing the detritus of the evening meal. Once the rush had died away, Collins began filling the sink with water.

"I can wash those." The words spilled from my mouth without me thinking much about them.

Collins looked surprised. "Are you sure?"

"Of course." I shrugged. "You look tired."

A smile broke over her face. "Well, if you don't mind, that would be great." She turned off the water and dried her hands on a towel. "Thanks, Quin. Really appreciate it."

She disappeared through the door and I took her place, running the water into the bowl and beginning to wash the plates which were stacked neatly on the side of the sink.

Baker seemed almost oblivious to my presence as she moved around the kitchen, tidying things and disposing of the minimal amount of leftover food. After several moments, she joined me at the sink and began to dry and put away the dishes that I had washed. As always, I admired her strength and her assurance, her familiarity with the room's set up lending a co-ordination to her movements as she returned the space to its usual order.

We worked in silence for a long time. Every time I attempted to share the information I had learned earlier, words failed me.

Eventually, Baker gave a loud sigh. "Well, spit it out then."

I was startled. "What?"

"You're a kind girl Quin, and I appreciate your help, but I'm not sure that giving Collins the night off was your sole motivation in coming in here." She paused, and when I didn't respond, continued just as swiftly. "You're not generally at home in the kitchen, so you must have a reason for being here, and if it was just to help me carry things, you've done that now and could have left. But you're still here, so I can only assume you have something else to say to me. So, like I said, spit it out. I've a lot to do."

Still, I stared at her, with no idea how to tell her. I opened my mouth to begin, then closed it, wincing internally at the growing frustration on Baker's face. I tried again.

"You're right. I did have... do have... something I wanted to tell you." I stopped, fingering the sheet of paper I had folded in my overall pocket. "The file Tyler has been looking over. It had other information in it. Information which relates to... well... me."

She stared at me, as though sensing for the first time the importance of what I might be about to reveal to her. "To you?"

"T-to me. Yes." I stumbled over the words. "And... to you."

"And to how many others?"

"No one else."

Her gaze was piercing, and I found myself utterly terrified of her reaction. Here was a woman, one of the oldest I had ever encountered, who had been so mentally scarred by the loss of her child that it had changed her, reshaped her personality irrevocably. Closed her off from the majority of people, shut her down, until she let very few people inside the protective walls that she had built around her. And I had the information which could destroy those walls in an instant.

"No one?" She frowned. "The information you have relates solely to you? And me?"

"Y-yes."

"Well let's have it then." When I still didn't continue, she raised her eyebrows. "How bad can it be?"

I almost laughed. "Not bad... exactly. Just... just a bit of a shock. Well, a lot of a shock."

The sound of voices, distant but inside the building, distracted me momentarily. My eyes flickered to the closed door and back.

"How long are you planning on keeping me waiting?" Her eyes on mine were unflinching.

I looked away, staring at the ground. In my pocket, my fingers closed around the piece of paper and I found myself withdrawing it and holding it out to her. She waited a fraction of a second before taking the proffered page and unfolding it, moving away to the counter to smooth out its rough edges so she could examine its contents. I found that my voice had somehow returned now that her eyes were not boring into me.

"It's a Meds list from several years ago. Tracking the babies born." Her back turned to me, she stared down at the page, her body rigid. "The names in the left column are those selected for Birthing. The columns that follow represent their Sector, and the outcome of the pregnancy. If it was a success, the final columns show the name of the child at birth and later."

Still, she didn't move. I waited, knowing she would work the rest out from the information in front of her. She was not a stupid woman. Now that the room outside had emptied, I felt the silence of the small space pressing in around us, weighing heavily on me as I waited for the woman who was my mother to react to the news. It seemed like an age.

"Do you..." I trailed off, hopelessly, no idea how to put my thoughts into words. "I know it's−"

But I never finished the sentence as the door was thrust open and Rogers burst through it.

"Are you done in here, Baker?" He didn't stop to hear his question answered, but pushed on, seemingly unaware of the tension which filled the kitchen. "Have we taken food to Thomas tonight?"

At last, the woman standing at the counter moved. Gesturing to the almost empty sink, she faced Rogers, as though I wasn't even present.

"Almost ready, yes. I'm sure that Quin wouldn't mind finishing up here. I was just about to take a tray through." She selected a knife from the drawer and began hacking chunks from a loaf of bread which had been standing on the counter. "Bread and water. Are we giving him anything else?"

Rogers shook his head. "Not at the moment, no."

Baker slid two hunks of bread onto a tray and busied herself filling a jug of water. "And did you make a decision?"

"About taking him to The Ridge? Not yet. I don't know how people will react, but Hughes assures me they have purpose-built cells for detaining prisoners over there, which will be much safer." He sighed. "The last thing I want to be doing is worrying about those left behind being at risk if he pulls any more of his stunts. If he's securely locked up over on The Ridge, we can all get on with things."

Completing the task, Baker picked up the tray and made for the door. "I'll deliver this and then head off to bed, unless there's anything else you need done before the morning?" She studiously avoided looking at me. "I'll make sure I'm up and have a good breakfast ready for you all before you set off."

"That's fine. Thanks, Baker. You have a good rest."

He smiled, as the woman who had just discovered that she was my mother turned and exited the room without even looking at me.

Like a zombie, I dried the last few dishes, then crossed the kitchen and collected the vital slip of paper from the counter where Baker had left it. Reeling from her total refusal to acknowledge the information I had just shown her, I slipped it back into my pocket and turned to face a curious Rogers.

"You ok, Quin?" He began. "You look a little pale."

"I'm fine." My voice sounded flat, and his look of concern increased.

"You sure? You don't look great. Get yourself to bed, Quin. Rest up, ok?"

Nodding dully, I passed him and opened the door of the kitchen, passing through the silent dining hall on my way out of the building. It was empty. There was no sign of Baker as I entered the darkened hallway. Clearly, she did not want to talk to me. I realised with a sinking heart that she really hadn't wanted to engage with the news.

In fact, it seemed that my mother had no interest in my presence at all.

Chapter Twelve

Over the next few days, things moved quickly. There were several other meetings where citizens were all given the chance to come forward and state their preferred choice of role in the coming weeks. Rogers and Green made their own suggestions for dividing the workforce, and between us we managed to make agreements about who would be where. A large number of people seemed willing to be trained to fight Adams, which demonstrated the strength of feeling among us. We had all lived under Beck rule, and none of us had liked it.

Decisions had been made. In total, eleven Crags citizens would be going to The Ridge. Those who were staying behind, either out of choice or because they had been persuaded to, were doing so for good reason: Harper, who was vital to our crop production on The Crags, her right-hand woman Price, and Blythe and Perry, for obvious reasons.

Mason had made some real progress in the mines. After some initial days of experimentation, his crew had settled on a method which worked well, and had since been bringing a consistent amount of raw lead down from the hills each day. The difficulty now was deciding where he would end up. Rogers felt he'd make an excellent soldier, already partially trained from Patrol in The Beck, but he had pioneered the mines project and was so far the only one who fully understood the best methods of excavation. Green was also concerned that he had only just recovered from the sickness and was not back to full strength yet.

The eventual decision was that Mason would remain on The Crags to begin with, training Shaw to take over as leader, and briefing the new Ridge citizens who were coming over. After that, he would move across to The Ridge and join in with the other recruits' training programme. Jackson was going immediately to The Ridge and was unhappy about their separation, but after some reassurance about the temporary nature of the posting, had accepted the situation.

After some discussion, Johnson had been released from the storeroom cell in the main building and permitted to rejoin the workforce, under close supervision. She was assigned to work alongside Harper, which surprised most people, but Harper had always been the forgiving type, and held no grudge against the young woman who it now seemed had been almost coerced into leaving with Thomas and Allen.

Johnson had originally come from the Agric Sector in The Beck, before volunteering as a Patrol recruit at the same time as Cass. She had not been from our pod but we had known her by sight. Harper was very aware that people's anger with the traitors was mostly linked to her own kidnapping, and knew that Johnson had had nothing to do with that part of Thomas' plot. In typical Harper style, she wanted to help Johnson be accepted back into the community, and knew that her own acceptance of the person most perceived as her enemy would go a long way to achieving this.

It had caused some issues with Walker, who was still

furious with Thomas and anyone associated with him. I had heard him arguing with her about the decision, but she always seemed able to calm him down and within a couple of days, Johnson was working hard in the fields and Harper and Walker seemed as close as ever. I noticed others glancing at Johnson with less negative expressions, and it was clear that Harper's actions were encouraging others to forgive.

I wondered if she or Walker would manage to be as forgiving of Thomas.

Two days later, Allen was also allowed to leave the storage-room cell. He worked with the fishing team to begin with, and Nelson was assigned to watch over him, which he did without complaint. Neither Johnson or Allen seemed prone to causing any kind of problem now, and both had worked quietly and diligently so far, clearly aware of the way their fellow citizens regarded them with suspicion and eager to prove their loyalty again. We had voted, deciding that both of them should stay on The Crags, at least for now.

Thomas, by a unanimous vote, remained in his cell. When Allen had been freed, Thomas had tried to force his way out of the storeroom, thrusting Nelson out of the way and only stopping when Rogers had floored him with a punch. He was now secured to the pipes at the rear of the room with rope, to prevent him causing any further trouble. His escape attempt had only confirmed most people's opinion that he needed to remain imprisoned for the time being.

Rogers planned to lead the party travelling to The Ridge, and train them to fight. He had put forward the idea of taking Thomas along to The Ridge, arguing that their purpose-built prison cells would be a better place to hold him. Most people were in agreement. Mistrust of the man who had abandoned and hurt us was still rife, and not many citizens were willing to take a chance on him causing trouble, once many of the stronger Crags citizens had left for The Ridge.

Throughout all of this, I moved in a daze, still struggling to come to terms with my recent discovery, and Baker's lack of reaction to it. My situation was unique. All Beck children were brought up communally, by the Meds Supers, from around twelve weeks old, and then transferred to Minors when they were five. This meant that no Beck citizen ever knew their parents. It just wasn't the way we were brought up. In fact, Blythe and Perry's was the first mother–child relationship I had ever seen. I had no idea how I should react, much less whether Baker's attitude was normal.

I had spent several hours talking with Tyler about the situation. She had explained that, according to some of the books she had read in the small library at The Crags, people in the old times had *always* lived in families. The majority of them spent their early lives with their own parents, from birth and throughout their childhood. Not just mothers, either, but fathers too. And they loved one another very deeply, mostly looking after their children very well. Caring for them, feeding them, educating them. I thought that it sounded like a nice way to live.

Only for us, it was sixteen years too late.

Sixteen years, where I had lived without a mother. Where Baker had lived with the pain of losing a daughter. She had spent much of that time hardening her heart to people and trying to live without affection.

Everyone knew Baker's history, though few ever brought up the subject around her. Her tendency to keep others at a distance stemmed directly from the emotional pain she had suffered after giving birth, because the bond she'd begun to forge with her own child had been severed.

And now we knew the truth. Her child, the one she had been separated from and believed she would never again know, was me.

I knew how badly Baker had reacted to having her child torn from her. But I felt no attachment to her. She was one of the least warm people I knew. I respected her, sure: her strength, her toughness, but I admired these qualities because I felt I did not have them myself. I admired them because they were a necessary part of making the difficult decisions a leader had to make.

In Rogers' absence, when the sickness had attacked more than half the citizens in the camp, she had taken charge. And done so well. She hadn't panicked or lost her head, and in doing so she had successfully kept The Crags going. In the end, we had only lost one citizen. When I had learned of her actions, I had been grateful that she was in charge.

But knowing that she was my mother was an entirely different thing.

Since the moment in the kitchen when she had found out, she had studiously avoided me. At mealtimes she ate quickly, and made sure that she was up and out of the canteen before most people had finished eating. And I knew for a fact she had changed the schedules in the kitchen so she could take on some shifts in the fields. As a result, I had barely seen her, and when we had been in the same room, she had refused to make eye contact with me.

After several days of this, I made a decision. I was going to The Ridge to train to be a soldier. My reasons were solid: I had been partially trained in Patrol on The Beck and had some weapons experience. I was strong, and despite my prior experience in Agric, I had never loved cultivating the crops the way that Harper did. I couldn't just sit on The Crags growing vegetables and hunting rabbits while a good number of my friends prepared to attack The Beck. I was also desperate to see Cam again, or at least find out what had happened to him. Rogers approved of my decision, and so did Jackson, Cass, and Green, all of whom were going to The Ridge too.

In the back of my mind though, I couldn't help but feel like I was running away.

On the morning of our planned voyage to The Ridge, I sought out Blythe, the only *real* mother we had on The Crags. She had been fairly withdrawn since the death of Barnes, and spent most of her time either quietly working up in the fields with Harper's team, or caring for her baby Perry. She had almost lost a child herself. And while I didn't feel ready to confess the reason for my curiosity, I knew speaking to her might help me to understand Baker's reaction better.

She was sitting at a table alone aside from her daughter when I approached her. She often arrived earlier than the others, and I knew she liked to get Perry fed before the rest of us arrived and distracted her from her meal. She looked up as I sat down and smiled gently at me.

"Hey Quin, how are you?"

I returned the greeting. "Ok thanks. How are things with you?"

She returned her attention to Perry, who was clasping a small spoon in her fist and banging it against the table top. "Alright, I suppose. She's eating better now, thank

117

goodness."

I watched as Blythe held out a small chunk of bread to her daughter. Dropping the spoon, the small girl took hold of the food and managed to raise it to her mouth, where she began to chew on it.

"Seems like she's getting the hang of solid food now."

Blythe chuckled. "She is. You know, a lot of it seems to be about letting her have some control over it."

Perry had now managed to smear pieces of the soggy bread over her cheeks and chin, but it was clear that she was eating some of it as well.

"It's hard, you know. Being the only one." Blythe's expression was frustrated. "There are no other mothers here. No one else to ask if I'm doing it right. What I might try to do if something isn't working." She stroked a finger down Perry's arm before continuing. "Green said they do things differently on The Ridge. I'm hoping at some point I could visit and speak to some of the parents over there."

"Sounds like a good idea." I hesitated before asking the question I really wanted the answer to, but pressed on, needing an answer. "Are you glad? I mean, even though it's difficult... you are... happy that Tyler rescued Perry and brought her here?"

She gazed at her daughter, running a tender hand across the soft hair on Perry's scalp. "Of course. You saw the state I was in without her." Perry knocked the spoon off the table and Blythe bent to retrieve it. "And even though it's hard, being the only one, and now that Barnes is..." She bit her lip and took a deep breath. "When I think of how many other Beck mothers have had to live with the knowledge that there is a child somewhere in the world who belongs to them but they can never see..." She shuddered. "Yes. I'll always be grateful for what Tyler did."

While we talked, the room had begun to fill with people, and around us the noise of chatter and the clatter of spoons and forks against plates grew louder. The mood seemed positive, if a little nervous. In a few hours, we would set off in the Clearance boat for The Ridge. And Shaw, who Rogers had been teaching to sail the boat, was going to bring some of The Ridge citizens back to assist with the lead mining production levels. Hughes had offered to let some of them come to The Crags temporarily, a further sign of his willingness to work in partnership with us.

Blythe and I were joined by Price and Marley, who sat down with a smile and began eating their morning rations. The conversation moved on to the impending arrival of The Ridge citizens. The three women were curious about what life would be like working alongside the unfamiliar people. I sat listening for another few moments, wondering how they felt about being left behind here on The Crags. As they talked, I watched Perry, noticing the way her smile and comical actions made everyone around her happy. If I was honest with myself, I could understand why missing out on this had made Baker the way she was.

Glancing around the room, I noticed that, yet again, there was no sign of her. She was definitely avoiding me. I felt the sting of rejection, and while I couldn't stop myself watching for her, I wondered at the same time why I wanted her to appear at all.

Chapter Thirteen

When Rogers arrived and began speaking to the group, I was glad of the distraction.

Even our usually calm leader seemed a little worried. He ran a hand over his hair with a tentative grin as he began to speak.

"So, the moment is here. Things are about to change. I hope we all feel happy with the place we have ended up. If not, remember that it is only temporary. We have all had to make difficult decisions over the past few days, but I really feel..." he paused and looked around the room, "...I really feel that we have the best chance we have ever had of defeating Adams and taking The Beck for ourselves."

There were a few muted cheers as he continued.

"I know we're all nervous. This is new to us. But when we set off from The Beck," he glanced at Green and Nelson, "when we *first* set off from The Beck, our only goal was to escape and build something better somewhere else. On the whole, we've managed that. But now we have the chance to go back. To rescue others. To take back the place which offers so much in the way of resources, if only it were better run. And we will run it better. But first, we have to take it from Adams, Carter, Reed, and their guards."

Now a low groan went through the group at the mention of our enemies. Rogers held up a hand to continue.

"There is no doubt that the next few weeks and months will be difficult. They will require sacrifice. But, in the end, when we take back The Beck as our own, it will have been worth it. Now, make sure you eat a good breakfast and check you have everything you need before we leave. We're scheduled to set sail in around two hours, so make sure that you're all down on the beach and ready in plenty of time."

The speech over, he sat down to eat his own food, and I took the opportunity to observe the others in the room. Rogers sat with Green, who was deep in conversation with Mason and Shaw, gesturing towards the mines as they discussed what would happen here while a good number of us were absent. At the next table sat Walker and Harper, leaning close together and not eating, but talking quietly. I knew that the separation was going to be hard on them, and could only hope that it was temporary, and brief.

Across from them, Nelson, Cass, and Collins sat together, not speaking but shovelling food into their mouths. Jackson was with them, and shot me a quizzical look. Although I hadn't spoken to her much lately, I knew she sensed that something was bothering me. I avoided her gaze, not ready to discuss Baker with anyone else yet, but knowing what her advice would be. Not one to shy away from a problem, she would tell me to try and speak to my mother again. Now, before I left and found myself on a different island, unable to have the conversation and regretting it.

She was right. Sighing, I got to my feet and headed for the kitchen, hoping Baker would be busy inside as usual. But when I pushed open the door, the room was empty. There was a tray lying on the surface, which contained the empty water jug and bread crumbs left over from Thomas' rations the previous night. Otherwise, the kitchen was as neat and tidy as usual.

A noise from behind me startled me, and I turned to see Green standing in the doorway.

"I was looking for Baker..." I began.

"Not here." Green tilted her head to one side. "She was up even earlier than usual... prepared all the breakfast for everyone before heading off somewhere. Said something about doing some extra hunting before the Ridge folk arrive, making sure we had as much food in our reserves as possible, you know... with the reduction in numbers here."

"Oh, I see."

"But I'm pretty sure she just wants to avoid the good-bye." Green smiled wryly. "She doesn't like to admit it, but she'll miss a lot of us when we're gone."

I tried hard to keep my face neutral, but knew as Green's expression changed that I had failed.

"What's wrong Quin?" She leaned closer. "Something to do with Baker? Do you know anything else about her disappearance?"

I paused. I trusted Green, and knew that she and Baker were close, but didn't feel right sharing information which was so personal when I had no idea how Baker herself felt about it. And if I couldn't talk to Jackson about it, I certainly didn't feel up to sharing the news with Green.

"Um, maybe." I considered my words carefully. "There was some other information in those papers," I began. "Not the kind which impacts us as a whole, I mean, nothing which you and Rogers would need to know about. Just... something which affects Baker, and…"

"I see." She smiled in her usual understanding way. "Well, I guess she'll tell me when she's ready. I can see you don't want to break a confidence, and I respect that."

I felt the tension leave my body at her understanding words. "Thanks. I'm not sure…"

"No. I totally understand. Look, if you want someone to talk to, I'm here. And the same goes for Baker. She knows that." She backed away. "Alright, I'm going to round up the troops, get people ready to leave. I'll see you in a little while."

The door swung shut as she left the kitchen and I stood alone in the space, wondering how Baker was feeling. I was certain she had left before most people awoke this morning in order to avoid any kind of contact with me, which seemed to suggest she just wasn't interested in accepting the fact that I was the child she had lost all those years ago. And perhaps she was right to leave it all in the past. Beck children were not brought up to have parents. Who was I to think that, because I could identify my mother, our relationship should be any different?

Taking a deep breath, I forced my mind to focus on the events of the day to come. Today, I was travelling to a whole new place to train to become a soldier in an army which would fight against Adams and attempt to retake The Beck, to save as many of its citizens as we could from its clutches, and to be reunited with Cam again. It was simple. There could be no room in my brain for anything else.

Squaring my shoulders, I headed for the door.

An hour later the majority of The Crags citizens were gathered on the shoreline. Walker and Shaw were readying the canoes to ferry those of us travelling to The Ridge out to the Clearance boat. Green was organising the various backpacks and boxes filled with the equipment we were taking along with us. Mason and his crew had been busy, and there was already some lead ready for transportation to The Ridge where it could be put to good use in the smelting plant. We had also packed a number of our weapons, including some of the small handheld explosives which we had brought with us when we left The Beck.

There were several excited faces among the crowd, but others seemed filled with trepidation, or a sense of sadness to be leaving close friends behind. Harper stood to one side, talking quietly with Marley, but the regular looks she shot at Walker were proof of her fears for him. Jackson and Mason were standing close together, their arms wrapped around one another, and I wondered if she would be able to let go of him and board the boat when the time came.

Baker and Rogers were conspicuous in their absence. Baker's I understood: I was doubtful that she would appear at all, but Rogers was supposed to be leading the mission. Walker and Shaw began to transport the equipment and some of the citizens on the beach over to the boat, and I could only presume that Rogers was on his way. I had just approached Green to question her when he appeared at the top of the cliff path.

Behind him, his hands still fastened together tightly with rope, walked Thomas. Many of the citizens had not seen Thomas since his capture, and whispers ignited around me as people reacted to his presence. The prisoner seemed reluctant, wearing his trademark scowl and pulling constantly on the ropes which held him as the pair neared the beach. Rogers simply ignored his resistance, pushing him forward and heading to a space further up the beach away from the rest of the community. It seemed that Thomas wasn't happy about coming to The Ridge with us. I wasn't surprised, but hoped that at some point he would start to show signs of regret for his past actions. Perhaps a new place would give him the chance he needed to prove he was a better man.

I noticed Walker frown as he assisted Cass into his canoe, and could see the difficulty he was experiencing just being near Thomas. As he did, Harper approached me. She looked sad, and I knew it must be difficult being left behind. But no matter how she felt about Walker and Cass and I, the best use of her talent was here on The Crags, continuing to care for and increase the crop yields in our new vegetable gardens. Harper was not a fighter, and Walker was. In the near future, I hoped we would be able to choose where to make our home. But for now, that simply wasn't an option.

"Take care of yourself, Quin."

She reached out and took both of my hands, and I was reminded of our first separation, after she had failed the assessment back in Agric. It seemed like a lifetime ago, yet the feelings were as painful as ever.

I bent my head and rested it against hers. "You too, Har. We'll be back faster than you know it."

She shrugged. "I don't think so. But I'll keep hoping."

Breaking away from me, she wandered further up the beach, returning to Marley and Price. Walker set off with Cass as Shaw returned to the beach. Feeling a sudden fear threaten to overwhelm me, I strode to the water's edge and nodded at him.

"You next, Quin?" He smiled a warm greeting. "Come on, then."

I took his hand and stepped inside the canoe, seating myself quickly. "Want help rowing?"

He shook his head. "I'm ok, but thanks for the offer."

Within seconds, the shoreline was receding from view. I could see what remained of the group on the beach getting smaller, both in terms of size and number. I looked away, feeling a confusing mixture of sadness at leaving and hope that our actions would lead to a better future for us all.

Shaw was silent, the only noise the rhythmic swishing of the oars entering and leaving the water as we moved away from The Crags. Swallowing my nerves, I blinked fiercely, and glanced back to the shore one last time. A solitary figure was making their way down the cliff path to where the others waited by the shoreline. It was difficult to make out who it was from this distance, but I squinted my eyes and eventually recognised the figure of Baker. It seemed she had changed her mind about staying away from the final good-bye.

But if she had come to see me, she was too late. I couldn't go back now, not without explaining my odd actions to Shaw. Blinking tears from my eyes, I again found myself filled with conflicting emotions. Surprise, that Baker had overcome her stubbornness and come to say good-bye. Frustration, that we had not discussed the life-changing news.

And finally, a tiny flare of a feeling I wasn't used to experiencing. Hope.

Chapter Fourteen

The journey went smoothly enough, and it did not take long before we reached the rocky coves of The Ridge. I remembered the first time we had passed the island, and how they had fired arrows at us from concealed positions along the shore. This time, our approach would be peaceful, cordial. Despite this, I couldn't help but feel a shudder of fear as we neared the foreign shore.

The boat was captained by Shaw, leaving Rogers free to keep a close eye on Thomas, who was fastened to the side of the boat's rail by the ropes. Green was close by his side, her decision to leave The Crags and be with her partner evident in every move she made. Clearly the only way she could stomach him leaving to fight was to make sure she was there by his side.

Making his disgust with Thomas clear, Walker was as far as he could possibly be from the prisoner. His tall form leaned on the rail at the rear of the craft, staring gloomily into the waters below. He looked tired, having worked hard ferrying his canoe back and forth, eventually leaving it behind and pulling Harper into a quick, hard embrace before joining Shaw in his boat for the final transport over.

Cass and Jackson had joined me close to the centre of the

boat, and others had grouped themselves in different sections of the craft as it motored towards The Ridge. The noise of the engine made it difficult to talk easily, but I got the impression that most of those aboard were lost in their own thoughts and did not wish to converse anyway.

Jackson had been too wrapped up in her sorrow at leaving Mason to ask me about my own bleak mood, but I suspected she would pin me down about it later on. As we had set off from The Crags, most of the small group on the land had waved their hands in farewell until we were out of sight, and although I hadn't looked for long, the one glimpse I had caught of them receding into the distance was branded in my brain.

I was fervently hoping that it would not be the last I saw of these people, of my people.

As we approached, I leaned over to Jackson. "How are we going to get ashore?"

"Hughes is sending the motorboat, I heard." She pointed to the shoreline, where the two Ridge motorboats were moored. "Can you see anyone aboard?"

I stood up and raised a hand above my eyes, squinting into the distance. Sure enough, the boats both seemed to have a driver, and several others were waiting on the shore. As we got closer, the motor boats began to head towards us, cutting through the water far more elegantly than the lumbering boat we found ourselves on.

Rogers cut our engine and waited. The boats had reached us within minutes, and pulled up alongside. McGrath was piloting one of them, the other was a tall man with a thick black beard and a friendly face. McGrath motioned for Rogers to drop anchor, and once we were stable, began to encourage people down the ladder and into one of the boats. The motorboats were smaller than the Clearance craft, but still held eight people each, and we would manage the voyage to shore in one go.

When it came for my turn, I stepped down into McGrath's boat. She smiled briefly in recognition as she offered me her hand while I stepped across. Minutes later we were speeding across the remaining gap between the boat and the shore. I felt a hand in mine, and looked down to see Cass clutching on to me tightly. Nodding at her, I squeezed it back, a sign of our reassurance that we would face whatever was to come together.

As I looked up, my eyes met those of Tyler, who grinned encouragement at me as she jerked her head towards the shore. Here was at least one person who was truly excited to be here, although I suspected a lot of this had to do with the camp's leader. I could see Hughes standing on the shore waiting for us, along with a number of Ridge citizens, presumably those who would be travelling back to The Crags to work alongside Baker, Harper, and the others. I wondered if they felt the same about leaving their home. I was willing to bet that they did.

The boat reached land faster than I was happy with, and soon we were all standing on a shore which looked similar to The Crags, but felt totally different. Hughes seemed even more assured than usual, and waved a hand as we walked up the beach, entering what I felt was, if not enemy territory, at least something alien and unfamiliar. There were around eight other people standing on the rocks alongside us, all of who waited to be transported to Shaw, waiting in the boat which would take them to The Crags. A few of them smiled, but they did not seem enthusiastic to be welcoming us to their home.

McGrath moored her own boat as the bearded man ushered the Ridge citizens aboard his. Once they were ready, McGrath slapped a hand on the side of the boat.

"Safe travels." Hughes smiled at the people as they settled themselves ready for their journey. "Get these folks to the boat quickly and report back to the hub, ok?"

"Aye-aye captain." The bearded man gave a mock salute.

McGrath stifled a smile and waved her hand briefly. "See you soon, Roberts."

The bearded man returned the wave as he roared off towards Shaw and the waiting Clearance boat. As soon as the noise of the engine had died away, Hughes stepped forward.

"Welcome." His smile widened. "If the nerves I've just sensed in those citizens leaving The Ridge are anything like what you're experiencing right now, I think we can identify with you. I know this is all new and strange, but I assure you we can be trusted." He glanced at our expressions. "But I also know that we'll probably have to prove that. Look... there's a lot to accomplish in the coming days, so I suggest we get started and work it out as we go along. Please follow me. It's just a short hike."

He set off at the highest end of the beach, moving along it rather than up out of it. The route we took seemed to hug the shore for a while, and as we reached some trees, we changed course, branching inland sharply and moving through a dense section of woodland which reminded me very much of those back on The Beck. Nostalgia hit me again as I thought of Cam and the woods close to Patrol. Despite The Ridge being physically closer to The Beck, he seemed further away than ever.

Feeling a presence to my right, I glanced over to see Jackson, who seemed as always to sense my mood. She smiled, a tight, sad smile which suggested that she too was struggling with our presence here. Her separation from Mason, however temporary, was a difficult one for her, and I knew she was putting on a brave face just as much as I was.

"It's a means to an end," she whispered. "That's all. Something that has to be done so that, in the end, we can get what we want."

Nodding fiercely at her, I said nothing. Just ahead of us, I noticed Thomas walking next to Rogers, his hands still roped together. There was nothing of the resistance he had shown back at The Crags. His head was down, but his eyes kept darting from one side of the path to the other as he took in our new surroundings. Clearly, Thomas was as nervous as the rest of us about The Ridge, and for the time being at least, was keeping his aggression at bay.

The woods around us were thinning out now and there appeared to be some buildings ahead. Unsure of what to expect, we all slowed our pace a little, until McGrath seemed to recognise our nerves and turned to Hughes, who stopped. She nodded at our reluctant group without speaking and he realised what the problem was.

"It's ok." He gestured to the buildings ahead. "Most people are out working this morning. I made sure that we carried on as normal. Didn't want you all to feel like you were being stared at. I know what that's like." I remembered their first visit to The Crags as he continued. "They'll be back at lunch, but by then you'll have had a chance to look around and settle in. Try not to worry."

131

He turned and strode into a large, open area. McGrath ushered us past her and brought up the rear, seemingly wanting to keep us all together. We gawked as one at the sight in front of us. From the water, the living quarters here had been hidden, but as we emerged from the woods the expanse of the buildings became clear. They were unlike any I'd ever seen.

Built from some kind of reddish stone, shaped into rectangular-shaped blocks, they seemed more solid than the wooden ones we had back at The Crags. But the set up was similar: built around a courtyard, which had benches ranged at regular intervals. There were several buildings, but they were far larger than those we were accustomed to. More like the main buildings at The Crags than the dorms, but larger still, there were at least five of them, and they rose higher into the sky than those we were used to.

"This is the hub, our communal living space." Hughes waved a hand around at the buildings. "They house things like canteens, storage, offices, kitchens, and so on. Our medical supplies, what there are of them, are kept in the building next door. We don't have much in the way of medical expertise, or medicines. That's part of what we're hoping to achieve from teaming up with you and gaining some kind of access to The Beck, which Rogers and Green lead us to believe has more advanced drug-developments."

He walked further still. "This building is generally used to cater to the children. There are a couple of rooms where the children are schooled, although not as often as I'd like. The older ones are often called on to do shifts alongside the adults." He shrugged, as though this didn't make him happy. "I'd like to have the children learning every day until they were at least twelve, but in reality, we often need the older ones."

He walked a few more steps and gestured through another window in the same building. "The older babies and infants are looked after in this room, while their parents are working. That helps to maximise our labour force. We currently only permit one child to be born per couple here, due to the constraints of the resources here on The Ridge, but I'm hoping in the future we might change that. Trading with you at The Crags, plus some access to Beck resources, would greatly improve things in that respect."

He continued on, until he was standing outside one of the largest of the buildings in the courtyard. "This is our main canteen. We have two, but we don't usually use the other. Not at the moment, anyway. Our population is served well enough by this one, especially as we don't eat all meals together. There are facilities for eating individually in the apartments."

He nodded at McGrath, letting her continue with the introduction. "Today we'll eat lunch together at midday. A sort of welcome meal for you, though I suspect you'll have to endure a lot of curious eyes."

Hughes chuckled. "You'll have to get that part over with at some point, though."

Rogers approached the front and turned to face us all. "I think we'd like to get that out of the way quickly. The people here have chosen to come because they want to train to fight Adams. We'd like to get on with that as soon as possible."

"Totally understand." Hughes nodded. "I'll show you your living quarters and let you get settled, then take you all on a bit of a tour before we eat. After that we can get straight on to some training, if you'd like?"

"Sounds good." Rogers nodded, then stopped, shooting a glance at Thomas. "Actually, we have a small issue. I mentioned it when Green and I were last here. The prisoner?"

"Ah yes." Hughes looked intrigued, glancing over at Thomas with open curiosity. "As I told you, one of these buildings has a number of secure cells. They were used to house soldiers on the base, those who had broken laws and so on. Only one of them is currently in use, which leaves several empty. Happy to house your friend...?"

"Thomas," Rogers supplied, "and he's not exactly a friend."

Hughes looked amused. "Happy to house Thomas there for the time being, then. Want to take him there now?"

Rogers glanced over at the remainder of the group, who looked expectantly at him. "Sure. The sooner the better."

Hughes nodded at McGrath. "Can you take him over while I show the others their accommodations?"

McGrath stepped forward, beckoning Rogers to follow.

For a second, Thomas resisted.

"Look, Rogers..." He was jolted sideways as our leader pulled on the ropes which fastened his wrists together and stumbled as he tried to stay upright. "...is a cell really necessary? I mean... couldn't I just... don't you want me close at hand, where you can keep an eye on me?"

"No, Thomas." Rogers smiled. "As long as you can't escape, I don't care where you are."

The other man's face fell. I was right: Thomas was far less confident of himself here on a strange new island, and the idea of being incarcerated in a cell purpose-built for prisoners in a place filled with strangers clearly did not appeal.

"But, I—"

"But nothing. You'll do as you're told, and go where I put you, until I change my mind."

Thomas fell silent, his look of vulnerability masked with the typical grimace.

"Let's go then." McGrath was a woman of few words, and set off in the direction of a building on the far side of the courtyard without waiting to check whether the other two men were following.

Hughes jerked his head in the other direction. "If the rest of you want to follow me, then."

He headed across the courtyard and walked between two of the larger buildings, closely followed by Green, who had taken Rogers' place at the head of the group in his absence. As we wandered past, I peered in through the glass. In one of them, I spotted a kitchen, much larger than ours at The Crags, with several people busy preparing food. In another there were people sitting at long tables with material spread out around them. It looked like they were crafting clothing of some kind. A few of them looked up as we passed by, and I glanced quickly away, not sure how welcome my curious gaze would be to these strangers.

Behind the main circle of buildings lay a wide, straight path, along which several smaller, two story buildings were situated. They were fairly uniform, and built from the same stone as the main buildings we had left behind.

"These are our living quarters." Hughes pointed. "We have a large number of them, and they're not all currently full. We've assigned you to one altogether. It's currently empty, so you won't be living alongside the rest of the citizens. We felt you'd be more comfortable that way, at least to start with."

He shot a sidelong glance at the group, as though monitoring how we might take this. It certainly seemed quite a leap, to presume that at some point in the future we might want to live alongside the Ridge people. I was certainly planning on being a temporary resident here, my goal being to learn, and be part of a force large enough to conquer Adams successfully and return to live somewhere more familiar. I could tell that the rest of the group felt a little uneasy at his suggestion, and he seemed to sense it too, moving briskly along the road and ignoring our silent response to his suggestion.

"Not sure how your dorms are set up at The Crags..." he paused, as though he thought Green might butt in with some information, but continued when she didn't, "...but we have two different types here. A long time ago this was an army base, and had families living here as well as single training recruits. That means we have dorms which house several soldiers in one large space, and also family quarters, which means smaller individual dwellings where couples or people with children live together, slightly separated from the rest."

This time Green did interject. "We do have rooms which can house couples, but no family accommodation. We're not used to that kind of set-up at all."

"Well we've put you up in one of the buildings which was created for families. It has several smaller units, called apartments, where several people can live together. There are two- or three-bedroom set-ups, so I suggest you divide up your number into the groupings they're most comfortable with, and place them into different apartments accordingly. You'll still be together in terms of one larger space, you'll just have more privacy."

He stopped walking as he reached one of the structures

towards the end of the long path. It looked in fairly good repair, though was less lived in than those we had already passed, where I had spotted colourful drapes at the windows, chairs outside on the porches, and various other items which suggested people had made their homes inside the buildings.

"Here you are." He looked a little nervous for the first time since we had stepped off the boat. "I hope it's ok. It hasn't been used in a while. I did have some people go in and clean it out for you."

"That's very thoughtful." Green surprised me by clasping Hughes' hands in her own. "I'm certain it will be lovely, and once we're used to it here, we'll feel very welcome. You might just have to allow us to adjust a little."

"Of course." He backed away slightly. "Want me to come inside, or...?"

"Thanks, but we'll be ok." Green seemed to sense our group's need to unload, and knew that Hughes' presence made it difficult. Not one of us had spoken since we got off the boat aside from Rogers and Green. "I'm sure we'll be able to work it out."

Hughes nodded. "No problem. I'll head back to the hub then, check that Rogers has got Thomas settled in alright."

"Sounds good." Green smiled at Hughes. "Thanks. We really appreciate this."

"Meet you back there in a few minutes, then." Hughes took a step away, almost seeming embarrassed. "Give you a chance to allocate rooms and unload. Then we can take a tour."

"Great." Green shot a smile at him as she turned away. "Fingers crossed this will all work out."

"It will. Hopefully, we can all benefit, in the end." He shot a final glance at the group, and shot a brief smile at Tyler, before turning and striding back to the hub.

Chapter Fifteen

We waited a few seconds until he was out of earshot before anyone spoke. Finally, the spell broke.

"Everyone ok?" Green was the first to speak.

There seemed to be a collective exhaling of breath as we visibly relaxed.

"Sure."

"I am now."

"Just about."

The space around me erupted into chatter about our new surroundings. Everyone wanted to discuss the differences between The Beck, The Crags, and here, and we broke into smaller groups, each one spilling out the words we had been saving, interrupting one another, all talking at once. The volume of our chatter became so loud that I saw Hughes, his figure now receding into the distance, turn back and observe us for a moment. I got the impression that he smiled to himself as he turned to walk away, although he was too far away for me to see his expression.

Green held up a hand to stop the chatter, and motioned for us to follow her. She walked through the front door of the building, the rest of us filing in behind her, eager to see how the interior differed from more familiar surroundings.

Inside, there was a large hallway, out of which led several doors and, facing us, was a staircase.

"How do we want to do this then?" Green asked. "Hughes mentioned apartments with two and three bedrooms, so I guess we split into groups and distribute ourselves throughout the building accordingly."

I looked around at the people around me, and knew I would be most comfortable with Jackson, Cass, and possibly Tyler. But there was also Collins, who knew Cass from their time as Patrol recruits together, and Marley, who was here as the most unlikely soldier, but had been among the first to volunteer and seemed as determined to fight as anyone. In the end, there were far more rooms than there were Crags citizens, so there was no need to fill every apartment to capacity.

Cass and I took a room with two single beds in a three-bedroom apartment, with Tyler in one of the other rooms and Jackson in the third. At first, I had been concerned that both Cass and Jackson would want to share with me, and thought perhaps we might share a room altogether, but when Jackson happily took a double room to herself, I figured that perhaps she was hopeful that, with the arrival of Mason, she would eventually have a roommate. A second three-bed apartment was taken by Nelson and Walker, taking a room each, joined by Collins and Marley sharing a double. Finally, Rogers and Green took a two-bedroom apartment to themselves.

After we had unloaded the few belongings we had, we headed back downstairs to find the others waiting. No one lingered in their apartments, and I suspected this was because the separation they provided was so unfamiliar. Hughes had spoken of privacy, but we were used to living in close quarters, and having everyone witness everything that happened to us. Just like gaining the freedom to speak after many years of having to whisper whenever we spoke, having our own space would take some getting used to, even if it was only a temporary situation.

Together, we set off back to what Hughes had called the hub, making the walk in almost half the time now that we knew where we were going, and felt more settled. Rogers and Hughes were waiting for us; Thomas was nowhere in sight.

"Ready?" Hughes smiled around at us.

His question was met with silence, but this time at least we felt able to nod or smile in response to the invitation. We were slowly warming to our host.

He began by gesturing in the direction from which we had come. "You've already seen the living accommodations. The majority of our citizens live in apartment buildings similar to the one you're in."

He now motioned around him at the circle of buildings. "This is the hub – like I said earlier – its where we meet... spend any time together communally. We try to make sure we do that at least once a day, though our differing shifts mean that we're never all together at the same time."

That, I thought, at least was similar to The Crags. We began walking into the woods we had entered through earlier, but this time took a turn in the opposite direction from the shore where our boat had landed. We walked for several minutes, in an uphill direction, until we came out of the woods and into an area which was clearly cultivated for growing crops. Smaller than The Beck, and not as flat, the fields were nonetheless planted with various grains and vegetables, and a number of Ridge citizens at work among the crops turned to eye us curiously as we passed by.

"Self-explanatory," Hughes waved a hand at the citizens at work. "Let's move on."

Skirting the edges of the fields, we headed uphill again, to a sector surrounded by high wire fencing. Inside, were a number of flattened sections of land with strange markings on them: lines ruled in various patterns across the ground. We stopped as one to stare at the space, so unlike anything we'd ever seen before.

"The sports pitches." Hughes explained, then seeing our confusion, he attempted to clarify. "Football? Basketball? We play games there sometimes."

"I'm afraid that kind of thing is a mystery to us." Rogers shook his head ruefully. "You'll have to explain it better sometime."

"I definitely will." Hughes looked amused. "Anyway, for now we've assigned that space to combat training for the new recruits. We'll start using it this afternoon."

We kept walking until we reached a long, low building which Hughes made a beeline for.

"The shooting range," he explained, ducking inside. He shook his head ruefully. "Though we haven't been able to practise firing anything for a long while."

He motioned to a bar which ran along the length of the space in the centre, and then pointed at a set of brightly painted circles which were ranged all along the walls at the far end of the space.

"The targets." He walked to the storage lockers at the side and opened two of them at once. "And the weaponry."

There was a collective gasp as we saw their contents. Row upon row of guns were stacked neatly inside.

"Of course, most of these are unused at the moment." Hughes sighed. "Without the ammo to supply them, they're useless."

Shaking his head, he closed the lockers and moved on, walking out of the range and into the building which lay directly behind it. It was a similar size, but built from sturdier material and with a stronger-looking door.

"This is the smelting plant." Hughes opened the door and walked inside. "Never before used by us, but we've had a small team in here working on clearing it out for a few weeks now, in the hopes that—"

"...that we'd agree to teaming up," Rogers finished.

"That's right." Hughes moved in through the door. "There isn't too much space in here, but I think we can pack ourselves in for a minute or two."

We stepped inside, and were greeted by another unfamiliar sight. The space was filled with large metal instruments and machinery, for the time being standing silent and still. The closest thing I'd seen to this previously was the Warehouse in Clearance, where The Beck made all of its clothes. I imagined a similar noise spilling out of the smelting plant as each of the metal giants vied for attention and I hoped silently that I would never have to spend much time here.

We managed eventually to cram inside the building. As we gawked at the unfamiliar sight, a tall young man and a petite older female with bright red hair wandered forward from the rear of the space, openly staring at us.

"Parker." He gestured at the man. "And this is Millett." He pointed at the woman, who was wiping greasy hands on an old rag. "They've been assigned to clear the place out for potential use."

"Good news on that score," Green interjected. "We've been able to bring the first of the lead with us today." She smiled at the two Ridge citizens. "You should be able to get this place working very soon. With the assistance provided by the citizens you sent over to The Crags, we'll soon be able to increase our collective ammunition levels."

Parker and Millett, who had until now been regarding us with something like suspicion, looked encouraged.

"That right?" Millett said. "Think we've almost got the machines up and running now. If you can bring the lead up, we can get going with it straight away."

"That's wonderful." Hughes smiled at the prospect, as a loud ringing sound cut through the air around us.

The majority of our group jumped, and stared in alarm at one another. I saw Millett stifle a smile behind her hand.

Hughes held a hand out to reassure us. "That's only the canteen bell." He laughed. "It just means there's food available."

Hughes stepped closer to Parker, muttering something in his ear, before motioning to the door again. "Let's get this over with, shall we? You're going to be the object of a lot of stares in the next hour, but it's only natural curiosity. After the meal we'll head back to the pitches, meet your fellow trainees, and begin training together. Who knows," he chuckled, "maybe we could teach you to play football, eventually."

Shooting a grin at Parker and Millett, he set off in the direction we had come. One by one, we filed out and followed him. We reached the hub to find a very different place. Instead of a large, open area, the space was almost entirely filled with people, milling around and slowly making their way into the canteen building. I suspected that on a normal day, the movement into the hall which served the citizens their food moved more quickly, but today, when there were far more interesting things to be seen, The Ridge citizens were taking their time.

A myriad of expressions greeted us: wide smiles, curious stares, determined indifference, and, occasionally, open hostility. Clearly, the residents of The Ridge were divided over our presence. What struck me was the wider mix of people here. For one, there was a larger number of older people than I had ever seen. For another, there were children mixed in with the adult community. Not too many, granted, but enough that it stood out as strange to me, so used to a population which separated its youngest members from the rest of the community.

The other startling difference was the clothing. The people here did not all wear uniform overalls. Some did, in fact there was still a large amount of what were clearly practical work clothes, yet there were a lot of others who were dressed in quite a different manner. Instead of trousers, many of the female citizens wore longer garments which did not have separate sections for each leg, and swished around their legs in a hypnotic way. Often, the garments they wore seemed to be all-in-one, covering the whole of their torso as well as their legs, yet some also had a separate shirt or top. And there were many different colours and fabrics on display within the crowd of people.

I realised that we were gaping at The Ridge community as much as they were at us. Though I did feel under scrutiny, I knew I was subjecting them to something similar, and somehow that made it feel less uncomfortable. I wondered how those citizens we had left back at The Crags were reacting to Shaw's boatload of Ridge folk. Probably the reaction was the same. From experience, I knew that Baker would not accept new people with open arms.

My heart gave a sudden jolt. I had not thought of Baker since I'd set foot on The Ridge, but now the crashing disappointment of her reaction to my revelation swept over me. I wasn't sure what reaction I had been hoping for, but it was not indifference. Tyler had assured me that she just needed time to adjust to the news, but now that we had been separated, I had no idea what she was thinking, nor when the next time was that I would see her.

I realised suddenly that the line in front of me had moved, and the people at my back were waiting impatiently for me to move ahead. Shaking off my depressing thoughts, I forced myself to put one foot in front of the other until I was standing just inside the door to the canteen. Ahead of me, people were filing into the large space and finding their way to tables where they sat down, chattering loudly. I followed the remainder of my own group as we were directed to a table at one side of the room which seemed to have been reserved specially for us.

As I took my seat, I noticed a small boy sitting at the table to my left. He, like most of the room, was staring at our table, but his expression was simply one of curiosity. There was no hint of discomfort or anger in his face. Catching me looking back at him, his eyes grew wide and he ducked behind the woman who sat next to him. She had not been looking at us, but as she felt the boy, her son, presumably, hide his head in the folds of the loose top she wore, she glanced over to see what he had been startled by.

Her eyes met mine, and I prepared to look away, not wanting to frighten or threaten anyone at The Ridge, but she surprised me. Instead of scowling, or staring with open curiosity, her lips simply curved into what looked like a genuine smile. Her good nature was infectious, and I found myself echoing her expression. Next, she bent and whispered something in the ear of the boy at her side. I watched as he shook his head vehemently, yet a moment later he peeped out from under her sleeve and his eyes met mine again.

Instinctively, I stuck out my tongue. Again, he darted behind his mother, but a moment later he peered out again and this time, he copied my expression, darting out his tongue in a mirror of me before disappearing again. We repeated this performance, his mother catching on and playing along, until the room grew silent and I turned to see Hughes at the front of the hall.

"Hello everyone," he began, "now I know we don't often meet here for a large meal in the middle of the day, but I felt it important that we all were here to greet and welcome our guests."

He gestured expansively to our table, and my original feeling of being under intense scrutiny returned full force.

"So here they are. Citizens from The Crags. Here, for now, to train with us, but with a view to building a working relationship in the future, so we can help one another to succeed. I know not all of you were comfortable with the idea of them being here, but I hope that you'll all give them a chance. We have long known about how short on ammo we are here. These people can help us solve that problem. And as for collaborating in other ways, well we'll see..." He trailed off for a moment and moved his gaze around the room, making steady eye contact with someone at every table. "For now, I ask you only to make them feel welcome, help them to settle in. I really believe that we'll be stronger together. Now let's eat."

As the room filled with chatter again, I considered my impressions of The Ridge so far. Hughes' welcome had certainly been warm, and said a lot about the start of our relationship with the community. I found myself daring to hope that this was the start of an effective working partnership with people who had the capacity to help us defeat Adams and retake The Beck.

Hopefully, it wouldn't be too late.

Chapter Sixteen

The canteen system here was quite different from what we were used to. As Hughes sat down, a number of citizens who had been standing at one side of the room came forward with trays and began passing out bowls of food to the tables. We were unused to being served food, but it was nice not to have to get up to fetch our own. The young girl who brought the food across to our table smiled shyly as she approached. Her head lowered and a cloud of frizzy hair flew in her face, while she bent to place a tray on the end of our table, next to me.

"Thank you." I smiled back at her.

She blushed pink and dropped her gaze, hurrying away to fetch another tray from the kitchen. When she returned, we repeated the same process, until I spoke again.

"Is this your job? Serving the food, I mean."

"T-the younger citizens take turns to serve on occasions like this."

"Occasions like this?" I queried.

She looked at me, puzzled at my lack of understanding. "Most of the time, we eat lunch in our own apartments, or take food with us to our jobs. But we all have dinner together a few times a week." She looked over her shoulder nervously, as though checking no one was watching. "And today, Hughes arranged this lunch so we could all meet each other." She grinned suddenly. "He suspended school for the afternoon, so we could join you all."

"That's nice." I considered Hughes' efforts. "It seems like he really wants to make this work."

She shrugged. "He's been talking about it ever since he first met you all."

She turned to go.

"What do you learn in school?"

"Learn?" Again, she looked startled. "Um... reading, and our history, and how to add and divide and multiply... sums, you know?" She nodded at a building on the opposite side of the yard. "We have it three days a week. The rest of the time, we work. Training on the job with the adults, so we can take over when we're old enough." She made a face. "But Hughes says school's important."

I nodded. "Well thanks. And it was nice to meet you, um..?"

She stared at me for several seconds before blushing again. "Simpson."

"How old are you, Simpson?"

She strained, perhaps trying to look taller. "I'm nine."

I hid a smile. "Ok. See you later maybe?"

Lowering her gaze again, she nodded slightly and scuttled away. I watched her serving several more tables before she was able to join her own and begin eating.

"What do you think?" Cass elbowed me, her mouth already crammed with food. "Pretty good, huh?"

I picked up a spoon and began helping myself to the food in the bowls Simpson had delivered. The trays contained bread which was softer than I was used to, plus a tureen of some kind of soup, again, finer than I had experienced before.

I grasped a spoon and tasted the yellowish liquid. It was a vegetable of some sort, and extremely tasty. Realising how hungry I was, I wasted no time, dipping the bread into the mixture and savouring its unusually smooth texture. The food here was good.

Once we had finished, I saw that Hughes had been right: the discomfort of the initial reaction was over, and most of the citizens had gone back to their usual routines. Having eaten their meals and shared stories about their morning, many of them began to leave, presumably heading off to their afternoon shifts. As they cleared out, only a few of them glanced over at our table, but mostly the stares were simply inquisitive.

Throughout the meal we had noticed that the community was different in the way that it grouped itself: mothers and fathers seated together, children scattered around the room, sandwiched in between the older citizens, a few tables which seemed to house groups of people in their late teens and twenties. I thought again of Baker as I remembered Tyler's claim that in the past, this was the way things had always been. The people here clearly lived that way, and, on the whole, seemed quite content.

Most of the inhabitants of the table next to me had yet to leave, and the little boy was still glancing in my direction every now and again, between shoving handfuls of bread into his mouth. In his other hand he grasped what looked like a rabbit made from some kind of material. His mother was chatting to a woman with white blonde hair who reminded me of Cass, patiently handing him small chunks of food when he became distracted and stopped eating. I thought of Blythe and Perry with a small pang of loss.

Suddenly, the boy dropped the stuffed animal on the floor and twisted in his seat, his eyes searching wildly for it. Spotting the cloth rabbit behind him, I stood up and retrieved it without thinking. I held it out to him, attempting to return it, but instead of taking it, he stared at me, his eyes huge and wary. The longer I stood holding out the treasured item, the more foolish I felt.

And then, his mother turned to me and smiled. Touching her child's cheek, she whispered soothingly in his ear. Glancing from his mother and back again to me, he reached out and wrapped his little fingers around one of the rabbit's arms. I held on to the other for a few seconds, and a puzzled look came over his face. When I tugged it back towards me gently, his eyes widened again and he tightened his grip. Finally, I let it go, and the delighted expression on his face as he won our little battle brought an echoing smile on my own.

"He likes you." His mother was also smiling. "If he's willing to let you hold Timmy, he definitely likes you."

"Timmy?"

She pointed at the rabbit. "His favourite toy. Had it since he was born." She smiled affectionately at the other woman. "Ross here made it for him."

I nodded at the little boy. "What's his name?"

"Rico. He's just turned two. And he's a little terror." She smiled affectionately at the blonde woman. "You've no idea what you're in for, Ross."

I glanced across at the second woman, surprised to see the swollen stomach underneath her clothing now that I was closer to her. She caught me staring and I glanced away, blushing.

"Maybe not, Coleman," she elbowed her friend, "But I

can't wait to find out."

I looked back at her, grateful that she didn't seem offended by my curiosity. "How long before…"

She gestured to her stomach. "Still a few weeks yet."

I nodded, thinking of my friend Riley who had been pregnant the last time I saw her in The Beck. I knew she was being kept safe from the sickness; Adams valued the Meds Sector, but I wondered when she would be due, and what kind of society her baby would be born into. I was certain that she would not be smiling and joking about the prospect of upcoming motherhood the way Ross was. Unhappy at the thought, I turned back to the small boy.

"Hey Rico," I tugged on the rabbit's arm again and he clutched it territorially. "I have to go. See you later, huh?"

"La-ta! La-ta!" He crowed loudly.

The noise of his screech drew more attention, and I began to back away. As I did, I almost bumped into a man who was coming to sit at one of the empty spaces at the table. He caught my arm before I tripped.

"Thanks!" I managed breathlessly before looking more closely at him.

It was Howard, the man who had guided our motorboat from The Crags to The Beck on our recent mission. He was not a tall man, but broad, and as a smile of recognition spread across his face, I couldn't help but reciprocate.

"I wondered if you'd be one of those who were coming from The Crags. How are you?"

"I–I'm good, thanks."

"Glad to hear it." He swung past me and slid into place beside Rico, tickling the little boy in the ribs and grinning even more broadly. "And how are *you*, my little love?"

153

Rico burst into laughter as Howard tickled him. "Daddy! Daddy, stop!"

Noting the look of adoration from Coleman, I felt a stab of jealousy. Howard, it was clear, had a partner and a son, and the entire group at the table seemed to welcome his arrival. Then there was Ross, with a baby on the way that she would get to keep and bring up, surrounded by supportive friends and family. Again, I marvelled at the different way the Ridge people lived, and hoped that Blythe would be able to come here at some point, to benefit from the support of others like her.

Turning to rejoin my own group, which was preparing to leave, I saw that the plates and trays had already been cleared to one end of the table. Marley was gazing around, trying to work out where to take them.

As she did, Simpson appeared out of nowhere. "Leave them there." She spoke quietly, her voice barely audible above the chatter in the rest of the room. "Thanks for stacking them."

"No problem." Marley smiled broadly at her. "Sure you don't want a hand?"

Simpson blushed. "No, it's fine. It's my job."

"Ok. See you later then." Marley shrugged, and went to join the rest of the group.

Throwing a last little wave at Rico and his family, I hurried to join them. Outside, Hughes and McGrath waited for us. Hughes was shouldering a large duffle which looked light as a feather, but I was willing to bet had a large number of heavy weapons contained within it. Waiting until we reached him, Hughes smiled around at us and nodded, as though satisfied with something.

"Ok folks," he began, "we're heading up to the pitches

to brush up on our knife work, and maybe look at bow and arrows. I have ten of my own citizens also assigned to this training. We've reorganised our work schedule to accommodate it."

He glanced at Rogers, as if prompting him to speak. It struck me what a good leader he was, so aware of the people around him and the way they perceived his actions. He knew that we were still wary of him, and by deferring to Rogers in some matters, he instilled confidence that he didn't hold all the cards.

"You will all be working together to form part of a larger team which can defend and fight against The Shadow Patrol, if and when it becomes necessary." Rogers sounded as calm and confident as ever.

"We're starting with twenty new citizens," Hughes continued, "but these will be supplemented by a larger force of Ridge guards who are already weapons-trained, and we can increase the number of newer soldiers we train in the future if it becomes necessary. Let's head on up to the pitches now and meet the rest of the team."

Hughes set off in the same direction we had gone earlier in the day. We followed, falling in line behind him. He and Rogers talked together at the front, while McGrath strode on ahead. I felt a presence next to me and turned to see Jackson at my side.

"Hey."

"Hey yourself." I looked more closely at her. "You ok?"

She shrugged. "Yes. And no. I just wish Mason were here."

There was a silence. I didn't know how to offer comfort to her when I had no idea how long it might be before the two of them were together again. Eventually, it was Jackson who broke the silence.

"How about you?"

I shrugged. "Oh, I'm ok."

"Liar." The word had no malice in it, but I could feel her sharp gaze penetrating me as we walked along. "There's been something wrong these last couple of days."

I bowed my head. "I just... I found something out. That's all. Something pretty big."

She waited patiently for me to continue.

"The papers from The Beck. The ones that told us about Adams' plans... well they had other information with them."

"You don't have to tell me if you don't want to." Jackson's voice was gentle. "I just figured maybe it would help to tell someone."

"Maybe." I sighed, and found myself glancing around to check that no one else was close enough to overhear. "Ok, here goes. You know Baker had a child once? One she was forced to give away, just like Blythe was at first?"

I could feel her nodding beside me.

"Well the papers from The Beck, among other things, confirmed the identity of that child."

"Oh, Quin!" Beside me, my friend stopped in her tracks and I knew she had, with her usual perception, worked it out. "Have you told her?"

I nodded, fighting to keep the tears from my eyes. "Yes. She doesn't want to know."

Jackson thought for a moment. "I guess, after all this time... it must be very difficult for her. We really did have a strange way of life in The Beck, didn't we?" She reached down and squeezed my hand. "Things here seem very different."

Thankful that she had seen fit to change the subject, I

agreed with her. "The meal was certainly an eyeopener."

"I know what you mean. Being in that hall with all those people... their lives are nothing like ours. It seems like their upbringing is... well, it seems nice, that's all."

"I know what you mean." I returned the squeeze briefly as we began walking again, but let go after a second. "Did you see the child at the table beside us. He was lovely."

"And being brought up with his actual parents in charge." Jackson made a face. "We really don't have much in common with these people, do we?"

"Well no, but... surely all we need is time to adjust? We've said we like the way they live... maybe we just need time to settle in here. Maybe we could live that way too."

"You really think so?" Jackson sounded doubtful.

"It would be nice to try, wouldn't it?"

"Guess so. But we have a whole lot of conflict to come before we get to that point." Jackson nodded as we approached the fencing surrounding the pitches. "Here we go. And Quin, don't give up on Baker. Give her a chance. She may come around."

She turned her attention to the pitches, which did indeed have a number of Ridge citizens already inside. Clearly, they were among the people who had left the canteen earlier. Rather than waiting around for instruction, they were engaged in a rapid game of some sort. From a distance, it almost looked like they were under attack, or fighting with one another, but as we got closer it became clear from the joyous shouts and laughter that the movements were linked to fun rather than defensive.

"What–?" Tyler spoke for us all.

The group were chasing a ball around and, once gained,

tossing it to the person in the centre, who then threw it towards another citizen standing on the other side of the pitch brandishing a long slender weapon. They used this to slam into the ball, which flew across the space, only for the whole process to begin again.

"Baseball." Hughes laughed at our incredulous expressions. "It's just a game. They'll stop now we're here."

Sure enough, as we approached the outer fence, one of the players called to the rest and they all came over to the gate. There were twenty of them, a mixture of male and female, and I guessed that they were all aged between twenty and forty. Unlike our own group, which was significantly smaller and younger.

"Ready to go, chief?" A tall, rangy man called out from the rear of the group. I recognized him as the man who had guided us over in the motorboat this morning with McGrath.

"Ready as always, Roberts." Hughes swung open the gate and motioned for one of the citizens to put away the ball and the long wooden instrument, which apparently did not count as a weapon.

We all walked into the pitch area, noting the stares from the Ridge group. Whilst not as open now (they had all seen enough of us at lunch) they were still clearly curious about our presence here, and the differences which existed between the two groups. Hughes walked to the far edge of the space, placed the bag on the ground and turned to face us.

"OK, the priority here is to train you all as soon as possible so that you can play a part in our force to both defend and also fight against the people at The Beck." Hughes pointed at McGrath. "You know that myself and McGrath are among the most experienced fighters here on The Ridge. We're here to teach you to fight well. Rogers and Tyler from The Crags are also experienced in combat. Between us, we'll divide you into groups."

He nodded at McGrath, who took over.

"These groups will rotate through the different instructors," she gestured at the four trainers, "practising with a number of weapons and participating in regular endurance-training sessions."

Rogers stepped forward. "This process will continue alongside our efforts to transfer lead over from The Crags in large quantities. That way, we can use the smelting plant here to create large amounts of ammunition as fast as possible—"

"—until we feel we have a strong enough force to mount a successful raid or takeover of The Beck." Hughes interrupted, seeming excited. "Right, enough talking. There's a lot to do, and limited time to do it in." He glanced from one side of the pitches to the other, noting the divisions between the Ridge and the Crags citizens. "First things first. We need to mix you up, so you can get to know each other. No good you fighting side by side if there's no trust."

He walked around the Ridge group, using his finger to point or prod the citizens into four even groups. Then he repeated the process with our side of the area, adding two or three Crags citizens to each of the groups he had created.

"Right." Now he looked satisfied. "Four groups. Four trainers." He directed McGrath, Rogers, and Tyler to a group each. "Let's begin."

Chapter Seventeen

The afternoon passed slowly, the training arduous and difficult in places. While I was fairly fit and could throw a knife
fairly well, I had never really got on well with the idea of hand-
to-hand combat, and we were learning how to use heavy
batons as well as knives. Add to that the fitness training
which McGrath was putting her group through, by the time
we had rotated through each trainer, the entire group was
exhausted.

I had been placed in a group with Collins and Nelson, not
Crags citizens I knew particularly well, and five others from
The Ridge, including Roberts. At first it was awkward, but by
the time our group joined Tyler, our second trainer of the day,
we had begun to gel as we worked in pairs to practise both
attack and defensive movements on one another. Most of The
Ridge citizens, in our team at least, seemed merely interested
in finding out more about us, and in between the instructive
talks from whichever trainer we were working with, we
managed to exchange simple questions which allowed us
to know each other better.

Tyler paired me with Roberts for her session, where we
were rehearsing defensive manoeuvres. I approached him
tentatively, aware that I would have to come into close prox-

imity with him in order to carry out the moves effectively.

He grinned widely, perhaps acknowledging my cautious expression. "Hey, Quin, is it?"

I managed a nod.

"All a bit awkward, isn't it?" He whispered, as Tyler demonstrated a move which required the entire side of her body to come into contact with Collins' as she slipped out of a choke hold. "Feel like we should've at least played some 'get to know each other' games first."

He was silenced by a sharp look from Tyler, but his comment brought a smile to my face and helped to dispel the tension. After the demonstration, we began rehearsing the movements slowly, and with Tyler's eyes elsewhere, he took up the conversation again.

"So how different are things in The Beck, then?" His voice drifted to me from behind, as he placed his hands lightly around my neck.

Twisting my body the way that Tyler had shown us, I managed to escape the hold, and we reversed positions before I responded. "Pretty different. We don't live the way you do at all."

He deflected my hold easily and we changed places again. "What do you mean?"

"We live communally, always. Like, there are no family units who share apartments and separate themselves from the rest of the community."

He stopped and stared at me. "How do you mean?"

I paused, thinking of how I could explain it. "We don't live with our parents. We don't even know who our parents are." His expression would have amused me had I not been describing such a difficult personal situation. "We grow up in a section where all children aged 5 to 14 live. Then we transfer to the adult section of The Beck and live together: shared rooms, shared mealtimes, shared everything."

"Wow, that must be tough. I'm guessing that's why you all tried to leave." He saw my look of shock and hurried to explain. "Sorry, Hughes has already told us some things about you. Just so we'd be able to understand the type of people you were. Clearly you left The Beck because you were unhappy."

I shrugged. "We did."

"I have a partner." He blushed. "She's expecting our first child soon, and I—"

"—is she—? Sorry! Is she blonde?" It was my turn to blush at the rudeness of my interruption. "Is she called Ross?"

He beamed. "Yes. Did you meet her?"

"At lunch."

His smile widened. "Well I can't wait. And the thought that I might not get to bring up my own child, well..." He trailed off, his sunny expression disappearing.

"Show me please?"

Tyler's voice came from behind, and she didn't sound happy. We demonstrated the movement and she took some time advising us how to improve on our efforts so far. After we had all mastered the basics of this move, she went on to teach us another, and the afternoon continued in a similar manner.

At moments when we paused in our training, Roberts continued to converse with me and I found myself liking his easy manner. I didn't think I'd ever met anyone who was so carefree. The excitement and nerves he felt about the upcoming birth of his child were always the main topic of conversation. His enthusiasm was infectious, and I decided that, however disconcerting the comparison of their lives to ours was, it was a necessary part of making sure that our own community changed for the better.

By the end of the day, Hughes called us all together, seemingly satisfied that we had made sufficient progress.

"We've really tried to put you through your paces today, and you've all risen to the challenge. Well done."

McGrath was less satisfied. "Yes, you're doing well, but don't get complacent. We've a long way to go before you'll be ready for a showdown in The Beck."

"Ease off, McGrath." The voice came from a Ridge recruit, and I heard the sharp intake of breath from my fellow Crags citizens at its impudence.

McGrath, however, seemed unruffled by it, and no more stern-faced than usual. She shook her head. "Store the weapons and go wash up before dinner, ok?"

"We're all eating together again tonight, people." Hughes, as usual, was beaming. "Now go on, all of you, get out of here!"

I had discovered from my conversations with Roberts and Simpson that they often cooked their own meals in their living quarters, though they did come together to eat in the canteen at least once every few days. I found their way of life intriguing: they felt part of a community, but also had their own privacy. I wondered if we Beck citizens could ever adjust to such a lifestyle.

McGrath waited until we had filled the bag with the various weapons, then hoisted it onto her back and set off out of the pitch area, the rest of the Ridge citizens following behind, joking around with one another and jostling for position close to the front of their group. Hughes lagged behind, seemingly waiting for Tyler as she tied her bootlaces, then engaged her in conversation as they headed off together.

The remaining citizens began to trail after them. I found myself falling into step next to Roberts, and for a while we didn't speak. As we approached the apartment blocks, there were other Ridge citizens wandering back from their own shifts. A small figure broke away from one of the groups of people and propelled herself towards Roberts with surprising speed considering the considerably swollen belly which jutted out in front of her. I recognized Ross from earlier.

"Hey, you." She smiled. "How was the training?"

He grinned, his pleasure at seeing his partner again evident in every line on his face. "It was good. Got to make some new friends." He turned to me. "This is Quin."

"Hi again." She gestured back towards the communal buildings as she turned back to Roberts. "We met at lunch."

"Quin said."

"He been giving you any trouble?" Ross' face was stern for a moment, but as she chuckled, I realised she was teasing.

"No, he was good company actually."

"High praise indeed from the newcomer." She nudged him. "Glad you weren't too much of a nuisance."

He waved her away before motioning to one of the buildings closer to the main hub of The Ridge community. "This is us. See you tomorrow, Quin?"

"Sure." I found myself looking forward to spending the day with him again.

The two of them smiled their good-bye and wandered away. As they entered the building, I noticed Roberts placing a protective arm around his partner and then holding open the door for her. She waved away his considerate gesture as she passed him and headed for the stairs, the door closing behind them.

"They're a little like Rogers and Green, right?" Cass' voice came from behind, startling me a little.

"I guess so." I turned to smile at her and Jackson who was walking with her. "But they get to live together and have a child together. It's so..."

"Strange, isn't it?" Jackson chimed in. "Like we said earlier, it's a long way from what we're used to."

"I kind of like it though," Cass replied, as we approached our own apartment door.

Turning to look back along the path, we could see the many Ridge citizens heading home. In pairs and threes, or larger groups, wandering along chatting to one another, they all seemed so comfortable. It was certainly unlike The Beck, and like Jackson, I envied them the simple friendships and family groupings.

Inside, we made our way to the small apartment we had been assigned and, as suggested, got ourselves ready for dinner. We were just leaving for the canteen when the door to Rogers and Green's apartment flew open and Green catapulted out, almost running into Jackson.

"Quin!" She was breathless. "You're right there. Come inside, quick. Rogers is talking to Anders!"

I glanced at the others, and she beckoned for them to come in too. At the rear of the apartment's communal area, Rogers was bent over a desk with a walkie-talkie in his hands. He spotted us and held a single finger over his mouth. The call for silence was unnecessary. The walkie-talkie in his hands was buzzing, and as we stood listening, the sound of the voice on the other end came hissing through. "…so you've moved… not…Crags anymore?"

Rogers shook his head as if Anders could see him, before pressing the button to reply. "No. We're on a different island. It should be easier to contact us now."

There was a short pause before the walkie-talkie crackled into life again. "I see. Well …still in a critical position… Adams hasn't been near the quarantine… happy to abandon them to live or die…"

The radio cut out for a minute. "That's just what we said!" Rogers hissed at Green in the momentary silence. "He's definitely not attempting to help most of the sick people." He punched his finger against the button on the side of the walkie-talkie. "So, Adams is using the sickness to eliminate large numbers of the population, is that right?"

There was further crackling and Rogers frowned. "Think we might have lost him."

"…one piece of good news…" We all drew nearer as Anders continued to speak. "Cam… improving… much better… seems to be pulling through…."

I stopped listening. Cam had never been far from my mind, even through all the upheaval of the past few days. Despite Anders' report being mostly negative, the news that Cam seemed to be recovering was extremely welcome. I blinked hard, attempting to prevent my tears of relief from escaping. The broadcast over, Rogers replaced the walkie-talkie on the desk, and sighed deeply.

Green took his hand. "At least he's aware we're within range now. He can attempt to get more regular information to us."

He closed his eyes for a moment and I noticed how tired he

looked. "I suppose."

"And maybe," Green began easing him to his feet, her voice encouraging, "once Cam's better, he and Anders will have more success with reforming the Resistance."

Rogers gave a slight nod, but I could tell he was still deeply troubled about the situation. As he and Green made their way to the door, Cass clutched my hand tightly, and Jackson gave me a small smile. Together, we made our way out of the apartment into the late afternoon sun.

***

Over the next few days, we settled into more of a pattern. Most days, we went on an early-morning run around the perimeter of The Ridge, aimed at building up our endurance. We then spent the rest of our morning participating in strength and fitness training on the pitch area, followed by a brief lunch, and a lengthy afternoon session with our different trainers, focusing on weapons and combat training.

In addition to our decent-sized portions at the communal meals in the canteen, we were also assigned some rations to use in our own apartments. Hughes wanted to make sure that all the training soldiers gained weight and had sufficient fuel to become stronger and more able to fight. When there was no prepared meal for the entire camp, we made ourselves something to eat as a Crags group, taking turns over which apartment would prepare the food. Some of us had started learning how to cook from a few Ridge citizens who were happy to teach us. It was fun, and many of us relished the chance to practise a new skill, as well as getting to know our new neighbours. Slowly, we had begun to adjust to having more freedom, and the majority of us thrived on it.

In terms of our trainers, Tyler and McGrath were always

with us, but after the first day, Rogers and Hughes divided their time between our training and the work at the smelting plant. Both endeavours were seen as vital. They were struggling to get the plant up and running properly, and initial experiments with the lead had not yet resulted in the production of gun-worthy ammo. They were also waiting for a second visit from The Crags with a delivery of additional lead which would provide those working at the plant with the raw materials to keep trying.

Until they managed to solve the issue, our group had to continue hand-to-hand combat training, and practise with hand-held weapons only. It was frustrating, as we all knew that our plan to takeover The Beck could only work if we had the numbers, the skills, *and* the ammunition to put up a strong enough fight against Shadow Patrol.

Now that we were here on The Ridge, news from The Beck came fairly regularly. Without the hills blocking the signal, messages were clearer. Adams, it appeared, was not keeping as close an eye on citizens like Anders, who were healthy, and not obviously causing a problem. Due to the sickness, our ex-leader was focusing on defending The Beck's boundaries and making sure there were sufficient citizens working in key areas such as food production. The messages came at different times of day, whenever Anders could manage to get private access to a walkie-talkie.

Green was in charge of responding to the messages, and the little black box was always attached to her belt. She was keeping a detailed record of the conversations in a large notebook Hughes had provided, and I knew that long after we had all retired to bed after a lengthy day of training, she, Rogers, and Hughes sat up well into the night discussing potential strategies for our attack on The Beck, whenever we considered ourselves ready.

During a period of particularly challenging endurance training one afternoon, Green left the training pitches to respond to a message. A few minutes later, I could see her gesturing to me from the other side of the fence. Noting her frantic hand gestures and checking that it was definitely me she wanted, I let McGrath know where I was going and raced out through the gate in the fencing. When I reached Green, she was beaming. She thrust the walkie-talkie into my hand and strode off to rejoin the others.

For a moment, I stared at the instrument as it lay silently in my palm. Then, recovering myself slightly, I pressed the call button and held the instrument to my mouth.

"Hello. This is Quin."

For a moment, the walkie-talkie remained stubbornly silent. But then it crackled, once, twice, and a voice came through.

"Quin?" I suddenly found it difficult to breathe. "Quin? Are you there?"

Raising the black box to my mouth, I managed to make my shaking hand obey me and pressed the call button hard. "C-Cam? Is that you?"

The reply was immediate. "Yes, it's me... first time I've been able to—"

I cut him off. "Are you alright... Anders said... the sickness... you were..."

"I'm alright yes. Still a little weak, but..."

My heart thundered in my chest. Glancing back at the other trainees I noticed Green watching me, a smile on her face, and turned away so I could focus.

"Are things... I mean... how are things?"

Despite the distance between us, I heard his tone change as he responded. "Not good. I... I recovered, but I was given meds... was fairly strong... others not so lucky..."

"I'm so sorry."

"...nothing... could have done."

"No..." I found it hard to find the words.

There were so many things I wanted to say to him, but it was impossible to have a proper conversation from such a distance. I wanted him to know how sincere I was, how much guilt I felt over my own part in what had happened. I sighed.

"You still there?"

I pressed the button. "I'm still here."

"Are *you* ok?"

"I'm fine. But..." I searched for the right words, "...I wanted to say I was sorry. For... for giving the sickness to you. I mean..." I blushed, again remembering the feeling of his lips on mine, "it was obviously me who gave it to you."

There was a brief pause before he spoke again. "How could I forget?"

Taken aback slightly, I wasn't sure how to reply. Before I could decide what to say, his voice came through again.

"Look, you didn't know... were sick. And it was me... kissed you..." His voice almost held a teasing tone. "an action I don't regret."

I felt a slight lifting of pressure in my chest. I had been so afraid that Cam would blame me, that he might die, that I would never see him again. Yet he was recovering, and didn't seem to blame me at all. My heart jolted at the thought of him thinking of our kisses as often as I did.

Taking a deep breath, I lifted the walkie-talkie again.

"Wish I was talking to you in person."

"Me too." I heard a noise which might have been a chuckle. "...better than not talking at all."

I nodded, then realised he couldn't see me, but he continued without a reply from me.

"...heard from Anders... the plan..."

"Yes!" I found myself anxious to reassure him. "We're gathering weapons... training a group of soldiers... I'm training... to fight..."

There was some static from the walkie-talkie before he continued. "Be careful Quin."

"I will."

"...now I'm better... talk to Anders... able to help... still some Resistance members active..."

"We'll be ready... soon..." I lowered the walkie-talkie, unconvinced by my own words.

"...could certainly use you..."

I found myself unable to respond. My eyes filled with tears as I imagined what they might be going through.

"Hey... you still there...?"

Taking a deep breath, I stabbed the button with more confidence than I truly felt. "I'm here. Just wish we could be there now helping you."

Again, his reply was rapid. "No point... too risky if... listen to Rogers and Tyler... don't even... if you don't have the firepower..."

I paused, then managed a reply. "You're right, I know, but..."

I stopped and stared at the little black box in my hands, wanting to say something which would make him understand how hard we were all working to help them. Before I could form a response though, the walkie-talkie crackled into life again.

"...have to go, but... wanted... tell you... happy you're taking action... makes a difference..."

It seemed he already knew. I raised the walkie-talkie one last time.

"Good. You have to keep fighting, Cam... now that you're better. Let everyone know that we're coming. I don't know when, but we're coming."

"Thanks. Talk soon maybe?"

"Sure."

"Good."

"Bye Cam. You take care."

"You too."

Though I stood there for several minutes after that, the walkie-talkie had retreated into stubborn silence. But Cam was alive. He was getting better. I'd been able to speak to him. The lead weight in my stomach could finally begin to ease.

I returned to Green and handed over the walkie-talkie. She took it wordlessly, simply smiling as she clipped it to her belt and continued training. As I rejoined my group, I must have seemed different, because both Collins and Roberts shot me quizzical looks. In return, I merely smiled and picked up a baton, readying myself for the next bout of sparring, spurred on to defeat Adams' forces at the thought of being reunited with Cam.

A little hope went a long way.

Chapter Eighteen

Rogers, Green, and Hughes were all missing from the pitches for the rest of the afternoon. We worked hard, training as two larger groups under McGrath and Tyler. McGrath was unforgiving at the best of times, and seemed in an even darker mood than usual. By the time we returned to the apartments at the end of the day we were all exhausted, and a little unsettled at our missing leaders. Trooping down to the canteen for a communal meal, we found our leaders were still absent.

"Think everything's ok?" Jackson muttered through a mouthful of the vegetable stew. "Not seen them since this morning, has anyone else?"

Various people shook their heads.

"Hughes isn't around either," Tyler commented, blushing slightly. "Perhaps they're working something out with him."

It amused but did not surprise me that she had noted Hughes' absence. Tyler had made quite a habit of staying in the canteen after communal meals and returning to the apartment block later in the evening, having spent several hours talking with Hughes. When he wasn't training us, and he didn't have any other Ridge business to attend to, he seemed equally as willing to spend time with her. I was happy for her, but also a little concerned.

Hughes was The Ridge leader. He had only taken over fairly recently, and while the majority of the citizens here supported him, I wondered what the reaction would be to him having a close friendship with a citizen from foreign shores. There were still some citizens here who went out of their way to avoid speaking to us. Roberts had told me they were generally supporters of the previous leader, who had died some weeks before Hughes had been voted in, but always been mistrustful of other communities.

The Ridge had generally been run more openly since Hughes had taken over, yet some people still preferred the style of the previous leader. Whilst so far nothing had been said openly, I feared people might doubt Hughes' loyalty to The Ridge if he spent too much time with Tyler. Still, it was nice to see her so happy. And I knew she would be the last person to throw herself into a serious relationship, particularly with a Ridge citizen, without thinking it over carefully.

We ate in silence for a while, each of us caught up in their own thoughts. As we were finishing the meal, Tyler stood up and went to speak to Simpson, who was serving us as usual. After a moment, Simpson disappeared and Tyler turned to scan the table. When her eyes settled on me, she beckoned me over.

"Could you do me a favour, Quin?" she asked, when I reached her.

"Sure," I managed, though the thought of dealing with an additional task today was not an appealing one.

"Rogers asked me to take Thomas his food this evening, but I need to check on something with McGrath. Would you take it to him for me please?"

I must have looked a little taken aback at her request, because she hurried on. "I wouldn't normally ask, but with the added pressure today I—"

"—no problem, Tyler." I held a hand out. "Of course, it's fine. Where do I need to go with it?"

"Simpson can show you." Tyler waved a hand as the young girl returned. "It's in the building just next door. There's a slot you can pass the food to him so you don't have to unlock the door or anything. Rogers just didn't want The Ridge folks feeling like he was their responsibility. That ok, Simpson?"

Simpson nodded and passed me the tray.

"Thanks, Quin," Tyler called to me as she hurried in McGrath's direction. "I owe you one."

I followed Simpson out through the side entrance of the canteen. We crossed a narrow passageway between the two buildings, and she pushed open the door opposite. Inside, there was a small entrance hall where a man sat behind a desk.

"Hi Bennett," Simpson greeted him shyly. "This is Quin. She'll be taking Thomas his food tonight."

The man looked up from the papers in front of him and nodded. "Sure." He lumbered to his feet. "It's this way."

"You alright finding your way back?" Simpson nodded encouragement and disappeared.

Bennett opened a door to the left of the desk he had been sitting at. Behind it was a corridor which stretched the length of the building. Holding it open, he motioned impatiently to me.

"He's in the last cell," he muttered, waving a hand down a dimly lit passageway. "On the right."

"Thank you."

I walked past him and through the door in the direction he had pointed. I had only gone a few steps when I heard the door bang shut behind him and the corridor was in shadow again. The cells consisted of openings in the sides of the corridor which had walls built to halfway up and bars fixed across the top of them which allowed guards to look in on prisoners. In the first cell I passed, a man was sleeping. I crept past him, not wanting to wake him to discover the reason he was incarcerated. The next three cells were thankfully empty.

I approached the final cell with great trepidation. They had nothing inside them except a small cot, and a table and chair, so once I passed into view, there would be no hiding from its occupant. For a second I was frightened, but then I took another look at the metal bars across the front of each cell and forced my stride to be more purposeful.

Thomas was sitting on his bed, leaning against the wall. At my approach, he stiffened slightly, but did not turn.

I headed for the section of the wall which slid up so I could pass the tray through. Lifting it up, I pushed the tray of food into the space beyond. Thomas never moved, but I saw his eyes flicker in my direction, as if wondering whether or not I would speak.

"Dinner time," I managed, as I turned to leave.

"Quin!" The word was whispered, barely audible.

I turned back to the cell, moving a little closer so that I could see the man inside. Thomas had angled his body, just slightly, so he was facing the opening at the front of his cell. Shadows darkened his face, so I couldn't see his expression. I felt a palpable sense of loneliness in the dark hallway.

"Thomas?"

"Why'd they send *you*?"

"Tyler was busy with something else." I shrugged. "I'm just doing her a favour."

He was silent for a moment. I could feel him brooding.

"Are you alright?" I asked after a moment.

"Guess so."

His response was a long way from the arrogant trouble-maker I had known. Yet even now, he could not admit to his misery, even though it enveloped him like a shroud. In the face of his stubbornness, I refused to offer him any words of comfort. The silence stretched out between us and I began to wonder why he had called me back.

"It's just..." he tried. "It's a long day in here."

"Guess you don't get many visitors."

He shrugged.

"Are you going to eat?" I gestured to the tray of food, which had better rations on it than we had been serving him over on The Crags.

Still, he didn't move. I turned to leave again, but hadn't managed more than a few steps before he continued.

"What's it like?"

I stopped.

"The Ridge, I mean. Are they very... different from us?"

"They are." I walked back to his cell, hesitating before I continued. I was unsure how much I wanted to talk to this man, but at the same time found myself unable to ignore the desperation in his voice. "They live in families, with their own children... they seem to have more choice and freedom. It's... well, it's refreshing."

He had stopped talking again, though I knew he was listening intently. Feeling the pangs of hunger myself, I turned to leave once more.

"I'm going, Thomas. I haven't eaten yet myself."

There was no response as I retraced my steps down the corridor, but as I reached the door, I heard the scrape of his tray moving across the ground. As I returned to the canteen, I found I was glad that he was at least still eating, and wondering when Rogers might revisit the idea of allowing him to leave his solitary confinement, at least for a little while. He seemed to be a changed man, on the surface, at least, but I could see that being alone for such lengthy periods of time wouldn't be good for anyone in the long term.

Once inside the main building I sat next to Cass and helped myself to a good portion of the fish and vegetables available. Glad to be back inside the warmth and the light, I did nothing but eat for the next few minutes, tuning out the conversations of those who had already eaten which were going on around me. I spotted Tyler who shot me a grateful look as she returned from her conversation with McGrath, and wondered where Rogers and Green had gone, that they still weren't back for the meal.

I had just begun to wonder whether or not we should be concerned about them when my thoughts were interrupted as the doors banged open and a new group made its way into the canteen. Hughes was at the front, deep in conversation with Rogers. They were followed by Green, and, to my surprise, Mason. I heard a shriek as Jackson flung herself off the bench next to me and rushed headlong to greet him.

"Must be the second shipment of lead from The Crags," Nelson commented. "They were talking about it a few days ago, but I wasn't sure it would arrive so soon. That's where they've been all afternoon."

"That's a good sign, surely." Cass strained her neck to see the group as they stood talking just inside the doorway.

Jackson and Mason were wrapped around one another in a tight embrace. I found myself hoping that he had finished perfecting the lead-extraction technique and taught it to Shaw, so he could remain here on The Ridge from now on. Jackson hadn't said much, she was never one to complain, but I knew she'd been miserable without him.

Hughes and Rogers continued their discussion as they walked, their faces serious, yet seeming earnest rather than angry or concerned. I wagered a guess that they were talking tactics as usual. Green remained close to the door, stepping back to hold it open once more, as though waiting for someone else to enter. I almost stopped breathing when the next figure entered. Striding in, the usual irritable expression marring her face, was Baker.

After noting Hughes' entrance, Tyler's eyes had also followed the group and she seemed to spot Baker at the same time as me. Anticipating my discomfort, she slid the empty bowl of bread at me, nodding at the counter to the side of the room.

"Why don't you go grab us some more Quin?"

It gave me an excuse to be away from the table when Baker arrived, and I was grateful for it. Slipping out of my seat, I walked quickly away, refusing to glance back to see if my mother had noticed me. I made it to the counter and selected a few more rolls, then turned to face the rest of the room. The little group had now made their way towards our usual table and were beginning to greet one another, chattering loudly as they exchanged news.

Glancing to one side, I caught sight of Simpson and beckoned to her. She came over, her usual shy smile lighting her face gently.

"Could you take the bread over to..." I gestured at our table. "Give it to Tyler please?"

"Sure!" She took the bowl out of my hand and peered more closely at me. "You ok, Quin?"

I attempted a laugh to shake off her concern but it came out a little strangled.

"I'm fine thanks. Just need to grab something from... from the apartment."

She stared at me a moment too long. "Ok. If you're sure." She turned and made her way to the table.

I moved in the opposite direction and made my way out to the courtyard via a circuitous route. Once outside, I dodged around the side of the building, leaned on the wall and tried to regain my breath.

When decisions were being made over where citizens would live in the weeks leading up to our attack on The Beck, I knew that Baker had insisted that she preferred to remain on The Crags. She had been pretty resistant to visiting The Ridge, saying she would leave it to the rest of us to communicate with 'the new folks' and let her know what she needed to know, while she kept things running on The Crags as she had during our previous Beck mission.

Her arrival here was therefore strange. Unless something serious had happened on The Crags, I couldn't see her suddenly deciding that she needed to see the Ridge for herself. Her arrival on the beach as we were leaving made me think that there was only one other likely reason for her visit. She had come to speak to me.

I found myself short of breath and feeling a little queasy.

Clearly, Baker mattered more to me than I knew. Trying to calm my breathing, I stumbled further away from the buildings in the direction of the water fountain. By the time I reached it, I felt dizzy. I bent over it, pushing hard on the lever to release the liquid. Splashing my face with copious amounts of water, I then sucked some of it down, making myself swallow as slowly as I could. Eventually, I felt my heartrate slow.

Still leaning heavily on the water fountain, I rested my head on my hand and breathed deeply, filling my lungs as full as I could. When I finally felt normal, I straightened up and wiped a sleeve across my face. As the courtyard came into focus, I could see a figure on the other side of the space. I knew it was Baker before she began to walk towards me, and was thankful that the panic I had experienced a moment ago did not return.

As she got closer, I noticed the absence of her usual impatient stride. In its place was a far more hesitant movement, and though her face remained impassive, something about the angle of her head told me she approached me with great caution, and was possibly just as frightened as me.

When she was just a few feet away she stopped. Stared at me. Said nothing.

I found myself wanting to fill the silence, and spoke the first words that came into my head.

"You came with the lead shipment?"

She looked slightly startled, as though this was not the question she had expected. After a moment's pause, she recovered herself and nodded.

"Mining's going well then?"

"It is."

I stared back at her, not knowing what else I could say. Had she come all this way to seek me out and then not speak to me?

And then she seemed to draw in a deep breath, and began to speak.

"I'm sorry." She dropped her gaze. "For my reaction to... well, you know what to."

The silence between us lengthened, swirling around us as we stood in the empty space.

"Want to walk?" The words were out of my mouth before I could stop them, and I had no idea where they had come from.

She nodded, and I gestured to the path which led to the apartment housing. We fell into step next to each other, a larger distance between us than there would have been had I been walking with Cass or Jackson. But without the pressure of making eye contact, Baker seemed to find her voice again.

"Look, when you've... well I've spent years..." She tried again. "I had no hope... I went through hell when they took my ch– when you were taken from me." I was aware that she glanced across at me, but didn't return the eye contact. "Quin, I still find it difficult to identify you with the baby I lost."

She sighed deeply. "Green tells me you've had first-hand experience of watching a suffering mother with Blythe... well, I was just like her. Except no one brought my baby back."

Her voice was hard, angry, filled with bitterness and re-sentment.

"That's why I hated the idea of Blythe and Perry coming to The Crags in the first place. But I... well I sort of got used to them..." She shrugged. "But I never thought... I just didn't ever imagine that... well that I'd ever find out who my child was. It's why I wanted to leave The Beck in the first place. I figured on The Crags I'd escape the constant wondering... " Her voice was almost a whisper. "You know, I knew that every day I could be walking past my own child and be totally unaware."

We were walking past the first blocks of darkened apartments now, most of them empty, as people were all at the communal dinner. We fell silent for a while, Baker seeming to have run out of steam, while I had no idea what I might say to make her feel better. The sky was clear tonight and the air fairly warm. A light breeze rustled the trees to each side of the path and set them whispering as we passed.

Baker stopped suddenly and turned towards me. "When you told me, it was a shock. I didn't know what to say. Since you left, I've... well I've sort of come to terms with the news, and I owe you an apology for reacting the way I did. So, I'm sorry."

I finally found my tongue and managed to get out a few words. "It's ok. I guess I understood. I felt the same way when I found out... didn't know how to react." I raised my eyes to meet hers. "It's not like we've ever seen anyone, aside from Perry, who has grown up with a parent."

She grimaced and began walking again. "Nope. Adams makes sure we don't know what family feels like."

Encouraged, I continued. "If you stay here on The Ridge for a little while you'll see how different it is. I mean, people live together in families here—they have children, they bring them up, they eat together, spend time together... it's totally new and strange, but once you've been here a little while you begin to see the benefits, how happy people are living like this... and—"

"I'm not staying." Again, Baker wouldn't meet my gaze, and instead stared off into the dark windows of the closest apartment.

"Oh." I didn't know what else to say, and found myself feeling stupid for making the suggestion.

Sighing, Baker continued. "Look Quin, I'd like to believe that we could become closer... perhaps... you don't know... you can't understand what I've–" She broke off and for a moment there was silence.

I waited, hardly daring to breathe as she made herself go on.

"I'm not good at this." She forced herself to look at me. "We've lived our whole lives apart, with no knowledge of one another. Your life hasn't included me for 16 years, Quin." She looked pained. "How can you miss what you've never had?"

I tried not to show how much her words hurt as she met my gaze one final time. "And as for me... I'd like to try, but... well I told you... I'm not sure I'll ever be ready to..." Her voice cracked and she backed away from me, shaking her head. "I can't do this."

And with that, she turned and stumbled away in the direction of the hub, leaving me standing alone.

Chapter Nineteen

I couldn't face returning to the canteen, so I wandered back to the apartment and made sure I was in bed by the time the others returned. I heard them later on, talking in lowered tones, Mason's deeper voice mingling with those of Cass and Jackson. Eventually it grew quiet, and I heard Cass creep into our room. As she slipped into the other bed, she whispered my name a couple of times, but I kept my breathing deep and didn't answer. Cass didn't even know of the connection between Baker and I, and my disappointment was still raw. I certainly didn't feel up to explaining the whole situation.

I was still awake when Tyler entered the apartment much later, but part of me was afraid that she might have spoken to Baker after she had left me, and I wasn't sure I wanted to hear what she'd had to say. Instead, I remained in my own bed, listening to the others settling down around me, willing sleep to come.

In the morning we woke to a heavy rainstorm and ate a quick breakfast in the apartment, none of us looking forward to training in the difficult conditions. When we were ready, we headed to the pitches to meet with the rest of the trainees. On the way, Tyler fell into step next to me.

"You ok?"

"Sure." I shrugged, not knowing what else I could say.

"She left," Tyler said.

"What?"

"Early this morning. They unloaded the lead last night after dinner, transported it to the smelting plant. Took a few of the early bullet samples back with them in return. But she was up very early and took the boat back to The Crags."

As I took in her words, the disappointment of the previous night flooded over me once more. I had spent most of the night trying to reason with myself that Baker's reaction was understandable. At least she had taken the first step, coming to The Ridge and trying to start a conversation with me. I had resolved to approach her again today, try to let her know I would wait until she was ready to speak to me. That had been my last thought before I had finally managed to drift off to sleep. But now, she had made that impossible.

I could feel Tyler's eyes on me. "She said she had to. She didn't want to leave Shaw for long without additional support, so she headed back early."

I turned and stared at Tyler, my eyes blazing. "You sure that was the only reason why?"

She had the grace to look a little ashamed, and dipped her gaze before she answered. "I don't know. I think Baker was just as eager to get back, make sure she wasn't leaving The Crags short on manpower for long."

I didn't reply.

"Did she...?" Tyler trailed off and then tried again, seemingly unsure of how to word her question. "What did she say to you?"

"Don't you know?"

"Well, I wasn't exactly sure, but..."

"She apologised for reacting badly to the news initially." I managed to keep my voice steady. "And she said that she'd like to think that we could get to know one another better, but... well that she isn't ready for that."

"Oh Quin, I'm so–"

I cut her off. "And from her hasty exit, it seems she didn't want to spend any more time with me than was absolutely necessary." I sighed. "I know she's finding it hard. But–"

"But so are you, right?" Tyler reached out and patted my shoulder awkwardly.

As the pitches came into sight, Tyler changed tack. "They might even let us train with guns today." I knew she was trying to distract me. "Should step things up, don't you think?"

I had to admit, though guns were not my weapon of choice, they would be necessary if we were to stand a chance of attacking The Beck with any kind of success. The idea that we might be ready to start working with them brought us one step closer to the fight, and that had to be a good thing. Now that I knew Cam was alive, had actually spoken to him, the planned attack on The Beck mattered even more.

I strode across the final few metres to the pitches, eager to bring that moment closer. But as I approached the gates, I noticed the crowd of people gathered just inside the entrance. Loud, angry voices rang out from the group.

"...can't believe you'd expect..." The strident voice definitely belonged to Walker.

"...just like us to try it ..." Rogers' tone was slightly calmer.

As Tyler and I slipped into the enclosure, I couldn't see Walker or Rogers. A few of the Ridge citizens on the outside of the crowd shifted slightly, but it was still difficult to make out what was going on at the centre of the group. The argument showed no signs of stopping though.

"...won't work alongside him, Rogers, when..."

"...not in your group though..." Rogers' voice had begun to sound strained.

"...nowhere near me..."

I found myself standing next to Roberts, who leaned closer, whispering in my ear. "Your man here doesn't seem too popular. Did he come across on the boat last night?"

I stood on tiptoe, straining to see the people in the centre of the crowd. Rogers and Walker were almost nose to nose, their faces red and angry. Behind Rogers stood a familiar figure, his eyes cast downwards. Suddenly, Walker's anger made sense.

"How can you expect us to work alongside him?" A vein on Walker's neck stood out as he glared at Thomas. "After what he did!"

Rogers laid a hand on Walker's chest. "Look. I knew you wouldn't be happy about this. I won't ask you to train alongside him. And he'll go right back to his cell every night." He paused for a moment, considering his words. "But his behaviour since we arrived here has been exemplary. He's never stepped out of line, not even once. And I'd like to reward him for that, see if we can integrate him again. You know he's strong. He'd be a good addition to our force–"

"No." Walker slapped Rogers' hand away and stepped back. "Not him."

"Look, Walker," I hadn't noticed Green standing to one side, but now she stepped forward, trying to diffuse the situation, "Anders says Adams is focusing all his time and energy on The Beck elite right now. It's extremely worrying."

Rogers ran a hand through his hair distractedly. "She's right. Reports are that Shadow Patrol are being given larger rations than anyone." I heard the angry murmur of the Crags citizens around me. "They're regularly being given drugs to heighten their fury, which is making them more violent. Adams is basically controlling them." He glanced at Green for support.

"More and more of the people in quarantine are dying, with no support from Adams, and those Upper Beck citizens who aren't Shadow Patrol are being asked to work long shifts manning various posts previously taken on by Lower Beck citizens." Green's voice was gentle, but insistent. "Adams isn't acting rationally. The situation is grave. Thomas has been nothing but calm and obedient since he's been in the cells here. We've spoken at length to him. We really believe that he understands the consequences if he steps out of line. And, in time, he'll be an effective addition to our forces."

Throughout the speech, Walker had stood motionless, his expression unreadable. Now, he sighed deeply.

"I know all that. But I can't work with him." He backed away. "I wish I'd known about this. Perhaps I would've gone back to The Crags last night."

For the first time, Thomas raised his head. He took a tentative step in Walker's direction.

"Look, Walker, I—" he began, his voice hesitant.

Walker recoiled from him. "Don't you try and talk to me!"

But Thomas continued, his hands clutched in fists by his side, his words coming slowly and haltingly. "I know we don't get along. I know that you—"

"Don't get along?" Walker spat at him, thrusting a hand against his chest. "You tried to kill me. And Harper."

189

Thomas' face flushed, but he continued, taking hold of Walker's hand and trying to remove it from his chest. "I did. But I'm not that man now. Being alone in those cells has almost—"

He didn't get any further. Yanking his hand from Thomas' grasp, Walker pulled his fist back and thrust it forward so fast that it sent Thomas reeling. He staggered backwards, but didn't fall. I expected him to retaliate, but instead he came forward with both hands held up in a definite gesture of surrender.

Walker seemed infuriated by the notion that Thomas was attempting to broker peace, and shoved both hands against Thomas' chest, thrusting him backwards roughly. This time, he hit the ground hard. Rogers and Nelson took hold of Walker's shoulders and pulled him back out of Thomas's reach.

"Go," Rogers muttered. "You need to calm down, alright? I won't make you work alongside him, but I want him to stay. On a trial basis." He shot a glance at Thomas. "He knows that."

Without a word, Walker turned and stalked off, leaving a yawning silence behind him. His outburst was not surprising, but his anger had seemed more intense than usual. I knew that he was missing Harper, and wondered if perhaps Mason and Jackson's reunion had made Walker feel even lonelier than usual.

Green attempted to smooth the waters. "Don't worry every-one. He'll calm down. He's upset, but it's understandable."

"Still think this is a good idea?"

The words were laced with bitterness, and came from Thomas, who was still sprawled on the ground. Everyone turned to look at him, Ridge and Crags citizens alike. He refused to meet anyone's gaze, his face flushed with anger and humiliation.

"Did you expect it to be any different?" Rogers' voice was impatient. "It's going to take time, after what you did. But you have to start somewhere."

McGrath stepped forward, clearly impatient to get on with the day's training. "Right, now that's out of the way, I suggest we get on with things. We've been doing well, making progress, but obviously not fast enough. And we have two new trainees today." She gestured to Mason and Thomas, who had begun to clamber to his feet. "There has been talk of us starting to train with guns now that we have more bullets available, but we've decided for now, until we're certain of a continuous supply of ammo, to continue training without the use of firearms." She glanced briefly at Thomas, who still had yet to raise his eyes above ground level.

"We also want to be very careful which hands we put guns into." Rogers nodded deliberately at Thomas, who flushed again. "We'd like to make it very clear that this decision is a joint one. Hughes, McGrath, and I all agree we have to be cautious with our guns, preserve precious ammunition, and make sure those who handle them are properly trained and can be trusted."

McGrath looked eager to begin. "So let's get started. Today we'll continue with fitness training, and work with knives and batons again later on." She frowned. "Start with some sprints up and down the pitches, while we rework the groups."

She turned away and we took the hint, lining up at one end of the area and starting the sprints. The only ones to remain

191

behind were Rogers, Tyler, Thomas, and McGrath. The three trainers bent their heads close together, presumably trying to work out which group would object to Thomas the least.

Roberts caught up with me, managing to sprint and speak at the same time. "Who's he then?"

"Thomas," I managed to gasp. "Been here since we first got here."

He looked surprised.

"In the cells."

There had been so much going on since we arrived at The Ridge that it had been easy to forget Thomas' presence. Aside from my one visit with his food tray, I had been totally unaware of him being here. By the look on Roberts' face, it was clear that Hughes had kept Thomas' presence from the rest of his people. But Rogers had clearly been visiting Thomas regularly, checking on him, perhaps working out when his punishment had had the desired effect. And Rogers was right, Thomas would be an asset, *if* we could control him.

When I had visited his cell, his misery had been obvious, and I knew he would jump at the chance of reintegrating with the group. But it was going to be more of a challenge than he had anticipated. And Rogers wouldn't allow it to continue if he couldn't be sure that everyone was able to work alongside him peaceably.

Slowing to a jog, Roberts continued to question me. "What'd he do?"

"Huh?" My thoughts snapped back to Roberts, and the question he had just asked.

"Why's he in the cells?"

"He betrayed us."

"How?"

I shrugged, not wanting to give all the details. "It's not important."

"But he must've done something pretty bad to Walker, I've never seen him angry like that."

"Trust me, he did."

I wasn't prepared to say any more. Feeling a little awkward, I changed the subject.

"How's Ross?" Every time I saw Roberts' partner lately, she looked exhausted. People here seemed to think this meant that her baby might come sooner than expected. Despite being given the option to stay home and rest, she continued to work some shifts in The Ridge kitchen and gardens.

Roberts grinned, never tired of talking about his partner and his child-to-be. "She's grand. A little tired, but still going. And the baby... he never stops! Kicking and shuffling and stretching his little fingers against Ross' belly!" He chuckled. "Makes it pretty difficult for her to sleep at all!"

"No wonder she's so tired. And 'he'? You sure?" Despite the fact that Roberts had no idea what gender his baby was going to be, he was insistent on it being a boy.

"Yup. He's going to be a right little fighter. Though I'll need to have a word or two about the discomfort he's been puttin' his mother through the past few weeks!"

We jogged across to the gates again as McGrath waved us over to begin the rest of our day's training. I liked Roberts more and more every day. He had a great sense of humour and his enthusiasm about his child-to-be was infectious. I thought again about Baker, her lack of ability to connect to people, and to me specifically. I was certain that it was a direct result of The Beck and its harsh, divisive practices. It only made me more determined to be part of the struggle to free its citizens from a life where children were wrenched from their mothers and denied the love and protection of a close family unit.

The groups were divided differently today. Most of us were fairly happy working alongside The Ridge citizens now, having done so for a while, so Rogers and McGrath had clearly decided we didn't need to be mixed any more to ensure our relationships were positive. Today, they opted for us to train in groups with members of our original home island, and whilst this originally surprised us, the reason behind the movement soon became clear.

The last person to be assigned a team was Thomas, and he was placed, perhaps sensibly, with a group of Ridge citizens who knew little or nothing about him. They were separated from the rest of the teams and sent to the far end of the pitches to train away from accusing eyes. Rogers stationed himself close by, keeping an eye on him. Within half an hour, the majority of The Crags citizens seemed able to ignore his presence and continue training harder than ever. Walker, though, did not return.

Thomas himself seemed to have decided it was better if he did not speak. When I glanced over at his group every now and again, he seemed to be participating well in every activity he was asked to, but I never once saw him open his mouth to comment or respond to a question. I had to admit he had changed. The old Thomas would not have allowed Walker to attack him without responding in a similarly violent manner. His imprisonment had definitely had some kind of positive effect on him. Yet every now and again as we trained, I noticed a Crags citizen shooting a look of curiosity or resentment at

Thomas, and I knew the conflict within our ranks was far from over.

Chapter Twenty

The next couple of weeks went by in a monotonous routine of eating, sleeping, and training. With little else to do, we grew stronger and fitter each day, and as we began a small amount of training with guns, it felt like we were creeping closer and closer to launching the planned attack.

The Crags had sent over several more shipments of lead, and Hughes assured us that a steady stream of bullets was now being produced in the smelting plant. He had sent another couple of workers over to The Crags to further increase extraction rates, and seemed excited that our working relationship was progressing well. Thomas continued to train alongside us, but was yet to work in a group directly with any Crags citizens, and Walker had eventually calmed down and been persuaded to rejoin the training programme, with the reassurance that Thomas would not come anywhere near him.

At night, as promised, Thomas returned to his cell at The Ridge. No one, not even Rogers, was comfortable having him eat and sleep alongside us for the moment. He continued to cooperate with the training programme and we were told he was being rewarded with an increase in his food rations, which he ate alone in his cell. He seemed to be a different man, from what I could tell. He said little, and always looked unhappy, but so far there was no sign of the old, argumentative Thomas.

Baker had reported to Green that all was going well over at The Crags. I was glad that she was managing to keep things running as efficiently as always, but I found myself walking away from conversations about her, the mere mention of her name bringing back the sense of disappointment I had felt the morning after her visit.

Pleased with the progress we were making in our training sessions, Hughes had begun introducing some of his more experienced guards to work alongside us when they were not posted on watch at various sentry posts around The Ridge. There were a good number of them, and the majority were experienced and well trained, so they made a welcome addition to our group. As a whole we had begun to gel, working well cooperatively, and our leaders had begun to feel fairly confident in our growing abilities.

We had heard a little more from The Beck Resistance. Green occasionally allowed me to man the walkie-talkie now that she knew Cam was alive, and I was always grateful for this. Now that he had recovered, he had resumed his role as Resistance leader, and was often the one to make contact. Things over on The Beck seemed little better though, and often the news was extremely worrying. Adams was continuing to ignore those in quarantine, and many of them had now succumbed to the sickness. Those still alive had attempted to deal with their corpses, but were mostly too weak to do anything other than separate them from the rest of the penned-in community and cover them over.

Meanwhile, Shadow Patrol were a stronger force than ever,

and additional patrols had been set up. Those who were not sick were left with additional shifts to work, and felt like the guards were spying on them before reporting back to Adams. Harsher punishments were being administered to anyone failing to follow orders, and the Shadows' recriminations were more violent than ever.

The only positive news was now that Cam was healthy again, he was attempting to resurrect the Resistance movement, and increase the number of people who pledged their allegiance to it. He had told them of our efforts to build a force to stand against their irrationally cruel leader, and there were many who had been glad of a force to join that was attempting to combat Adams. Cam always sounded exhausted, but he seemed hopeful that there were more citizens in The Beck willing to act, when the time came.

I relished the times when Green handed me the walkie-talkie and I had hope that I might hear his voice, no matter for how brief a time. I often spent long, frustrated nights sitting up in the vain hope that he would call with an update, only to collapse into bed way after everyone else had gone to sleep without so much as a word from him.

I was always tired, but not in the way I had been when I had lived on The Beck. Here, there were far more opportunities for citizens to relax and enjoy themselves, and after a few weeks at The Ridge, we Crags citizens had embraced this strange and wonderful phenomenon. It definitely helped to take my mind off my concerns for Cam. We could often be found on more pleasant evenings, sitting outdoors on the grass, talking together. When we did this, we were occasionally joined by some of our Ridge counterparts, who seemed to enjoy spending time with us and were curious about our lives on The Beck.

While there were still a few Ridge people who regarded us suspiciously, I had never felt unsafe here. Those who were less friendly tended to be the older citizens, and most of us had come to the conclusion that this was only because we were unfamiliar to them. The people here had little or no knowledge of anyone from the world beyond their island's border. The younger Ridge members, on the whole, found us quite fascinating, and were happy to spend time listening to stories about our time in The Beck and our escape to The Crags.

In return, they occasionally entertained us with various strange objects they used to create what they called music. Roberts, in particular, played the guitar, a wooden instrument with strings which created a pleasant melody when plucked the right way. Ross often accompanied him, playing a smaller, rounder instrument they called a banjo. One of my favourite things to do in any down time we had was listen to the two of them as they played us a wide variety of songs, from hauntingly beautiful melodies to raucous and rousing numbers, with which the other Ridge citizens joined in. I loved the sounds they could create, and the way their music brought the different members of The Ridge together.

I had begun to get to know Ross better. She was a warm, funny woman, and I could see why Roberts loved her. The pair shared an apartment with Howard, Coleman, and Rico, and a large part of me envied their friendly, supportive setup. I often found myself finding reasons to visit their apartment to see Rico and share a drink with them. When I had gone several days without contact from Cam, spending time with the two couples made me feel a lot less lonely, and I had even confided in them my feelings for the man who I was now separated from. They had been sympathetic, and both joked about how they couldn't wait to meet him when all this was over.

One particular evening after we had eaten in our apartment, a group of us gathered outside. Despite being fairly close to giving birth and finding it more difficult to get around, Ross managed to join us for a little while. Typically thoughtful, Roberts brought her a chair and cushions to sit on while she played. I gazed around at the group: Jackson and Mason curled up together on a chair; Cass, laughing and chattering with Marley and Coleman; Howard, trying desperately to get Rico to catch a small ball while others laughed at his frustration; even Walker had joined us, and looked, if not happy, then more at ease than he had in a while. Despite missing Cam, I felt happier than I had in as long as I could remember.

After half an hour, Ross struggled to her feet and, apologising for the shortness of the set, said she was too uncomfortable to continue. Roberts took her arm and escorted her back to their apartment, waving a hand and calling over his shoulder that he would see us all tomorrow. The entertainment over, most of the others wandered off to bed, and a few minutes later only myself, Cass, and Tyler remained outside.

The sky was growing darker, but Cam hadn't called and, as we hadn't heard from him in over a week, I felt sure he would be in touch tonight. Cass tutted as I checked the volume on the walkie-talkie for the hundredth time.

"It's on, Quin. You know it is."

I blushed. "I know. I'm just..."

Tyler shot a warning look at Cass. "She's worried, that's all. It's difficult being so far away from him."

I nodded but didn't respond.

"He'll be ok. He came through the sickness, didn't he?"

"But it's been a week." I shrugged. "A week since the last message. We know how bad things are over there. Who knows what Adams is going to do next?"

"You think he has worse planned?" Cass' eyes were wide. "What more could he do? He's already abandoned most of the citizens in the Lower Beck."

"We don't know that for sure." Tyler's tone held a warning. "Last time he was in touch, Cam said it had been harder to gain access. The Resistance had been trying to check on the people in quarantine, sneak them some food and so on. They're not supposed to be inside the area at all, only to guard it from the perimeter."

"But Adams knows how many people are in there, right? And that many of them are dead?" Cass's voice echoed the disgust we all felt at The Beck leader's behaviour.

Tyler sighed, defeated. "Of course he does."

"Then why aren't we on a boat over there already?" She threw up her hands in frustration. "If we wait much longer, we might be too late for all of them!"

I understood her anger. "You're right Cass, but going before we're ready will do more harm than good."

"Quin's right." Tyler nodded. "Rogers and Hughes have very clear targets: numbers of bullets produced, numbers of effectively-trained soldiers. They've thought about it carefully, tried to plan so we have the best chance of overcoming Adams' forces."

"I suppose." Cass sighed. "Waiting is hard though, knowing how things are over there."

"Better than racing over there with no backup and no plan." Tyler's tone was no-nonsense now. "Rogers seems to think Hughes is a great ally. Thankfully, it looks like we were right to trust him. There's no way we could ever have attempted to take on Adams without The Ridge's assistance."

Cass shot a sideways look at Tyler, a wry smile crossing her face. "Rogers isn't the only one who thinks Hughes is a great ally."

"Stop it, Cass," I said, seeing how uncomfortable the comment made Tyler feel. "Leave her alone."

"You're right. I agree with Rogers. Hughes is an excellent ally and we're lucky to have him." Tyler straightened up, looking down her nose at my other friend. "And now, I'm going to bed."

We waited until she had walked back into the apartment before chuckling.

"I'm right though, aren't I?" Cass grinned. "She can't take her eyes off him during training. Is something going on between them?"

"I'm not sure." I stared at the door Tyler had disappeared through. "I know they spend a lot of time together, but don't know that anything has actually happened between them. Think she's too focused on the mission."

Cass snorted rudely. "Too scared, you mean."

"No." I glanced at Cass, annoyed. "Think about how concerned you just were about the citizens left on The Beck. Tyler cares about them just as much as you. She'd never put her personal feelings ahead of potentially saving their lives."

Cass stared at me, and I held her gaze seriously for a moment before continuing. "I do think she likes him though."

She giggled again at my admission, and then quickly grew more serious. "She does. Which means she doesn't feel that way about Cam anymore, presumably."

I shot her a look. "What would you know about that?"

She shrugged. "Jackson told me. When you were training together at the start of your Patrol promotion, Tyler liked Cam. But Cam," she leaned forward, wriggling her eyebrows at me, "liked you."

I swatted her away, embarrassed.

"No, he always liked you. That very first night on the wall, he liked you."

I stared at her. "How could you know that?"

"I could just tell." She smiled again. "He couldn't stop looking at you."

"Rubbish." I tried to shrug it off, and was relieved when she fell silent for a moment.

The sky was almost completely black now, and the only light came from a small lantern we had brought out with us. The calls of nighttime birds swirled around us and despite me wishing desperately that the walkie-talkie would crackle to life in my hand, it remained stubbornly silent.

"You miss him."

It was a statement, not a question. Cass had always been headstrong and impetuous, but in recent weeks, I had seen a different side to her. Her understanding that I might be miserable without Cam demonstrated this perfectly.

"It's just hard, you know?" I turned to her, my eyes suddenly heavy with tears. "It was worse when I knew he was sick and was afraid that he might actually..." I stumbled over my words. "...and obviously it's better now that I know he's alive... but it's still hard. I worry about him all the time, and then I see Jackson and Mason or Rogers and Green, and even... even Tyler and Hughes, whatever might be happening between them, and Cam and I never... we never had a chance to be together without there being some awful crisis."

She shook her head. "Well, when the mission's a success, then..."

I squeezed her hand. "Thanks, Cass. That's what I'm hoping."

She pushed herself to her feet. "We should get some rest before tomorrow."

I glanced down at the walkie-talkie again.

"You're not coming, are you?"

Shooting her a baleful glance, I shook my head.

"I get it. Just don't wait up all night, ok?"

"I won't."

Leaning down to give me a quick hug, she hurried inside, closing the door after her with a typical, Cass-like bang. I winced, knowing how late it was. Glancing around at the empty area around me, I sighed, knowing I should have gone inside with her. It was too late to be waiting up to hear the voice of a man who might well be totally unable to send a message at this particular moment in time.

From my position on the grass, I could see along the entire row of apartment blocks, and I had been watching them go out one by one as we had been talking. Now there was only one lamp lit, in a block a couple down from us. It was the one where Roberts and Ross lived, and I wondered idly if she had managed to get comfortable enough to sleep yet, or if she was still as wide awake as I was.

Making me jump, the walkie-talkie suddenly hissed loudly into the silence surrounding me. It took a moment, but when I realised what was happening, I grabbed it and pulled it closer to my ear. For a few minutes, there was only silence, and occasional hissing, but eventually, my heart racing, I heard the familiar voice.

"This is Cam. Anyone there?"

"Hey Cam." My hand was shaking. "It's Quin."

"...good to hear..." The reception was poor tonight, and I couldn't hear him as well as I usually could.

"Is everything ok?"

"...more deaths... difficult to... Anders... Dev Sector... been trying..."

The sound cut out for a moment. I sat in the darkness, blinking away tears, willing him to continue. A bitter wind cut through the trees on the far side of the path and I shivered. It was going to rain soon, I could feel it.

"...still there?"

"Yes! Yes, I'm still here."

"...need to... how soon... think you'll be ready?"

"Ready for the attack? Not sure. Rogers said a few weeks yet. We're trying to build up a larger amount of ammo."

"...not sure how... longer we... there's a... not managing to... "

"You're cutting out, Cam." I sighed in frustration. "Can you repeat that please?"

"...not managing... many... too many..."

The walkie-talkie cut out again abruptly. I had to stop myself from hurling it across the grass. Instead, I clung to it, desperately hoping for more. But after several minutes of silence, I had to admit defeat. Clearly, he had stopped broadcasting, or had to abandon his efforts to speak to me.

But what I had heard from him was not promising. I racked

my brain trying to recall the words I had been able to make out. Deaths. Difficulties. Not managing to do something. And, the most clarity I had heard from him, his eagerness to hear when we would be launching an attack. Which, above everything else, implied that he needed to know we would come soon. My heart sank, as I released my hold on the walkie-talkie and sank back onto the grass, my hand aching from the tight grip I'd had on the instrument.

The ground at my back felt cold now, and I knew I'd regret staying out here so long when I had to get up in the morning. I knew I had to report the call to Rogers and Green, but for a moment, I couldn't force my reluctant body to move. I lay there and let the tears roll down my face, knowing from experience that I needed to cry it out if I wanted to regain control before I went inside.

I had waited to hear from Cam for a week. And now that I had, the contact hadn't made me feel any better. Reluctantly, I pushed myself to my feet. I was not relishing the prospect of waking Rogers to deliver the depressing news. Sighing, I glanced at the sky once more as a light rain began to fall, and turned towards the apartment.

I had only gone a few steps when a scream of pain ripped through the night.

Chapter Twenty One

Alarmed, I spun round to face the direction the sound had come from. It had seemed to originate from one of the apartments further down the row. In the silence which followed though, I could only hear the rain pattering softly on the grass around me. Peering into the darkness, I saw Roberts' light was still on, and, as I watched, more of the windows in the building lit up, one after another, in rapid succession.

And then the scream came again.

I started running. It took me less than a minute to jog to Roberts' block, and as I approached, I could see several citizens silhouetted in the doorway. One of them hurried off towards the hub and the others disappeared inside before I could reach the building, so when I got there, the door was closed again. My heart in my mouth, I knocked tentatively.

For several moments, there was no response. Inside, I could hear muffled sounds: insistent whispers, footsteps, and a low, moaning underpinning it all. Alarmed, I tried the handle of the door, easing it open when I discovered it wasn't locked. The hallway which lay in front of me was dark, but its layout was similar to ours, so I could find my way without too much difficulty. I crept up the stairs, seeing no one, knowing the noises were emanating from the upper floor, where I knew Ross and Roberts' apartment was.

On the landing above, I came across two citizens standing together, casting glances at the door to my friends' apartment.

"Hey." I approached with caution. "What's going on?"

I recognised the citizen standing closest to me as Millett, the red-haired woman I had met at the Smelting Plant on my first day at The Ridge.

"It's Ross." She turned and looked curiously at me. "Baby's coming."

I heard the scream again, chilling in its intensity now I was so close. "Is she ok?"

"She'll be fine." Millett grimaced. "It hurts, that's all."

The second citizen was a tall, older woman who I hadn't seen before. She shook her head at Millett's words. "If Jones has gone for McGrath, I'm off to bed. Not that any of us'll be sleeping well tonight with that racket going on."

I noticed that she didn't even look at me. Evidently, she was one of the Ridge citizens who still mistrusted those of us from the Crags. As she shuffled away to an apartment on the other side of the hall, the redhead turned back to me.

"You Crags people never known a baby be born?" She chuckled. "It can be long, and it's painful. Might take the poor girl 'til sometime tomorrow."

I stared in horror. "Does it hurt the whole time?"

She laughed again. "On and off it does. It's worse towards the end." Her eyes gained a faraway look. "I've one of my own. He's nineteen now, but I still remember his birth."

"How long did it...?" I let the question hang in the air.

"It was a full day's work, let me tell you. But so worth it."

She looked sad. "I always wanted another."

I stared at her, something Hughes had said to us when we first reached The Ridge coming back to me. "Ah yes, you're only–"

"–only permitted one, that's right. The old leader made it law. For good reason, mind you," she added hurriedly. "He was afraid too many people would... well, that The Ridge wouldn't support a much larger community."

"Why not?"

"Various reasons: food production issues, defence, the problems associated with the power source required to cater to more people." She shrugged. "He was cautious, that's all. Didn't want us to end up in a situation where we were putting existing citizens at risk."

I considered her words. "The Beck controls the births pretty closely too. More so than just limiting people to a single child."

"So I heard." She smiled sympathetically. "Whilst I'm sad I only had the one child, at least I got to bring him up myself."

I dropped my gaze, thinking of Baker. "Where I'm from we don't know any different. I'd forgotten you had similar restrictions here, that's all."

"They're hardly similar. We get a child, if we want one. And there's always the potential for the rules to change."

I thought back to Hughes' conversation. "Helping us like this, Hughes is hoping...?"

"...to broaden our horizons," she finished. "Make our lives a little easier. His interest in the Beck? This alliance?" She gestured between herself and me. "He sees it as a long-term strategy for improving things all round. For everyone."

I considered her words. "Let's hope we're successful then.

You think people will be permitted to have more than one child in the end then?'"

"Maybe. If things work out right for us." Millett cast one more sideways look at me before turning back to her own apartment. "Too late for me, anyway."

"I'm sorry." Suddenly, I wanted to stop her leaving. "Did you say they'd sent for McGrath? Why?"

Millett stopped and turned before she reached her door. "She's our resident midwife." I thought of Montgomery, the scientist at The Beck who was skilled at creating various meds. "Not a doctor, exactly. We don't have anyone who's properly trained, medically I mean." She frowned. "But McGrath has the most experience with delivering babies, taught by her mother, who did the same before she died. We do better generally when she's here."

"Better?"

A shadow crossed the woman's face. "Babies don't always come easy."

There was a silence, as the moaning coming from the apartment stopped momentarily. We waited a few seconds, until it resumed.

"Anyway, I'm off to bed now. See if I can get at least a little rest." The woman grinned wryly. "Work'll have to continue tomorrow, baby or not."

She turned away and disappeared into her own apartment, leaving me staring at the door she closed behind her. This time, I couldn't stop her. I stood still, unsure of what to do. I had raced over believing someone to be in danger, and wanting to help. But now, knowing there was a baby being born, I just felt like I was interfering in something private in which I had no part.

Deciding to return to my own apartment, I turned to creep in the direction I had come from. I'd barely reached the top of the stairs when I heard a door opening behind me. I tried to hurry out of sight before I was spotted, but tripped on a loose board and had to slam a hand on the bannister to stop myself falling. Wincing in pain as I nicked my hand on a stray splinter of wood, I knew I had been spotted.

"Quin?" This voice was more familiar, and louder. "Quin, is that you?"

I turned slowly to find myself facing Coleman. Her face was pale in the darkness of the hallway, and she looked worried.

"Hey." I had never felt so awkward. "I heard the screams and came running over, but... I mean... I didn't realise what was happening."

"You didn't?" She looked puzzled, and then understanding dawned on her. "Ah, you Crags folk aren't used to this kind of thing, are you?"

"No. Not really." I knew I was blushing. "Things are done quite differently on The Beck. Listen, I didn't mean to intrude. I was just leaving."

"It's fine." She came a couple of steps out onto the landing. "Ross won't mind that you came. She'll be glad to know you care."

"Would you tell her... good luck with it... for me?"

"Sure."

There was a slight noise from inside the apartment, and a small head with rumpled hair peeped out from behind her.

"Quin?" Rico's voice was sleepy and he was rubbing his eyes. "Why'y here?"

"I'm just visiting, that's all." I smiled. "I'm going off to bed now though."

"That's where you should be, little man." Coleman grimaced. "I was hoping you'd sleep through this, but I guess not."

"S'goin' on?"

She knelt down beside him. "Ross is having her baby, that's all. Could you go back to bed for me please?"

"No!" He regarded her with wide eyes. "Wan' see bay-bee."

"But the baby isn't here yet. It might not be here until morning."

Rico's eyes became mutinous. "Wan' see bay-bee."

"You can't." Her voice took on a pleading tone as the moans behind her grew louder. "I need you to be a good boy, because Mummy has to help Ross, ok? Can you go back to bed please?"

He frowned, and stuck a thumb in his mouth. "No."

She sighed, and cast a despairing look at me. "Any chance you could...? I mean, you're so good with him."

For a moment, I didn't understand, but then I realised what she meant. Flushing with pride that she trusted me enough, I stepped forward.

"Hey Rico, how about I take you on a little adventure?"

He looked at me suspiciously. "N'adven-ta?"

"Sure. Tonight's a special night, and I think it'd be fun if you came and stayed at my place."

He looked back and forth from his mother to me. We both nodded encouragingly, as he began to digest what was being offered. The chance to sleep over at my apartment. The idea was clearly appealing, yet he also seemed wary. I realised he had probably never spent a night away from Coleman and Howard. I needed to sweeten the offer.

Stepping forward, I held out a hand. "How about I give you

a piggy back?"

His eyes widened. "Alla way?"

"Sure. All the way." I smiled. "And when we get there, how about I fix us a late-night snack?"

Now his eyes were like dinner plates. "A'nack?"

"Of course."

I stepped forward and knelt next to him, bending so he could clamber onto my back, but he stepped away, looking up at Coleman. "Can get Timmy?"

He looked once more at his mother, who nodded and smiled her permission. "Of course. He'd be lonely without you."

Rico toddled back into the apartment, a determined expression on his face.

"Thanks so much for this." Coleman pulled the apartment door closed behind her as I straightened up. "Ross will need me, and I don't want Rico seeing anything he shouldn't. He'll just be in the way here. He likes you, and this way hopefully he won't feel like I'm sending him away. You can bring him back right away in the morning."

"Of course."

The door eased open again and Howard appeared behind her, a wriggling Rico in his arms. "This little man tells me he and Timmy are off on a secret sleepover adventure with Quin. That right?"

"Yeeees!" The boy giggled, waving the stuffed rabbit in the air in triumph. "Got Timmy."

"Hi, Timmy." I waved at the toy, which was apparently Rico's favourite. "Yes, he's coming home with me for the night," I confirmed for Howard's benefit, noting the slight strain in his eyes as he smiled his thanks.

"You'll be back in the morning, right kid? I don't think I

can manage too long without you."

Rico grinned as his father carried him over to me. "Back mornin'."

"And you look after Quin, mind," Coleman added.

Rico nodded solemnly, as Howard stepped closer and lifted him onto my back. I felt his warm arms wrap around my neck and made sure he was hanging on securely before I walked away.

"See you tomorrow, little man." Howard waved a hand as we walked away.

"Byeeee!" Rico squealed at his parents, clutching Timmy close to his cheek and resting his head trustingly on my shoulder as we descended the stairs. I found myself concerned by the uneasy eyes of his parents, who seemed keen to return to Ross even as they waved good-bye.

As we reached the bottom, the front door of the apartment burst open abruptly. McGrath stood in the doorway, her hair mussed up from sleep. Pausing for a moment and blinking in surprise, she took in the situation, eventually understanding what I was doing with Howard and Coleman's son. She nodded her satisfaction.

"Was wondering what they'd do with you, Rico." She glanced at me, lowering her voice. "Better he's out of the way for now. Thanks, Quin."

I smiled. "No problem. Glad to be able to–"

But she was gone, moving past me and striding up the stairs rapidly. I heard a low rumble of voices on the upper landing and the door to the apartment shutting. The hallway was silent for a moment, before the moaning began again. Concerned that Rico might hear and question the noise, I hurried to the door and let myself out.

"Just you and me for now, little man," I muttered, shifting his weight on my back carefully as I eased the door closed behind us.

He wriggled slightly, but his head remained on my shoulder and there was no response. Taking a deep breath and praying that Ross would be alright, I set off back to my own apartment, carrying my precious cargo.

Chapter Twenty Two

When I reached our apartment, it was silent. I let myself in through the door, struggling slightly. Rico was not heavy, but carrying him for a prolonged period of time had been more difficult than I had anticipated, and I was pretty sure he had fallen asleep on my back, as he had become a dead weight somewhere between Coleman's building and my own. The door banged shut behind me as I struggled to keep the boy steady, and a moment later the outer door to one of the downstairs apartments opened.

A faint light filtered out into the hallway, silhouetting a figure. Green. She stared at me, her eyes puzzled and sleepy. "Everything alright?"

"Ross is having the baby," I whispered. "Coleman asked me to take Rico for the rest of the night."

An expression I couldn't identify flickered across her face for a moment and she came further out into the corridor. She approached, and ran a finger across Rico's cheek.

"Fast asleep," she murmured. "Isn't he good?"

I frowned, thinking how he'd tried to resist leaving his mother. "He is now he's asleep."

She chuckled, gesturing into her apartment. "Want to bring him inside?"

I hesitated. All the way from Coleman's apartment I had been wondering what I would do with Rico when I got here. My own apartment had three bedrooms, but two were otherwise occupied, and my own was shared with Cass. Green's invitation solved the problem. She and Rogers shared a two-bedroom apartment but only used one of them, so there was definitely space for Rico.

"Sure." I followed her inside. "Is it ok if he and I spend the night here? I don't want to leave him, but there's not really enough room in my apartment."

She nodded and led the way to a door on the other side of the room. On the other side of it lay a comfortable bed, ready made up with sheets and blankets.

"He'll be ok here." Green gestured to the soft toy. "Cute."

"He's called Timmy," I whispered.

She helped me to ease the small child onto the bed. I moved slowly, certain that he would wake. A moment later we were staring down at his little face, serene in sleep.

"I promised him a late-night snack when we got here." I smiled.

"When he wakes up, he'll be cross that he missed out." She wrinkled her nose. "Bless him."

I returned her grin, as I eased the blanket out from underneath him and covered him up. Smoothing the surface of it over his sleeping form, I backed towards the door.

Outside, Green gestured to a jug which rested on the counter back into the communal area. "Want a drink?"

"Don't you want to go back to bed?" I questioned, not wanting to intrude.

She shrugged, motioning to the room where Rico slept. "I won't sleep, at least not for a while. Not now that I know he's here."

Nodding my agreement, I settled on the sofa while she poured us both a glass of water.

"How's Ross doing?" she enquired.

"I'm not sure," I hesitated. "She was screaming. That's why I went over in the first place. I was frightened someone was being attacked."

"I believe it's very painful." She smiled, but it didn't reach her eyes. "Worth it, though."

I thought back to the conversation I'd had with Millett. "That's the second time someone's said that tonight."

She was staring off into the middle distance, almost as though I wasn't even there. "Not that I'd know, of course."

I recalled that she and Rogers were both eager to have a child together, and understood her wistful expression. The Beck's imposed drug, the one which blocked a woman's ability to conceive a child, was administered at the age of fourteen and only reversed if and when that woman was selected for Birthing. At the moment, not one of the female citizens on The Crags would be able to get pregnant. Not until we had gotten our hands on the reversal serum. It was another reason we had to return to The Beck.

"I was talking to a woman over in Ross' apartment about the fact that the citizens here are only allowed to have one child. Did you know that?"

"I did." Her expression was unreadable. "It seems fair. More than we'll ever get, if we don't manage to take The Beck."

"We will." I remembered the earlier radio call. "Cam was in touch. Before..." I waved my hand back in the direction of Ross' apartment.

Green's attention refocused, and her face immediately reflected a different concern. "Everything ok over there?"

I bit my lip. "Not sure. He sort of... got cut off. And the signal was poor, so I couldn't hear a lot of what he said."

She squeezed my arm. "Could be nothing. We've had issues with the signal before. Bad weather, or..."

"I know. But what he did say didn't sound good."

She cocked her head to one side. "What was it?"

"He was asking how soon we'd be ready. Said something about them not managing to do... well, something. I couldn't work out what." I sighed.

She finished her glass of water before she replied. "Try not to worry. There's little we can do, until..."

"...until when though?" I couldn't keep the frustration from my voice. "When will Rogers and Hughes decide we're ready?"

"Shh, you'll wake him." She shot a look at the closed door of the room where Rico slept. "It won't be too much longer now. They just want a couple more shipments of lead from The Crags to make some more bullets, and a few more training sessions, so you're all as ready as you can be." She pushed her chair away from the table and stood up. "And now, I think perhaps we should both try and get some sleep."

She stacked the glasses in the sink and wandered back to Rico's door, pushing it open slightly to check on him. The look of yearning on her face spoke volumes. Closing the door quietly, she waved a hand at me and slid inside the room she shared with Rogers. Once she had disappeared, I decided she was right, used the washroom quickly, and slipped into the unfamiliar bedroom.

Rico lay spread-eagled on the bed, his little mouth wide

open, arms flung out, legs tangled in the blankets which I had placed carefully over him when I had first laid him down. Sliding them out from under him, I straightened them and gently shifted his little form on to the other side of the bed so I could lie beside him. He snuffled once or twice, his face twitching as though his dreams were troubling him. I smoothed his hair away from his forehead and located Timmy, who had slipped off the bed and onto the floor. Once I returned the soft toy to him, he clutched it tightly and was comforted enough to return to a peaceful sleep.

I settled back myself, doubting that I'd be able to sleep in this unfamiliar room, the child I had been given responsibility for lying beside me. But it was not long before I drifted into a sleep which was more restful than I had experienced in weeks.

***

When I woke it was too light. Something was wrong. I should have been up by now, awake and eating breakfast ready to head for the pitches for another day of training. But the light which flooded into the room told me it was later than it should have been. Glancing at the other side of the bed, I noticed the rumpled covers, but sat bolt upright with a start as I saw that the space beside me was empty.

Hearing voices from the communal area, I bounded to the door and sprung through it, panic making my heart pound furiously. On the other side, Rico was seated at the table, and Green was speaking softly in his ear. Timmy lay next to the child, and Rogers stood at the stove. As I entered, Rico burst into a further fit of giggles at something Green had just said.

Spotting me, Rogers waved a hand. "Heard we had a late-night visitor. Two, in fact." He waved a spatula at Rico and made a funny face, which sent the child into further gales of laughter. "Breakfast?"

"What's going on?" I blurted, ignoring his question. "Why didn't you wake me? Why aren't we already up at the pitches?"

Green came over to me, lowering her voice. "It hasn't happened yet. The baby. Apparently, Ross is struggling a little."

My eyes widened in alarm. "But– but–"

She shot a pointed look at Rico. "So we're just extending the adventure and having the snack you promised this little man last night, aren't we Rico?"

"'nack! 'nack!" He beat his little fists on the table and beamed at me.

"Where's everyone else?" I re-entered the bedroom and started to pull on my jacket.

"Already up at the pitches. We can join them later, Quin." Rogers spoke quietly, keeping his tone even. "Sooooo, who's for a little oatmeal?" He turned to Green. "We're running a little low. We'll need to ask if we can have some more from the hub at some point."

"Who'd have thought someone would've made a cook out of you?" She smiled affectionately.

"I enjoy it." Rogers narrowed his eyes at her before carrying the pan across to the table. "I still can't believe how generous they're being to us. I mean, I know we're providing for their citizens over on The Crags, but there are more of us here and...well, it's surprising."

"I'm not sure everyone is happy with it," Green mused, "but Hughes wants to cement the relationship between our communities, and I guess this is his way of doing it."

Rogers shrugged, and began spooning some of the oatmeal

into Rico's bowl. Once the child had his food, Rogers served another three portions, and beckoned for us to come and join them. Shaking my head, I stood undecided at the door.

"Ross doesn't need you, Quin," Green muttered under her breath. "Rico does. And he can't go back there, not just yet. Let's eat with him."

Sighing, I stepped away from the door and reluctantly joined the trio at the table. Rico beamed as I sat down, and I could see that Green was right. He was my responsibility, and though I was worried about Ross, the best I could do for her now was to care for Coleman's child so that her closest friend could be there for her.

We made the meal last as long as we could. Eventually we had all consumed a bowl of oatmeal and Rico was playing on the floor of the apartment, banging on some pans with a wooden spoon. We retreated to the bedroom to talk privately.

"Howard came over this morning early. Asked if we'd keep Rico a little longer," Green explained. "Apparently the birth isn't progressing as they'd like. Ross is exhausted and there's no sign of the baby yet. Hughes has instructed that people continue with shifts as much as possible, but obviously certain people aren't working today because they're helping Ross."

"But how... I mean... what...?" I couldn't finish the thought.

"We don't know. Apparently, it's not uncommon for a woman to struggle like this. Giving birth is difficult, but they're a little concerned that, if it takes too much longer, the baby... and Ross... will be in danger."

"Tyler went over earlier." Rogers saw my confused expression. "She used to work quite closely with the Meds Sector at The Beck, didn't you know?"

I nodded, remembering my own trip over there with her. It seemed so long ago now.

"Well she's not an expert, but she has experience of viewing and assisting with births, so we figured she might be of some use."

"I hope so."

"Me too." Green peered through the door at the small human playing in the room beyond. "He seems quite happy right now. Rogers, do you want to go up to the pitches now? No point us all being stuck here."

He nodded. "Sure. I'll be back for lunch later."

As he disappeared into the second room to collect his things, Green nodded at Rico. "You alright to keep an eye on him while I go and get an update on what's happening?"

"Sure." I opened the door wider, smiling as I approached the little boy again. "Hey Rico, can I play?"

He nodded enthusiastically, handing me one of his spoons and grinning broadly.

We played games for the next few hours, and I found it helped to take my mind off what was going on in Roberts' and Ross' apartment. Rico was an easy child to be around, but keeping him amused for a prolonged period of time was quite a challenge. By the end of the morning, we had turned the entire apartment upside down as we created a fort from bedsheets and chairbacks, and I was exhausted. When the door opened again a little while later, I barely heard it.

Chapter Twenty Three

Only when Green was standing directly in front of the entrance to the makeshift tent I was crouched inside, did I know she was there.

"Hi!" My voice carried a tone of alarm, which had returned the moment she had burst the bubble of escapism Rico and I had created. I clambered to my feet and stood up, clumsily. "What's... I mean, how's...?"

She looked strained, and for several moments I was frightened of her response.

"Oh no..." I began, clambering to my feet and attempting to extricate myself from the tent. "What's... I mean, how's...?"

She raised a hand to stop me.

"It's ok." She looked down as Rico crawled out from the fort and stared up at her in alarm. "She's ok. The baby was born half an hour ago." She bent down so she was on a level with Rico. "Ross had her baby. A boy, just like you. Isn't that great?"

Straightening up, she walked to the table and sat down heavily. Rico's wide eyes followed her, as though he wasn't sure whether he believed her or not. Seeking to distract him, I took his hand quickly and pointed at the bedroom.

"Did you hear that? You have a new little friend." I glanced at Green, who hadn't moved. "Hey Rico, I think Green's tired. Where's Timmy? Think he could make her feel better?"

He nodded earnestly. "Yes. Timmy can."

"Can you go get him then?"

He hurried to the bedroom and disappeared out of sight.

Knowing I didn't have long, I hurried to Green's side, placing a tentative hand on her arm.

"Green, is something wrong?"

She turned to look at me, her eyes filled with tears.

"Green!" Shaking her slightly, I bent closer to her ear. "What is it?"

She seemed to shake herself, and rubbed the heel of her hand across her face. "Sorry. Ross is ok, I promise. She's weak, and she lost some blood, but McGrath thinks she'll be ok."

"And the baby?" I kept my eyes glued on the door to the bedroom, which was still closed.

"He's fine too." She took a long, shuddering breath. "Sorry, it's just that... I was there when it... when it happened, and to see her... to see him b-being born... well, it's all I want to do Quin, and I can't... and I'm so..."

I bent down and placed my arms around her gently. The tears were not for Ross then, nor the baby, but for Green herself. A noise from the bedroom door alerted us to Rico's presence. He came back into the room cautiously, peering with concern at Green. When he finally reached us, he clutched Timmy to his chest, as though Green might hurt him.

She managed a weak smile. "I'm sorry if I scared you, Rico. Could I hold Timmy please?"

A wavering hand offered the toy. Green took it, and gently cradled it to her chest. Slowly, Rico crept closer to her, until he stood beside her, then he put a small hand on her knee. She took it in her own, but didn't appear able to speak.

"It's exciting news, isn't it Rico?" I smiled as widely as I could, attempting to put him at ease.

Green found her voice. "Your mum says you can go and meet him soon."

A smile spread across Rico's face as the news sunk in. He ran to the window, peering out.

"Where mummy? Where mum?"

We exchanged a glance. "Not yet, Rico. They need a little time to get ready for you. Why don't you come and show Green your den?"

It turned out that Rico was fairly easy to distract as long as we kept on playing games with him. The next hour was spent keeping his mind off the baby until he could go home and meet his new little friend. This had the added benefit of diverting Green, who became quite entranced with our game, once we explained how it worked. I did catch some occasional sadness clouding her features, but there were no more tears, and she managed to keep it together fairly well. When it came time to return Rico to his parents, however, I understood her insistence that Rico and I go without her.

"They entrusted him to you, Quin." She nodded firmly. "You need to take him back. Anyway, I should be getting up to the training grounds. I'll let them know where you are."

"Alright." I swallowed my nerves at taking Rico back to his parents alone. "I'll take him over there now. Be up as soon as I can."

She nodded. Her face was a mask of indifference, but I knew

she was hiding her earlier pain. She did not want to come face to face with Ross' and Roberts' child again just yet. She strode to the door and pulled it open, turning only briefly to wave a hand before disappearing through it.

I stood up too, walking to Rico and ruffling a hand through his unkempt hair. "Coming, little guy? I can take you back to your mum now."

Nodding eagerly, he dropped the cups he held in each hand and sprang to his feet. "Comin'!"

"Don't forget Timmy," I reminded him.

It only took a few minutes for us to walk the distance to the apartment, despite Rico's little legs. I remembered the walk the night before and grimaced: with the child on my back, it had taken an age. When we arrived at the apartment there was none of the awkwardness I had felt the evening before. Rico didn't knock, he just powered through the door and sprinted up the staircase before I could caution him not to run. He reached the apartment long before I did, and stood waiting for it to open.

"Did you knock?" I called, from the top of the stairs.

In answer, he began hammering his little fists on the door and calling out loudly. "Baby! Baaaaaby? Wan' meet baaaaby!"

As I drew level with him, the door swung open and Howard was standing there. His face was drawn and he looked exhausted, but he managed a smile as he swung his son up into his arms.

"Rico! My little man." He smothered the boy's face and neck with kisses. "I missed you!"

Rico giggled and wrestled out of his father's grasp, pushing past him and inside the apartment.

"Roberts! Incoming!" Howard called over his shoulder, before turning to grin at me.

"Is everything ok?" I managed.

"It is now." He beckoned me in. "There were a few rough moments, but we got there in the end. Tyler was a real lifesaver. Knew some things even McGrath didn't."

"Is Ross alright?" I still hovered on the threshold.

"Sure she is. Well, she will be." He stepped forward and took me by the arm, encouraging me through the doorway. "Coleman's had to go to work her shift. Thanks for having Rico. Was he good?"

"He was no trouble at all."

"We really appreciate it."

I found myself on the other side of the door, still feeling a little like I was intruding. Inside, the apartment was quiet, the drama over and done with, for now at least.

Howard was at the far end of the space already, heading for a door which was slightly ajar. He turned back to see me lurking just inside the door and looked surprised.

"You coming?" He frowned. "You want to meet the newest addition to the family, don't you?"

Grinning, he disappeared through the door of the bedroom. Tentatively, I followed. The way they were so close, referring to one another as family even when they weren't related by blood, was so strange. Lovely, but strange. I thought again of Baker, but quickly quashed the waves of negative thoughts which washed over me. Stepping through the bedroom door, I surveyed the scene.

Ross lay sleeping in a large bed in the centre of the room. Her face was pale and she was clearly exhausted, but she seemed, at least, peaceful. My eyes were drawn to the corner, where Howard had joined Roberts, who was unsuccessfully trying to contain a wriggling Rico in his arms.

He spotted me and smiled. "Hey. Come meet this little one."

As he glanced down at the child in the crib beneath him, his face shone with pride. He didn't seem able to tear his eyes away from the baby for longer than a few seconds at a time. His eyes were ringed with black circles and his entire body radiated fatigue, but his happiness was indisputable. As I approached, I marvelled at the joy on his face.

The crib had been standing in the corner of Ross and Roberts' room for several weeks now. Empty, but made up with sheets and a small blanket that Ross had spent ages sewing together, it had stood waiting patiently for the new arrival. Now I stared down into it, at the miniature human who lay inside.

For now, the baby slept. All that was visible was his face, which was red and puffy. The blankets were tucked tightly around his small form, and his tiny rosebud lips were puckered, as though he was thinking of something unpleasant. As I stood there, he wriggled slightly and let out a small whimper, a darker expression shadowing his features.

Immediately Roberts passed Rico to his father and bent close, stroking the baby's cheek with a hand which dwarfed the tiny figure. The moment passed, and the baby seemed to relax into a more peaceful slumber.

Howard chuckled. "Enjoy this peace. You won't have a lot of it later on."

"Baby! Baby!" Rico, clearly tired of staying quiet, pointed his tiny finger, eager to show off his new playmate.

Roberts turned to me with a tired smile. "What'd'ya think,

then?"

"He's... um... he's small?" I tried.

Howard and Roberts burst into laughter.

"And... well, beautiful? ...I guess."

"Thanks, Quin." Roberts patted me on the shoulder. "Such compliments."

"Are you not totally amazed by the tiny human I managed to produce?" Ross' voice came from behind us, and we turned to see her, a small, satisfied smile on her face.

"Hey," I said, moving to her side. "How are you?"

"I've been better." She grinned. "I'm a little tired. And sore. That's all."

Roberts left the crib and sat on the bed next to his partner. "She was amazing. Even when..." He stopped.

"...even when things looked a little... um... dicey," Ross finished for him. "Tyler was a great help, by the way."

"I'm glad. I knew she had some experience in Meds, our Birthing Sector," I mused. "But I didn't know how practical the experience had been."

Ross smiled tiredly and yawned. "Well she had some good advice. McGrath was pleased to have her here, even if she wouldn't admit it."

"Not sure about pleased." Roberts frowned.

"Oh hush," Ross chided. "She's not one to be warm and friendly, but I think by the end even she had to admit how helpful Tyler had been."

"Where's Tyler now?"

Roberts shook his head. "She and McGrath headed for the pitches."

My heart thudded at the thought. "Really? After being up all night?"

"Yup." Howard frowned. "I don't think they'll stay all day. They just wanted to make sure they were there to run their training sessions this morning." Seeing the expression on my face, he relinquished his hold on Rico, who raced off to play. "Are you worried because you didn't make it yet?"

I nodded.

"But everyone knows you were helping us out last night." He stared at me, puzzled. "What happened if you missed a shift in The Beck?"

I shrugged. "We didn't miss shifts."

"Clearly. But seriously, what kind of punishments did that Adams guy hand out?"

I paused, thinking back to the unpleasantness of my time at The Beck. The Reckonings had seemed normal, when we had lived there and known no different. With hindsight I was almost ashamed to admit the treatment we could potentially suffer at the hands of our Supers.

"Generally, they were physical. Whippings, beatings, and so on. Our Supers had electric cattle prods that were supposed to be used with the animals, but they were often used to give us a short, sharp shock. Usually when our work output wasn't what it should have been."

"Really?" Howard looked appalled. "That's terrible!"

I could feel my face flushing. "It wasn't always so bad. It depended on your particular Super. Some were far worse than others. Those who wanted to get ahead, to impress their superiors and be recognized by Adams, were usually the worst."

"Well, surely you know it isn't like that here?" Howard soothed. "Look, go up there now and explain where you've been, if it makes you feel better. And stop fretting. The fact that you stepped in and helped out in an emergency situation says a lot about you. Hughes'll be glad you were around. I'm guessing he'll alter the training schedule for today anyway. He won't want people who aren't with it handling weapons. He'll probably dismiss Tyler and McGrath and let the rest of you work on endurance and strength training today with him and Rogers." He paused, peering into my eyes closely. "Does that reassure you at all?"

"A little." I managed a smile. "I'll get going up there now anyway, make sure I'm no later than I need to be. Are you ok taking care of Rico now?"

"Sure. I'll have him until later today when Coleman gets back from her shift. Then she'll take over while I'm on guard duty at the hilltop. Means one of us can keep an eye on Ross and Roberts too."

"Alright. I'll head off then."

I walked to the door of the bedroom again and peered inside. Roberts had curled up behind Ross and the two of them were fast asleep. Tiptoeing away, I hoped they would manage to get at least some sleep before the baby woke them. As I reached the door of the apartment, I turned to wave at Rico, who beamed at me. I glanced back at Howard, who was fixing some food for his son.

"Thank you."

"For what? It was *you* doing us the favour." He smiled. "Have a good day, Quin."

Leaving the building I stepped out into the sunshine, feeling more positive than I had done in a long while.

Chapter Twenty Four

Howard was right about Hughes' intentions. That day, he sent Tyler and McGrath away to catch up on their rest, and he and Rogers simply doubled the number of trainees in their own groups and carried on as usual. It meant that some of The Crags citizens, including myself, had to work more closely with Thomas, but he barely spoke a word all afternoon and was easy to ignore. Walker was purposefully placed in the opposing group, so no problems arose.

When I did occasionally find myself watching Thomas, he did nothing other than rehearse the manoeuvres diligently and with a fierce focus I had rarely witnessed in any of the other trainees. When he did have to work with a partner he was always placed with a citizen from The Ridge, and I could see what a skilled soldier he was becoming. By the end of the session, sweat was streaming down his face and he returned to his cell looking totally exhausted, but satisfied.

Over the next few days, Hughes made sure that both our female trainers had shorter shifts so they were well rested before they returned to their usual pattern. He took on extra training shifts himself to make sure that their absence didn't impact our schedule, and when he announced the joyful news of the new arrival at the communal dinner that night, he told us all that he was allowing Roberts the usual week off to be with Ross and Fenn, the name they had decided on for their son.

A week later we were all in the canteen again when Hughes rose and banged on the table, as he always did to make any announcements after dinner. As the crowd slowly fell silent, he beckoned for Rogers to come and join him, and waited until he had reached the front of the hall before he started to speak.

"Evening!" he began. "I hope we're all feeling positive tonight. Rogers and I are happy that the training of our new recruits is progressing well. We are pleased with the number of bullets now being produced regularly in the smelting plant and we've been busy making plans in relation to our attack on The Beck. We're pretty confident that, in the very near future, we'll finally be ready to launch an attack which is well planned and stands an excellent chance of success."

Rogers took over. "The soldiers we are training have begun to work with guns now, and this, along with the amount of ammo we now have available to us, is the key to beating Adams."

I thought back over the past week, when we had indeed been training with guns. While I still wasn't totally confident about using them, I had now managed to fire off a few rounds and had found myself to be a surprisingly good shot. My fear was that when I was aiming at a human being rather than a brightly-coloured, circular target, I would be less enthusiastic about pulling the trigger.

"Our main concern," Rogers continued, "is the lack of contact with The Beck. It has been more than a week now since our last communication, and before that we were receiving messages once every couple of days. That's not to say there is anything majorly wrong, of course," he was quick to reassure, "...but still, we'd feel happier to hear something from them soon."

He glanced at Hughes, who continued. "So with the idea that we are going to set sail for an attack on the Beck fairly soon, and to celebrate the birth of our newest arrival, we invite you all to our customary birth party."

The room erupted in cheers from The Ridge citizens, and those of us at the Crags table exchanged perplexed glances.

"It will take place tomorrow night, in the courtyard outside this canteen, and everyone, aside from a small unit of guards who will of course complete short rotations on duty at our major outposts, is welcome to come and raise a glass to toast the newest member of our community." He nodded at Rogers.

"Now I know my fellow Crags citizens are looking a little confused, and to explain to all you Ridge folk, we people from The Beck don't actually know what parties are."

A few of The Ridge citizens laughed as Hughes butted in. "No, seriously. When I mentioned the planned party to Rogers, I had to explain the concept to him."

Rogers held up a hand to stop the buzz of appalled conversation that had sprung up at Hughes' comment. "Listen, at the Beck, we hardly had any leisure time. We certainly didn't have large gatherings to celebrate our achievements, nor did we prepare special meals to commemorate a particular occasion. But that," he turned to our table and grinned, "is what they do here at The Ridge, and I'm excited that we're going to be able to join them in their celebration."

A small thrill of excitement ran down our table, tempered with more than a few nerves. A party would certainly be a new experience for us all, and none of us knew what to expect.

Hughes carried on. "Anyway, tomorrow afternoon, the majority of the Crags citizens are going to come over here for the evening and join us."

More than one person in the room exclaimed at this news. I watched Walker punch the air in delight at the idea of being reunited with Harper, and many faces lit up at the prospect of seeing family and friends they had been long separated from.

Rogers grinned at the reaction. "As well as celebrating Fenn's birth, we'd like also to raise a toast to the successful collaboration we have experienced over the past few weeks." He paused and grew more serious. "I know there are still a few of you Ridgers out there who are less than happy that we're here at the moment. But I'm hopeful that we are steadily gaining your trust, and that together, in the end, we can achieve what we all want and secure that bond of trust for good."

"Anyway, enough of the serious talk," Hughes interrupted. "This is about celebrating! We look forward to seeing you relaxing and enjoying yourselves for a change. You deserve it. Oh," he paused, a mischievous expression crossing his features, "and the customary day off for most of us will follow the day after the party. Reduced shifts for those of us who have to work, but a generally relaxed day off for all of us to nurse our sore heads."

With a cheerful nod, he dismissed us and went back to speaking to Rogers. The room erupted into a louder chatter than usual as everyone discussed the announcement. I sat thinking of what it meant for us: the chance to see friends we had been apart from for some time now, and a large dinner to celebrate. The idea that we might relax and enjoy what we had achieved was at the same time daunting and exciting.

Of course, it might mean seeing Baker again. Recalling our last words, I wasn't sure how I felt about this. Very possibly, she would decide not to come. She wasn't one for socialising at the best of times, and I suspected the thought of seeing me again would not be very appealing. No, she had probably volunteered to remain on The Crags as one of the guards Rogers had mentioned. I swallowed my disappointment, annoyed that I was still letting her get to me.

Turning my attention to the rest of the table, I tuned into the excited conversations going on around me. Walker was looking happier than I had seen him in a long time; Marley was chattering away with Collins, both of them clearly excited by the prospect of a celebration and the possibility of seeing and spending time with the friends they had not seen for so long; Nelson and Green had gone to join Rogers at the front; and Tyler gazed around the table with a satisfied smile on her face that told me she had already known about the party, probably from Hughes.

"What do you think it'll be like?" Cass' words in my ear startled me slightly.

I looked over at her. "Not sure. What do you think people *do* at a party?"

"It's fun." The small voice came from my left and I turned to see Simpson, clearing the plates quietly as usual.

"How?" Cass asked, her expression curious.

"You really don't know what a party is? Like, you don't know what happens at one?" Simpson's expression was incredulous.

"Nope. No idea!" Cass leaned closer, grabbing Simpson's arm and pulling her down to sit on the bench beside us. "Tell us!"

For a moment Simpson looked uncomfortable, but then she glanced around and saw that the whole room was busy chatting about the upcoming event, and relaxed.

"Well, there'll be food – good food – they always save some of the great stuff for a party. And, um... no one really works. I mean, there'll be people working, but the shifts are lighter and they'll be on a quicker rotation so everyone gets some time to join in. There'll be music, and dancing, and–"

"Wait!" Cass interrupted. "Dancing? What's that?"

Simpson giggled. "You don't know what dancing is?"

"No. We definitely don't," I murmured.

"It's like, um... moving to music?" Simpson tried to define this new activity. "There are different types of movement... like swaying or skipping or kind of bouncing... or stepping different ways, just moving your feet in time to the music, I guess."

Cass and I were stunned into silence. Simpson stood up and smiled. "I'd better get on. But honestly, everybody loves a party."

She picked up a large pile of plates from the surface and moved away. Cass and I helped to clear a few more of the dishes before setting off back to the apartment. She kept up a non-stop chatter all the way.

"Can't wait to see Harper again. Mind you, think we'll get a minute with her? Not if Walker has his way. He'll want to keep her all to himself." She hardly paused for breath before ploughing on. "And Blythe and Perry – they'll come, right? Bet she's so big now!"

My own thoughts had so far been preoccupied with Baker, but they brightened at my friend's words, looking forward to seeing both Harper and Perry.

"Thank goodness!"

I turned to my friend in surprise. "What?"

"That's the first sign of enthusiasm you've shown." She sniffed. "I know it'd be better if Cam was there, but you know you'll be seeing him soon now. Hughes said we're almost ready. Can't you be at least a little bit happy about the party?"

I hadn't realised quite how much Cass had noticed my mood, and felt guilty for not managing to at least fake a little happiness. I still hadn't confided in my friend the news that Baker was my mother; until she managed to make up her mind whether she wanted to attempt some kind of relationship with me, it had seemed silly to make a big thing about it. But it meant that she interpreted my low mood as linked to my separation from Cam, when that wasn't always the case. I resolved to work harder at being positive. Baker wouldn't attend the party, so I wouldn't feel the need to hide my feelings, and there would be plenty of people there who I wanted to see.

I reached out a squeezed my friend's hand. "Sorry, Cass. I am excited. I'll enjoy it when it gets here, I promise."

"You'd better."

We were passing Ross' and Roberts' apartment and I had a sudden urge to check on them. Pointing towards their building, I set off towards it, calling over my shoulder.

"Hey, I'll just look in on Ross and Fenn, ok? See you in a little while?"

Cass waved a hand and continued on her way. I jogged to the door of the building, no longer feeling awkward about my visit. In the hallway I encountered Millett, her red hair twisted into a knot on the top of her head. She stopped when she saw me.

"How are you, Quin? Excited about tomorrow's celebration?" She chuckled. "I can't believe you all don't know what a party is!"

I shrugged not knowing how to respond. "We were brought up so differently... I mean..."

"Hey, don't worry about it." She grinned and patted my shoulder. "They're not difficult to adjust to, parties I mean. We'll show you how it's done and you'll be up and dancing with the rest of us within the first hour." She grew more serious. "I don't think the people here realised quite how different your lives have been from our own. Not at first. But now... well put it this way, even the most hostile Ridgers are starting to see how bad you had it, and what benefits we all can have from bringing down that Adams of yours."

Touched by her words, I searched for something to say, but she had already passed me and was on her way out. I headed up the stairs and made my way to Ross' apartment. A timid knock brought a tired-but-happy-looking Roberts to the door.

"Quin!" He opened the door wide and beckoned me inside. "How are you?"

"Good, thanks. Missed you all at dinner."

"Did you now? Well, as of tomorrow, you won't need to."

The little family had not been taking meals in the canteen lately. Since Fenn's birth Ross had preferred to feed him at the apartment, as she adjusted to life with a little one. But the party marked the beginnings of them rejoining community life.

"Great! We just heard about the party."

"Looking forward to it?" Roberts questioned, as he returned to washing the dishes in the sink.

Ross was sitting on the sofa, breastfeeding a hungry Fenn who was clamped firmly to her chest and swaddled in numerous blankets.

"Hey there, Quin. You ok?"

"I'm fine thanks. And yes," I turned to Roberts, "the party sounds... interesting."

"Not something you're used to, huh?" Ross was as perceptive as always. "And I bet you're wishing that your Cam could be there, right?"

"It's not that," I insisted, feeling my cheeks flushing red. "But we actually had to have the word 'party' explained to us. It's just... just that we... we've never had those kinds of celebrations."

"Well it's about time you did!" Roberts brought me a drink.

"Don't worry." She caught sight of my expression and smiled gently. "We'll show you how it's done. By the end of the evening, you'll be loving it!"

As I lowered myself onto the sofa beside her, she continued to gossip about previous parties. Listening to her enthusiasm, I found myself feeling like I might actually enjoy the occasion.

Chapter Twenty Five

The next night arrived faster than I would have thought possible. We had done the usual morning's training, but were allowed the afternoon off to get ready for the party. None of The Crags citizens understood why, until we wandered down to the hub, where we found people stringing up chains of the wild flowers which grew in abundance on the Ridge hillsides, candles being placed in holders at regular intervals around the courtyard, barrels of drink on the long tables which had been moved outside, and delicious smells emanating from both canteens.

We all helped out for a while, gathering wildflowers and bringing them to those in charge of what they called 'decorating', but later in the afternoon the area seemed to empty. When we enquired where people were going, we were told they were going to get dressed for the event. None of us had any different clothes to change into, but we returned to our apartment anyway, unsure of what else to do.

On the way, Cass and I came across Coleman, who stopped for a moment to talk. Once she realised that we had nothing else to wear, she hurried away, promising to return. Within half an hour she was knocking on the door to our apartment, her arms filled with various items she had borrowed from others.

"There isn't a lot, but there should be a few things you can use." She sounded out of breath, and I wondered how many places she had gone to in her quest to make us feel included.

A perplexed Green accepted the bundle from her. "What do we... I mean... what are all these for? Why do we need them?"

"They're just clothes." Coleman grinned at Green's confusion. "But a bit different than the usual. We wear them to... to make us feel a bit special. To kind of... mark the occasion, I suppose. There are some dresses and skirts, blouses, a few smart shirts. There won't be enough for everyone to wear a complete outfit, but there are enough ties and scarves that you all should manage something to supplement your usual stuff."

Coleman worked in the department responsible for producing all the garments worn on The Ridge. She mostly made practical workwear, but had previously told me that her real passion was creating fancy items of clothing to wear on special occasions. She found it frustrating that there was so little occasion to make and wear such outfits. I hadn't known what she meant at the time, but now I understood.

"Have fun!" She cried over her shoulder as she jogged back to her own apartment. "See you in an hour."

Green brought the clothing into our apartment, and invited everyone to take a look. We divided up the borrowed items so that everyone had at least one new thing to wear. I ended up with a soft, cream-coloured blouse, which I wore over my vest with my usual overall trousers, and I tied a blue scarf around my neck to finish. It felt strange to be dressed so differently, but I enjoyed the sensation of the silky fabric against my skin and found myself wishing that Cam could see me dressed this way. I rejected anything with a skirt, imagining it would make me feel uncomfortable, but when I saw the way Mason looked at Jackson in the pretty yellow dress she wore, I was a little sad that I hadn't had the confidence to wear one myself.

We made our way to the hub as one, a little self-conscious about our new attire and unsure about the expected behaviour for a party. When we reached the courtyard, it was already filling with people. The candles had been lit and were already glowing in the dusk. The small garlands of wild flowers smelled wonderful, and one of the tables already held some dishes of food which looked to be steaming hot. Stools were being set up in the corner for the band to play music. The air was filled with chatter and laughter. The Ridge citizens were already sipping drinks and circulating, looking far more comfortable in their smart clothing than we did. We stood awkwardly at the edge of the courtyard until we were spotted by Hughes, who strode forward, abandoning the group he had been speaking to in his haste to greet us.

"Welcome! Welcome!" he boomed, turning the heads of most of the citizens in the area. "Come on, let's get you all a drink."

He ushered us towards the table which contained trays with cups, and several barrels which had taps fixed to the sides of them. When the tap was released, a gold-coloured liquid flowed into the cup beneath it.

"Whisky!" Hughes declared. "There are some barrels in the stores here. We save it for special occasions only. Don't drink too much though, or mix it with water. It can have a bit of a... funny effect on the brain."

When I was finally handed a glass, I took a sip. The liquid had a sharp, woody flavour. It was also extremely strong, and

I was glad I hadn't gulped the entire glass down the way that Cass, who was now spluttering and coughing violently, had.

Further encouraged by Hughes, we headed into the centre of the party with our drinks. The area hummed with conversation, warmth radiating from every corner. Cass and I exchanged a sly glance as Hughes poured Tyler's drink last, and the two of them headed to one side of the space, seating themselves close together on a bench which was slightly apart from the rest of the crowd.

Moments later, there was a commotion at the far end of the courtyard. We all turned to see what had caused it, and the next thing I knew, a group headed by Harper and Blythe, Perry clutched tightly in her arms, arrived in the courtyard. There was a slightly awkward moment, where it was clear that our old friends were wary of their new surroundings. But then Green rushed forward, followed by Cass and Jackson, and soon we were all hurrying towards one another, our conversations overlapping as we attempted to express our joy at the long-awaited get-together. Hugs were exchanged and couples brought together as both The Crags and The Ridge citizens were reunited with people they had been apart from for many weeks.

I spotted Harper approaching and thrust through the crowd to fling my arms around her, realising how much I had missed my friend.

"So good to see you, Quin," she whispered. "Catch up properly later?"

I nodded, as she repeated the greeting with Cass before heading for Walker and throwing herself into his arms.

Behind her came Shaw, who delivered a friendly slap on the back before heading off to get a drink, and finally I saw Blythe, who handed Perry to me while she exchanged tearful hugs with the other Crags citizens. Perry seemed just as surprised as me by the commotion, but instead of it upsetting her, she beamed, clapping her little hands together.

"Hey little lady," I made a silly face at the girl, "haven't you grown?"

She hiccupped, and looked startled, blinking and staring around until she found her mother. Once she had spotted Blythe, she pointed her finger and babbled something unintelligible. I made sure I moved closer to Blythe so that Perry felt safe.

"How are you, Quin?" Blythe asked me softly, when she had finished greeting everyone.

"Ok, thanks." It wasn't difficult to find a smile for my friend. "You're looking well."

"Thanks. I'm actually starting to be ok. Most days, at least." She gestured to her daughter, who was wriggling wildly in my arms. "You can't just shut down when you have a little one."

"I'm sure." I smiled. "Well at least here you'll finally get to meet some other parents."

She glanced around nervously. "I'd like that."

"And this little one will get to make some friends her own age."

I rubbed my nose against Perry's cheek. Abruptly, she stopped squirming and stared at me, wide-eyed. I thought she might burst into tears, but a second later she grinned, displaying four new teeth.

"Oh, be careful what she gets in her mouth," Blythe chuckled, "if it's your finger, she won't show you any mercy!"

"She's so big now!" The voice belonged to Collins, who

had come across to say hello. "And she has so many teeth!"

"I know," Blythe said. "I was just saying how she's developed a nasty habit of biting people when they least expect it."

"Oh, she'd never do a mean thing like that. Would you, Perry?" Collins tickled the baby under the chin.

Blythe and I exchanged a look, as Perry giggled and held out her hands to Collins.

"Can I?" Collins glanced at Blythe, who nodded.

Spotting Coleman and Rico, Collins' face lit up. "Oh, come with me, you have to see some of the other children here!"

I handed the small child over and backed away as Collins whisked Perry off to meet the others. Blythe followed close behind, clearly relieved to have someone to introduce her around. I stared around at the new influx of people, trying to pretend that I wasn't searching for Baker. Spotting Price close by, I headed over to say hello.

She gave me a brief hug before backing off and glancing around. "Wow. I mean we've met The Ridge folk who came across to us... they described this place, but..."

"It's really something, isn't it?" I remembered how I had felt when I had first arrived. "They live quite differently over here... it's refreshing."

"It really sounds like it." She smiled broadly. "So how are you, Quin? What's the news?"

I shrugged. "Not much really. We've been training hard since we got here. How are things with you?"

"Ah, they're ok. I mean it's been quiet. Less people around, you know. But—"

"Listen," I interrupted her, unable to stop myself. "I heard some people volunteered to guard The Crags while you all came here. Who stayed behind?"

She looked a little startled at my sudden interruption but rallied and managed an answer. "Johnson and Allen. Plus a couple of Ridgers they've become friends with."

I must have looked surprised, as she went on to clarify. "Listen, they've been good as gold since you all left." She shrugged. "Honestly. We were very cautious when allowing them to do anything to begin with, but the two of them have been desperate to prove themselves with Thomas gone. I guess when we needed people to stay, they were prepared to step up."

"I wonder if..." I broke off and considered their reasoning. "Maybe they didn't want to come across Thomas."

Price glanced around in alarm. "He's out and about? With everyone else?"

"No. But he has been training alongside us. To be honest, his attitude has improved too," I admitted. "I guess the punishments we decided on worked, then? They've all been behaving themselves."

I glanced around as I spoke, my eyes searching for Baker. Because if Price hadn't mentioned her name as staying behind, then she might be...

"They do seem to have changed their behaviour." A familiar voice from behind stopped me dead. My heart pounding, I turned to see Baker standing a few feet away, as though she had been watching me. Her expression was carefully neutral. "They've been working hard, kept themselves to themselves mostly, but have cooperated at all times."

I didn't have time to react to Baker's approach before Price continued, unaware of the tension in the air between us.

"Johnson was never an issue." She shrugged. "Been quiet

as a mouse the whole time, and works almost as hard as Harper in the fields. We've needed her since you've all been gone. With fewer people working the shifts, well..."

Baker continued, as though she carried on such conversations with me every day. "They've been a great help actually. We put Allen on cleaning and foraging duties at first, heavily supervised of course, but once we were sure he wouldn't cause any trouble, we let him join the fishing group. Now, we even trust him to go out alone. It lightens the burden when we have such reduced numbers, and he's actually become very good at it. Brings home a decent catch most days, and never comes back until he's caught something."

"He's dedicated alright," Price confirmed. "And the two of them seem to have become something of a couple. At least, they've spent a lot of time together since..." she trailed off, looking a little guilty. "Look, people didn't fully trust them at first, so they ended up without too many people to talk to for a while. It's why they made friends with some of the people from The Ridge. And..." she smiled almost fondly, "well I guess they've grown pretty close to one another."

I considered what both women had said, wondering if things back at The Crags were more difficult now that there were fewer citizens to work the fields and hunt. A stab of guilt lanced into me when I considered the fairly generous rations we received here at The Ridge.

"What's that?" Baker pointed abruptly to the cup in my hand.

I managed to find my voice. "It's called whisky."

"Is it good?"

"Um... yes? Tastes a little funny at first – sweet, but sort of heavy too."

249

She bent closer. "Smells interesting. Where did you get it?"

Unable to speak, I pointed at the barrels.

"Want some, Price?" she asked brightly.

Without waiting for the other woman to reply, she strode off. I wondered why she was acting so strangely. Baker was not one to chat, nor was she the sort of person who relished a party. But here she was, voluntarily joining in a conversation and welcoming the idea of a shared drink.

Price shot me a strange smile before going to follow Baker. I stopped her with a hand on her arm.

"Look, we were told not to drink too much of it. I think... I don't know. I've had half a glass and already my head feels a little light."

"Warning appreciated. I'd better let Baker know before she downs a glass in her determined efforts to appear sociable!" She laughed before she walked away, shaking her head at Baker's unfamiliar behaviour.

As she wandered off in pursuit of the older woman, I caught my breath. Baker had spoken to me quite pleasantly. And she had clearly made the journey here again, despite her general resistance to social occasions. Did this mark the start of her adjusting to our hidden connection?

I turned as I heard the band strike up at the other end of the space. Ross and Roberts would not be taking a turn this evening, as they were the guests of honour, but there were plenty of other musicians who could play the upbeat songs which were apparently traditional at a party. I smiled at the now-familiar tune. I was curious to witness the dancing which we had been promised would accompany the music later on, and found myself tapping my foot as the musicians began to play their first number.

I wondered again at Baker's behaviour. I honestly hadn't thought she would attend the party, yet here she was. But as I watched her pouring herself a drink and sipping it, glancing around the crowd as though determined to enjoy herself, I couldn't help but feel a tiny seed of hope take root within me.

Finishing my drink, I wandered to the side of the courtyard and placed the cup down on the table. For now, I decided, I wouldn't have any more. It had left me feeling a little dizzy and strange, and I wasn't at all sure that I liked the feeling. Heading for the washrooms on the side of the canteen, I smiled at a few people as I passed: Cass and Marley, who waved at me as they chatted away happily with a group of the younger Ridge citizens; Jackson and Mason, nodding at me whilst deep in a conversation with Shaw that I sincerely hoped wasn't all about lead yields; Walker and Harper, seated on a bench at one side of the courtyard, their heads bent so close together that they didn't even notice me.

The washrooms were blissfully empty for the moment, and I took my time, splashing my face with cool water from the basin. Eventually my head felt slightly clearer. I decided that I wouldn't drink any more whisky for now. Glancing into the cracked mirror above the sink, I caught sight of myself in the unusual outfit. My cheeks were flushed slightly and the unusually light colour of the blouse made my eyes stand out. For a second time, I wished that Cam was here to see me looking so different, though I wasn't quite sure why.

Sighing, I headed for the washroom door, hoping that the promised food would be ready soon. Outside, the air was getting cold as the darkness drew in, and I wrapped my arms more tightly around my body. The thin blouse might look attractive, but it was doing nothing to protect me from the chill. At the far end of the passage which led to the courtyard I could see a shape, which as I came closer, seemed to morph into a person. But an odd-shaped person. It seemed almost too big to be...

And then I realised. It wasn't one person. It was two. Leaning against the wall—their bodies so close they appeared to be glued together—was a couple. I faltered, not wanting to disturb their privacy, but having nowhere else to go in the narrow passageway. The shadows hid the identities of the pair from me, but as I stood there, they separated, one stepping away from the other. For a moment, they seemed to pause, looking into one another's eyes, and then the person farthest from the wall leaned in for a brief, sweet kiss, and slipped away to the party again.

I waited for the other person to move, but they did not. For an age, I stood, thinking that they would at any moment turn around and return to the more communal area beyond, but whoever it was remained, leaning against the wall, unmoving. As we stood there frozen in time, the music ended and a booming voice from the courtyard behind me announced that the feast had begun. My stomach growled in anticipation.

Making my decision, I strode in the direction of the party, determined to pass the person, whoever they were, as though I had not just witnessed the intensely private moment. But when I reached the figure, I realised that it was Tyler. She didn't notice my approach, and seemed startled when I arrived directly in front of her.

"Oh... hi Quin." I had never known her to be so inattentive to her surroundings. It said a lot about the kiss I had just stumbled upon.

CHAPTER TWENTY FIVE

"Hey." I stifled a smile. "You alright?"

"What?"

"Are you alright?"

"Sure! I'm..." Shaking her head slightly, she focused on my face for the first time and caught my knowing smile. "Oh. I see. You, um... saw that?"

I nodded. "Sorry. I was on my way from the washroom and... well... I couldn't really help it."

Although the shadows hid her face, I could tell from her tone she was blushing. We paused for a moment as two Ridge citizens passed by.

Tyler waited until they had disappeared from view before continuing. "Hughes. He's never... kissed me before."

"I see." I waited for a moment, prompting her when she didn't continue. "Was it nice?"

"Um...." She hesitated, shy, "...yes. It was."

"And it was only the first time he'd...?"

"Yes." Her reply was hurried. "He's wanted to for... well, for ages, but I told him no."

"Why? Are you worried about what others will think? The Ridge citizens?"

Another nod. "They're already a little unsure of us. He's their leader. What will it look like, if he... well if he forges a partnership with someone from elsewhere?"

"You don't know what they'll think," I tried. "There are a lot of Ridge citizens who've been working closely with us since the training started. They like us. Respect us. You know they do."

"But... it's one thing for him to be our ally. But if he became my partner..." Her shoulders slumped a little. "I'm not sure that they'd... accept it."

"You don't know that. It's early days." I shrugged. "Once we've got The Beck attack out of the way, then maybe... well, if the attack's a success... I mean, I think we stand a good chance of becoming permanent allies, don't you?"

"That's what I told him." She turned away, her hands bunching into fists. "I told him that we had to wait, and he's usually patient. He even agrees with me. But tonight... I don't know, with the whisky and all the excitement..."

"You got carried away?"

She nodded mutely.

"Well there's no one but me who knows about it. What's the problem?"

"You won't mention it?" She peered into my face closely.

"Of course not."

Satisfied, she smiled again. "Ok. Well I'm just going to... before I..." she gestured to the washrooms. "Be out in a minute, ok?"

"Sure." I backed off and watched her walk down the passageway, following the same exact pattern I had a moment ago. I understood her hesitancy with Hughes. But at the same time, life was very short, and I knew I'd have given anything to kiss Cam right now.

Chapter Twenty Six

The cheerful sounds of chatter and laughter increased in volume as I entered the courtyard and I felt my spirits lift. On the area designated as a dancefloor many of the children, who had eaten earlier than the rest of us, were spinning around, leaping and playing happily. I couldn't help but smile as I watched Rico shrieking with laughter as a beaming Howard twirled him around. Coleman grinned from the sidelines where she stood talking to Blythe. Next to them, Marley had Perry on her knee and was repeatedly sticking her tongue out to make the small girl giggle. Blythe was eating and listening intently to Coleman, who I could already see was helping my old friend to feel more supported in parenthood.

It made me happy to see how well the other Crags citizens were mixing with the Ridge folk. I could see barriers being broken down all around me, as I headed for the tables of food on the far side of the courtyard. When I reached them, I couldn't fail to brighten up. The tables which had been brought out of the canteen were now laden with numerous dishes. There were the usual stews, but with more choices than usual, and bread which was warm and freshly baked. Accompanying this were potatoes which had been baked in their skins in a firepit, and a variety of vegetables mixed with herbs, which smelled delicious.

Helping myself to a plateful of food, I sat down at a table next to Roberts, who had Fenn cradled tenderly in his arms. Oblivious to what was going on around him, the baby was fast asleep. I dug into the food with enthusiasm, exclaiming out loud as I did so.

"Ohmgh!"

I had never tasted potatoes like this before, but they were delicious when cut open, their crispy skins sheltering the fluffy white softness inside. I had just shoveled a large forkful into my mouth when Roberts seated himself next to me, Fenn cradled tenderly in his arms.

Roberts chuckled softly. "Enjoying the food, Quin?"

I nodded, waving a hand to my mouth to indicate that I couldn't reply.

"So I've just been talking to Walker and Harper. She a friend of yours?" I nodded. "Seems like a nice girl. Cheered Walker up a *whole* lot, I can tell you. Never seen him so happy." He peered into my face. "You enjoying your first party?"

I finally swallowed the food and faced him, considering my response. "Well, it's a lot to take in, but... I am actually."

He adjusted his position slightly, shifting Fenn so he was more comfortably settled against his chest. "I'm glad. I mean, I can't imagine what this is like for you. We've grown up with it." He waved a hand at the merriment going on around us. "I mean, not regularly, but festivities have always been a part of life here. Even when Stewart was in charge, and before that, we've always recognised the need to take time out to celebrate. He paused, gesturing all around us. "This isn't just about Fenn's birth, you know. Hughes is happy. He feels really positive about the connection we've been making with you all. The lead mining, the bullet production, the weapons training... it's going well. We have so much to hope for right now." He glanced over at me. "But it must be kind of strange for you to experience this when you've never known anything like it. I'm happy it's made you happy."

As he finished speaking, his eyes sought those of his partner. Ross had joined Coleman and Blythe at the other side of the courtyard, where they were quick to find her a seat. She caught his eye and gave him a wave, her expression tender.

I rolled my eyes. "Could you be any more gooey-eyed? I mean–"

My teasing remark was cut off as we were joined by Shaw, who sat down with a plateful of his own, beaming at us both.

"Hey," he held out a hand to Roberts. "I'm Shaw. You're the motor boat driver, aren't you?"

"I'm one of them. One of the better ones here on The Ridge, actually." Roberts winked at me. "And you were the guy driving that monstrosity of a boat back to The Crags." Roberts grinned broadly. "I'm Roberts."

The two men started up a friendly argument about boats. I tuned out, glad that they were getting along, but not in the least bit interested in the conversation. At least Shaw had stopped any more lingering looks between Roberts and Ross, for now.

Moments later we were joined by Marley and Cass. Marley immediately began cooing over Fenn, and swooped him into her arms. Cass looked amused. They were followed by Green and Baker, who were deep in conversation. The two had always been close, having been the only two females to flee The Beck during the original escape. They had spent a year with no other female company, and understood one another well. I had not considered their separation before, but as they seated themselves together, I recognized the sacrifice that they'd had to make.

As I gazed at them, Baker glanced over and caught my eye. Embarrassed at being caught staring, I looked away, my face burning and focused on finishing my food. When I glanced back along the table a few minutes later, I saw that Baker's eyes still rested on me. Green was still chatting with her, and, in the end, realising she had lost her friend's attention, she followed Baker's gaze until she was also looking directly at me.

Flicking my gaze between the two women, I registered the gentle smile on Green's face, which seemed to indicate her approval of whatever was going on between myself and Baker. And when I looked back at my mother, though she wasn't smiling, her expression was softer than usual, and she held my gaze for a moment or two before she looked back at Green and continued their conversation.

Perplexed, I slid out from behind the bench and was about to pick up my plate when the band began to play again. I had just turned to watch when someone suddenly grasped hold of my arm. Startled, I turned to see Roberts, grinning like a loon.

"This is one of my favourites!" He jerked his head back at Marley, who was holding the still-sleeping Fenn, and pulled me in the direction of the dancefloor. "Quick, before he wakes up."

Horrified, I tried to pull away. "I don't want..." I tried to shout, but my voice was drowned out by the band's enthusiastic introduction to the new song.

We were halfway to the dance space when I managed to stop Roberts.

"What is it?" he bellowed in my ear.

I waved a hand at the quickly crowding dancefloor – clearly this was not just Roberts' favourite. "I don't know how. Wouldn't you rather dance with–?" I gestured helplessly to Ross.

"Ah no. She's not up for dancing just now." He gestured at his body. "Still too sore."

I had noticed that Ross looked a little pale, and she had not yet returned to her usual working shifts. In fact, tonight was the first time I had seen her up and about at all. I had to admit that, if she was still in pain, the last thing she'd want to do was dance, which, from what I'd heard, was a fairly energetic activity.

He nodded his head in Ross' direction. "She won't mind, if that's what's stopping you."

I still hesitated, until Roberts leaned towards me again. "Wouldn't you like to learn how to dance, so you can show your man Cam how it's done in the future?"

He winked, and I knew he wouldn't take no for an answer. Reluctantly, I allowed him to drag me the rest of the way to the dancefloor, comforted only by the fact that there were now so many bodies on it that it would be difficult for anyone to pick me out as the most inexperienced dancer there.

When we reached the mass of swaying bodies, there were very few, if any, Crags citizens present. A quick glance over my shoulder told me that although many of them were crowding closer to the dancefloor, it was only so that they could get a firsthand look at this dancing they'd heard so much about. Groaning inwardly that I was among the first to give it a try, I firmly guided Roberts so that we would be dancing at the very back of the crowd.

When I was happy with our position, Roberts took hold of my arm, guiding me towards him. Copying the movements of the others around us, we began to twist and sway in time to the music. At first it felt very strange, but as we continued, I began to relax a little. No one could really see me in amongst the many dancers, and it felt nice to be appreciated, though I suspected that Roberts had singled me out because he knew how much I was missing Cam.

The music changed, the beat slowing until the song was much gentler. Roberts hesitated for a moment and then held out his arms. Feeling slightly awkward, I stepped towards him, but he only rested his hands loosely on my waist and used them to guide me around the dance floor in a series of gentler movements. For a moment it crossed my mind how nice it would be to be able to do this with the man who I missed so much. I knew that, if I were dancing with Cam, I would have been pressed a lot closer to his body. I shivered slightly at the thought. Closing my eyes, I sighed and tried to enjoy the pleasure that the swaying movement brought, even if it wasn't with the man I was thinking of. When I opened them, I found Roberts grinning down at me.

"Not bad for a beginner!"

I swatted his arm playfully and he swung me round in an exaggerated manner, wriggling his eyebrows at me. Smiling broadly, I realised how lucky I was to have such a friend.

The next hour or so saw most of The Crags citizens up on the dancefloor at one point or another. The Ridge people took it in turns to partner a 'Crag' and it wasn't long before all signs of discomfort had dissolved and everyone, good dancer or not, had been up and moving at some point. The only ones I hadn't seen dancing were Ross and Baker.

Despite her dislike of social occasions, my mother remained at the party and watched the dancing quietly from the side of the courtyard. I felt her eyes on me at various times during the evening, though she never approached me again. I wondered if she might be trying to pluck up the courage so I didn't approach her, hoping she would manage to conquer whatever it was that made her keep her distance before the evening was over.

I was amazed at how late the children had been allowed to stay up, and how much energy they had, despite the late hour. They were gathered at one end of the dancefloor, right in the centre of the courtyard, and were flinging themselves about to the music with total abandon. In between dances, they ran to the tables at the side of the space, grabbing drinks and small pieces of the sweet cake which had been made for the occasion, before racing back to the games in the middle.

A little while later, I was sitting at one of the tables talking to Roberts when the band finished a particularly rousing song and the crowd around me fell silent. I turned to see Hughes standing on one of the benches at the end of the courtyard, raising his hand for quiet. When he had achieved it, he gazed around at us all, smiling broadly at the scene before him.

"I just wanted very briefly to say a few words. Tonight is very special. We welcome the birth of Fenn, the newest arrival to our community, the way we always welcome additions." He paused, and glanced around at Rogers and Green. "But Fenn is not our only new addition. For the past few weeks, we have been living alongside several members of The Crags community, and in return, some of our number have been made welcome over at The Crags. It was an experimental move, and required a lot of trust on both sides."

I looked around at the crowd, who were all listening to Hughes, whether Crags or Ridge, and seeming to believe in his words and his entire ethos. He was a decent man, who wanted the best for his own people, but also for those of us from The Crags. As he continued, I could see that I wasn't the only one who felt this.

"Tonight is the first time we have been able to get together as one, and it could well have been a difficult, awkward occasion. Instead," he beamed around, an expansive hand encompassing the entire crowd, "we have Ridge and Crags citizens mixing as though they've known one another for years.

"I won't go on too long," he held out a hand at the crowd who still stood on the dancefloor," as I'm sure you all want to get back to your dancing, but I wanted to mark the occasion and just say, thanks!" He raised a glass high in the direction of the crowd. "Thanks for being prepared to put aside your fears, and trust that, together, we can achieve something great. I hope that y–"

A noise came from somewhere behind me, and suddenly Hughes faltered. His gaze travelled slowly to his arm, and then he looked up at something behind us. An expression of horror crossed his features. Following his gaze, the group turned as one.

At the very edge of the courtyard, standing in the pools of dusky shadows which lent them their name, were several figures who made my heart go cold. Guns raised and pointing straight into the crowd of unarmed, unprepared dancers, two Ridge guards captive at their side, stood several members of

CHAPTER TWENTY SIX

The Beck Shadow Patrol, with Director Reed at their head.

Chapter Twenty Seven

Chaos broke out all around me. Even though The Ridge citizens didn't know what Shadow Patrol looked like, they knew an enemy when they saw one. People ran in all directions as they tried to escape the danger zone. For a moment, the Shadow Patrol stood motionless. Roberts and I ducked quickly under the table we had been sitting at. I glanced back at the place where Hughes had stood only moments ago, to see him on the ground. McGrath crouched at one side of him, Tyler at the other. There was no sign of Rogers for a moment, but then I spotted him, barking orders at Mason and McGrath and ushering people into the canteen.

Whatever he asked of his two soldiers, they immediately took notice. I watched as they slipped around the side of the canteen building and headed off, managing to escape before the first bullets started to fly. Screams of panic mingled with cries of pain as the first few bullets hit their targets. I glanced left and right, trying to decide which way to move. On the far side of the courtyard, the doorway to the canteen was starting to jam up as people crammed through it. I recognized the familiar face of Simpson, waiting at the rear of the crowd, her face white with shock and terror.

Immediately behind her was Jackson, who had spotted

the issue with the narrow doorway and was taking action. Prodding Simpson sharply in the back, she gestured wildly to the exit door of the canteen. It was around the side of the building, and would require a brief dash back into the danger zone, but it would allow twice as many people to enter the building and reach safety. Passing Simpson, Jackson continued down the line, alerting people to the alternative route to safety. I watched as Simpson hesitated, clearly unsure what to do.

She wasn't the only one. Many of the citizens Jackson was attempting to speak to were from The Ridge, and it was immediately clear that, whilst some barriers had been broken down, they didn't trust Jackson the way they would have trusted a Ridge citizen. While a few made their way around the side of the building, too many stood dithering, the sound of bullets growing thick in the air around them.

Finally, Simpson made up her mind and turned to run. She made it two steps before she was caught by a stray bullet. Her body seemed to twitch unnaturally, and I cried aloud as she crumpled to the ground, a stain of scarlet clear on the back of the pale dress she had worn for the party. Close by, others in the crowd were hit, and collapsed in a similar way, clutching at their wounds. Watching their friends fall, the Ridge citizens who had been frozen in indecision suddenly bolted in the direction of the exit door, and I watched Jackson heave a sigh of relief before picking up Simpson and carrying her off in the same direction.

There were too many people heading for the canteen though, and I knew it would be the wrong path to take. Glancing in the other direction, I realised that there were still a large number of children in the courtyard, and not enough people trying to get them out of harm's way. Most of them were standing frozen in their own little area of the dance floor, alarmed to see members of their community lying bleeding on the ground close by, the tables of food partially blocking their exit from the courtyard. Green and Cass were doing their best to guide them around the tables and into the closest building, the one which housed the school, but many of them seemed unwilling or unable to move. My heart beat faster as I saw the terrified expressions on their faces.

We had brought this attack on The Ridge. Our presence here. The thought spurred me into action. As there was a momentary lull in the bullets, I bent low and raced across to them, Roberts close behind me. We reached them safely, noting the grateful expression on Green's face as we arrived. There were still a lot of youngsters to move, and many of them were frozen in shock or simply sitting and crying. I watched as Cass attempted to bring a couple of the youngest citizens with her across the space to the building. She was almost carrying one of them by the time she reached the door and thrust them into the arms of a waiting Marley.

Spotting the banquet tables, I had an idea. Grasping Roberts by the arm, I pulled him away from the children. For a moment, he resisted, but seeing the pleading look on my face, reluctantly followed me to the tables.

"Flip them!" I gestured wildly with my hands, trying to get him to understand my meaning. "Turn them over!" I bent down and held on to the leg at my side of the table, hoping he would catch on.

With a thumbs up, he grasped the leg at his side of the table and together we pushed it on its side and thrust it forward, its contents spilling everywhere. We managed to place it in front of the remaining children, providing a shelter, of sorts, from the bullets. Returning to the tables, we continued with our efforts. They were heavy, but large, and within a few seconds we had two of them lying across our section of the yard, providing a makeshift shield which gave us at least some protection while we worked out what to do next.

Catching on, Green pulled the last remaining children behind it. Cass was now standing in the doorway of the schoolroom with those she had already managed to move. I signaled to her to stay with them for the time being and sat back behind the table, trying to catch my breath. I felt a small hand creep into mine and looked down to see Rico, his face streaked with tears. I squeezed his hand in comfort, noticing how violently it was trembling. His other hand held on to Timmy, as though he would never let go.

Momentarily safe, we had a second to look around and take stock. There were fewer bullets flying through the air, as though Reed had given the signal to stop for now. I noticed that he and his guards had not managed to advance across the courtyard yet. Instead, they were using some of the additional barrels of whisky as cover. I wondered why they hadn't simply swept across the entire space, but when I glanced at the other side of the yard, I could see. Mason and McGrath had returned from their mission with a number of weapons. Rogers had been quick to hand them out and now there were at least six of our own soldiers lined up behind upended tables on the other side of the courtyard, returning fire.

I sighed with relief that we now stood a chance of fighting back, but without a weapon between us, our little group behind the tables was still very vulnerable. The school building was some distance away. A distance in which we would be totally exposed, should the bullets start to fly again.

Nudging me, Roberts came close enough to hiss a question in my ear. "Can we move the table along with the children? Protect them as we head for the building?"

I looked back along at the group we had with us behind the tables. There were around eleven children of differing ages, and only three adults. The tables were heavy and would need two of us, which meant we could only move one at a time. The group was currently positioned behind two, which was ample shelter, but I didn't think a single table would provide enough protection for the whole group.

"It might work." Green seemed to share my doubts. "But what if the kids won't move? Look at them. They're absolutely petrified."

She was right. Having witnessed Cass having to physically carry at least one child away from the danger area, I knew there was no guarantee we could get them all to move at once. With two of us occupied trying to shift the heavy tables and only one adult to encourage them to move, I wasn't confident it would work.

For now, we stayed where we were. I wrapped my arms around Rico and tried to stay calm. Peering out through the space between the tables, I could see several bodies lying in the space beyond. The ones who hadn't managed to escape the bullets in time. No one I could immediately recognise, from this distance at least. The majority of the citizens, though, seemed to have managed to make the dash inside the doors of the canteen and the courtyard was now empty aside from those who lay dead and the two opposing groups of soldiers. I glanced over at where Hughes had fallen, to find the space quite empty. I hoped they had managed to get him to safety, and that he was alive.

Moments later my glance travelled to Rogers, who was crouching behind the wall on the other side of the courtyard, and signaling wildly to us.

I nudged Roberts. "What's he saying?"

He shrugged. "Not sure. Green?"

Green shuffled closer so that she could see her partner clearly. This time, he motioned to McGrath, who was kneeling on the ground next to him. In her hand was a bow and arrow. We watched as Rogers pointed in Reed's direction, then gestured back to McGrath.

"I'm presuming he has a plan which is linked to McGrath firing her arrows at the guards over there." Green's face was puzzled as she tried to work out what Rogers was doing. "Perhaps distracting them with her fire, so that we can get the children into the schoolroom safely. I'm sorry. I'm not sure exactly what he's doing."

"Why just McGrath?" Roberts gestured to the other soldiers, some of whom held guns. "Wouldn't bullets do a better job?"

"Who knows?" Green's face was grim. "It's better than nothing, though. You both ready?"

I nodded, and turned to Roberts, who looked nervous, but determined. I realised for the first time that he was separated from Ross and Fenn, and must be frantic about them. I had no idea where they were. In the school building already, or the canteen, or maybe they had left the party early and were back in the apartment. I could only hope that they were well out of harm's way. A wave of anger surged over me as I thought of all the worry and heartbreak Adams was causing, particularly with people who were not his own.

I watched as Green gave Rogers a thumbs up. Returning the gesture, I saw him lean across to McGrath and speak into her ear, pointing at the area where the Beck guards were crouched.

"Allocate yourself three or four children. Now!" I hissed. "Whatever they're planning, we need to be ready."

Green tapped the four closest to her on the arm and pointed at herself. "You're with me, right? When I say so, you run! Stay with me, unless I fall over. In which case," she glanced grimly at the rest of us, "Get to that door as fast as you can."

Every one of the children's eyes followed her finger to the schoolroom door, where Cass and Marley were waiting with encouraging smiles on their faces. Roberts and I quickly divided the remaining children between us. I ended up with only three: Rico, who had refused to relinquish his hold on my hand, a trembling blond boy who looked even younger, and an older girl who thankfully seemed more in control of her fear.

"We should decide on an order," I whispered to Green. "That way, we minimise the chance of anyone tripping or bumping into others."

She nodded grimly. "Ok. Quin, you first. Roberts to follow. I'll go last."

"But you have more children with you."

She frowned. "OK. I'll take the lead then. Roberts follow me. Quin, you last. Ok?"

We nodded, and Green glanced at Rogers, who watched us with a concerned expression.

"Time to go now." She even managed a smile for the children as she readied herself for action. "When I shout 'GO' we run, ok?"

I could feel my own hands shaking even as I tried to hold on to the children I had been assigned. Reed and his patrol seemed to be regrouping, but I knew it wouldn't be long before they began shooting again. We watched as Rogers gave another command, and Howard and Mason began firing rapidly. But their shots went wide. Instead of hitting the Shadow guards, several of the shots plunged into the barrels holding the whisky. The amber liquid began to flow out, draining into an ever-growing puddle on the ground.

As I watched Rogers strike a match, I knew. The flame flared brightly and he leaned towards McGrath, lighting the tip of her arrow. She fired, the tip of the dart drawing a graceful arc in the sky. It skittered to a stop in front of the barrels, and I saw more than one of the Shadow guards smirk at what they saw as McGrath's poor aim.

For a moment, nothing happened. And then, very slowly at first, the whisky caught fire, a tiny flame snaking its way across the pool of liquid. The Shadow guards looked startled, their panic mounting as the fire began to grow, a number of sparks leaping in the direction of the barrels, which held even more fuel. They backed away rapidly, terror emblazoned on their faces.

"Go!" I screamed.

Green wasted no time, racing for the schoolroom with four children clutched tightly to her sides. When I glanced back, the fire had grown. The area where the guards had stood was filled with smoke, and the barrels were blazing fiercely. I could hear various shouts and screams, and Reed's men had definitely backed off. The plan was working.

A hand squeezing my arm made me look back. Roberts cast a quick smile my way, before letting go of me and herding

271

his own children across the gap to safety. Both groups had made it so far, and there was now only mine to go. Flexing my muscles to ease the tension bunched up in them, I turned to the three children left behind the shelter with me.

"Ready?" Three pale, wide-eyed faces stared at me from the shadows. "Look, see how the others got there safely?" I pointed at the doorway which Roberts had just disappeared into. Both Cass and Marley stood there, their hands out-stretched. "See? Just head for my friends, they're waiting for us."

Letting go of Rico's hand, I hoisted the smallest boy into my arms. I turned to go, making sure that the other two were close by. The girl nodded that she was ready, but since I had relinquished my hold on Rico's, his face had crumpled.

I bent close to his ear. "Hold on tight to Timmy, won't you? I won't be able to look after him too! He's your responsibility, ok?"

I watched his face change as he stared at the grubby stuffed rabbit in his hand. Holding my breath, I was relieved when he finally looked back at me and nodded, a serious expression on his face. He clutched the toy tightly to his chest, and managed a weak smile. Forcing one of my own in return, I took a deep breath and thrust my little group out into the open, striding across the gap as fast as I could without running.

The sound of bullets ripped through the air again. I hoped they were coming from our side. I stumbled on, determined to reach the doorway where Cass and Marley were waiting. I fixed my eyes on Cass. Her mouth was opening and closing, and though I couldn't hear her, I knew that she was screaming words of encouragement. Her face blazed with the effort.

After what seemed like forever, we reached the door. I

ushered the children inside, extricating the youngest boy's arms from around my neck before placing him on the ground safely. Glancing back, I could see that the bullets I had heard were coming mostly from Rogers' side of the battlefield. Reed's forces had managed to regroup, and were beginning to return fire from a different location, but the fire had delayed their attack. I allowed myself a small sigh of relief.

As I did, I heard Marley shriek behind me.

I spun to face her, but was too late to stop a small figure from racing back past. Horror washed over my body as I saw Rico heading for the tiny crumpled rabbit, which had slipped from his grasp on the way across. Before I could react, Cass was barging past me, dodging Marley's hands which reached out to try and stop her. When Cass managed to catch up with the small boy, he resisted her, determined to rescue his beloved Timmy.

I watched them struggling for a second, hearing Marley's frightened whimpers beside me. Rico was stronger than he looked, and though Cass tried to scoop him up and forcibly carry him back inside, he was wriggling so much it was impossible. Stepping out through the doorway and trying not to look at the numerous bodies which littered the courtyard, I headed back into the chaos to help them. I had barely reached Cass when I heard a noise behind me. Turning, I could see three shadowy figures had emerged from behind the building we were sheltering in. They were blocking our escape route, their tall forms foreboding and immoveable.

In desperation, I sprinted the short distance to Cass, who was still wrestling with the now-hysterical Rico.

"Move!" I hissed, pushing them in the opposite direction, knowing it was useless to head back the way we had come.

Reaching past the struggling pair, I scooped up the rabbit and pressed it into Rico's hands.

"Go!"

He stared blankly at me for a second, then his eyes followed the direction my finger was pointing in. Clearly confused that he was now being given instructions to run in the opposite direction from the one we had previously told him to travel in, he looked back at me, a puzzled expression mingling with the panic on his small face.

I tried to push him, aware of another pause in the bullets. Glancing at Rogers, I saw him holding out a hand to his soldiers, warning them not to fire while we were in harm's way.

Turning to Rico, I screamed, "Run!"

It was too late. Within seconds, the three Shadow Patrol guards had us surrounded, their weapons primed and focused at our heads. Instinctively, Cass and I placed the young boy between us and stood back to back.

One of the men spoke, his tone almost robotic. "We're not here for him."

We stared at him dumbly. In response, he jerked his head at the schoolroom door, still open. I could see Marley standing on the threshold, her eyes glued to Cass, her face pale and frightened. Beside her stood an anxious Roberts, and Green, who was visibly holding him back.

"You won't hurt him?" I checked, unsure of whether this was a horrible trap.

"We're not interested in him." A short pause before the toneless voice continued. "Send him over there. Now."

The command was clear. I bent down to Rico and whispered in his ear.

"They're letting you go. See Roberts, at the schoolroom door there?" He nodded. "Take Timmy. Walk quickly to the schoolroom and go straight inside."

His eyes were huge as he stared at me. "What about you?"

"We'll be right over." I suppressed a shudder, forcing myself to keep my eyes on his. "You just look after Timmy, ok?"

Rico glanced at Cass, disbelief on his face. She nodded at him, even managing a weak smile. It seemed to be enough. Stepping away from us, the small boy began walking slowly past the Shadow Patrol, who took a small step away to allow him space. Once past them, he ignored my command and raced towards the door, throwing himself into Roberts' arms as he reached the familiar face.

Cass and I straightened up, meeting the gaze of the three Shadow Patrol guards. I felt her take my hand in hers and squeeze it ever so slightly before she was pulled roughly away from me. Suddenly Reed was standing beside us, shining a flashlight directly into my face. I blinked rapidly, trying to see as stars exploded in my gaze.

"This one's definitely Beck. I recognise her from Patrol." I could feel his breath on my face as he leaned closer. "Take her."

Two other guards appeared from nowhere and took hold of my arms roughly. Beside me, Cass leapt forward and lashed out, scratching Reed's face with her nails.

"Take her where, scum? Leave her alone!"

I heard him curse under his breath as he backed away. "This one too."

Marley's sob echoed from the doorway of the building Rico had just run through. My heart sank as I realised Cass' attempted defence had led her to the same fate as my own. I wondered if she'd done it on purpose, to make sure I wasn't alone. Wincing, I felt the sting of rope cutting into my skin as my hands were fastened behind my back. Cass received the same treatment.

The bullets from Rogers' side of the courtyard no longer came, but I knew why. If they fired in our general direction now, they were just as likely to kill us as they were the invaders. The smoke from the explosions had all but cleared now, and Reed's men had been able to advance into the centre of the courtyard. Several of them formed a barrier across the space, dividing us from the rest of our people.

The shield of Shadow Patrol converging behind us meant that not a single one of our friends was able to penetrate it and do anything to stop them. With two guards either side, Cass and I found ourselves being frisked for weapons, turned abruptly about and marched from the hub.

Chapter Twenty Eight

Before we knew what was happening, Cass and I were being marched through the woods. At first, I assumed that we would head for the harbour. I remembered the captive Ridge guards who Reed had arrived at the hub with. The Shadow Patrol had clearly taken at least two of our guards prisoner when they came ashore, so I didn't hold out a lot of hope for gaining their assistance. Reed's men took a different turn as we were travelling through the woods, however.

Before long we were moving along The Ridge shoreline in the opposite direction from the harbour. The shore was rockier here, and the growing darkness made it even more difficult to keep our footing, but Reed set a punishing pace anyway. I estimated that we had walked for at least fifteen minutes before a Clearance boat came into view, very like the one we had taken when we left The Beck. It was moored a little distance from shore and floating silently on calm waters.

Reed called a halt when we got to a point where there was a small flattened shelf of land which was less littered with hazardous rocks. This was where Reed had come ashore to mount his attack. Too clever to approach from the harbour, which he knew would most likely be guarded, his team had obviously circled the island the long way around to make sure their presence went undetected until it was too late.

There were two small rowboats tethered to the shoreline, and Cass and I found ourselves being thrust into them. Reed dispatched three guards in each boat, one to keep guard and two to row, and sent us over to the Clearance vessel. He had staggered the movement of his troops back to the landing stages carefully, leaving enough of his crew behind to distract Rogers with the continual onslaught of bullets, while the rest of us headed for the safety of the boat.

I considered struggling, but the barrel of a gun was jabbing into my side, so it seemed like a dangerous action to take. Cass had put up more of a fight to begin with, but had received a couple of punches to the face for her trouble, and had soon come to the same conclusion as I had: for now, it was safer to just go along with them. They hadn't killed us yet, and they had let Rico go free, which suggested they weren't entirely inhuman, and that they had something else in mind for us.

As I sat in the boat waiting for the last guard to cast off, I found myself fighting against tears of panic and anger. The guard by my side felt my body shaking, and thrust his gun more tightly into my side as the boat was pushed away from the bank. The shores of The Ridge gradually retreated into the distance and I felt a cold terror creeping over me.

The journey to the larger boat did not take long, and soon we were handed over to the guards who had been left onboard. There were three of them, and they took Cass and I to the rear and tied us together, back to back, securing us to the rail which ran around the edge of the boat. I could feel Cass shivering and, despite the ropes, managed to entwine my fingers with hers. We sat like that, silent and unmoving, while the rest of the guards went back and forth to collect the remaining soldiers. This process seemed to take forever, and I waited in vain for the time when Rogers and Mason might appear on the shore, brandishing weapons and ready to rescue us.

Reed's plan had worked well, however, and as the final set of guards reached the rowboats, there was a strange glowing light in the distance. I stared at it for several minutes, confused, as it grew brighter. And then it hit me. Like Rogers earlier, they had needed a distraction to delay anyone who tried to follow them. They had set some of the trees in the wood alight, and the fire which had taken hold of them would provide a screen through which they couldn't progress until they had dealt with the flames. I watched in horrified fascination as the orange glow spread through the trees.

For a moment, I considered what might be happening back up in the hub, now that the immediate danger had passed. Scenes of sorrow and despair played over and over in my head, as Ridge citizens began to take stock, extinguishing the fire, treating the injured, and attempting to soothe the children. Those were the immediate concerns. I shuddered when I considered the most difficult job, that of retrieving the bodies of the citizens they had lost. My thoughts kept returning to Simpson, and Hughes, and I found myself hoping desperately that they were not among those who would have to be buried.

Hearing the engines beneath us roar, I felt, rather than heard, Cass' sob. All I could do was squeeze her hand more tightly, as we motored off into the darkness, heading to our old home, to Adams, to a community filled with dying people, and to the very real danger that was the Shadow Patrol.

***

We travelled for several hours, the larger Clearance boat taking far longer than The Ridge motorboats. Aside from checking that our bindings were sufficiently tight, the guards left us alone. They knew we posed no threat to them, shackled as we were. Instead, they stood in groups around the perimeter of the boat, strangely silent. Reed stood at the helm, not piloting the boat, but keeping a close eye on the man who was. Not once did he look back at us: his focus remained entirely on the waters ahead.

There were thirty guards on the boat in total. Insufficient numbers to have had much of an impact on The Ridge, had we not had our guard down and a smaller patrol than usual due to the celebration. I wondered what Reed's aim had been. To simply attack and weaken? He had managed to hurt a few of us, but not sufficient numbers to truly damage our chance of resistance. Once he had taken hold of myself and Cass, the first citizens he had come into direct contact with, he had left The Ridge without further action. Had his sole intention been to kidnap us? And had the light he shone in our faces been to make sure of who we were? He had identified us as 'Beck'. Perhaps his objective was simply to abduct some Beck citizens and bring them back with him.

I shuddered when I began to contemplate the reason why.

Fearing they would overwhelm me, I forced my bleak thoughts elsewhere. I leaned back against Cass, closed my eyes and attempted to empty my mind. Eventually, I managed to slip into an uncomfortable doze, stirring every now and then as Cass shifted or a gust of wind shivered across the deck.

When I opened my eyes again, the light of dawn was in the sky, and I could clearly see the cliffs of the Clearance hills looming ever closer. I was cold: the thin blouse I wore did not compensate for the chilly breeze which blew over us as the boat cut through the water. Cass, too, was shivering. I cursed the dressing up we had done for the party, which seemed so foolish given our current situation.

Once we reached the shore, more Shadow Patrol were waiting for us, larger numbers than I had ever seen before. This made sense, given what Anders and Cam had been telling us recently. Adams was increasing his defences. The guards pulled us roughly to our feet and untied the ropes which bound us to one another. As I straightened up, I could see Cass' face for the first time since we had boarded the boat. I recognised her mutinous expression, and shook my head imperceptibly at her, warning her not to struggle. What would be the point? Even if we escaped the numerous guards, where would we run to?

She avoided my gaze and I knew she wasn't going to pay attention to me. As we were hurried to the boat's gangplank, a sickening feeling overtook me. The guards holding on to her were expecting us to come quietly and weren't ready when she kicked out at them, using one of the moves we had learned from Hughes' training. For a second I felt proud of her, but a moment later the guard to her left turned and slapped his hand full across her face. She staggered sideways, but somehow managed to stay upright.

Calling for another guard to assist him, they proceeded to tie her feet together loosely, so she was able to walk, but not to move her feet far enough from one another to cause any further damage. He repeated the process with me before dragging us both off the boat and handing us over to the Shadow Patrol who were waiting on the shore.

The journey over had been strangely still and silent, but now things started to happen. Reed stood to one side, muttering into his walkie-talkie, and then he gestured with his hand to the guards holding us to begin moving.

"Take them to Adams in Gov," he barked. "He wants to speak to them straight away."

The guards guided us up the beach and toward the familiar path up the hillside. I gazed around as widely as I dared, darting my eyes from side to side so the guards didn't notice my curiosity. Clearance didn't seem very different. The ragged pods which housed the citizens were still there, and one or two people who were beginning to make their way into the washrooms in preparation for the day ahead shot us a curious glance, but the usual noise of The Warehouse was strangely absent. I wondered if it had been closed down for now as a result of the sickness.

We trekked up the path, the guards close by our sides. Cass seemed to have given up struggling for the time being. It was difficult to walk with our legs so closely tied together, and the hillside was fairly steep. The ropes at my ankles were beginning to chafe, and I feared they would have broken the skin by the time we reached our destination.

I wondered again what Adams was going to do to us. Memories of Wade's execution flashed into my head and I found myself seized by a fear which threatened to overwhelm me. Stumbling, I fought to stay upright and control my racing heart. Our kidnapping had been calculated and deliberate. Adams wanted escaped Beck citizens for a purpose. I shuddered when I considered what he might have planned.

As we reached the pass which led through the mountains, the guards either side of me seemed to relax a little, perhaps realising that I didn't intend to cause any trouble. We entered the thickset bushes and began to pass through them. We hadn't gone far when, without my hands to guide me, I stumbled and fell sideways, slamming my hip against the ground as I landed. I cried out, and the guard to my right sniggered, but the other one grabbed my hand and pulled me up.

"This is ridiculous," he muttered, bending down and scanning his flashlight across my feet. "We'll never get there at this rate."

The second guard stopped laughing. "What are you doing, Bell?"

Sliding his fingers in between my ankles, the first man worked on the knots in the ropes until he had loosened them, and finally, released them altogether.

"That's on your head." The other guard seemed frightened. "If she tries to run—"

"Where exactly is she going to run to?" Bell sounded exasperated. "How far could she get?"

As we started walking again, I could feel my ankles throbbing. I didn't think the rope had broken the skin as yet, and hoped that my guard would not see the benefit of replacing it once we had made it through the bushes. It was easier to walk now, but my hands were still tied, and my face was being constantly whipped by branches. I managed, barely, to keep my footing. When I did stumble, Bell, always right behind me, was quick to grasp my arm and thrust me onward. After several instances of this, I tried my hardest to stay upright, feeling the bruises blooming on my arm from his rough treatment.

The rest of the journey passed uneventfully. The woods

on the other side of Clearance looked much the same, the guard hut on the other side manned by two more Shadow Patrol guards who nodded as we walked by. We passed the Patrol Sector without entering. Continuing on, we headed in an unfamiliar direction, the path sloping steeply upwards to Gov, which I knew had to be situated somewhere higher up in the woods. Of course, Adams would want his haven to be well protected, secluded, situated well away from the rest of his citizens, who he considered so far beneath him.

Eventually, the trees thinned out somewhat, and we approached a hut similar to the one at the entrance to Clearance. Two members of Shadow Patrol stood outside it, already alert to our approach. Bell held out a hand to stop me moving any further. We waited until the guards who were holding Cass had caught up. She was quiet now, but the ropes around her ankles remained, and I noted the thin lines of red which ran down her leg and into her boots. Reed came from the rear of the group, his face focused and serious. He approached the guards, his stride confident as ever.

"Prisoners to see Governor Adams."

"He's in his office." One of the guards gestured over his shoulder. "Said to send you right up."

Reed nodded curtly and beckoned to our guards. They pulled us forward and, reluctantly, we were guided into Governance. I was surprised to discover as we approached the buildings, that this area was very similar to Patrol. It was smaller in size, and its accommodation consisted more of buildings like the dorms we slept in on The Crags than pods, but otherwise the style it had been built in was very familiar. I wondered briefly which of these buildings Anders had stolen the meds from on our last visit, and how he had managed to get Rogers past the guard hut at the entrance.

We made our way towards a larger structure not unlike the Jefferson Building. I guessed that its function was similar, and that this was where Adams' office would be located. My heart was pounding and my breathing shallow as I contemplated meeting him face to face. I had never actually spoken directly to our leader, only experienced him at ceremonies and public meetings. I could feel a trickle of sweat making its way down my spine as the sign above the doorway became visible. Finally, we passed through the entrance of the Washington Building, and headed down the hallway inside it. Most of the doors along the corridor were closed, but as we reached the end, I spotted that one of them stood ajar. Voices were floating from within, and I strained to hear what was being said.

"...have to act now, act quickly..."

Cass and I exchanged glances at Carter's familiar tone. I wondered if I looked as stricken as she did.

"...understand your eagerness, but..." This was Adams, his tone far less steady than I had ever heard it before. He sounded almost excited. "...want them to understand the trouble... to suffer..."

"...know how you feel..." I had never heard Carter sound soothing before, "but if we wait... delay... further issues..."

"Alright." Adams sounded annoyed. "Bring it forward... if only to... this afternoon..."

Reed approached the door and rapped on it sharply. The conversation stopped. There was a moment's pause, and then Adams spoke again.

"Enter."

Motioning to the guards who held us to wait, Reed marched

inside. The voices resumed, but far lower now, and it was impossible to catch anything that was being said. We waited in silence for a few minutes, but it wasn't long before Reed's head appeared around the door again. I took a deep breath and tried to control my racing heart as he spoke.

"Bring them in."

Chapter Twenty Nine

I felt Bell's baton prodding me from behind and took the first few steps towards the open door. Behind me, I heard Cass follow suit. Reed moved aside so that we could pass through, and I got my first glimpse of Adams' sanctuary. It was larger than any other office I'd ever seen. Its walls were covered with dark wooden panels, giving an impression of luxury, and the enormous table which dominated the centre of the room was also made from highly polished wood. I thought angrily of the Rep citizens who had no doubt spent precious time building it.

Behind the table, seated on a highbacked chair, was the man himself. He stared at me as I was brought in, his lips curving into a strange half-smile and his eyes glittering dangerously. As Cass was thrust into place beside me, I felt her stiffen. Following her gaze to the opposite side of the room, I understood. In front of a large window which looked out over the darkened forest beyond, Superintendent Carter was standing with her back to us.

Behind us, Reed had a whispered conversation with the guards. A moment later, I heard the door close and felt Reed take up position directly behind us. Only when we were surrounded by the three most powerful people in the entire

Beck, did Adams begin to speak.

"Welcome back, *deserters*." His tone was now menacing, and his eyes flickered constantly between mine and Cass' as if he couldn't decide who to focus on. "You thought you could escape The Beck, escape the life provided for you here, escape... me."

A harsh laugh escaped him as he turned to Carter. "You know, I don't even recognise them. Ridiculous, that these... specimens... believed they could get away with leaving us, that they wouldn't have to face the consequences... of their betrayal."

"Ridiculous," Carter agreed, turning to face us, her expression mocking. She stared at Cass. "I remember this one. I've dealt with her before."

Beside me, I felt Cass tense and prayed she wouldn't do anything stupid as Adams continued.

"Yes, clearly the message you delivered didn't... get through. They abandoned The Beck. And then to return, to have the audacity to come back here to... to... to steal," he spat the words out, "from us... infect us with their *foreign* diseases..."

He paused for so long that I wondered if he had forgotten what he was going to say. Out of the corner of my eye I saw Carter exchanging glances with Reed, as though even they were a little concerned by Adams' behaviour.

Carter had just opened her mouth to speak when Adams finally spoke again. "Well your little escape has stirred something up in the people here... whispers of rebellion abound," he slammed a hand against the desk and lunged to his feet, "and I am *not* about to let these whispers grow in volume."

Without taking his eyes off us, he thrust his chair back and began a slow stroll around the table.

"I have to quash these rumours. Stop the people believing they can change things, escape from the place which feeds and clothes them, provides them with a job and a purpose..." I wondered if he actually believed his own words, "...eradicate talk of rebellion once and for all."

His slow walk had brought him into position right in front of me, where he stopped and leaned closer, his breath hot on my face. "At first I thought the sickness would be devastating. But then I realised that I could spin it to my advantage. Blame you, the heroic escapees, for infecting us. And when I reveal that you purposefully brought the sickness which killed so many of us here, you will go from hero to villain in a matter of minutes."

Beside me, I heard Cass gasp. Adams moved on, this time thrusting his face close to hers. I felt her recoil, but he grasped hold of the top of her arm and pulled her closer.

"Today is a big day. Today is the day that I free the remaining citizens from the quarantine and bring together all of the Beck community for the first time in weeks. And later today, in front of this *momentous* assembly, there will be an execution."

He let go of Cass' arm suddenly and she fell backwards. As Reed caught her and pushed her back into place beside me, Adams circumnavigated the table again and took his seat.

"You," he jabbed a finger at us, "are a symbol of the rebellion. And when I expose you, execute you, right in front of them, their rebellion will be crushed."

I felt my heart contract at his words. An execution. My fears about his reasons for bringing us here had been accurate.

He meant to lie about us, use us, as symbols of a failed rebellion, escapees who had returned not to rescue, but to inflict death and misery on those citizens left here. And once he had blamed us, turned all The Beck citizens against us, he would extinguish us and those citizens he had left would be compliant, believing that any thought of rebellion was futile. My heart sank.

But Adams hadn't finished. "Executing you, however, will not be quite enough."

He motioned to Reed. Behind us, I felt him turn, heard him open the door, and then close it softly behind him.

"You are not the only ones who have caused me a problem." Adams went on. "Oh no. I have recently discovered that some of the rebellion has come from within."

My heart lurched in my chest at his ominous words.

"In addition to you two..." he almost spat the next word, "*traitors* being publicly executed, we also need to deal with a disloyal citizen who has never even left these shores."

I felt a cool draft as the door swung open again. Behind us, there was a scuffle of some kind. Adams gestured with his hand, granting us permission to turn and look as Reed re-entered the room. He was accompanied by two Shadow Patrol officers. With them was a struggling figure whose head was covered with some kind of sacking. They dragged him through the doorway and around the table. When the strange group were standing at the opposite side of the room from Carter, Adams gestured to Reed, who stepped forward and tore the sacking away.

Suddenly, the reason for the recent lack of communication between The Ridge and The Beck Resistance became abundantly clear. Beneath the sacking, his shoulders hunched, his face peppered with bruises, his hair matted with what looked like blood, was Cam.

I found I couldn't tear my eyes away from the man I had waited so long to see. His hands were bound and his head was lowered, his eyes staring down at the thick carpet on the floor beneath us. For a moment, he was still.

But then, he looked up. As his eyes met mine, they flared: first with shock and fear, then with fury. Finally, as I watched, they filled with darkness and despair. I understood. He had not anticipated my presence there. He had been ready to face his own death.

But he was not ready to face mine.

As quickly as the look of anguish had crossed his features it disappeared, and we looked away from one another. I heard Cass give a soft gasp of shock, and dug an elbow into her side to shut her up.

Adams chuckled, a low, sinister sound which came from deep in his throat. "I take it you know Cameron, then? Don't bother hiding your reaction. I'm aware that he's been leading the Rebellion from within. Seeing him brought so..." he paused and cast his glance at Cam, "*low* must be... difficult."

My heart sank. I knew that Cam had been working hard since his recovery trying to revitalise the Resistance efforts, attempting to bring the citizens together to rise up and fight. Adams was using him as an example: brutally executing him in front of his supporters was a stroke of genius. With their leader dead, the Resistance would be devastated, and many of the ordinary citizens who had been persuaded to join him would be too frightened to do so again in the future. I glanced at him again and could feel him quivering with anger, his gaze cast down as he fought to remain in control.

Adams looked back at Cass and I, the mocking smile firmly in place. "A triple execution," he crowed, "three of you at once, and a very strong message delivered to my remaining citizens to ensure that they remain... faithful to me."

He turned to Carter. "This afternoon, then? Once you have time to empty out the quarantine area and gather the rest of the citizens together?" He paused, shooting a sideways glance at the three of us. "You're *sure* I can't leave it a day longer, let them sweat over their fate a little?"

Carter blanched. "I don't think it's a good idea... the quicker the message is delivered, the better."

Reed chimed in, "Then we can work on getting back to normal. Go ahead with our plans. There's been enough upheaval recently, don't you think?"

"Alright, this afternoon. Give us some time to... prepare..." Adams gave an exaggerated sigh.

Reed and Carter nodded, both of them looking relieved.

There was a momentary silence, until Adams tutted impatiently. "What are you waiting for then? Get them out of my sight!"

Heading for the door, Reed jerked his head at the guards, who thrust Cam in the same direction. Reed held it open and nodded to the other guards who were standing outside. Seconds later, we too were being manhandled out of Adams' office and down the hall.

My head was buzzing with questions. We hadn't heard from Cam in more than a week. Was that how long he had been their prisoner? The marks on his face clearly demonstrated that he had not been treated well. I wondered if the sudden attack on The Ridge had anything to do with his capture, and if he had been forced to tell them our whereabouts.

Watching him walking ahead of me, I noticed that he moved more slowly than usual, and wondered at the full extent of his injuries. Being back on the same shore as him, only to find him wounded and about to be executed, was torture.

Adams' plan for our very public deaths was not a surprise: he had executed Wade in a similar manner for her attack on Donnelly, a particularly nasty Shadow Patrol guard, and was well aware of how witnessing a fellow citizen die was a surefire way to keep people's behaviour in check. But waiting until he had three of us here was brilliant. All the Resistance's hopes: for escape, for rescue, for freedom, quashed in one fell swoop. I shuddered at the thought.

Rather than heading back towards the entrance to the Washington Building, this time, the guards took us to the rear, where they pushed us out into the courtyard beyond. On the opposite side was a large, forbidding-looking building marked 'No Admittance'. The door was protected with an access pad, not unlike the ones I had seen used in Dev. The area was obviously very secure.

One of the guards used an access card to open it, and we were all guided through. On the other side was a dimly lit area with chairs and a table, and beyond it, a narrow hallway with four doors. We were brought down to the very last one, which was secured in the same way. Finally, the three of us were pushed inside the room, a small square of space which was empty of any furniture. A single window set high in one wall of the room let in a small amount of light.

"We'll be back for you later," one of the guards grunted at us, checking that the bindings on our hands were still secure. He jerked his head back towards the lobby area. "There are two of us outside at all times, so don't try anything stupid."

He backed away, slammed the door shut and bolted it. We listened as footsteps retreated down the hallway outside. Eventually, there was silence.

I turned to Cam first, unsure of how to approach him and also very aware that we weren't alone. He too, was looking at me, his expression unreadable. He took a faltering step towards me, then stopped. Unable to prevent myself, I closed the gap between us, stopping when I realised that I couldn't free my hands to reach for him as I wanted to. Frustrated, I leaned into him awkwardly, attempting to convey my happiness at our reunion.

As our bodies made contact, he cried out in pain.

Instantly, I shifted backwards. "I–I'm sorry! What...?"

"He's hurt." Cass stood at the door, staring at him knowingly. "They tortured you, didn't they?"

He nodded.

"Carter?"

"Yes." His voice was quiet, so quiet that it was difficult to hear him. I couldn't work out if he was angry or just in pain.

Cass looked away. "That bitch."

I backed up and slid down the wall a little distance away from the man I had been so desperate to see.

Cass turned away and began running her tethered hands around the door, testing the edges of the frame as best she could.

"You won't manage it." Cam's voice was louder now, more confident. "I've been locked in here for a week now. Don't you think I've tried everything?"

Ignoring him, she continued to explore. The room was built from stone and had only one unreachable window. Cass worked her way around the room with difficulty, searching for any small weaknesses in the construction.

Cam sighed in disgust. I couldn't decide whether he was irritated by our general situation, or the fact that Cass had not heeded his advice. I decided not to enquire. We watched Cass' frustration growing as she discovered that Cam had been right: our cell was totally secure, even if our hands had been free to attempt escape. I avoided Cam's gaze, not knowing how to approach him. He alternated between watching me and following Cass' progress, and I couldn't judge his mood at all.

Eventually, Cass returned to the door of the cell. Having exhausted every other possibility, she began hammering both fists against it, screaming her rage at whichever guards were stationed on the other side.

"Tried that too."

I glanced over to find Cam looking at me again, his expression guarded.

"Do any good?" I attempted a smile.

"Nope." He shrugged. "I give it one more minute before..."

There was a pounding on the door which, this time, came from the other side.

"Stop that!" The guard's voice was loud and threatening. "Unless you want me to come in there and execute you right now."

"Bring it on, you–"

But Cass was cut off as the door opened and the larger of the two guards stood there, his considerable bulk filling the entire frame. He advanced into the room, backing Cass into the far corner.

"You've already had a knock from me." He shook his

clenched fist close to my friend's face. "Are you asking for another?"

Cass glared up at him defiantly and I feared for what she might say next. Pushing myself to my feet, I advanced on the guard, my bound hands outstretched in a gesture of surrender.

"Leave it, Cass." I met the guard's gaze directly. "She'll stop now, ok?"

He glared down at me. "She'd better had, or..."

I knew from Cass' expression that he wasn't going to like what she said next. "Or what?"

Turning back to her, he drew his fist back and I watched in horror as the punch connected with her chin and her head recoiled back. Her expression flashed from outrage to agony.

"Or that," he snarled, and gave her a shove which sent her reeling backwards. "Keep quiet now."

He turned and exited, leaving a yawning silence behind him.

Chapter Thirty

Once the door had slammed shut, I hurried to Cass' side. The force of the attack had knocked her halfway across the small cell, and she was now lying sprawled on the floor, her hands nursing her cheek.

"Are you alright?"

She removed her hands, moaning a little. The side of her face was red, and I could see the impact had jarred her. She tried to calm her breathing as she digested what had just happened, all the fight seeping out of her.

"Hey, Cass. That was brave," I tried.

"It was stupid."

I shot a look at Cam.

"Well, it was. Not that I didn't try it myself, but there's no easy route out of here and all you've done is made sure you'll have a pounding headache for the rest of what could be your last day on earth." I winced inwardly at the bitterness which laced his tone.

Despite his criticism, Cass looked at him with admiration. "You tried it yourself?"

He nodded, a small, tired smile creeping on to his face. "I did."

Managing to help Cass into a position where she was

leaning against the wall more comfortably, I stood midway between my fellow prisoners. "What happened to you?"

He raised his eyes to meet mine. "What happened to *you*?"

I shook my head. "You first."

He sighed. "Sit down, this could be a long night."

With a little difficulty, I slid down the wall and faced Cam expectantly. He grimaced as he began to speak.

"Look, we told you that things have been getting worse here for a while now. The people in quarantine died in huge numbers, but no one was sent in to take away the bodies, so the place was becoming unbearable. Adams needed workers to keep things going in the fields, the kitchens, and with the livestock, so he demoted some of the Upper Beck citizens, said it was a temporary measure, sent them back down to work the Lower Beck shifts. I've been working in LS, Will was placed back in Agric, Anders was transferred back to the Dev Sector. Adams even brought some of the healthier Clearance citizens back in the end."

I thought back to how The Warehouse had not been operational. It made sense, if many of its workers had been transferred to work in the Lower Beck instead.

"But it still wasn't enough. Eventually, he made the decision to bring across any Minors above the age of ten."

"Ten!" Cass' eyes widened.

"Yes, ten. Those kids have been working themselves to death for the past couple of weeks trying to do the jobs that were previously done by much older, better trained citizens. He's been working with Montgomery to administer drugs to the Shadow Patrol, similar to those which were about to be tested on you," he nodded at Cass, "and your fellow trainees the night you escaped."

She shuddered visibly. "What effect do they have?"

"I don't know exactly. They seem to make the Shadow guards angrier, less rational." He gestured to the door with his hands. "You saw his reaction just then. So extreme. It's like... they follow orders but when they're asked to attack, their actions seem more fuelled by anger, even when there's nothing specific to anger them personally." He paused. "Does that make sense?"

I nodded, thinking of the glazed expressions on the guards' faces, the strange quiet which had fallen over the boat as we had travelled back from The Ridge, and the guard's vicious punch.

"I told you he'd recruited more Shadow Patrol guards, and I know for a fact he's been giving them larger food rations. They were also the first to be given the meds to fend off the sickness, after Adams, Reed, and Carter, of course, and they received larger doses than anyone else." He sighed. "All his efforts have gone into defensive measures. Nothing's been done to care for or protect the weaker amongst us."

Tired of waiting to hear Cam's own story, I burst out, "What about *you* though? What happened to *you*?"

He looked back at me, his eyes weary. "I told you I'd been trying to rebuild the Resistance. You know, get the word out about what Adams was really doing, try to persuade people to make some kind of stand, to be ready for when you all came over here to fight from The Crags." He slammed his clenched fists into the wall beside him. "And it was working. They were listening. When they heard you'd all escaped to safety and were building a larger alliance, they started to really *believe* that we could do something about it."

I shifted closer to him, desperately aware of his frustration as he continued.

"But now Adams has us all captive: the Resistance leader and some of the very people I promised were coming to help save us! They'll just... give up again," he fumed. "As of tomorrow, when he executes us in full public view, any confidence in a potential rebellion will disintegrate."

He slumped back against the wall, his eyes bitter. There was a silence for a moment, before he spoke again. "What about you then?"

I glanced at Cass, who seemed happy to allow me to do the storytelling.

"We were doing well. We'd been training, like we told you, lots of us, and working hard." His eyes felt like they were burning into me and I shook as I continued to speak. "We were mining lead and making bullets... amassing a good quantity of ammunition. We were almost ready."

"But almost isn't good enough. Don't you see? We needed you earlier than this." Cam frowned. "What was Rogers waiting for?"

I paused, unsure how to respond when he looked so angry. "He was trying to make sure that we had enough ammo, enough trained soldiers, enough of us to, well... to stand a chance against Adams' forces."

He didn't look convinced.

I tried again, hurt by the anger in his eyes. "There were plans in place. Last night, *literally* last night, Rogers announced that we were almost there. We were coming."

"Not fast enough though."

"You cannot possibly be blaming us." Cass spoke up at last, and she was no less furious than Cam. "Look, we've been working hard, training every day, for *hours*. Quin's right.

Rogers and Hughes had been planning..."

"They'll still be planning."

I felt both sets of eyes jerk to meet mine, but Cam was the first to speak. "What?"

"I said, they'll still be planning. I bet they're planning right now." Swallowing an image of the pain on Hughes' face when the bullet hit him, I met Cam's gaze with more confidence now. "Don't think they'll have given up. We've been working on this for weeks. When Reed showed up last night it was a shock. We weren't expecting it. He and his soldiers... did some... damage..." I trailed off for a moment, but pressed on when I saw the doubt on Cam's face. "But the fact that Adams dared to send people to The Ridge, to hurt people, to kidnap Cass and I, will only make Rogers and the others more determined."

"You think they'll still come?" Cam sounded doubtful.

"I do." I searched for the words which would make a difference. "And what's more, after what happened last night, I don't think they'll wait."

Cass perked up a little. "You're right. We only needed a few more days... and for what? To make extra bullets and do a bit more training? It won't make that much of a difference. Not now. I think they'll come straight away."

"What good will it do though?" Cam sighed, the anger seeming to drain out of him. "They won't be in time to prevent our executions, and by the time they get here, Adams' plan will have destroyed the Beck citizens' confidence. They won't have the confidence to fight."

"You don't know that." I glared at him. "Not for certain. The Ridge boats are much faster than the Clearance ones."

"Maybe. But we don't have long. And we most likely won't

be alive long enough to see it."

I shifted forward a little, trying to get him to believe me. "I think you're wrong."

"I sincerely hope so."

"You've been here, on The Beck, with no hope..." I tried to keep my tone even. "You haven't seen–"

I struggled to find the words to explain The Ridge community. I wanted Cam to share my hope, that a free and cooperative community could succeed, but knew that without ever having left The Beck, I would never have been able to imagine it. But I had to try.

"Look, things are run differently on The Ridge. I know that you're angry and frightened right now, and probably can't imagine a life which is better than this, but please..." I realised that my hands were balled into twin fists on my lap and forced myself to relax them, "...please trust that it can."

"Alright. I take your point." He sighed again. "But I don't see anything we can do from in here, do you?"

"Not from in here, perhaps." Cass' words were quiet now, but edged with a steely determination. "But we can still fight. When the time is right. At the very last minute. If they're going to kill us, we won't let them do it without a struggle. Let's wait 'til we're up on that stage, then kick and scream and hit out at those guards. Show The Beck we haven't given up."

There was another silence, as Cam considered her words. Eventually, he managed a wry smile.

"Ok. Let's go out with a bang."

I nodded my agreement, relieved at his change of heart. Now the decision was made, none of us spoke for a while. Cass rubbed her already-swollen cheek, where the red mark was developing into a nasty bruise.

"You alright?" I asked.

"My cheek's sore, that's all. And my head aches."

"Why don't you try and get some rest." Cam's voice was gentle. "Attempt a couple of hours at least. I presume you didn't get any sleep on the boat?" Cass shook her head. "You must be exhausted. There's nothing else we can do. And you'll be in better shape to fight back if you're not as tired."

Cass looked as though she might argue, but then her expression changed. "Guess you're right. I could do with some rest." She shifted position, lowering her body to the floor of our cell. "And if I want to give them a taste of their own medicine, I need to be strong, right?"

She grinned and turned away from us, curling her body into a ball and sliding both arms under her head. Never one to struggle with sleep, even in stressful situations, it wasn't long before her breathing evened out and her body relaxed.

When Cam finally returned his gaze to mine, I gestured at her. "Thanks. You were right. She was exhausted. All that fight takes a lot of energy."

"I'll bet." He managed a chuckle. "What about you?"

"Ah, I'm alright." We both knew it was a lie, but I smiled to soften it. "I don't fight as hard as she does."

We fell silent again. Now we were practically alone, there were other things to discuss, but neither of us seemed able to find the words. Eventually, I shifted slightly closer to him.

"Mind if I sit here?" I stopped as I felt his body stiffen. "I promise I won't... touch you."

"Believe me, it's not that I don't want you to touch me." He grimaced. "It just hurts, that's all."

I hovered awkwardly, still waiting for his response to my

question. Eventually he gave a small nod.

Relieved, I eased myself into place next to him and leaned my head on his shoulder, welcoming the warmth of his body. Once there was no eye contact between us, it was easier to speak.

"So, they tortured you."

I felt his shrug. "For a couple of days, yes. Then they stopped. I guess they decided on this course of action instead..." he gestured at me, "...the execution, alongside you two, and... well, the torture wasn't necessary anymore."

"Is it very sore still?"

"If you want me to be honest, yes." I raised my head as I felt him shift, and then he was facing me, but I couldn't meet his gaze. "It's not as bad as it was. After they left me the first night, I lay here in agony. Bleeding. Not sure if they'd come back for more."

"But now... well it's more of an ache than excruciating pain." He waited for a response, then went on. "Quin, look at me."

I shifted my body so I mirrored him. After a couple of deep breaths, I raised my eyes to meet his. The anger and bitterness were gone. I reached out, cursing the ropes which bound my hands together, and placed a tentative hand on his arm, feeling a surge of joy as he didn't recoil from my touch.

"I'm sorry about earlier. I just... well, I was disappointed." He sighed. "A week ago, I was in regular contact with The Ridge, I had more citizens convinced that joining the Resistance was a good idea than *ever* before, and I knew..." he coloured slightly, "...well, I knew I'd be seeing you again soon."

"Cam, I–"

He held up his hands to stop me. "Hold on, let me finish please. What has kept me going... these last few weeks... was the thought that resistance might finally... *finally* be possible. And... the thought that I would get to see you again. I know things haven't been easy for us... but I care about you, Quin, I do, and..." He looked away and his words trailed off.

I let the silence roll on, hoping that he would find the courage to finish his sentence. After a long moment of quiet, he finally brought his gaze back to mine.

"Look, if this is the last time we'll ever be together, well... " he stumbled over the words, "...it's not what I wanted... I mean, I've imagined this reunion so many times, and this is..." he glanced at me, his face flushing, "...well it's about as far from what I imagined as it could be... you know?"

He fell silent, dropping his gaze to the floor. I squeezed his hand gently, swallowing the lump in my throat as I willed him to continue.

"What I mean is... I don't want to spend this time regretting what... um... what could have been. I want us to just, be together... be glad that we knew one another." He cleared his throat softly. "Because you've been... one of the better experiences of my life, and well... if this is it..."

I leaned forward and placed my lips on his. For a second he resisted, wincing slightly at the pain he felt, but then he returned the gesture. It was a sweet kiss, filled with longing and sadness, and it didn't last long. But when we broke apart and stared at each other, we were both slightly breathless.

He grinned suddenly. "That's more like it."

Glancing over at Cass, to check she was still sleeping, I shifted even closer to him.

"Where does it hurt?"

"Oh, just about everywhere."

I started to back away, but he stopped me with a hand on my arm. "No, don't move. Let's just... be careful."

He lay down on the ground, easing his body into the most comfortable position he could manage. I waited until he was still, and slid my body alongside his, taking care to make no sudden movements. We lay still, my back cocooned against his chest, our bodies curled around one another.

"Damned ropes," he cursed, "can't put my arms around you."

My heart raced at the thought and I felt the soft laughter rumble through his chest.

"What is this you're wearing?" he whispered, his voice close to my ear.

I had forgotten the unfamiliar garments Cass and I had been dressed in when Reed had kidnapped us. Blushing, I attempted to explain.

"It's called a... a blouse. They have different clothing on The Ridge for... well, for what they call parties. Like, special occasions when they have something to celebrate, you know, if... if something great has happened."

He ran a finger awkwardly up my arm, tracing the thin material. As the rough bristle of the ropes which bound him brushed against the fabric, I was suddenly very conscious of how flimsy it was.

"Hmm. Not very practical. Are you cold?"

I wriggled against him. "Not now, I'm not."

"I like it." I felt his lips brushing the back of my neck and shivered slightly. "Sure you don't want me to warm you up?"

I ignored his teasing tone, but snuggled a little closer.

"Tell me more about these, parties, then. What are they all

about?"

I smiled to myself. "You'd love them, Cam. I mean... it's a totally different way of life." I sighed. "I wish you could've been there to see it."

"Me too."

"We were having a party when Reed arrived. To celebrate the birth of a *baby*. A baby who was going to live with his own parents. Cam, you wouldn't believe–"

"Ssshh!"

Behind me, he froze. I stopped speaking abruptly. From the hallway outside we could suddenly hear noises: voices, and rapid footsteps approaching. Cam and I separated, both scrambling to a sitting position as the bolt scraped against the outside of the door.

Someone was coming in.

Chapter Thirty One

Instinctively, the two of us slid across the room to Cass. Once positioned in front of her, we stared at the door as it began to ease open. Cam had spoken of the torture he had suffered in this very cell, and I wondered if we were about to have a similar experience. My entire body shook with fear as a vaguely familiar voice drifted into the room.

"...won't take long. Adams' orders, you know. Make sure they're compliant."

"Good idea," one of the guards replied. "Wouldn't trust any of 'em."

There were murmurs of agreement at his comment as the door slid open wider.

"Back up against the wall, all of you!" The tone of our visitor's voice changed as he entered the room and began directing his commands at us.

Cass woke with a start and, realising the danger, huddled closer to me. I shrank back from the figure, unsure of what was coming. Beside me though, I felt Cam relax. I stared at him, not understanding, and then looked back at the doorway, where the figure now stood. The light behind him made it difficult to see, and he immediately turned his back to us, pulling the door of our cell closed. But as he turned back, I understood.

It was Anders.

"Alright," he continued, in the same loud, demanding tone. "I need you to remain still. I'll deal with you one at a time. If you don't struggle, this won't take long."

We remained silent, unsure what Anders was planning. As he knelt down on the floor, I spotted the gun which was in a holster fastened to his shoulder, but he didn't touch it. In his other hand was a small case, which he laid on the floor and began to unpack. Laying a small bottle of liquid on the ground, he proceeded to unpack three glass syringes, similar to those I had seen only a few times before. They were used to administer medicines, or other concoctions which could do far more damage. For a second, I wondered if Anders had changed sides, but then he began to talk in a totally different tone.

"Listen," he whispered quietly, his voice close to Cam's ear, "I'm here with a plan."

Glancing back over his shoulder, he switched back to his previous tone. "You first. I just need your arm."

Catching on, I shuffled towards him, making noises to support his ruse, so the guard outside would continue to be fooled. Anders had originated from the Dev Sector and transferred to Patrol at the same time as I had. He was quiet, but had been a hardworking guard. He was even better at the Dev stuff, and had a real brain for science. As Cam had mentioned, he was now working in Dev again, and using this as an excuse to get to us at a time when we couldn't have needed him more.

He dropped his voice as he continued. "Look, I've been speaking to those citizens who survived the quarantine."

He grimaced. "The ones who Adams wants to witness your execution. Montgomery was recently instructed by Carter to check them over, verify they were sufficiently recovered from the sickness to work safely alongside the rest of the surviving society. She asked me to help out with the checks. The conversations were interesting."

"What are people saying?"

Cam's voice was barely a whisper, but Anders shot him a look anyway, and put a finger to his lips.

"Hold still!" Anders took the bottle of liquid, slipping off the lid as he continued to speak in a much softer tone. "This is a drug, supposed to keep you calm and stable, make you sleepy. Adams wants you as docile as possible, so there is no chance of you looking rebellious. He wants all the fight gone out of you, so he can persuade everyone that resisting him is useless."

I stared at Anders in horror and backed away as he filled the first syringe. As we watched, he lifted his overall jacket and tugged at the undershirt which he wore beneath it. Taking a section of it in is hand, he squeezed the liquid from the glass vial into the material, which soaked it up and only looked a little wet by the time he was finished.

Finally, I understood. Adams was paranoid. He would want evidence that those people who came into contact with us did as instructed. If Montgomery had been told to check that we had been injected with the drug, Anders couldn't return to the Dev Sector with unused syringes and a full bottle of meds. Hopefully, she would accept the empty bottle and no one would think to check Anders' clothing. As far as I knew, no one suspected him of any involvement with the Resistance.

"Move it now! I don't have a lot of time." Anders made sure

his commands sounded even more frustrated and louder than before. Then he dropped his voice again. "Many of the folks from quarantine don't like what's happened. Spending weeks in that hell, watching people close to them die and being able to do nothing to help them... honestly, they're furious."

We shifted closer, straining to hear him.

"Now you." He paused. "Yes, you next. Over here, girl! Don't give me any trouble. You can see that I'm armed, and there are two guards right outside."

We moved round, keeping up the pretence. Anders shifted closer to Cass, as though she would be his next victim.

"Everything alright in there, Anders?" One of the guards' voices floated in from the corridor outside. We froze.

Before Anders could respond, Cass pushed away from him and shouted. "Get off me! What are you trying to– Ow!"

She cried out, and then went silent, slumping back against the wall. As the guard reached the door and poked his head through, Anders leaned away from her, empty syringe in hand. I made sure I also went limp next to her.

"You ok?" The guard stared hard at the scene in front of him.

"F-fine, thanks." Recovering himself, Anders waved a hand at him. "This one was giving me a little trouble, but she's all good now that I've administered the meds."

"You don't need me then?" The guard sounded doubtful.

"No. I'm alright." Anders patted the gun, then made a show of picking up the final syringe as he spoke.

The guard waited. Anders filled the syringe slowly, taking as long as he could. Beside me, I could feel Cam tensing, wondering if Anders would have to actually administer the drug. After an agonising moment, the guard seemed satisfied, and turned to leave, his footsteps moving away down the corridor. We heaved a collective sigh of relief.

Anders motioned to Cam, who shifted slightly, making sounds like he was moving closer to Anders. He shot an uneasy look at the door, which remained ajar. There was no sign of life however, and the footsteps had died away now as the guard returned to his position.

"That's it. Keep still for me."

We leaned closer still, waiting for Anders' final instructions.

"Once I'm gone, you need to act like you've been drugged.." He paused, and called over his shoulder. "Almost done now." The whisper resumed. "You need to seem... sleepy, not with it, like your limbs are heavy... you know... so when they come for you, drag your feet, walk slowly, stare off into space, try not to react suddenly to anything."

He emptied the last of the liquid into his shirt and tucked it back into his trousers, shuddering slightly as the wet fabric came to rest on his skin. "When you're up on the stage and they're about to start the execution, there'll be a distraction. Once it comes, there are people in the audience in front of you, among the quarantined citizens, who'll continue the disturbance, diverting the guards' attention. That's when you fight. Until then, you do *nothing*."

He reached inside the bag once more and brought something out. As he held his hand out in front of us, it flashed silver. Bending closer, I could see he held three slender blades, each one the size of a small pen.

"These are scalpels, the tiny knives used in the Dev Sector." He handed one to each of us. "Their blades are very sharp. Find somewhere to hide them, and use them to try and escape from the stage if you need to."

He paused, glancing at the door once more and looking afraid. "I'm sorry I couldn't bring you anything more substantial, but they might search you for weapons, and these are small... should hopefully not be found... at least they might give you a chance."

I reached out a hand and took hold of his, squeezing it gently. *Thank you*, I mouthed.

He blushed. "Don't thank me yet."

He began packing up the bag with more noise than was strictly necessary. "After the distraction, no one can know for sure what'll happen. The plan is that people will fight. Pick up whatever weapons they can, and hit back at Adams and the Shadow Patrol. But there are no guarantees. Not everyone will fight... and it probably won't be enough... but perhaps we can have some impact, and then, if Rogers and the others are still able to... able to come, then maybe... It's something, at least." He trailed off.

Cam placed a hand on his shoulder, keeping his voice low. "Thank you."

Anders turned to go, but stopped abruptly as Cass shifted towards him. Silently, she clasped both his hands in her own and leaned forward until her forehead rested against his. When she let go, his face was flushed with embarrassment. He nodded briefly at Cam before clambering to his feet and making for the door.

"Coming out now!" he called ahead, turning for one last glimpse of us before he closed the door behind him. We heard the bolt shoot into the lock once more.

Once he had gone, we shifted into the most comfortable positions we could, choosing to lie fairly close together on the ground at the far side of the cell. The guard returned to check on us, sliding the bolt across and staring in through the door for a long time, but he didn't come inside, and must have been convinced of the docile condition induced by the meds, as he eventually closed the door and slid the lock back into place. His footsteps faded and didn't return.

It was a long time before we dared to move. Eventually, we felt confident enough to shift slightly, but knew that we didn't want to go far: he had seen the positions we had settled in, and if we were drugged it would be realistic to expect us not to move very far. But we did huddle a little closer together and conversed in voices lower than whisper level.

"Where are we going to hide these?" Cass asked, staring at the silver blade in her hand.

Cam was turning the blade back and forth. "They're sharp. Needs to be somewhere they won't hurt us accidentally." He considered for a moment. "I think inside our clothes would be best. But we need to have access to them when the time comes. And concealing them isn't going to be easy without proper access to our hands."

I glanced down at my blouse, which offered no secure hiding places. Considering my trousers, I lent down and looked at the cuffs along the base of each leg.

"In here?" Twisting my hands until the ropes burned the skin on my wrist, I managed to angle the blade so I could run the sharp edge along the seam.

Cam nodded in agreement. "Might be tricky, but I think if we can slide them inside the seams, they'll be less notice-able."

It took a long time, but eventually, I managed to make a hole large enough to slide the blade in, but hopefully not be noticed. "The material's pretty thick. I think even if they patted us down for weapons, we'd get away with it."

Cass had done the same, and Cam followed suit, working to create a slit in the side seam of his overall jacket so it was a little closer to his hand. Again, I cursed the flimsy costumes that Cass and I wore, but there wasn't a better place for the blades in our impractical outfits.

Having concealed the blades, there wasn't much more we could do.

"Let's all try to get some rest," Cam advised. "Like I said, we'll need our strength if we're really going to fight back. Listen, when the time comes, we need to move as one. We probably won't be able to use the blades to begin with, so try and use your fists, kick out, whatever you can do without a weapon, until you can figure out some way to retrieve it." He reached over and squeezed Cass' hand. "Best of luck, Cass. I'm glad Quin has you to look out for her."

She blushed, but returned the squeeze before turning to me. "Quin... I hope..." she trailed off.

"I know. Me too." I leaned into her as silently as I could, trying to convey my concern and affection without the ability to give her the hug I wanted to.

She shifted away and laid down, making sure her position echoed the one she had been in when the guard had looked in on us earlier. Turning back to Cam, I could see nothing but warmth in his eyes. He leaned closer, so Cass couldn't hear.

"I'd like nothing better than to lie with my arms around you." He glanced down at the ropes which bound him and rolled his eyes. "Or at least close to you." My heart pounded at the thought. "But if we fall asleep like that, and don't wake before the guards come in... I mean, it would be stupid to..."

I placed a hand against his chest, quieting him. "I know."

He stopped speaking and just looked at me. "Whatever happens... well, I hope we both get through tomorrow. And get to spend some time together where we don't have to lie several feet apart."

I shuffled closer to him, aligning my body with his. He stiffened.

"Just for a little while," I managed to whisper.

Finally, he relaxed into me. Through his overalls, I could feel his heart beating as fast as my own, but I wasn't sure if it was caused by being near me or the threat of what was to come. Closing my eyes, I breathed slowly, wanting to savour the moment. For now, at least, we could be together without separation or interruption.

Eventually, I found my voice again. "Things look better than they did an hour ago anyway," I managed. "I mean... there's hope."

"There is." Cam leaned forward and pressed his lips to mine, wincing slightly. "There really is."

Shifting away from me, he lay down, tucking both his hands underneath his head. I did the same, lying facing him, still breathless from the promise of his kiss. I watched as his eyes began to flutter shut and he drifted off to sleep gazing at me. Wondering what the rest of the day held in store for us, I attempted to follow suit.

Chapter Thirty Two

A few hours later we were disturbed by the scraping of the bolt against the door and the rough shaking of several guards who burst in and roused us. I was hugely glad that Cam and I had separated ourselves and not been caught together. It was vital that the guards believe we were drowsy, kept calm by the drugs. In the end, having had so little rest, it wasn't too hard to pretend.

Another thought which had haunted me after Cam had drifted off to sleep was of Adams working out the connection between us. Visions of Cam being tortured in front of me had flashed through my head, and the horrible images had taunted me as I watched him. Should we survive to fight another day, I knew that Adams and Carter wouldn't hesitate to use our relationship against us.

I didn't have long to dwell on that though, as we were pulled to our feet and hustled out the door. I had half been hoping that the guards would untie the ropes, believing the drugs would render us helpless, but we were marched out of the cell and down the corridor with our hands still bound. In no time at all, we were back on the path through the woods.

We took our time, plodding along as though our heads were muddied by the meds Anders had supposedly administered.

I didn't look closely at the others, but kept my gaze on the ground, focusing on nothing in particular. I was aware of Cam and Cass acting in a similar manner, the guards having to actually prod Cass in the back several times in an effort to keep her moving. I would have been amused at how good an actress she had become, had the situation not been so serious.

Eventually, we reached the lower end of the woods. As the trees thinned out, I realised that we were approaching the square where the Transfer Ceremonies took place. Clearly Adams wanted the execution to be as public as possible. By the time we reached the square, I was trembling. We were directed to sit under a tree at the rear of the stage so we could not be seen too early by the people being gathered in front of it.

The guards had spoken little as we had made our way here, but once we were in place, they checked our bindings again and retreated a little distance away, talking in quiet tones. In the background, we could hear the sounds of other citizens arriving: the pounding of feet, the sharp commands from the Shadow Patrol who were directing people, the shifting of those already in position.

I risked a glance at Cam, who was slumped against the trunk of the tree in a very convincing portrayal of near-slumber. A moment later, he seemed to feel my eyes on him, and raised his own to meet mine for just a fraction of a second. His eyes warmed and he slid his hands slowly to the seam of his overall jacket, fingering the place where I knew the scalpel blade to be concealed, but not removing it.

The guards had not patted us down as we had predicted, presumably satisfied that we had been searched for weapons when we were captured. I wondered for a moment about trying to retrieve the blade from my trouser seam while no one was looking, but a glance over at the guards in charge of us warned me not to. They were relaxed, and believed we were drugged, but their eyes still flickered over to us every few minutes, and I knew a purposeful movement would be a mistake. Cam's gesture was merely a symbol of encouragement and hope.

Cheered by his positivity, I began mentally running through all the defensive moves we had been taught in our time with McGrath and Hughes and wondering which would still be effective with my hands bound. For now, the idea was to simply get away from the stage and as far from the guards as possible until we could free ourselves and get hold of a better weapon. I knew that we'd be useless unless we managed to get our hands on something we could fight back with. I said a silent prayer that Anders had managed to arm the rebellious citizens with something more dangerous than their fists.

From where we were sitting, it was difficult to see the whole of the stage. Adams had talked of the execution, but not stated what form it would take, and another thought which had haunted my dreams had been the method he might use. The only public execution I had ever seen had been Wade's. When Adams had instructed that she be made an example of, Carter had stabbed her in the chest with a knife. I shivered a little, wondering how I would cope with such pain.

My thoughts were interrupted by the arrival of some additional guards, one of whom was indeed carrying a large knife. Behind these guards came a smaller knot of people which contained Adams and Carter. They came to a stop directly in front of us.

"All in order?" Adams asked one of the guards who had

brought us down from the cells.

"Yes, Sir. They haven't given us any trouble at all."

"Just look at them," another of the guards sneered. "The mighty rebellion."

"Look at them now," Carter crowed, giving Cass' foot a sharp kick. "Completely tamed."

She bent closer to Cass and hissed something in her ear. For a moment, I was terrified that my friend would lash out, but she remained remarkably still. As Carter leaned away from her, I breathed again.

"Not so tough now, are you?" she sniggered. "Just like your little friend Wade in the end. And we know what happened to her."

I could feel how badly Cass wanted to strike her, but kept my eyes almost closed, hoping desperately that my friend could keep her cool for another few seconds.

Adams seemed to tire of Carter's taunting and cleared his throat impatiently. He turned to the guards, gesturing at the ropes which bound our hands.

"Untie them."

The guard closest to me looked confused. "But—"

Adams held up a hand to stop him. "The drugs have done their job. I want the crowd to feel like they've given up." He pointed at Cass. "No restraints, but they don't even struggle. Show that lot out there that their little *rebellion* is dead."

"Shall we accompany them on to the stage, then?" another guard asked.

"Sure. If you think it's necessary." Adams sounded irritated. Clearly, he didn't think there was any chance of us fighting back, and I had to fight to prevent myself from glancing at Cam. "I hardly think they'll cause any trouble now."

He nodded to Carter, and as the pair moved on, I heaved a sigh of relief. When I caught Cass' eye I could see the fury that the female Superintendent's comments had provoked, but she kept her body in check, remaining limp and docile, even as the guard bent to untie her bindings. I suspected she would be the first to lash out at Carter, her thirst for revenge understandably strong, but I was proud of my friend's self-control.

The sounds from the other side of the stage had grown louder, and it was clear that almost everyone was here now. After a last nod from the guards who had finished removing the ropes and forced us to our feet, Adams and Carter made their way onto the raised platform. The crowd was immediately silent.

"Good morning citizens," Adams began, his voice ringing out over the square. "I have called you together to witness a momentous event. As you know, over the past few months, our community has suffered. The terrible sickness which swept through our community has taken its toll. But today I am able, finally, to call together the strongest among us. Those who did not succumb to the illness. Those who had strength enough to fight it off. Those who have been under tremendous pressure, taking on the work of others who lay ill and dying. Today, at last, all those who have survived can begin to return The Beck to greatness."

I felt sick at his words, wondering if any of the citizens standing mute in the square believed them.

"I understand how frustrating this time has been for you all," Adams continued, "but you must understand that it was vital we kept those who were sick separate from the rest of the community while they were a danger to others." He swept an arm across the heads of the crowd in front of him. "I'm certain that you're anxious to ease the burden of work which has fallen on the Upper Beck citizens and the Minors who have been fulfilling your duties while you were recovering."

For the first time since he had reached the stage, he shot a glance in our direction.

"Before we can do that though, there is something else which must be dealt with." His tone grew more powerful. "You will be aware, I'm sure, that some months ago, a number of citizens attempted an escape from The Beck."

For the first time, there was a slight murmur from the crowd, as though the mention of our flight had stirred something in the remaining citizens. As Adams continued, I found myself being pulled to my feet and steered towards the stage.

"I say *attempted*," Adams gave a mirthless laugh, "though up until today, I'm sure that many of you thought they had succeeded. Well I'm here today to let you know that they have not."

I felt the guard's arms on my own and allowed myself to be guided up the steps onto the platform. Keeping the act up to the very end, I moved my feet slowly, as though I was walking through thick mud. Ahead of me, Cass was doing the same. As we reached the top, the whispers of the crowd grew louder. Our sudden appearance was having the effect Adams wanted. The muttering grew in volume as his words sunk in.

Cass and I were positioned next to one another on the far side of the stage, a guard remaining behind each of us. We were close enough to exchange a look, but not to touch one another. Adams glared at each of us in turn, then looked back at the people in front of him. His tone grew arrogant, no doubt enjoying the effect our appearance had on the crowd.

"Two of those very citizens stand before you today, and I want you to know what their *real* plans were." Another dramatic pause. "The sickness I mentioned, the one which almost wiped us out, was brought here by them, deliberately. And as I'm sure you agree, this kind of betrayal simply cannot be allowed. It must be punished in the most severe manner, to protect those of us who work hard, who are loyal, who follow the rules which are designed to keep us safe."

A chill ran down my spine as I listened. I had always had a healthy dislike of Adams, but, in the old days, his words had been delivered under a veneer of pleasantry. This man was different, barely disguising his threats at all. My legs shook as I stared down at the wooden platform beneath me. Memories of Wade's brutal execution flooded my mind.

Raising my head slightly, I began to see the faces of the crowd, their horrified expressions reflecting their devastation at our capture. Without moving my body, I ran my eyes slowly along the line of people as far as they would go without alerting the guard at my back to what I was doing. Just below me, in the second row back, my eyes locked on a pair of eyes which flared with the same fury as mine.

The face was vaguely familiar. It took a moment, but eventually I placed her. It was a long time ago now, but back in Minors we had sometimes mixed with the younger citizens: passing them on the way to our shifts, helping to train them, eating meals beside them in the canteen. Some of their faces became more familiar to us than others. I remembered this girl distinctly from my final day in Minors, when I had been about to leave for the Ceremony which would mark me as an adult member of The Beck.

Unlike the others, who had been happy to wish us well as they sent us off, she had seemed upset. So much so that I had asked her what was wrong. Through tears, she'd told me about a friend of hers who hadn't been seen for several days. At the time, I remembered dismissing the girl's fears, being certain that she was wrong, that her friend would turn up. Knowing what I knew now about the way The Beck was run, I doubted that anything good had happened to the friend she was searching for.

"Today, I want to show you these deserters for what they really are." Adams' next words broke into my thoughts. "Show you how they returned, not to save you, but to hurt you. I want to let you know... actually let you *see*, what happens to citizens who believe they can abandon or attack their friends and allies in The Beck without consequences."

Tuning out his empty words, I searched my mind for the girl's name. Freeman. She must have been brought up from Minors early, one of those to fill the gap in the workforce caused by the sickness. She was skinny, and too young to be here, working hard at a job she was barely qualified for. But she had lost the teary-eyed look of innocence I remembered so clearly. The barely veiled anger in her eyes told me that, despite her youth, she was one of the ones on our side.

I forced myself to remain expressionless, only widening my eyes slightly in an attempt to show my gratitude. She was too smart to show any visible sign of recognition, but something flashed in her own eyes as she stared up at me and I knew she understood. Hope burned in my chest as I waited for Adams' next words.

"I want to rebuild our community, strengthen it, so we are

able to move forward. But with the threat of these deserters hanging over us, I don't feel that we can." The murmuring ceased as Adams turned again to glare at me. "So today, as a symbol of our reunion and the rebuilding of the society and the ridding ourselves of those who seek to weaken and destroy us, there will be a number of executions."

A ripple of fear ran through the crowd, but Adams hadn't finished. He held out a hand for silence.

"I say a number, because it isn't only those who have escaped The Beck and travelled to places further afield who we have to fear. Oh no. Some rebellion comes from within. So, in addition to these two..." he almost spat the next word, "*traitors*, we also need to deal with a citizen who will be familiar to many of you. A citizen who has never left these shores, yet who has been attempting to plot resistance from within the very woods which surround and protect us." He paused again as the frightened murmurs returned.

He turned in the opposite direction and nodded at another guard, who began to bring Cam up onto the stage. My heart lurched as his feet shuffled slowly up the steps and he was guided into position on the opposite side of the platform. His hands were limp at his sides, his head was lowered and his eyes stared down at the wood of the platform beneath us. He looked utterly defeated. The citizens gasped out loud now, and again I had to credit Adams with a dramatically effective performance.

Sensing he had an advantage, he pressed on. "I'm sure many of you have come into contact with Cameron. He seems, on the surface, a model Beck citizen. However, recent information has come to light which leaves no doubt as to where his loyalties lie."

The crowd's reaction was evidence of the great admiration and affection they had for Cam as Resistance leader. Adams knew it, and this was exactly why he was being made an example of. Brutally executing Cam in front of his supporters was a stroke of genius. With their leader dead, the Resistance would be devastated, and many of the ordinary citizens who had been persuaded to join him would be too frightened to do so again in the future.

But Anders' words came back to me. There were many citizens in that crowd who, like Freeman, hated Adams. Who wanted to oust him as much as we did. These people had been left to die, and now their leader was expecting them to spring into action, working themselves to the bone again for the good of the 'many', which, in reality, meant the good of the few at the top. While these people were scared, at least some of them were prepared to stand up and do something about it.

When those few led the way, hopefully others would follow. I felt a sense of determination take hold of me as Adams went on, waving another arm wildly above the crowd.

"To conclude, all three of these citizens are guilty of defying Beck rule. They have demonstrated, among other things, violent conduct towards those who seek to protect us," he nodded at the Shadow Patrol either side of the stage, "they have shirked their Sector duties and run away from a place to which they owe their lives. And, as a recent mission to infiltrate their new home has demonstrated, they directly threaten the lives of all Beck citizens." He paused and jabbed a finger pointedly out into the crowd. "That means *you*, with their greedy desire to take over here and run our community for their own ends."

I didn't know why, after everything he had done, I felt shocked by his lies. My heart sank. Clearly, he was trying to fool his citizens into believing that *we* were the enemy. I hoped desperately that most of them would be able to see through him. In fact, the list of crimes he was blaming us for could just as easily be applied to his own governing body. As I struggled to keep my expression blank, I vowed to be ready when Anders made his move.

Feeling the heat emanating from the solid body of the guard who stood directly behind me, one hand on my right shoulder, the other around my left wrist, I shifted slightly. His hands tightened automatically at my movement. This man would be the first I would have to fight. I had already noted that his gun was in a holster at his waist, and that he would waste precious seconds taking it out. When the time came, if I acted fast, I could escape from his clutches before he had the chance to even aim it at me, let alone fire.

Beside me, Adams was working up to a big finish. "Citizens, today marks the end of *any* talk of rebellion. All three of these citizens, these *ex*-citizens, will die. And once their executions are over, I'm certain you'll see how vital it is that we all work together, as a single, united society," he jabbed a finger at the people in front of him, punctuating each word, "to strengthen and defend our home."

He took a deep breath and stepped forward. "Well, the moment has come."

Adams cast a glance at Cam, then turned his eyes in our direction. Nodding at the guard who stood behind Cass, he gestured for her to be brought forward. My admiration for her acting skills grew as Cass allowed herself to be moved to the very centre of the stage with no sign of resistance. When

Adams was certain that the eyes of the entire crowd rested on her, he began to speak.

"Citizen, you are aware that you have done wrong, and as a result must suffer the consequences."

For a moment, I wondered if he was going to execute her himself, but then he nodded at Carter, who took the knife from the Shadow Patrol guard and strode forward.

"You will be executed by the knife, a fittingly violent end to your own violent rebellion against our society's rules." He took a step back, as Carter stepped forward. "Superintendent Carter, if you would."

I held my breath, unable to prevent my gaze from snapping to Freeman, the only person in my sight who might know when the distraction would occur. I felt the hand on my shoulder press down with more force and made myself relax again. We'd been instructed to wait, had trusted that Anders knew what he was doing, but now that Cass had a knife to her throat, terror swept over me. What if the distraction was delayed? What if we had come all the way here, docile and meek, hoping for salvation that never came?

My eyes met Freeman's as Carter positioned herself to one side of Cass, readying the knife for use. She nodded imperceptibly, as though to reassure me.

And then the stage behind me exploded.

For a few seconds, I was unable to work out quite what had happened. There was a sharp ringing in my ears, and the smoke that enveloped the stage clouded my vision. But as I glanced backwards, I could see that the disturbance had come from behind. Close enough to have a dramatic effect on those of us standing on it, plus the crowd beyond, but not enough to hurt any of us. This was surely Anders' distraction, and the reason, perhaps that he had been nowhere in sight so far today.

For a second, the guard behind me had relaxed his hold, but now he had recovered from the shock, he grasped hold of me once more. Acting quickly, I twisted and dropped as low as I could, silently thanking McGrath for teaching us the defensive movements that worked when an opponent had the advantage of size. The guard shouted in alarm, and I felt his hands brushing against one of my legs as he groped blindly, trying to work out where I was.

Feeling for the edge of the stage with one hand, I thrust myself to my feet and snapped my leg out in what I hoped was the right direction. I heard a yell of pain as my foot made contact with something hard, his knee perhaps, and I heard a thud as he buckled, dropping to the platform. Wasting no more time, I moved out of range before he recovered.

Now I was free of him, I became aware of the world around me again.

Chaos reigned. My heart thundering in my chest, I thought immediately of Cass, and the knife which had been held so close to her throat the last time I had seen her. Carter would not let this setback stop her. Taking advantage of the smokescreen, I moved towards the centre of the platform. I grasped around blindly, but there was no trace of her.

The noise around me had intensified. Immediately after the explosions, there had been a silence broken by nothing but the ringing in my ears, but now other sounds emerged from the confusion: heavy breathing, grunts, thuds and thumps, and the occasional strangled scream. I took a few more tentative steps, hoping I hadn't totally lost my bearings, and my foot bumped against something very solid.

Instinctively, I grasped hold of it, though it quickly slipped from my grasp, rolling in the opposite direction. An arm. Something slammed into me, and I bent to try and see what it was. On the ground, grappling like a couple of wild animals, were Carter and Cass. I reached out, trying to lend Cass some assistance, but they were thrashing around so violently that I couldn't guarantee anything I hit would be attached to our enemy.

There was no sign of the knife. Instead, the two women fought with their bare hands: punching, slapping, scratching. Cass was the slighter of the two figures, but she was wiry, and determined. Several times she slid out from under the older woman, only to roll on top and underneath her again. I realised she was trying to tire Carter out, a technique we had been taught by Hughes. Keep your opponent moving for long enough and they'll weaken. I only hoped Cass had enough fight in her to outlast Carter. Circling the pair, dodging Cass' Shadow Patrol guard who was stumbling around clutching hold of a head that streamed with blood, I tried to get into a position where I could help my friend.

But in the end, she didn't need me. As I watched, she continued to wrestle with Carter, again allowing the other woman to get the upper hand and roll on top of her. To my horror, she seemed to give in for a second, her arms going limp in Carter's. Surprised, the Superintendent loosened her hold, and Cass grabbed her chance.

Twisting to one side, she doubled over, ducking out of Carter's reach with the unexpected move. As the older woman recovered herself and moved forward again, Cass seemed to fumble with her boot. I began to panic, but suddenly she grasped hold of something I couldn't see, brought it across her body and drove it upwards, deep into Carter's chest. The other woman struggled, a startled expression crossing her features before she let go of Cass altogether, her hands clutching uselessly at the hilt of the silver scalpel.

Finally, she collapsed forward on to Cass and lay, motionless.

Chapter Thirty Three

For a moment it seemed like time had stopped. Carter was dead. But then I took in her position, slumped over Cass' body, her weight pinning my friend to the ground. Dashing forward, I took hold of Carter's arm and hauled with all my might. It took some doing, but eventually I moved her far enough, and Cass was able to crawl out from underneath. She surfaced, gasping for breath, her face pale, the whole of her chest soaked scarlet with blood. She stared down at the other woman's body, her eyes huge.

We needed to get out of here. From our position at the rear of the stage I had not been fully aware of what was happening, but now I stopped and gazed in wonder. The area beneath the stage was slowly coming into view as the smoke cleared. Clearly frightened by the explosion, some people had run away, and more still were hovering uncertainly on the sidelines. But a small, determined few, were actually fighting. Some with large wooden staffs that must have been hacked out of tree branches, a few with knives, and even more armed with nothing but large rocks, they had headed straight for the Shadow Patrol and attacked.

In response, many of the Shadow Patrol had leapt down from their elevated positions, which had gone a long way to reducing the threat upon the platform itself. But there were still a few enemies up here too. There was no sign of Cam or Adams, but there were at least two Shadow Patrol, struggling with a small band of Resistance citizens who had clearly been specifically instructed to defend us.

We needed better weapons, but there were none within our reach here.

"Cass!" I called out to my friend. "Cass, let's go."

She didn't even register my voice, but continued to stare in horror at the blood on her hands and clothes. Behind her, the Shadow guards had managed to strike down two of their Resistance assailants. I watched as one of them heard me call out and, leaving his companion to fight off the remaining two citizens who were not heavily armed, he headed straight for us.

It was time to leave. Grasping Cass by the hand, I leaned close to her ear. "Move. Now!"

I tugged at her hand, and said a silent thank you as she came without a struggle. Together, we raced across the stage and down the steps. I glanced around, searching for Cam, but could see no sign of him. He had been on the far side of the stage, and could easily have taken the other exit. I knew that he wouldn't have stood still for long after the explosion, so I could only assume that he had made it to safety. Cass and I needed to find somewhere safe too. And fast.

But where? My mind raced over the possibilities. Patrol would be a good place to find a weapon, but it was a good distance from here. It had been so long since I had been at The Beck that I wasn't sure of where the quarantine was situated, nor whether it would be a good place for us to hide. The woods perhaps, were an option, but I was certain that once Adams regained control, he would commission a search of them. We wouldn't be allowed to escape him easily.

The Shadow Patrol guard was still hot on our heels and had now made it to the bottom of the steps. Glancing around, he spotted us and I knew we were out of time. I was about to turn and run into the woods, hoping we could lose him there, when a figure leaped in between us, a large wooden club in hand. The Shadow guard stopped, startled, but was too late to throw his hands up to protect his face from the blow which collided with it. He collapsed sideways, hands to his head, a scarlet wound emblazoning his forehead. When he hit the ground, he didn't get up.

Hope surged through me as the figure who had saved us turned. It was a Lower Beck citizen named Duff. I had met him what seemed like a long time ago now, helping a friend of his called Lewis, who had been badly injured in a chemical spillage. Duff was clearly one of the ones who had survived the sickness, but I knew he had as much reason as I did to hate those in charge. Anxious to remove us from harm's way, he pulled hard on my arm before heading off into the woods. Nodding to Cass, I followed suit.

He led us into the trees via a different route, snaking in through some tangled roots which took some time to clamber over. I felt my hands and arms becoming scratched and sore from the branches that whipped against them, but knew that this less-travelled route would be safer. Checking every now and again that Cass was behind me also slowed me down, but I was frightened about her state of mind and didn't trust that she would follow.

Duff did not afford us the same consideration. It was difficult to follow his retreating figure as he got farther and farther ahead. When he did look back, very occasionally, I could see the frustration on his face. I waved a hand to show him we were on our way, and he set off again, keeping up the punishing pace. Behind us, the sounds of struggle faded.

Eventually, we broke through a particularly dense section of bushes and reached a small clearing. I helped Cass out of the foliage and we crouched on the ground, panting. Seconds later, I realised that we were not alone. Crouched on the other side of the space, a relieved expression on his face, was Cam. I dived across the clearing and flung my arms around him, holding on so tightly that we fell sideways, ending up in a tangle of limbs on the ground.

Duff cleared his throat. "No time for that, I'm afraid."

We pushed ourselves to our feet.

"Sorry. And thanks." I managed. "It's Duff, isn't it?"

"Yes." He smiled a little in recognition. "You remember?"

I nodded.

"Just repaying a favour."

"Is she ok?" Cam gestured to Cass, bending a little closer to my friend, whose face was still drawn and white. "What happened, Cass?"

She didn't reply. Anxious eyes rested on her pale face as I attempted to explain her condition.

"She... um... we were attacked, and had to fight back... she... " I faltered.

"She stabbed Carter," Duff's voice echoed his pride. "I saw it happen."

I watched as the expression on Cam's face changed. "Cass! Wow, I mean..." He glanced between Duff and me. "Is Carter–?"

"Dead?" Duff's expression was grim. "Yes. I'm pretty sure

335

she is."

"And Cass... are you–?" Cam turned to me, concern on his face. "Is she–?"

I shook my head. "I don't know. It's obviously..." I glanced down at Cass.

"Listen to me." His expression determined, Cam bent close to her. "This is it. We can't fail now."

Cass continued to stare into space.

"Look around you," he continued. "There are so many of us prepared to do something now... to stop Adams..."

He broke off, glancing at me worriedly. I shrugged, unsure how to snap her out of her current state.

"Look, Cass," Cam tried again, taking hold of her by the arms. "When I first came across you on that wall, you were prepared to go to any lengths to protect your friends. The girl I met that night was fierce and determined. You need to find her again. Because now, more than anything, we need everyone we've got."

Finally, she turned to look at him, blinking slowly.

"Cass, if we can arm you with a weapon, are you up to joining the fight?" Duff said softly.

A silence followed his words, and for a moment I thought they'd had no effect, but then, slowly, something seemed to come into focus in Cass' eyes.

"M'ok," she mumbled, turning to look at us, blinking hard. "Sorry. I'm... I'm ok now."

Cam smiled, and Duff heaved an audible sigh of relief. I wasn't sure that my friend's words rang true, but at least the fixed expression had faded, and she seemed able to speak again.

"Good." Cam stood up, seeming to have no time to make

sure of more. "Ready to go back, then?"

We nodded. Cam held out his hand briefly and pulled me to my feet. He held on an instant too long before letting go. Duff helped Cass up, and we turned to face one another.

"What now?"

Cam turned to Duff. "You know what the plan was?"

Duff shrugged. "We were told to wait for Anders' explosion, which would happen the moment one of the prisoners was about to be executed, then fight like hell."

"And after that?"

Duff shrugged. "That was pretty much the gist of it for most of us. Attack the Shadow Patrol and take down as many as possible. Try to persuade others to join in. There were a few people with more specific orders: to protect the youngest, to engage the leaders in combat. But most of us were just told to arm ourselves as best we could and fight."

Cam looked thoughtful. "Have you seen Anders?"

Duff shook his head. "Not since yesterday. He passed the order round via others. We had to communicate it between ourselves. I never actually spoke to him."

"But the main fight was focused on the square?"

"Yes. The Resistance knew that the largest concentration of Shadow Patrol would be there."

It made sense. If we took out large numbers of Shadow Patrol from the outset, we would stand a far better chance of success.

"I'm guessing the main targets are Adams, Reed, Carter?" Cam continued.

"Yes." Duff's eyes came to rest on Cass again. "And you already took care of one of them."

She didn't seem to notice. I took her hand and squeezed it.

337

"You ok?"

"Sure. Well, I'll have to be, won't I?"

"We should get back to the square and join the fighting. It's all we can do at the moment. We need weapons, though." Cam glanced at Duff. "Any ideas?"

Duff looked worried. "There was a small stash of knives." He reached down and pulled something from his boot. "I managed to snag this one, but I don't think there were any left." He brandished the club with which he had felled the Shadow Patrol earlier. "A stout branch, maybe?"

"I think that's probably the best we can do for now," I agreed with him.

Though clearly not wanting to give up his own weapons, Duff was willing to let us use his knife to create weapons of our own. We searched until we found several limbs which had fallen from the trees. Making sure they were heavy enough to do some damage but not too cumbersome to carry, we stripped off any remaining twigs and attempted to sharpen the ends. Once we were all armed, Duff replaced the knife in his boot and led the way back through the undergrowth, Cam right behind him, Cass and I taking up the rear. We crept as silently as we could back to the square.

As we approached, it seemed quiet. Too quiet for a battle-field. We skirted the edge of the area until we were hidden in a clump of trees which would conceal us but give us a better view of the area. Once there, we peered out through the tree branches. I let out a breath which I realised I had long been holding, and tried to calm my thundering heart.

Hearing Cam's hissed expletive in front of me, I crept to his side to get a better view. Ahead of us, the square was still filled with people, but now they were separated into two groups. One cluster of people stood on the fringes, cowering to the back and sides of the square, frozen in fear. These were the ones whose terror had prevented them from joining the fight. They were safe, for now at least.

The other group was distinctly smaller. Gathered in the very centre were around sixty people. Surrounding them was a ring of around ten Shadow Patrol guards, who had clearly managed, despite the fighting, to round up those who had tried to rebel. They each had a rifle aimed at their prisoners. A quick glance around the rest of the area told me that, whilst there were a few Shadow Patrol bodies scattered across the stage and the ground in front of it, the number of ordinary Beck citizens lying dead was far larger.

Now the remaining few who were willing to fight had been rounded up and were at Adams' mercy. And, armed with nothing but rough tree branches and a couple of small blades, there was little we could do to help them.

Adams and Reed stood centre-stage, a knot of Shadow Patrol guards surrounding them. Our leader's face was steely.

"It is clear that some of you still think resistance is worth pursuing. I am here to show you it is not."

He pointed a finger at the small group of people who stood in front of him. The Shadow guards prodded guns into their backs and thrust them up to the area beneath the stage.

Adams continued. "We may have lost sight of those traitors we were going to execute this morning, but I assure you they will be apprehended. And in the meantime, you can still see what happens to those who attempt to resist."

The rebellious citizens were moving towards the stage as slowly as possible in an effort to delay proceedings and no doubt frustrate Adams. The Shadow guards began to increase the pressure on them, prods with guns turning into stabs, and eventually to blows to the head. The rest of the witnesses waited with an air of silent dread as the group reached the stage.

When it did, Reed dispatched two guards down the steps. They grasped the closest Resistance citizen and hauled him up the steps. A second later he was standing on the platform in front of the entire crowd, Adams on one side of him and Reed on the other. I didn't recognise the man, but Duff's sharp intake of breath beside me told me that he did.

"You think you can take me on?" Adams' words were a threatening hiss.

The man opened his mouth to respond, but was rewarded by a sharp crack across the skull with Reed's rifle. He staggered sideways, but managed to right himself as Reed beckoned across a Shadow Patrol guard to secure him.

"You cannot," Adams spoke sharply, turning once more to the crowd who were hovering in the shadows at the sides of the area. "No one can. And, as I said earlier, traitors will not be tolerated."

He stepped back and nodded curtly at Reed, who took a step back, raised his gun to the man's temple, and fired. Instantly, the man slumped to the ground. I felt Cam tense beside me, and Duff slammed a hand into the ground. Two of the Shadow guards grasped the fallen man by the arms and hauled him to one side of the stage as Adams continued to speak.

"Everyone who picked up a weapon today and fought against those who work to keep this society running will be executed." He waved another hand at the guards waiting at the side of the stage. "Bring more of them this time."

A further ten Resistance citizens were forced onto the stage.

To my horror, I recognised Freeman among them. Many of the group struggled, kicking out and shouting, but they were quickly silenced by a smash over the head from a Shadow Officer's baton. One woman collapsed after such a blow, and did not get up. She was quickly replaced by another prisoner from the waiting group. Eventually, they were lined up across the stage, either staring down at their feet or glaring defiantly at the crowd in front of them.

Cass and I clung together, cringing, as Adams positioned one Shadow Guard behind every pair of Resistance citizens, their guns primed to shoot them both in quick succession. Soon, there would be ten more dead bodies on the stage. The crowd around the edges of the square was already beginning to shrink back, whimpering and even crying aloud at the prospect of so many deaths. I couldn't help but share their fear. And, in the back of my mind, I knew that those who might have been prepared to resist earlier would be far less likely to do so with every shot which rang out from the stage in front of them.

Adams knew what he was doing.

"You will see how defiance of this kind will get you nowhere," Adams called. "Only by following our rules can our society survive, thrive, prosper."

He gave the signal for the Shadow guards to ready themselves. Five guns were raised into position. Five fingers hovered on triggers.

"On my count." He turned to face the remaining citizens ahead of him. "Three, two, one. FIRE!"

A volley of shots rattled through the air. In neat orderly fashion, five of the citizens, spaced alternately along the line, collapsed. Those left standing turned pale as their comrades hit the ground. I could see Freeman sobbing uncontrollably at the sight of the people lying dead at her feet.

Adams shook his head, as though the sight pained him slightly. "And now for the rest."

He raised his hand again, readying himself. As he did, I closed my eyes, unable to watch. But the countdown never came.

Instead, a volley of shots, too many to execute just five citizens, came from somewhere behind me. I opened my eyes to find the five prisoners still standing, and the guards surrounding them glancing around in confusion.

As the familiar figures of Rogers and Mason emerged from the trees on the other side of the square, my heart soared.

Chapter Thirty Four

Confusion filled the square again, as our backup arrived. I heard Cam's shout of triumph as Rogers and Mason led a tight knot of citizens, all armed with guns, right to the centre of the square. I spotted Roberts, Jackson, and several other familiar faces among the group. Seconds later, McGrath came from the opposite direction, also followed by a number of the citizens I had been training alongside in The Ridge for so many weeks. My heart pounded when I noticed Baker in the midst of the group.

"We have to help them." Cam stood up and glanced around urgently.

Duff was also on his feet, brandishing his club. "I'm ready."

I placed a hand on Cam's arm. "We don't have proper weapons."

He grunted in frustration. "I won't let them fight without me!"

A noise to our left startled us all and we spun round, prepared to face a new opponent. The bushes rustled as something moved through them towards us. Cam motioned for us to crouch down and hide, the element of surprise being all we had. We all clutched our makeshift weapons and waited, as a voice drifted through the foliage.

"...approach from this direction..." The voice was familiar. "...flank them... surrounded...."

"Anders?" Cam hissed into the greenery.

The noise stopped as its owner froze.

"Anders!" Cam tried again.

The rustling continued, more slowly now, and a moment later a familiar face appeared through the undergrowth. Anders was followed by several others, some citizens whom I recognized from my days in Patrol.

"Cam!" Anders' face lit up. "You're safe!"

"Thanks to you!" Cam grinned at his ally.

"He made it then?" Anders peered past Cam, nodding at Rogers.

"You knew?"

He nodded. "Finally managed to get through to them last night after I left you. They were already on their way. They regrouped pretty quickly after Quin and Cass were kidnapped. Got straight into their boats."

I sighed with relief. "How many of them are there?"

"A fair few," Anders managed. "Not as many as there are Shadow Patrol, but with these as well..." he gestured at the group behind him, "...and any others we can persuade to join the fight again, well... we should at least stand a chance."

"Where have they come from?" I nodded over his shoulder at the group who had taken up crouched positions behind him.

"All Upper Beck, and mostly Resistance. People who saw what happened with the group who were in quarantine. Felt bad they received meds while the Lower Beck was abandoned to live or die with no support."

"And there are more of you?"

He nodded. "Will's guiding a second group in from the east side of the square and, if we're lucky, Harris might have managed to round up a few from Gov as well."

He turned to the citizens behind him. "Go ahead without me. You know your instructions. I'll follow in a minute."

We moved aside as his group rushed past us, shunting their way through the remaining foliage and heading out into the square with their weapons ready. In pairs, they fanned out across the space, moving swiftly and determinedly in the direction of the stage and its guards. It took several minutes before the citizens had all passed us by, and I marvelled at how many people Anders and Cam had managed to recruit.

When they were gone, Anders rummaged in the backpack behind him. "Got a few extra weapons here." He jerked his head over his shoulder. "Not as many as I'd hoped were prepared to join us." He brought out two additional guns and a small cloth bag, handing them to Cam. "Still, it means we can arm you properly now."

Cam nodded his thanks and held out a gun to Cass. "Take this. Go with Duff." He nodded at Duff's staff. "You ok with that?"

The other man nodded. "I've no experience with a gun. This will do me fine."

"Stay together. Use the smoke from the explosives to screen you as far as possible. Try to eliminate as many Shadow Patrol as you can."

He turned back to Anders. "I'll go with Quin. Anything I should know?"

"The aim is to take out the main players, like we planned. We're hoping that will be enough to stop the Shadows from continuing to fight. Without those in charge there to give orders, we're hoping the onslaught will stop."

Cam peered over at the stage again. "So, we're aiming for Adams, Reed, and Carter then?"

"Carter's already out," Cam informed him. "So, there's one less to worry about."

"That's great." Anders looked relieved. "How did you manage that?"

Cam nodded at Cass. "This one here took her on. And won."

"You took Carter out?" Anders appraised Cass with a look of respect. "Amazing!"

"I've had experience with her before," Cass muttered. "I know what she's like."

"Well she was a huge target, one we knew would be difficult to stop. Knowing she's already been dealt with.... well, let's just say you've saved us a job."

Cass shrugged, looking embarrassed. There was a pause, into which shouts and the sound of gunfire intruded.

"We'd better get going, hadn't we?" I murmured. "We'll need every citizen we've got."

Anders nodded curtly. "You're right."

"Quin and I will head for the far side of the platform, try to get up on the stage and see how we can help."

"Right." Anders nodded. "I'll go with these two then, take the left."

"Good luck." Cam slapped Anders' shoulder.

Cass reached across and gave my hand a quick squeeze, before racing from the bushes, her gun poised. Duff and Anders set off behind her. Thankfully, she seemed to have gotten over the initial shock of Carter's death. I hoped she could find enough strength to get through the remainder of the day.

We waited until they had made it some distance away, then Cam and I headed in the opposite direction. He went first, the gun cocked and ready to fire. We skirted the edges of the square, which was now packed with people fighting. It seemed that some of those who had been cowering at the edges of the area had been encouraged by the arrival of the promised support. Many of them had taken up weapons and joined the battle. Others, I suspected, perhaps the younger or weaker citizens, had seized the chance to run away. I hoped they had made it somewhere safe where they could hide until this was over.

We crept slowly forward, taking care when stepping over any bodies which were already on the ground, and slipping past Resistance citizens who were engaged in combat with the Shadow Patrol. As we began to make slow progress, I spotted familiar faces among the warriors. I briefly caught sight of Baker, concealed behind a tree in the woods at the side of the square. She was well hidden, and doing a good job of picking off Shadow Patrol whenever she had a clean shot. She hesitated as she saw us coming, and our gazes locked for a second. Slowly, she retracted her gun to demonstrate that it was safe to pass. I felt her gaze on me as I hurried by, but when I turned back a few seconds later she had begun firing at the Shadow guards again.

As we continued, we passed several other small skirmishes. I was surprised and relieved to see Hughes, one arm bandaged at the shoulder, fighting beside Green, and a little further away, Nelson and Tyler, tackling several more of Adams' guard. Thankfully, the number of active Shadow Patrol Officers in the area seemed to be reducing. Cam and I ducked past another group of our own citizens who were battling two seemingly unarmed Shadow guards. I was happy to see Roberts among them, fighting fiercely alongside Marley and Collins.

About halfway across the square, we came across McGrath, who waved us past impatiently as she took aim at a Shadow Officer who was reloading his weapon. Cam dodged out of her way, and I was about to follow when something went wrong. McGrath's expression flashed from triumph to panic, and she glanced with horror at her gun. Spotting her hesitation, the Shadow Officer seized the advantage. Thrusting his newly reloaded weapon at her, he pulled the trigger. I watched McGrath's face twist with pain as the bullet ripped through her body. She grasped a hand in front of her, fingers closing on nothing as she staggered forward. A small spot of red bloomed on her chest as I stood watching.

Finally, McGrath raised another hand as she sank to her knees. This time, it was in surrender.

Before she had even hit the ground, the Shadow guard turned to face a new opponent: me. For a moment, I froze. Then, as the guard raised his gun once more, I found the ability to move. Fumbling with the staff, made clumsy by my fear, I attempted to pull it round in front of me to fend off the attack. Behind him, I saw Cam falter. Realising the danger I was in, he swung round, raising his own gun in an attempt to protect me. But I knew he wouldn't be fast enough. The gun was almost level with my chest.

The guard raised his eyes to meet mine, and suddenly I recognised him. His name was Mitchell, and he was one of the Supers who had been assigned to Cass and Wade's Patrol training sessions after their Transfer. Whilst he was not someone I knew well, I had dealt with him in the past, sat alongside him in the canteen, and occasionally taken over from him on shift around The Beck. His promotion to Shadow Patrol must have been fairly recent.

"Mitchell!" I gasped.

I saw the flash of recognition in his eyes and, for a second, he faltered, his hand wavering slightly. It was all the time I needed. Swinging the staff across my body, I slammed it as hard as I could into the hand which held the gun. He yelped loudly as the heavy wood made contact with the fingers holding it steady and he dropped it in shock. As he bent to retrieve it, I readied myself again, balancing the staff in my hands and deciding where it could do the most damage.

The preparation was unnecessary. As Mitchell straightened up, Cam was right behind him. Smashing his gun against the side of Mitchell's head, we watched as he fell sideways heavily, landing with a thud on the wooden floor of the stage. Cam bent closer, readying his gun to fire a final shot which would finish Mitchell off, but I laid a hand on his arm, shaking my head.

"He hesitated."

Cam stared at me, a confused expression on his face

"Mitchell. He recognised me. And he hesitated." I stepped over Mitchell's body, taking Cam by the arm. "I don't think he was going to shoot."

"You can't be sure Quin, he's just as danger–"

"Well he can't kill anyone right now, can he?" I gestured at the man who lay still on the ground behind me. "Leave him. It's Reed we want, isn't it? And Adams. After that we're hoping the Shadows'll stand down, right? Give him a chance."

Cam frowned, but accepting my words, he turned and

continued towards the stage. This area was less densely packed with struggling figures, and it didn't take us long to reach the steps, where we looked for our major targets. Adams was nowhere to be seen, but we could see Reed crouching with several Shadow guards behind the wooden supports at the back of the stage. Rogers and Mason were advancing up the steps, their guns aimed at the group. Just behind them, to my surprise, was Thomas, though he was only armed with a baseball bat.

"They're closing in." Cam elbowed me, gesturing across at Walker and Jackson, who were armed and waiting at the opposite side of the stage. "He can't make a run for it that way."

We crouched at the foot of the steps, wondering how best to help our comrades. Bullets flew furiously in both directions, and I could see it was only a matter of time before both sides ran out. Realising this for themselves, three of the Shadow Officers beside Reed rushed headlong towards the trio at the top of the steps above us, taking them by surprise. Clearly, the guards were among those who had run out of bullets, as they all wielded knives.

Taken by surprise by this fresh onslaught, Rogers and Mason managed to recover themselves swiftly enough to fire repeatedly at the approaching enemy. Outnumbered and outgunned, two of them didn't make it. But the hail of bullets missed the last guard, and he leapt the last couple of feet, his knife outstretched. I heard Mason cry out as the blade pierced his arm. He recoiled from the attack in surprise, a look of agony on his face.

The Shadow guard took full advantage, pushing forward and attempting to drive the knife at Mason again. Cam raised his gun to fire at the enemy guard, but as he did, another figure leapt in the way, blocking the knife's progress.

It took me a moment to register, but the citizen who was now shielding Mason was Thomas.

Chapter Thirty Five

Time stood still as the Shadow guard tried to work out what had happened. Instead of his knife connecting with the softness of flesh, it had landed in the wood of Thomas' bat and was now stuck there. The guard attempted to free his weapon, panic crossing his features as he realised it was stuck fast.

I didn't want to think about how deeply embedded it was in the wood and what kind of an impact it would have had on Mason's body if it had made contact in the wrong place. Thomas' move had been extremely well timed, and his aim very accurate. If the blow had not hit the wooden shield, it would surely have made contact with his own flesh and caused just as much damage. But now the guard was stuck.

Realising his difficult position, he let go of the knife and took to fighting with his fists instead. This time though, taking the lone guard out was an easy task. Saving his ammunition for when we might need it more, Rogers used the butt of his gun to knock the guard out. When he stood back, all three of them were panting from the exertion. Thomas, looking slightly uncomfortable, wrenched the knife from his staff and tucked it into his boot.

Mason stepped forward. "Thomas, I... well, I–"

"No problem."

"But you don't even have..." Mason trailed off as he gestured at his own weapon.

Shrugging, Thomas turned away, his eyes meeting mine abruptly before jerking away to stare down into the square below.

"I'm out." Rogers had recovered himself and was checking his ammo stock. "But they must be too."

We all glanced up at the stage to see Reed's face blanch as he realised he had little left in the way of defence. There were only two Shadows left on the stage beside him now, and neither were firing their guns.

Rogers jerked his head at Cam. "You still have bullets?"

Cam nodded.

"Mason?"

"A couple."

"Together then?" Rogers turned to face Reed and his remaining protectors.

We walked up the steps slowly, joining the others to form a line at the top and steadily bearing down on what was left of the enemy. One of the guards stood bravely in front of Reed, wielding his knife in a hand which was shaking slightly. Cam fired his gun once, hitting the guard in the leg. He collapsed with a stifled scream. At the same time, the second guard was felled by a bullet from the opposite side of the stage. I turned to see Walker and Jackson, echoing our actions. Behind them came Will, who I was extremely glad to see. Between us, we advanced on Reed, cornering him at the rear of the stage.

Realising that this was it, Reed turned to face us. He had abandoned his gun, useless without bullets, yet he held a nasty-looking long-bladed knife in front of him and did not

353

look afraid. Given that some of us still had ammunition left, he didn't stand a chance. The cordon we had formed moved steadily towards him, flanking Cam, who raised his gun ready to fire.

"Do you honestly think you can beat us?" Reed's deep voice was sarcastic. "With all our ammunition? Our guards? Do you *actually* believe you can win?"

Cam paused, glancing sideways at Rogers, who had frozen, glaring at Reed.

"I remember you," Reed waved his knife at Rogers. "Used to be such a big man over here. A powerful soldier. You could've gone far. But you ran away. You and your little lady... *Green*, wasn't it?"

There was an audible intake of breath from Rogers, who was visibly shaking with anger. "We left, yes. But we came back. And we won't be running again."

A harsh laugh burst from Reed's throat. "You won't get the chance. Adams has more power than you can imagine. He'll get you. He'll get *Green*. He'll get all of you, in the end."

He took a step closer, daring us to shoot. Beside me, I felt Cam's arm tighten as he fingered the trigger.

But Rogers hadn't finished. "You'll die first though. You deserve to. After all you've done—"

He stopped talking. I could see his hands at his sides, and even though his fists were clenched, they were shaking. He seemed to fight for several minutes, trying to regain control. Finally, he lost the battle, leaping at Reed and totally obscuring Cam's shot.

There were several cries of shock as Reed and Rogers tumbled to the floor together. Reed's knife clattering out of his grip. I winced, as one of the men's heads slammed against the hard wood, though I couldn't be sure which one of them had suffered the blow. They grappled fiercely with one another, neither seeming able to get the upper hand. Again and again, Cam aimed his gun at the pair, but they were moving so rapidly it was impossible for him to fire and guarantee with any certainty that he would hit Reed and not Rogers.

Time seemed frozen, every single citizen, aside from the two men who continued to wrestle on the ground, standing still. Finally, Rogers managed to roll his body on top of Reed's and started to tighten his hands around the other man's throat. Reed struggled, writhing from one side to the other and attempting to find his weapon again, but Rogers had one leg either side of his enemy and was using his weight to pin his opponent down.

His face turned red as he fought to throw Rogers off, but we could see that he was weakening. His expression was one of panic, and for a man who had spent a lifetime forcing others to bend to his will, it almost seemed fair. Reed's eyes rolled backwards, as he fought to draw some breath into his exhausted lungs. Suddenly, Rogers loosened his hands from the choke-hold, and we saw Reed snatch a breath.

For a horrible second, I thought Reed might summon some kind of desperate strength and fight back. Rogers was clearly exhausted, and Cam moved towards the pair, ready to help his friend end it, but Rogers jerked forward and once again resumed the assault. Reed's eyes went wide with alarm, but his struggles were weaker now, and his movements slow. Finally, he collapsed backwards, and lay still, his eyes empty and staring at the sky. Only then did Rogers stop, sinking back on to his heels with a huge sigh of relief.

Will was the first to move towards him.

"Are you alright?" She bent over Reed's body and then nodded, confirming what was already clear.

Rogers sat back on his heels, his breathing ragged. For a moment, he stared down at the man lying dead in front of him. When Will placed a gentle hand on his arm though, he jumped and stood up abruptly.

"Two targets down."

Seeing the bleak look in our leader's eyes, Will tried again. "You had to, Rogers. *We* had to. It's not your–"

"Don't say it." Rogers' tone was harsh.

He stood still for a moment, his entire body tense. Around him, we waited for him to regain control. Eventually, he dragged his eyes from Reed's body and turned to call out across the square.

"All clear?"

Various Resistance citizens replied, confirming there was no further danger for the moment. There were certainly no more Shadow guards left standing in the immediate vicinity. One by one, the others wandered over to join us. I saw Hughes pause on his way, leaning over the body of McGrath. Once he was certain she could not be helped, he knelt down next to her, and took her hand in his. From this distance she seemed so frail and small. As he bowed his head close to hers, I felt a presence at my side and turned to see Tyler, shaking her head.

"It'll hit him hard, won't it?"

She sighed. "They've known each other for a long time."

I turned back to the stage to see Jackson fussing over Mason, a concerned look on her face. "Does it hurt?"

He groaned slightly but allowed her to help him up.

CHAPTER THIRTY FIVE

"Not that much."

"A likely story." Jackson helped him remove his jacket and pulled up the arm of his white undershirt. Baker, who had just arrived on the stage, came over to examine his wound.

"Not as bad as it looks." She nodded to Rogers. "We need to stop the bleeding though."

"I'll take care of it." Jackson tore off a strip of her own undershirt and began binding it tightly around Mason's arm.

Baker backed away slightly, avoiding my gaze now that we were in more close quarters. I wondered why, after all her protestations about not training with the soldiers on The Ridge, she had decided to come. As I did, my gaze was drawn back to Mason, who was wincing at the pressure Jackson had placed on the wound. He was still staring at Thomas in wonder.

"He jumped... he jumped in the way..." he gestured to the ex-prisoner, who had retreated alone to the far side of the stage, "...if he hadn't..."

He broke off, clearly surprised by the actions of the man we had ostracised for so long. I wondered if this was the reason Thomas had separated himself from the group. Anyone could see this was not the same man who had run away, stolen from his own community, threatened violence. Whilst Thomas was a difficult man to understand, it was clear that his punishment had changed him for the better.

The awkward moment was interrupted by the arrival of Hughes. His footsteps were heavy and slow, and his expression bleaker than I'd ever seen it. His gaze sought out Tyler, who was still standing next to me. Aware of his focus, she glanced awkwardly around at all the people on the stage. Hughes continued to look at her, his eyes empty. Eventually, she gave in to the impulse and approached the grieving man.

"I'm so sorry." She placed a tentative hand on his shoulder.

For a moment, he didn't move, but a second later he turned and thrust his arms around Tyler, burying his head in her neck. After hesitating for a brief second, she returned the embrace, wrapping her arms tightly around him as though she could erase the pain.

Rogers cleared his throat. "Right. Um... Sorry to push, but..." He ran a distracted hand across the top of his head. "Look, we need to take stock. We got Reed." He studiously avoided looking at the place where our fallen enemy lay. Instead, he gestured at the area in front of the stage, which had emptied out somewhat. "And I'm not sure where everybody went, but this definitely doesn't account for everyone. Anyone seen Adams. Or Carter?"

"Cass already dealt with Carter, before you arrived." I gestured to my friend, who was blushing. "I guess they must have taken her body somewhere else already."

Roger's eyes had widened. "That's great."

Again, he glanced out at the area below the stage, where a small group of Resistance had gathered and seemed to be waiting for further guidance. With them stood Roberts and Howard, who thankfully looked unscathed.

"Did anyone see where Adams went?" Rogers enquired.

Tyler broke gently away from Hughes and turned to the rest of us. "I overheard one of the guards calling something about a retreat."

"Did we take out a lot of the Shadows?" Will stared out across the area in front of her, which was mostly filled with those who were dead or injured. The only ones left were lying still on the ground.

"A fair few, I think, but as Rogers said, definitely not all of them." Jackson moved away from Mason now that she had finished tending to his wound. "I had a better vantage point than most. I'm pretty sure a large number of them disappeared at the same time as Adams. Presumably they had some kind of secondary plan."

Baker joined in. "She's right. They were here when we arrived, and several of them left at the same time." She glanced around the group. "Headed back into the woods."

Mason finished easing his jacket back on and turned to stare into the trees behind the stage. "Where would Adams retreat to?"

Putting some distance between himself and Reed, Rogers walked to the rear of the platform and gazed out in the same direction. "Somewhere well protected? Where he has reserve stores of ammunition, perhaps?"

As he spoke, I noticed another familiar figure emerge from the group below the stage. Her face pale and her hands stained scarlet, Green approached the stage and began to climb the steps. I heaved a sigh of relief to see that she was still alive.

"Looks like we dealt with all the Shadow Patrol in this area." Green looked exhausted, and I wondered how many Resistance citizens she had seen fall. She gestured to Collins, who had just finished securing a bandage around one of the Resistance citizens' legs. "We've done what we can to patch up those who have minor injuries for now at least." Her face clouding over, she moved to Rogers and took hold of his hand. "What's the plan?"

He sighed. "We're just trying to work out where Adams might have gone."

"I just heard some chatter from one of the Shadow's walkie-talkies." Collins called as she came to join us. "They're heading for Meds."

"What?" Green's head whipped around to face her fellow medic. "Like, there aren't enough people dead as it is, and he wants to put the most vulnerable people at risk?"

Cam found his voice at last. "Typical. He's running scared, so he takes a group of Shadows, probably his personal guard, up to Meds to hide out." His chest rose and fell rapidly as he fought for control. "Anyone seen Anders? He might know more."

"Here." Our friend and saviour had just appeared on the opposite side of the stage. "Adams was seen by several citizens going into the woods in the direction of the Upper Beck. But he definitely sent a second group of guards in the opposite direction."

Rogers and Cam continued to discuss possibilities. "You think Adams would go to Meds?

Anders gestured towards the Lower Beck. "Very possibly. It's a good place to defend, if you think about it. And I know there are stores of vital meds up there. Ones he'll want to protect."

Cam frowned, "And you said there was another group of guards?"

Anders nodded. "A smaller one, but yes. I think he sent them to Minors. And that would be a real problem. I instructed a good number of Beck citizens to retreat there during the battle. Those who I really didn't think were strong enough to fight. I figured they could hide there in relative safety until we had beaten Adams, and then we could go and release them. But if there's a posse of guards over there, the citizens will be difficult to get to, plus, their lives could be in danger, along with those of the children."

"Our main priority has to be Adams." Rogers paused at the expression on Anders' face. "But I can spare a few citizens to go over there with you and check it out, if you like."

Anders looked relieved. "Thanks. I'd appreciate it."

"What if he's sent the Shadows to Minors to *protect* the younger sector? To make sure that we don't get our hands on them?" Green said. "Even if he loses the majority of the adult population, he'll still have enough new bodies to populate The Beck in the future if he shields those in Minors, keeping the youngest citizens ready to step into the shoes of the ones who die today."

"You might be right." Rogers' tone was thoughtful. "So, I guess they wouldn't be in danger from the guards…"

"But I'm not sure he's thinking rationally right now," Anders pressed on.

Baker snorted. "He certainly isn't *acting* rationally.

"If he can protect Minors and get rid of us all," Tyler mused, "he can start again."

Jackson sighed. "It might even be what he wants."

"It might," Anders continued, "but I wouldn't want to leave them there with no protection."

"What next then?" Mason pushed himself to his feet, eager to act now that his injury had been dealt with.

"I guess we have to split up." I could see Rogers mentally adding up the number of soldiers he had left. "But the bulk of us has to go to Meds, focus our efforts on getting to Adams."

"Agreed." Hughes' expression was fierce. I knew that the deaths of the Ridge citizens and the loss of McGrath had made the fight personal for him. "Is there somewhere we can get hold of additional weapons? I mean, we left a store of ammo and a few extra guns hidden up in the woods, so we can restock, but it won't last forever..."

"Steal Beck weapons and use them against Adams, you mean?" Rogers looked interested.

"I could take a team to Dev." Cam jabbed a finger in the opposite direction and I thought of Montgomery's experiments. "I know they've developed certain... devices we could use, if we can get hold of some."

Rogers looked around at the group. "Alright. A small group to Minors. Another to Dev. The rest of us head for Meds, guard the entrance, and wait for the Dev group to return with additional weaponry."

"If his forces are split between Meds and Minors, he should be easier to defeat." Mason had rallied, and his expression was more positive now.

"But if his forces are divided, so are ours." Rogers cautioned, looking around at the assembled group.

"We've done ok so far, though," Mason tried again. "And if we wait for Cam to get back, we'll have the strongest force we can muster ready to attack Meds and–"

"Not attack." Tyler cut him off. "Remember, Meds is full of pregnant women and babies. It's the reason Adams has gone there."

There was a bleak silence as we considered the task which lay ahead. Eventually, Green was the one to speak.

"Tyler's right. Adams is selfish. But clever. An attack on the *esteemed* Beck leader needs to be swift and forceful. But an invasion of the Meds Sector..."

She trailed off, sighing, and Rogers finished for her. "Well, put it this way, we can't make any mistakes."

Chapter Thirty Six

With nothing else to be done, Hughes and Rogers got to work deciding which of us could be dispatched elsewhere without leaving the central team too vulnerable. Marley, Collins, Walker, and Howard were sent with Anders to Minors to protect the citizens who had retreated there, while Cam and I were directed, along with Roberts and Baker, to the Dev Sector to gather additional weapons. The plan was for us to rejoin the main group later, who would hold off on attacking Adams until we did.

Roberts' presence in the Dev team pleased me, but I wasn't sure how I felt about Baker coming with us. The four of us made our way to the compound as fast as we could, none of us mentioning how much we feared what we might find there. Cam strode ahead in total silence, leaving the rest of us to hurry in his wake. I walked alongside Roberts, feeling distinctly uncomfortable with Baker's presence, and concerned by Cam's strange mood.

When we arrived at the Dev Sector it seemed deserted. Instead of feeling relieved, the fact that there were no guards at this usually well-protected entrance made me nervous. Cam stepped up to the forbidding gate, which was closed as usual, took a pass out of his pocket and scanned it against the pad to the left of the entry.

"Where did you–?" I motioned to the pass.

"This? Oh, it belongs to Anders."

The gate clicked as it accepted Anders' access card. Cautiously, Cam pushed it open.

"Like I told you, Anders has been working over here since... well, since the sickness hit. People have been fairly mobile in terms of Sector while others were unable to work."

I felt a stab of guilt at bringing the illness here in the first place. "How many, I mean, in total how many citizens...?"

He turned to face me as he swung the gate shut and secured it behind us. "Dead? Over two hundred we think."

He turned away abruptly, wasting no more time. The rest of us fell in behind him, moving as quietly as we could. We approached the buildings slowly, our weapons raised. Before we had left the rest of the team, I had been armed with a gun, and the others had been able to restock their ammo from the supply in the woods. I couldn't decide if the cold, heavy hunk of metal I clutched in my hand made me feel secure or nervous.

Cam had reached the first unit, and waved a hand for us to wait as he used the card again to release the door. Pulling it open cautiously, he peered inside, then gestured for Roberts to cover him while he slid inside. A moment later, Roberts followed him in.

Baker and I were left outside alone. I glanced over to find her actually looking at me this time. She looked away as our eyes met, but I felt the avoidance of my gaze demonstrated her nerves rather than her displeasure at being around me. We waited in awkward silence as the two men moved around inside, and eventually returned to the front entrance, waving the all clear.

"Be careful won't you, Quin?" Baker gave my hand an unexpected squeeze, but I had no time to respond before she had hopped up the steps and into the building.

Ducking in through the door behind her, I was cautious not to make any sudden movements. Inside, the hallway was dark.

"Why aren't there any guards here?" I whispered.

Cam shrugged. "Not sure. I guess Adams has diverted them elsewhere."

We began walking down the corridor as a group, our eyes darting from one side to the other as we travelled.

"But aren't there..." I strove to make sense of it all, "... supplies here he'd want to protect?"

"You'd think so, wouldn't you?" The voice startled us.

Immediately on high alert, the four of us raised our guns and swung round as one. Striding towards us, her ice-blonde hair as perfect as usual and the obligatory mask pulled down around her neck so she could speak to us without difficulty, was Montgomery.

It frightened me to know that she had been in the building all along without us knowing. Despite noting that she didn't seem to be armed, I kept my weapon steady. She didn't seem fazed by the four guns which were all trained on her, though. Before any of us had the chance to respond, she continued.

"Well if it isn't the rescue squad. Good to see you, Cam. Quin." She gave me a brief nod before continuing to run her eyes across our group. "Well, *Baker*, I never thought I'd see you again."

I watched my mother's expression sour and wondered how well the two of them knew one another. Ignoring Baker's scowl, Montgomery's gaze came to rest on Roberts. "And who do we have here? *You're* not someone I know."

Wisely perhaps, Roberts chose not to respond. After a moment of silence, Montgomery continued, chatting as though the situation was a perfectly normal one.

"I suspect you're wondering why Dev is unguarded." She waved a hand airily. "Adams' decisions of late have been... somewhat erratic, shall we say. He's been moving a lot of resources around, *concealing* them in various places."

She came to a stop in front of us, her smile broad and her eyes flashing. Cam lowered the arm holding his weapon. After a few seconds, I reluctantly forced myself to do the same.

"Montgomery."

"Cam." She barely glanced at me. "Heard you got yourself into a little trouble."

He looked past her. "I did. But it's dealt with now, as you can see. I'm free."

"I see."

"What are you doing in here alone?" Cam peered at her closely. She didn't look at all perturbed, but I could see he was waiting to see a crack in her cool facade. "Are you hiding?"

"Hiding? Of course not." A jerk of her blonde head was the only suggestion of any nerves. She nodded to the door. "What's going on out there?"

Cam, his voice calm, continued. "A battle."

"Many dead?"

I found myself digging my nails into my palms to prevent myself from butting in at her cold tone. Beside me, Baker's body was rigid and I could feel curiosity radiating from Roberts.

Cam shrugged. "A good number."

"On both sides?"

"Yes. On both sides."

"I heard the noise." She shrugged. "And there's been a lot of chatter over the walkie-talkies this past couple of hours."

Cam and I exchanged glances. I wondered if bumping into Montgomery might well prove useful.

Cam took a small step forward. "So, Montgomery, we're here for a reason. Are you going to get in our way?" He deliberately tapped his gun against his palm.

Montgomery's gaze travelled to the gun, but didn't flinch. "Is Adams...?"

"He's not dead, if that's what you're asking. Not *yet*, anyway."

"I see." Montgomery looked like a snake trying to fathom how she might slither away without getting trapped. "And Reed?"

"Oh, *he's* dead."

The tiniest glimpse of panic crossed the scientist's face before she shut it down. "Carter?"

"Her too." Cam shifted his gun from one hand to the other. "But you didn't answer my question."

Montgomery seemed to make a decision. "I won't get in your way, no."

Cam's shoulders relaxed the tiniest bit. "And will you help us? We're after weapons. I know you have various... devices you've created... bombs, grenades and the like. Will you take us to them?"

"What's in it for me?" she purred.

This time Cam's step was not small, and he thrust his gun towards her as he spoke. "What's in it for you is that you don't end up dead."

Barely flinching, Montgomery took a step back and nodded. "Alright then."

She turned and began walking back down the corridor in the direction she had originated from. Cam looked startled, but didn't immediately move after her. She had reached the halfway point before she turned, her face a picture of innocence.

"Well?" Her voice was inviting, welcoming almost. "Are you coming?"

I glanced at Cam, who jerked his head at us to follow her. As we did, Roberts shot me an inquiring glance. Baker's eyes remained fixed on the retreating form of the scientist who she seemed to trust even less than I did. Moments later, we stood in a store room at the rear of the Dev building.

In the centre of the space, Montgomery waved a hand around at the mostly-empty shelving. "As you can see... there's not a lot left."

"Adams moved everything?" Cam strode to a cupboard at the far end of the room, hauling the door open and staring at the almost-empty shelves.

"He did, I'm afraid."

"Where to?" Baker took a menacing step towards Montgomery.

She sneered down at my mother. "I couldn't honestly say."

Baker grabbed hold of the collar of Montgomery's white coat and pulled her closer. "Or you won't."

For the first time, Montgomery seemed to lose her cool. Her usually pale face was flushed and she let out a small whimper at my mother's rough treatment. Baker pressed her advantage, placing the end of her gun against her temple.

"Where did he take it?"

Hands shaking slightly, Montgomery opened her mouth to respond. "He took most of it to Meds."

Behind her Cam shot a glance at me. This fit in with what we already suspected. She was, for now at least, telling the truth.

"Alright." Baker continued her interrogation. "Is there anything left here that we can use?"

For a moment, there was silence. And then Montgomery nodded.

"Now we're getting somewhere." Baker took a small step back, relaxing the pressure of the gun against Montgomery's head. "Take us to it."

"I don't need to take you anywhere." Montgomery stuck out a hand, pointing to the floor at the side of the room. "Underneath."

Baker jerked her head at Cam, who came forward. Together, he and Roberts pulled a shelf forward to reveal a tiny, circular hole in the floor.

"I've shown you I'm willing to work with you." Montgomery took a step away from Baker. "May I?"

Cam nodded, and Baker reluctantly released her. Taking a step forward, Montgomery slid a delicate finger into the hole and hauled up a trapdoor with surprising strength for so slight a woman. Once it was lifted, she secured it with a section of rope and gestured below, where a secret storage area had been revealed. It was packed with various boxes and packages.

"What's all this?" Cam bent to take a closer look.

"Personal supplies." Montgomery had backed a couple of paces away and allowed us to pull out some of the items in her secret haul. "Call it my insurance policy."

Hidden under the floor were a number of large bottles of meds, some syringes, and a good number of small, hand-held explosives. We had taken some of them from The Beck when we had first escaped, but I had yet to see their effect.

"You hid all this?" I spoke for the first time, shock making me blurt out the words before I could stop myself.

"Yes, I hid it." Montgomery turned slowly, gesturing at the gun in Baker's hand. "You never know when you might need something to bargain with."

Baker huffed out a breath with disgust, the gun still trained on the other woman.

"Look," Montgomery ignored the weapon, smoothing back her hair as she spoke, "I get it. You're here to take over... to eliminate those in charge. Let me help you." She gestured at the equipment in the storage area below. "I've amassed a lot over the past few months in preparation for... this kind of situation."

"Just what do you see happening here?" Cam's voice was steady, but I caught a hint of the anger he was keeping under control in his question.

"Cameron, this isn't the only place I have things stored. *Useful* things. Chemical weapons, meds, poisons..." Her voice trailed off almost seductively. "The list is endless."

Cam glared at her. "And?"

"We used to be friends. I can help you, Cam." She stepped closer to him. "Let me help you."

He didn't move away from her and I had to fight to stop myself from thrusting my body between them. "And in return...?"

"In return, you keep me safe. And allow me a place in the new Beck, whatever you decide is going to happen with it. I can be a useful person to have around. I'm very... *resourceful.*" She let her sentence trail off, her gaze lingering on Cam's.

"I'm very well aware of that."

"So you'll let me help?"

He snorted. "I don't trust you, Montgomery."

Her face flashed with fury for a brief second before she had it under control again. "Don't forget, there are many things I know how to do that..." she broke off and looked at me, and Baker, and back to Cam again, "...no one else does. Adams knows what an asset I am. You might want to keep me safe."

I thought of the various meds she was able to create. The infertility serum, which had the power to grant The Beck women the ability to bear children; the salve, which would have been capable of treating Lewis' chemical burns if she had allowed it; the drugs which had saved us from the sickness. Letting out a long hissing breath, I clenched my fists at my side, hating the fact that she was right.

I felt Cam glance briefly at me before turning back to Montgomery. "Alright. You may have a point. But that doesn't mean we trust you." He turned to the rest of us. "Let's take some of this. Just the things we can use, for now."

Baker stood guard over Montgomery again while Roberts moved to the trapdoor and began sorting through the various packages. Cam and I removed our packs and we began filling them with a number of the grenades and explosives which were stacked neatly beneath the floorboards.

"Let me help you." Ignoring Baker's gun, Montgomery smiled silkily and tried to move towards the trapdoor.

"No, thanks. I'm sure we can manage." The scientist yelped slightly as Cam grasped hold of her slender arm and tightened his grip. "You stay right there, where we can see you." He reached across to where I was leaning over the open hole in the ground. "There was some rope down there, Quin. Could you pass it to me?"

I reached for the rope and handed it over. As my fingers grazed his briefly, he looped his thumb around mine and held on for the briefest of seconds. When he let go, I immediately missed the warmth of his touch. Indicating that we should continue to pack up the explosives, he moved to Montgomery's side.

"You want us to trust you?" he continued, securing her hands tightly behind her back. "Then don't give us any trouble."

Roberts handed me the packs and hopped up out of the hole. Cam glanced over and I indicated they were both full as Roberts pulled the trapdoor back into place.

Shouldering his pack, Cam turned to his prisoner. "One thing I won't do is guarantee you *anything* until the situation with Adams is resolved. For now, you stay with us and you behave."

"Fair enough." I marveled at her ability to smile even in the bleakest of situations. "Shall we?" She nodded at the door and even took a step towards it before Cam caught hold of the ropes which bound her hands again.

I could see him seething at her arrogance, but he managed to control his reaction and nodded to the rest of us. "Let's go."

As we followed him, I feared that Montgomery might prove more of a burden than an asset.

Chapter Thirty Seven

A few minutes later we were standing outside the gates to Dev once more. Cam had handed Montgomery over to Baker for a moment while he moved away to contact Rogers on the walkie-talkie out of the scientist's earshot. While we waited, Roberts moved closer to me, dropping his voice so only I could hear him.

"Who *is* she?" He jerked his head towards Montgomery, who stood serenely gazing into the distance, ignoring Baker's pointed glare.

"She's a scientist who works here in Dev," I explained. "She's brilliant, but... well let's just say she doesn't always use her genius for good."

"Certainly doesn't seem like it," he muttered, eyeing Montgomery closely. "I don't like her at all."

"I don't know many people who do."

There was a pause, where I could feel him watching me before he spoke again. "Happy to be back with Cam, then?"

My gaze shot to the man who stood with his back to us, speaking into the walkie-talkie, his shoulders tense. I felt my face flushing, remembered conversations I had had with Ross and Roberts, where I had confided my feelings for the man I had left behind.

"I... um... we haven't really had a chance to..." I tailed off uncertainly.

"I don't think you've got anything to worry about." Roberts leaned closer, nudging me gently as Cam lowered the walkie-talkie and turned to walk back to us. "I've seen the way he looks at you."

I shot him a swift sideways look to silence him as Cam returned, oblivious to the topic of our conversation.

"Take over for a second would you, Roberts?" Cam jerked his head at Baker.

Roberts shot me a wicked grin as he went to relieve her. Taking advantage of the brief solitude, Cam took me by the elbow and led me a little way away.

"Are you alright?" I asked, while we waited for Baker.

"I will be when this is all over." He shrugged, his expression grim. "I just can't wait for a time when we can actually..."

He trailed off, frustrated, as Baker approached, and I found myself wondering how he would have finished his sentence.

"What's happening?" My mother was all business, as always.

"I spoke to Rogers, told him we had the explosives." Cam glared at our fugitive. "And that we were bringing a hostage along."

"You think Adams cares about her enough to want to save her?" Baker's tone was sceptical.

"Probably not, but she's right about being useful. To Adams, at least. That's why we can't leave her here. She's too dangerous." Cam turned back to us. "Ok, so the group led by Anders and Walker have already made it to Minors. There were only a few Shadow guards posted on the Minors gate, and they managed to take them down. They're either dead or imprisoned in one of the buildings down there now."

Baker gave a low whistle. "That's fast work."

Cam nodded. "Turns out there are *a lot* of people in Minors, and they're not just children. Many of them wanted to fight once they heard that Carter and Reed were already dead." He turned to give me a weary smile. "A lot of them have started believing in the Resistance again."

"They hadn't given up, then." I returned his grin. "And they'll join us? Fight?"

"I don't know about fight." He smiled wearily. "But Anders is in the process of arming some of the more able citizens. He's going to station them along the Minors wall and gate. Hopefully, it will free them up to help out elsewhere... I mean if they're able to leave those in Minors to look after themselves, for a little while, at least."

"That's good news," I blurted. "What's the situation in Meds, then?"

"Rogers and the rest made it up there without issue. No sign of Adams himself, but there's an extremely large number of Shadow Patrol covering the entrance." Cam paused and glanced at Montgomery. "Add that to Montgomery's confirmation that Adams has hidden lots of supplies up there, and it seems likely that's where he is. I'm certain he's gone there because he knows we can't launch a major attack without risking the lives of the women and infants."

Baker and I exchanged a disgusted glance, united in our hatred of the coward who was choosing to hide behind the most innocent members of his own society. We had to stop him.

"Good job we have these additional weapons then, isn't it?"

Baker gestured at the pack on my back. She paused, looking frustrated. "Shall we get going, then? We've a fair way to walk yet."

Cam nodded. "Look, I don't think we'll run into any trouble, but stay behind me, just in case. I'll take the lead. Quin, you assist Roberts with keeping Montgomery in check. Baker? You take up the rear. Don't let anything approach us from behind."

As he strode off in the direction of the woods, I hurried to join Roberts with our prisoner. Jerking my head to indicate that we should follow, we set off, and Baker fell into step just behind us.

We hadn't gone very far before Montgomery started to speak.

"Headed for Meds, then?"

I nodded, but didn't respond.

"You've been away for a while, Quin." Her tone was friendly, but I didn't let it fool me. "Been missing our Cam, have you?"

On the other side of her, I felt Roberts tug harder on the ropes which bound her. She winced slightly, and fell silent for a moment, her eyes fixed on the broad shoulders of the man who walked ahead of us.

Suddenly, she turned to face me. "You're together."

It was not a question.

Painfully aware of the presence of both Roberts and Baker, I played dumb. "Sorry?"

"You and Cameron. You're together, aren't you?"

I looked away.

"Ah you can refuse to confirm it, if you like." She chuckled. "But it's pretty obvious."

I had forgotten how shrewd she was. But I hadn't forgotten the unrequited feelings she had long held for Cam, which meant she watched him far too closely. Clearly, she had noticed the way we acted around one another, and put two and two together. Knowing how easy it would be for Adams to use the knowledge of our feelings for one another against us, I cursed her perceptiveness. Knowledge, as I very well knew, was power. And she had just gained some.

"I don't know what you mean–" I struggled to backtrack, stumbling over my words unconvincingly as a voice cut across me from behind.

"So, Adams is in Meds because he thinks it'll save him, is he?"

I glanced over my shoulder at Baker, who wore an unreadable expression. I wondered why she was bothering to speak to a woman she so clearly hated. Montgomery said nothing as she continued.

"I mean, I remember it well. Meds, I mean... it's difficult to access. That narrow opening, the cliff climb... Adams knows we'll struggle to get to him, and be cautious when we do."

Baker sounded almost chatty, which was totally out of character. I shot her another curious look. "I'm guessing that he's gone there because he thinks he can pick us off one at a time until there are none of us left."

"I suspect you're right." Montgomery sneered openly at Baker. "You always were clever."

Baker didn't reply. She met my gaze steadily, and I realised what her aim had been. Her incessant chatter had successfully diverted Montgomery's attention from me. I smiled, and after a short hesitation, she returned the gesture before dropping back again as we continued to make progress through the woods.

"Where is this Meds then?" Roberts enquired.

"Not too far." I paused, very aware of Montgomery's presence between us, but then decided that informing Roberts about the place he was approaching with no prior knowledge was of benefit to him, and nothing I said would be anything the woman beside me didn't already know. "Adams has gone there because it's full of vulnerable people. Pregnant women and the very youngest babies."

"What a hero." Roberts sounded disgusted.

"We'll have to be very careful how we go in. We can't just blast our way through without risking the lives of the mothers inside."

"I get it." Roberts glanced across at me. "What's the entrance like?"

"That's the issue." I sighed, thinking back to my one and only visit to Meds Sector, which felt like a lifetime ago. "It's pretty narrow, and will be easy for Adams to defend. He had a good head start on us. You can bet he's already hidden away in one of the buildings up there, with his best guards stationed at the main entrance to the Sector."

"Hush."

The command came from behind us, and I knew Baker was warning us to stop speaking in front of Montgomery. I shot an apologetic glance over my shoulder and was grateful to see that she didn't look angry, only worried.

I wondered again why she had come, and if it was because she felt differently about me now that she'd had time to get used to our connection. But this was not the time to ask.

When we were within sight of the path which led up to the Meds entrance, I heard her sharp intake of breath. Glancing back again, it hit me how difficult this must be for her. Returning to The Beck had been difficult enough for me, but Baker's memories were far more traumatic than mine.

I couldn't imagine how painful it was to revisit the very spot where she had given birth, the place where I had been wrenched from her so long ago. I kept my eyes on her, waiting until she looked up and met my gaze, hoping that the look on my face would convey my understanding and provide some sort of comfort to her.

Ahead of us we heard Cam hiss triumphantly, and I was the first to break the gaze.

I spotted what he had already seen. We had found Rogers and he was accompanied by lots of familiar faces: Mason, Tyler, Jackson, Nelson, Hughes, Roberts, Green, and Thomas among them. A few feet away in a slightly separate group stood Will, and a significant number of Resistance citizens who I didn't know.

As we got closer, Cam called over his shoulder to us. "Roberts, keep Montgomery back here a minute, would you?"

Montgomery gave a low chuckle. "He really doesn't trust me, does he?"

Roberts exchanged glances with me, before halting sharply, pulling on Montgomery's bindings so she was forced to an abrupt stop. She was glaring at him as Baker and I passed by and followed Cam towards the others.

Rogers nodded curtly at our approach. "Glad you're all ok. We've gathered here out of Adams' sight, for the moment at least. Anders' group have secured Minors. They're hoping to head out soon. I've asked them to scout around other Sectors. I don't want any surprises. If there are other potential threats out there, I want to know about them."

"Good plan." Cam glanced around the group. "Do we have confirmation that Adams is definitely up there? Did anyone manage to get within earshot of the Shadow Patrol at the entrance?"

"I did." Mason stepped forward, the hint of a smile on his lips. "Heard several walkie-talkie conversations. He's up there alright." The smile faded. "And he plans to stay there, hiding behind the women, until his Shadow Patrol have picked off anyone attempting to get close."

"Always was a coward." I was the only one close enough to hear Baker's whispered insult as Rogers continued.

"Now you're here with the additional weapons, we can get on with this. He's been up there too long now, without being challenged. I don't like it." For a moment, Rogers looked uncomfortable. "Look, before we go up there, I have something I need to say to you all."

There was total silence as the group gathered closer.

Rogers sighed, and took a deep breath before continuing. "We don't have much time, so I'll be brief." He shot a look at Green, who gave him an encouraging smile. "Earlier on, as you all know, I killed Reed. And that is a fact that we have been celebrating, since he has been our enemy for so long, but I... I find myself..."

He paused for a second, and Green moved close enough to stand by his side. Taking strength in his partner's support, he continued.

"In truth, I murdered Reed. Strangled him with my bare hands, when Cam had a clean shot and could have killed him painlessly. We have spoken of how we want to take over The Beck so we can run it more fairly, more equally..." He stared at the ground. "Well, today I behaved as badly as Reed and

Adams. I allowed my anger to get the better of me... acted like... an animal. The Beck I want to live in does not tolerate that kind of behaviour."

He looked up suddenly and met the gazes of the people standing in the group. "So, while our fight is not over, and we may have to kill many more in our struggle to free The Beck, I'd like to try, where possible, to take prisoners and incapacitate, rather than kill, people. Alright?"

There were various nods from the crowd who stood around Rogers. An awkward silence hung over the group for a few moments, and I saw Montgomery glance over at us curiously.

Following my gaze, Rogers noted the same thing and grimaced. "She behaving herself?"

"So far." Cam nodded. "And she's in big trouble if we take all The Beck leaders out. She's already offered her expertise to us if we guarantee her safety... later."

"We'll see about that." Dismissing Montgomery for the moment, Rogers turned to Tyler. "Meds is your area of expertise. Any inside information that might help?"

"Not really." Tyler frowned. "It's going to be difficult. The entrance is so narrow. And you heard what Mason said. If we're to have any chance of success, we'll need to try and sneak up on them. Take any guards who are up there at the entrance out, then be ready to force our way through before they can be replaced."

"It's risky." Rogers frowned.

"It's the very reason he chose this specific spot," Baker muttered beside me.

"I don't have any better ideas, I'm afraid." Tyler shrugged. "Once we're inside we'll need to be careful how we proceed. There are a lot of vulnerable citizens up there."

"We need a backup plan." The words were quiet, and again came from the woman standing to my left. All eyes turned to Baker, whose expression was pained, but determined.

"What do you suggest?" Rogers' tone was quiet, his respect for the older woman clear.

"We need to be clever," Baker considered. "Attack from two angles. Confuse Adams."

"I don't see how we can do that when the access to Meds is so limited." Cam sounded impatient.

"Hear her out, Cam." My tone was sharper than I had intended, and he shot me a look of surprise. I glanced away, embarrassed.

"It's limited," Baker continued steadily, "but there's something else. Something that not many people are aware of."

Rogers cocked his head to one side. "We're listening."

"There's another way to get into Meds." My mother paused for a second, glancing in the other direction, before leaning closer and continuing. "And I'm willing to bet Adams doesn't think any of us know about it."

Chapter Thirty Eight

The citizens around me stared at Baker in disbelief.

Undaunted, she continued. "It's a tunnel, and fairly narrow, but it's accessible."

"But how do you–?" Rogers looked perplexed.

Baker sighed. "Before I left Patrol, I explored the area thoroughly. At the back of Meds there are some caves. I don't think many people know about them. When I was in Meds I used to go and hide there for a bit of peace, when I could get away with it. I discovered a tunnel at the back of one of them and followed it one day... It comes out in the woods," she pointed into the distance, "over there somewhere."

"You mean the tunnel exists?" Tyler's eyes were wide.

Roger's eyes darted back to Tyler. "You knew about it?"

She turned to face our leader. "Not really, I mean, I heard rumours... that's all... but I didn't realise there was any truth in them."

"I heard there was a tunnel too." The voice came from the rear of the group, where Will was standing. She came forward, her expression serious. "I was never selected for Birthing myself, but I had a friend who was. She mentioned it once or twice. But she wasn't sure it was real either. I always figured it was just a story, you know, made up by women who dreamed they might see their children again…"

"I concealed the entrance a little, and I never mentioned it to anyone." Baker studied the ground as she spoke. "Once I was sent back to Patrol, I used it to…" She broke off.

"You mean you used to… come and see m– your daughter?" I flushed at my error.

She nodded. "I tried to. And I kept the tunnel a secret. In case… well in case someone told on me… stopped me from coming."

There was a silence as I took in her words. Pausing for a moment to take a breath which seemed difficult for her, she continued.

"I thought I might be able to see her… check on her progress." Her eyes locked on to mine as she spoke. "But it was too hard. From that distance, all the babies looked the same. I could never be sure whether… whether…"

Green moved closer to her, placing a hand on her arm. "It's alright. You don't need to–"

But Baker cut her off, seeming determined to get it all out. "Of course, I knew that when she was one, they would take her away from here and then I'd never be able to…" She sighed. "I gave up after a while."

The silence surrounding us was all-encompassing. I could see the Resistance citizens casting curious glances at the strange stillness which had fallen over our group. Finally, my mother took a deep breath and ploughed on.

"But the tunnel definitely exists."

I found myself unable to look away. This time, she was the first to break the eye contact as Cam interrupted.

"How do we know it's still operational?"

Baker shrugged. "I guess we don't. But it's worth a try."

"Think you can get us up there?" Rogers sounded more positive. "Remember where it is?"

She rolled her eyes, back to her usual sardonic self. "I'd know the way blindfolded."

"Alright." Rogers glanced around. "Adams might well have it guarded, at either end, so we'll need to be prepared for that. Can we approach it from the outside without being noticed?"

Baker thought for a second. "Probably. It's in a fairly dense section of woodland. Lots of trees and bushes to conceal ourselves in, as long as the group isn't too large. And, once we get through, we'll be cautious as we exit, check for guards on the Meds side as well."

"Just how narrow is the tunnel?" Rogers ran his eyes over the group in front of him. "Could we concentrate the bulk of our force that way?"

Baker shook her head. "It's pretty cramped. Single file in some places. We couldn't get a large number of people in or out quickly."

"Ok. Two teams, then." Rogers looked back at Baker. "We'll use a smaller one to access the tunnel, the rest of us ready to push in through the main entrance. No point getting large numbers of us trapped in there, unable to fight."

"If some of us distract the guards at the front, where he expects us," Green considered, "could we try to get the pregnant women and babies out? To safety?"

"Is that even possible?" Tyler voiced the same doubts that were plaguing me. "If it's so confined? Can the women who are heavily pregnant manage the tunnel?"

"With help, the majority of them probably could. It's not very wide, but it's tall enough to stand in all the way, and a little rough in places, but I think it could work, especially if we could do it without Adams noticing." Baker frowned. "And even if we only manage to free a few of them, it's better than none, right?"

"I guess so." Rogers looked around, considering who would be best approaching Meds from which direction.

"We brought explosives from a store Montgomery gave up." I remembered. "Could they be helpful in some way?"

Rogers beckoned Roberts over with Montgomery in tow.

"You told Cam you wanted to be helpful. Now's the time to prove it." He jabbed a finger at her. "Quin says you gave us some additional weapons. Anything we could use as a distraction?"

"Sure." Montgomery jerked a thumb at my pack. "There are some ordinary explosives, but I'm guessing you'll feel they are too dangerous to use close to the women." I clenched my fists at her lack of empathy for the vulnerable citizens trapped inside the Sector as she continued, unaware of the effect she was having. "However, there are a few grenades which simply emit a lot of smoke. That the kind of thing you were after?"

"They'd be worth a try, I suppose." Rogers stared hard at Montgomery, not bothering to hide his mistrust. "*If* they do what you say they do. You'll be happy to set off the explosives yourself, I assume? Just so we know that they have the effects you're describing, and not any other, *unexpected* surprises."

"Sure. Whatever you want." She shrugged, as if it meant nothing to her. "I told you. I'm on your side."

"*Sure* you are." Cam swung his pack from his back. "Ok, which of these are we going to be able to use, then?"

Rogers glared at Montgomery for a second, and then began

to make his way around the group, dividing people up into the two teams. Approaching Montgomery with reluctance, Cam set his pack in front of her and released her hands from their bindings. She gave him an appreciative smile as she massaged her wrists briefly, before bending down to sort out the pack's contents, swiftly dividing the different items up and selecting the ones she needed. Cam watched her like a hawk. Eventually, she sat back on her heels, three small black cylinders in her hands.

"These will do nicely."

Rogers called the group to order again. "Right. Who haven't I spoken to yet?"

Cam raised his hand. "Me. But I'm coming with you." He nodded meaningfully at Montgomery as she began to prime the explosives beside him.

Rogers nodded. "Fine." He turned to me. "Quin, you go with Baker's group. Since the majority of citizens up there are female, you'll blend in more successfully if necessary. A couple of you try and get inside the Sector. The rest of you hide in the cave at the top of the tunnel. Be ready to help those citizens who need it."

Glancing around, there was only one citizen, Thomas, left without an assignment. I knew now why Walker had been directed elsewhere. Despite his earlier defence of Mason, there was still a long way to go before that bridge would be mended.

"Go with Baker's group." Rogers moved towards him, "And here—" reaching into his pack for something, he drew his hand out and pressed a gun into Thomas' hand. "I figure you've earned this. But do not make me regret giving it to you."

"I won't." Thomas' face burned, but he looked determined as he shook his head.

Satisfied, Rogers turned back to Baker. "How long before you'll reach the top?"

Baker considered. "Twenty minutes, maybe?"

"Alright. That gives us a chance to get things ready down here." He held her gaze. "Radio when you're in place. And be careful."

Baker nodded and turned to leave. Satisfied, Rogers turned to speak further to his own group. Cam looked at me as I moved to go, holding my gaze for a moment longer than necessary. I realised that, as always, this was the only good-bye I was going to get. Summoning a brief smile, I hurried quickly after the second group.

It was smaller, consisting of myself and Jackson, Tyler, Green and, of course, Thomas. I suspected Rogers had put him in the mostly-female group on purpose. He easily kept up with the rest of us, walking along without a word to anyone, the newly-issued gun resting at his side. When I considered his courageous defence of Mason in the earlier battle, I understood Rogers' newfound trust, and was quite glad he was coming along.

We hadn't gone far when Baker held a hand out for us to stop.

"It's not far now. Stay here. I'm going to creep ahead and check the entrance, see if Adams has stationed guards on it."

Before anyone could stop her, she had ducked into the dense undergrowth and was gone.

We stood for several minutes in silence, the nerves growing. Beside me, Jackson held my gaze, and I knew she had many questions for me. But now wasn't the time to ask them. Staring back at the bushes into which my mother had disappeared, I tried to breathe slowly, but couldn't prevent my heart from pounding and my palms from sweating. I knew they wouldn't stop until she was back safe.

What seemed like several long minutes later, there was a rustling in the greenery before us. We had barely had time to aim our weapons in the right direction when Baker slid back out from the undergrowth and stood in front of us again.

"There's no one there." There was a broad smile on her face. "He's so arrogant. He believes no one could possibly know about it, so he's left it unguarded."

"Really?" Tyler looked doubtful.

"Really." Baker reassured. "The entrance is concealed with some pretty thick bushes. It's well hidden."

She jerked her head for us to follow her, and began cutting through some of the dense branches with her knife. The rest of us joined in, helping her to hack away at the thickest of the branches and creating an easier pathway to the legendary tunnel.

"Doesn't look like it's been used in a long while. Must be why Adams assumes no one knows it's here," Baker muttered. "Getting us all through might just take a little work."

Tyler paused for a moment. "It won't be hidden any more though."

"One way or another," Baker motioned for her to continue, "after today it's not going to matter whether the entrance is disguised or not."

Her words sent a shiver through my entire body.

Within a few minutes of working together, we had removed enough of the foliage to create a path which led to a small, dark entrance in the rockface. Bending down, Baker gestured to it.

"The tunnel is fairly narrow in places. You can walk most of it, but occasionally it will be necessary to get down on your hands and knees. We should leave one person here, to keep watch. We'll have to assess what's happening at the top when we get there, but hopefully a couple of us will be able to sneak into Meds while the guards are distracted."

"I'll stay here." Green nodded, her face a little pale.

I wondered if it was the idea of entering the dark, narrow tunnel that had put her off. I wasn't relishing the thought myself.

"Fine," Baker continued. "The rest of us will walk along the tunnel together. Quin and I will be the only ones entering Meds. When we've reached the top, the rest of you can wait just inside the tunnel entrance, out of sight, ready to guide small groups of women down the passageway when they arrive. Everybody ok with that?"

There were several nervous nods, but no one asked any questions. Wasting no more time, Baker dropped to her knees and crawled through the small space in the rock. The rest of us followed in her wake. We only had to crawl for a minute before the tunnel widened and we were able to stand. It was dark, and we only had three flashlights between us, which cast eerie shadows on the tunnel walls.

As we walked, I was hugely aware of the volume of rock which towered above our heads, and the slow tapping sound of what was presumably water dripping down from above. After a while, the tunnel became steeper, and we were almost climbing upwards at certain points, holding on to crevices in the rock to keep our balance. Thankfully, it wasn't long before the ground flattened out slightly, and eventually we began to see a faint light in the distance.

Slowing our pace, we approached the end of the passage with extreme caution. I was close to the back of the line, and by the time I caught up with the rest, Baker and Tyler were peering out through the mouth of the tunnel into dense greenery.

"Can't see anything out of the ordinary," Baker said, creeping a little further out. "Oh wait!" She thrust out a sudden hand. "There are a couple of guards on duty."

Sure enough, there was a Shadow Officer posted on the rear exit of both buildings.

Thomas raised his gun, aiming it in the direction of the closest guard. "I could take him out. I'm a decent shot."

Baker glared at him, placing a hand on the barrel and lowering the weapon firmly. "And have the other one come running? Our advantage is the element of surprise. The second they know we're here, we lose that."

Thomas raised his eyebrows, but didn't argue.

"What do we do then?" I asked.

Baker glanced both ways. "You stay here. I'll let Rogers know we made it."

She hurried a little way back down the tunnel and I could hear the faint crackling of the walkie-talkie. The rest of us waited in tense silence. A few seconds later, she was back.

"Now, we wait. Once the explosives go off, we hope those two guards react and disappear in the opposite direction." She shot a warning glance at Thomas. "*Then* we act. Get to the buildings and try to get the mothers out." She motioned her hand forward. "We're probably safe to come out a little further, Quin; the trees will cover us."

"Be careful." Jackson grasped my hand and squeezed it

hard.

"I will." Our eyes met and, as with Cam, it flashed through my head that this could be the last time I saw her.

Shaking away the gloomy thoughts, I followed Baker, leaving the others waiting in the mouth of the tunnel. We only had to wriggle a little further forward, until we could settle in the undergrowth close enough to the field to get a good view.

"Ever been here before?" Baker asked, not looking at me. "As an adult, I mean."

I nodded. "Once. On a shift with Tyler, when I was injured." She shot me a quizzical look.

"It's a long story. I'll tell you sometime. Basically, Cam had Tyler bring me here on her shift once. I was exhausted... needed to rest. She let me hide here while she was on duty."

I thought back to the day I had spent here, when I had realised the different way the Meds citizens were treated. The food they received was far superior to that which citizens in the other areas of The Beck were given, and the women did little but rest and relax as they prepared for the birth of their babies. It was a blissful time, until a few weeks after the baby was born, when the mothers were forced back to their old positions.

I thought of Riley, a Super I had known back in Agric. She had been assigned to Birthing at the same Assessments when I had been transferred to Patrol. The last time I saw her, she had been a few weeks pregnant. I wondered how far along she would be now. She had been a very sympathetic Super, and I knew she would support a rebellion of any kind. As far as we knew, the sickness had never reached Meds, so I assumed that she was still alive.

Baker looked intrigued at my response to her question, but didn't ask any more. "That building to the left is the one which houses the citizens who are pregnant. The other contains the babies. Bringing them out is going to be trickier, as they'll all have to be carried, and they may be noisy."

"Can we coordinate the two efforts? Have the women who aren't yet heavily pregnant and those who've given birth already carry a child each?"

She nodded approvingly. "That's what I was thinking. We need to move fast when the time comes. Ideally get in there, inform them of the plan, then get them out fast."

"Is there any guarantee they'll come with us?" I glanced at my mother, fear in my eyes. "What if they alert Adams instead?"

Her expression was grim. "We'll have to deal with it, if that's the case. I'm hoping that Adams' presence here is strange enough to ring alarm bells. And if they're presented with the knowledge that a lot of The Beck leaders have already fallen, I think they'll see the sense in going with us."

"I hope so."

"Which building do you want to take?"

I considered the options and thought of Riley again. "Can I take the one with the pregnant mothers? If I'm right, there's a woman in there who knows me. She'll help me to convince the others to follow us, I'm certain of it."

"Sounds like a plan. I'll do my best to organise things in the other one then. If you can bring the mothers across, we can get them all out together."

She turned to speak to the others in the tunnel, but had barely opened her mouth when we both spotted a large cloud of smoke which was billowing up into the sky from somewhere behind the buildings. Its appearance was accompanied by shouts, the crackle of walkie-talkies, and a second later, the two guards left their posts to race round the front.

"Be ready!" Baker hissed at Tyler and the others, who nodded. She turned to me. "Let's go."

Together, we burst out of the woods and raced into the open. The area behind the buildings was usually used for exercise and leisure time, but at the moment it was empty. I wondered whether Adams had instructed the women to stay inside until the standoff was over. There was no sign of them so far.

With a brief nod, Baker swerved away from me. I approached the entrance to the building with the expectant mothers hesitantly. Feeling suddenly nervous, I wondered how they would react to my appearance. I reached the door and wrenched it open, heaving a sigh of relief when it wasn't locked.

Inside, I found myself in a hallway which I knew ran the length of the building. Although I had entered from the other side the last time I was here, the corridor was the same from either end, with several doors opening off it. I hurried down the hall, heading for the canteen, the largest room in the building and the one I guessed most of the mothers would be in.

As I neared it, I knew I was right. Whilst the hallway was quiet, I could hear the muted sound of voices, softly murmuring behind the door. Stuffing my gun into the back of my overall pants, I pushed it open as slowly as I could. As I did, the quiet chatter stopped.

Stepping inside, I made sure that my hands were stretched in front of me in an unthreatening gesture. As the citizens on the other side came into view, I was glad that I had. The room was crammed with people, both expectant mothers *and* babies. Some were grouped on benches and others sat on the floor. Most were huddled together in small, frightened-looking groups.

But several women were standing in front of all the others. Three of them held knives, all of which were aimed directly at me.

Chapter Thirty Nine

Acting on instinct, I raised my hands even higher, to make it totally clear that I was not a threat. As I did, a vaguely familiar voice came from behind one of the weapons which threatened me.

"Quin? Is that you?" The knife was lowered slightly.

I raised my gaze over the blade and tried to focus on the woman wielding it. "Riley?"

Holding out a hand to show the others I was not a threat, Riley lowered the weapon and approached me. "I thought you were..." She looked puzzled. "I mean, I was told you had escaped...What are you doing back?"

Glancing behind me, I took a step into the room. "It's a long story. And we haven't much time." I dropped my voice. "Do you trust me, Riley?"

She looked surprised. "Of course."

"Well, trust that you're all in danger. Adams is outside, and–"

"No, he's not."

I faltered for a moment, concerned that she didn't believe me. "He is, Riley, he–"

"He's in the building next door." She jerked her head. "Why do you think he moved us all in here?"

I glanced again at the large number of women in the room, and then the infants. A sudden panic overtook me and I spun around. Hauling on the door handle, I dashed out again, breathless with terror. When I saw what was at the other end of the hallway, I froze.

Standing just inside the door, her face flushed and clearly out of breath, was Baker. She moved swiftly towards me, hustling me quickly in through the door and closing it firmly behind her.

"Are... are you... were you–?" I struggled to form words.

"I'm fine." She jerked her head in the direction she had come. "I'd just got the door open... was about to go in when I heard male voices. Coming from *inside.*"

"But did they–?"

Baker caught the panic in my face and smiled wearily. "I got out pretty fast, before any of them knew I was there. I'm pretty sure they were too distracted by the smoke to notice me." She wiped an exhausted hand across her face before looking around the room. "Ah. I wondered where the babies had ended up."

One of the other armed women approached warily. "Adams turned up an hour ago. Moved us all in here together and told us not to go anywhere. Threatened us, if we tried to leave. So, we're a little... um, on edge."

"Hence the knives," Riley continued. She let the hand holding the weapon drop to her side. "Sorry about that."

"No." Baker shook her head. "It was a sensible move."

"Where did you both come from?" the other woman questioned. "And what are you doing here?"

I waited a moment for Baker to speak, but when she didn't, I tried to explain for us both. "As you obviously heard, a little while ago a group of us escaped from the Beck. We always intended to come back. Try and... improve things for everyone. Today... well, we're trying to get rid of Adams for good." I glanced around. Every single young woman in the room was listening. "There isn't time to explain right now, but the smoke you see over there? It's not a fire. It's my friends. They're at the Meds entrance, causing a distraction so that we can get to you. Look, Adams is hiding up here because he thinks we won't attack a Sector which shelters babies and pregnant women."

A few of the women whimpered in fear, but Riley waved a hand at them and they silenced, waiting for me to continue.

"And he's right." I looked around at the doubtful faces. "We have to get you all out before we can attack Adams."

"Look," Baker stepped forward to speak, "we've already succeeded in eliminating both Carter and Reed." More positive exclamations followed her announcement. "But we have to take out Adams. He's the key. If we can get rid of him, and the Shadow Patrol don't have anyone to take orders from, then we're hoping it will all be over."

"But we need to keep you safe." I hoped they couldn't hear my voice shaking. "Once you're elsewhere, we'll be able to attack Adams with everything we've got."

"But how will you get us out?" Riley gestured to the front entrance to Meds. "Adams has an awful lot of Shadow Officers over there. Heading that way while his men are still in position is pointless. We decided that over an hour ago." She waved the knife at me. "Why do you think we attempted to arm ourselves?"

"There's another way." Baker gestured at the door. "A tunnel, hidden... at the back of the caves in the woods."

There were gasps of surprise.

"You mean..." the woman beside Riley stared at me, "...the tunnel actually *exists*?"

"We've just come through it." Baker's face was growing anxious. Ignoring the growing chatter, knowing we didn't have time, she hurried on. "Look, we have others, waiting to help you. But there's very little time. And it won't be easy, especially for those of you who are quite far along with your pregnancies. And there are the babies to consider too. You'll have to help us."

Riley turned to the women in front of her. "Alright. We talked about this. Said we didn't want to be left here at Adams' mercy. Most of us said we'd fight, if we had to. Well, now's the time."

"You don't have to fight," I added quickly.

I walked to the door and peered out into the hallway, grateful to see it was still empty.

"Just follow Quin. She'll get you to safety." Riley's voice was soothing, yet also commanding. "Those of you who aren't heavily pregnant, take one of the babies as well."

She clasped Baker's hand tightly for a second. "Thank you." My mother's cheeks pinked slightly, and she looked away.

"All clear?" Riley crossed the room to me.

I nodded. Turning back to the other occupants of the room, she beckoned to the first of the women. "Go quietly. But quickly."

I marvelled at the way Riley had united the mothers-to-be in Meds. They stood a good chance at surviving, whatever the outcome of this battle, because they listened to her. Although some of them seemed too scared to move, the majority were beginning to stand, and some were gathering around the babies and picking them up, before getting in line at the door.

Seeing that Riley had the mothers in fairly good order, I raced back to the rear door of the building and eased it open. I breathed deeply when I realised that the area behind the buildings was still empty of guards. The continuing commotion from around the front told me that the struggle with the Shadow forces had begun. Glancing over at the door to the other building, I could see no sign of life.

I turned as the young mothers began to creep up the passageway towards me. Those who were only just pregnant came first, each of them clutching a small bundle tightly. When the first one reached me, I slid the door open a crack, checking that the coast was clear. Pushing it wider, I motioned to the young woman to move through. She looked at me uncertainly, and I realised that without being directed, none of them would be able to find the tunnel entrance.

I whispered back over my shoulder. "Riley, can you man the door?"

She waved a yes and hurried to take over. I stepped outside and began to make my way across the grass, beckoning the first young woman forward. Her progress hampered slightly by the precious burden she carried, she began following me across the grass to the woods. Behind her came a line of others.

When I reached the woods, I dived into their shelter and called out softly.

"Tyler!" For a moment there was no reply and my heart began pounding in my ears. "Jackson! You there?"

There was a slight rustling, and Tyler's face peered out from inside the tunnel.

As my heart rate slowed again, I waved a hand. "Here are

the first few, Tyler."

She nodded, and beckoned to the young women who stood beside me, their eyes wide with terror.

"Come on. I'll get you somewhere safe, don't worry." Her voice was remarkably soothing, and the woman did not hesitate to approach her.

"I'll send more down with Thomas and Jackson in a minute," I added. "When you get to Green, come straight back."

As I turned back to check that the women were all heading in the right direction, I said a silent thank you that none of the infants had started to cry yet. I could see Riley and Baker dispatching the women a couple at a time from the building, staggering the numbers so we didn't have too many arriving at the tunnel entrance at once.

We continued ferrying across women and infants for several minutes, the three citizens in the passage keeping the steady stream of women moving down the tunnel. Trusting that the system was working well, I left my position at the edge of the wood and raced back to Riley.

"Everything ok?"

She nodded and glanced behind her. "How many left?"

From the rear of the line, Baker called. "Just five more women to go now. And only three more infants."

I sighed with relief. "Thank goodness."

The air was suddenly filled with the rattle of gunshots. They came from the other side of the building, but were enough to heighten my sense of dread. Following the noise, there was a brief silence. Then several things happened at once.

A young girl, standing just behind Riley, screamed. Some of the babies, startled by either the shriek or the bullets, began to wail. Finally, a single Shadow Patrol guard appeared around the corner of the building. Spotting us, his face blanched, but within seconds he had recovered his composure and raised the walkie-talkie to his lips.

Panicked, three of the women directly behind Riley bolted, racing across the grass without waiting for Baker to pass them a child.

Riley turned to look at the other women who were left. One of them was hugely pregnant, and could not realistically manage to run whilst carrying a baby. Riley waved her through. The other did not look to be pregnant at all. Baker managed to press a child into her arms and thrust her through the door, shouting after them.

"Run!"

The two young women took off without needing further instruction. I glanced back at the Shadow guard, who had lowered his walkie-talkie and was now raising his gun. Fumbling to retrieve my own from the back of my trousers, I let out a groan of frustration when it snagged in my belt loop.

And then several more shots rang out. Devastated, I turned to look at the running women, relieved when I saw them plunge into the woods safely. When I looked back at the guard, he was on the ground, his weapon useless beside him. For a second I was confused, but then I saw Thomas racing out of the woods, gun in hand, his expression determined.

"Get out of there!" he screamed.

A glance around showed that there were two more guards emerging from the building where Adams was hiding.

"The babies!"

Baker brought forward the remaining infants, thrusting one at me and holding the last one herself. We stepped outside, Riley bringing up the rear, as Thomas raced towards us, firing wildly at the Shadow Officers who were exiting the building next door.

Unfortunately, they were closer to us than he was.

We froze on the steps, unsure whether to make a run for it or not. As we did, Thomas continued to empty his clip of bullets in the enemy's direction. He managed to hit one of them, who doubled over and collapsed on the steps, tripping up the man behind him. As he struggled to recover, we surged down to the field, the children clasped tightly in our arms.

"Cover us!" Baker commanded, as Thomas approached.

Nodding, he circled our little group and walked at the rear as we headed for the woods. We moved as quickly as we could, pushing Riley ahead of us, Baker and I following. For the first time, I glanced down at the child in my arms to find a pair of enormous eyes staring up at me. For a second, we gazed at one another, and then the child opened its mouth and started to wail. I cradled it closer to my body, the way I had seen Blythe do with Perry, and continued to hurry after the others.

We made it half way before Thomas shouted another warning. Without looking back, the three of us burst into a sprint. In my arms, the baby stopped crying, shocked at my sudden change of speed. The trees were close now; we didn't have far to go. I had no idea whether Adams would order his Shadows to shoot at the innocent children, but I didn't want to find out.

Baker reached the trees first, to find Jackson waiting at the passage entrance. There was no sign of anyone else.

"Take him!" Baker thrust the baby she was carrying into her hands.

With no hesitation, Jackson turned and set off down the

tunnel.

We looked back to see Riley entering the tree line, Thomas only metres behind her. In hot pursuit were two more Shadow Patrol guards. As he reached the trees, Thomas fired a single shot back at them. Undeterred, the men kept coming. I retreated towards the tunnel with my own precious cargo, readying myself to run.

Backing up slightly, Thomas fired again, but his shot went wide. A look of panic crossed his face. Beside him, Baker reached for her own weapon, grasping at her waist with her eyes fixed on the enemy. As she pulled it from its holster, it caught on the walkie-talkie which was also clipped to her belt. Out of time, she wrenched it free and the bulky black radio came with it, flying into the air and landing several feet away.

Baker thrust her gun into position, aiming for the guards. Thomas had continued to shoot, letting off a constant stream of bullets as the guards came ever closer. Finally, one of the shots hit home and the guard closest to us stumbled, fell, and didn't get up again. Startled, Thomas paused in his fire, but Baker was ready, and finished off the guard behind with a single shot.

For the moment, there were no other guards in sight.

Certain the danger was gone for the time being, Baker dropped to the ground and began searching for the lost walkie-talkie. It took her a few seconds to locate it, and when she did, her face fell.

"Cracked," she muttered, examining its surface.

My heart sank.

Tentatively, Baker brought the walkie-talkie to her lips. "Rogers?" Her voice seemed softer than usual. "Come in,

Rogers."

There was a moment of static, and then nothing.

"Green? Rogers?" This time, there was more urgency in her tone. "This is Baker. Come in please."

Again, there was a brief crackling, and the walkie-talkie cut out.

Baker sighed loudly, flicking the switch off, then back on again. Slowly, she raised it to her lips and pushed the button.

"Rogers. Green. Come in." Her face was pale, and she closed her eyes momentarily as she paused for a second, then went on. "This is Baker. Are you there?"

This time, there was no static. And no response.

"Damnit!" She was clutching the useless walkie-talkie so hard her knuckles had turned white. "Damnit!"

Riley and I exchanged glances. Without the ability to inform Rogers that the women were safe, we had a big problem.

I looked back at Baker, who seemed to have regained control, and gestured to Riley and the remaining baby. "What do we do now?"

I could see her calculating our next move, her eyes focusing on each member of our group one by one. "First, make sure the women and children waiting at the bottom of the tunnel are taken somewhere safe."

"But..." I looked out into the woods, "...Rogers won't attack if he thinks the women are... I mean we have to–"

"–we have to find some other way to let them know the women are safe." Baker's tone was low, determined. "I know. But the babies are our priority." She glanced down at the infant in my arms, then gestured to the tunnel entrance. "Off you go then."

Disappointed that she wanted to send me away, I began to protest, but she held up a hand. "The others will be waiting." She glanced worriedly at the still-empty field, then turned back to Thomas. "You can stay with me."

He blanched slightly, but took a tentative step forward.

"I'd really rather—" But she cut me off before I could finish.

"Off you *go*, Quin." Baker's tone was firm. "Show Riley the way."

Dismissing us, Baker slid closer to the cave entrance and listened. "Thomas, I'm going to sneak a little further out, see if I can work out what's happening. Figure out the best way to proceed. Stay here. I won't be long."

Without a backwards glance at me, she disappeared. Riley took a step towards the tunnel mouth, stopping in surprise when I didn't follow. Always astute, she glanced back at me, then at the space Baker had vacated.

"You're not coming, are you?"

I shook my head. Thomas turned to stare.

"What?" He looked confused.

Knowing Baker would be back any moment, I took a step towards the man I used to hate, and thrust the tiny child at him. "So, leading all the women and children to safety. Think you're up to the job?"

"Me?" His forehead wrinkled as he tried to understand the sudden turn of events. "But she said—"

"I don't care what she said. You've done an excellent job of protecting them so far. Why not see the job through?"

He still stood there, unmoving. I tried a different tack.

"Look, I want to stay here and help Baker. You don't need to know why." I touched his arm gently. "Just... just... go, would you?"

"Do you have enough ammo?" He began to rifle through his pockets, offering me more, but I stopped him.

"You heard her. These women and children are our priority." I pushed his hand, filled with bullets, away. "You might need them as much as we do. I have enough, for now at least."

For a moment longer, he hesitated, but then he pocketed the ammunition and, giving a brief nod, turned to Riley. Following suit, I placed the infant into her arms.

"Can you manage? I think Thomas would be of better service bringing up the rear with his gun primed." I paused to make sure the baby was secure and then glanced up at Riley. "Are you alright going with Thomas? You don't mind, I mean?" I peered out of the cave in the direction my mother had gone. "I don't want to leave Baker alone, dealing with..."

"I'm fine." Riley hugged me awkwardly with one arm. "Thanks, you know... for..." I tried to smile. "No problem."

"And take good care of yourselves." Turning to Thomas, Riley took a deep breath. "Ready to go?"

"Sure." With a terse nod and a final glance at me, Thomas gestured for her to enter the tunnel ahead of him. As she disappeared into the darkness, he turned back to me. "Well... good luck, I guess."

"Thanks." I watched as he entered the tunnel, suddenly feeling vulnerable.

As I listened to their footsteps dying away, I hoped desperately that my mother would forgive my actions. Creeping to the edge of the cave, I found I didn't have long to wait. Seconds later, she reappeared, her face clearly shocked at my appearance rather than Thomas'. Slipping past me, her eyes swept the empty cave before returning to mine.

"I'm sorry." I shrugged. "I couldn't just..."

She ran a tired hand across her forehead and sighed. I waited for the inevitable onslaught of criticism, but instead she merely shook her head.

"Your decision, I suppose. Well. You're stuck here with me now." She pointed out at the field beyond. "Looks like it's all clear for the moment. Shall we?"

I nodded grimly. Together, we crept forward through the trees towards the field beyond, preparing to cross it once more.

As we did, the door to the building which contained Adams burst open, and this time a line of at least ten Shadow Patrol Officers exited, their guns raised and at the ready.

Chapter Forty

Baker and I froze for a second, waiting to see what the guards would do. If they knew of our existence and headed straight for us, there would be little chance of escaping them, unless we fled down the tunnel. While that was an option, I knew neither of us wanted to leave without the others knowing that our mission had been a success.

Baker was the first to act. Keeping her movements slow, she slid a hand inside her pack, drawing out her remaining store of bullets. Wordlessly, she began to count them. I doubted we would last long if the Shadows headed straight for us. Reaching into my own pack, I was about to follow suit when I noticed that the guards had stopped.

"Baker," I kept my voice as low as possible.

"Mmmm?"

"Baker! Look."

Reluctantly, she abandoned her task and followed my gaze.

"What are they doing?" I whispered.

She shrugged but didn't respond. Her expression, however, had grown hopeful. We kept our eyes fixed on the men. Instead of heading in any specific direction, they had come out of the building and circled it, each one stopping a similar distance from the next, until they formed a human barrier around the building which contained Adams.

"Defensive move," Baker muttered. "Lining them up to protect him."

We continued to watch, but the soldiers took no further action. Instead, they remained still, their guns focused outwards, but in no specific direction. I wondered what they were waiting for.

"What do we do now?" I hissed at Baker.

She turned to me. "For now, we wait. There's nothing we can do at the moment. We can't get to Adams without marching right into that cordon, and if we try to do that, just the two of us with no backup, it's a suicide mission. We might take out two or three of the guards, but they'll get us before we're even halfway across the field, with only two targets to aim for."

"But–"

She held up a hand to silence me as a voice boomed out across the Compound.

"Ex-Beck citizens! And current Beck citizens who have joined the Resistance. Listen."

The voice came from somewhere inside the building, but was amplified. There was no mistaking its owner, though. Adams sounded as calm and unruffled as ever, though I had no facial expression to support my theory, since he was clearly speaking from somewhere safe inside the building, using something to project his voice so we could all hear him.

"This has gone too far. I am here inside Meds with some very frightened young women. Many of these citizens are with child, yet you continue to threaten them."

I felt my breath catch in my throat at his lie, and started forward, but Baker's hand on my arm was fiercely tight. I sat back on my heels as Adams continued.

"I came up here, bringing a large number of Shadow Patrol, because I knew these were the citizens that needed my protection the most. Despite this fact, you continue to attack the guards who only attempt to protect the vulnerable inside this compound. These young women are terrified, and this has to stop. Now."

The guards around the outside of the buildings seemed frozen in place, their faces blank and emotionless. They were waiting for Adams' command, I realised, and completely under his control. I shuddered at the thought.

Adams' tone had grown more passionate as his speech went on. "If you do not cease this attack on the innocent Beck citizens, we will be forced to take swift and definitive action. Up until now, I have attempted to be patient. But when it comes to protecting my own citizens, I will not hesitate. You should know that a second wave of Shadow Patrol is on its way up here. More than your pathetic little forces could *ever* cope with." His voice reached a crescendo as he delivered his final edict. "This is your last chance. Surrender *now*, or face the consequences."

Baker and I looked at one another as Adams' final words echoed across Meds.

"We *have* to get the message to Rogers." I whispered. "More than anything, now. He needs to know that Adams is lying, that we've taken all the citizens to safety."

"You're right." Baker's look was grim. "It's going to be dangerous though."

Fighting the sense of dread that crept over me, I took a breath. "What do we do?"

Baker pointed at the woods which surrounded us. "These

trees circle Meds, more or less. If we stay inside them, under their cover, we should be able to navigate around the Sector, head for the front of the buildings. Then all we have to do is find Rogers."

"Hide, you mean?" I ran my gaze along the tree line, following it as far as I could.

"Yes. Well, at least until the tree cover runs out." She shrugged. "If we both go, in opposite directions, we stand a better chance of at least one us of reaching the others."

Her words sent a shudder through me.

"Alright." I squared my shoulders. "So, get around the front without being seen, find Rogers and tell him we can attack the buildings without fear of harming innocents?"

She nodded, then hesitated, her eyes piercing mine. "Are you sure you're up for this? I'd go alone, but..."

"We stand a better chance if we both go." I smiled weakly. "I know."

"I'd feel a whole lot better if it was Thomas I was sending out into the danger zone," she muttered.

I stared at her, unable to prevent myself from smiling. "You almost sound like you care about me, Baker."

She shot me a startled look but quickly masked it, and in seconds her usual business-like attitude was back. "Hopefully this way, at least one of us will make it." She peered out at the tree line again. "There are only a few spots where the cover runs out. When you get to them, all I can suggest is that you move fast."

"I will."

We stared at one another for a second, neither of us knowing what to say.

"Good luck then, I guess," I tried.

"And to you." Baker nodded. "You can do this."

"*We* can do this," I amended.

She smiled momentarily, and then turned, heading off in the opposite direction, crouching low and moving swiftly but silently. I watched her for a moment, before turning and heading in the opposite direction. It wasn't long before I felt the sweat rolling down my back as I fought through the tangled roots and bushes, which scratched at my skin constantly.

I made fairly good progress for a while; the silence occasionally punctured by the sound of gunfire as I moved towards the area in front of the buildings. The shots were not regular enough to signal the start of a large battle, and I knew that Rogers was holding off until he knew that the area was clear. Desperate to reach him with the truth, I pushed on, forcing my way through the foliage as fast as I dared.

As I passed through a section of particularly dense bushes, I found my progress abruptly halted, as my body jerked backwards. Straining to see what had happened, I caught sight of my backpack, which had snagged on one of the lower branches. I pulled at it, gently at first, and then more firmly, desperate to free myself. The branch clung stubbornly to my pack for a few seconds, until it was abruptly released and I was thrust forward onto my hands and knees.

The movement caused by the backpack's release was sudden and violent. Glancing at the guards in horror, I froze, waiting to see whether any of them might spot the place where the foliage was swaying back and forth. Most of the guards were focused on the action at the front of the buildings, but one or two were still looking this way. Praying they would dismiss any movement as caused by an animal, I continued

413

onwards, creeping even lower.

I wondered where Baker was. Had she made it around the front yet? The bushes and trees on the side that she had taken had looked less dense, and I knew that her choice for me to travel in this direction was no accident. Ahead of me, the trees were consistently thick and sufficient to hide me until I was parallel with the side of the Meds buildings. At the point they petered out, there was a large gap which I would have to breach before I could get to the rest of the Resistance.

Reaching the break in the trees, I considered my next move. I could see the Meds entrance now, where the others had clearly defeated the Shadow Patrol presence. Numerous members of Adams' guard lay dead, and as I stared, I began to notice various members of the Resistance concealed behind the trees, spreading out in a semicircle from the point where they had entered the Sector. They all looked primed and ready to fire at the line of Shadow Guards, but as yet they were not taking action. Rogers' instructions to protect the citizens inside were being followed to the letter, but this meant the Shadows could fire at us without fear of reprisal, hence we were making no progress towards our goal. The injustice of it spurred me on.

We were wasting precious time. Every second we waited to attack the buildings, every second that the Shadow Patrol continued to fire at my friends hiding in the trees, we risked reducing our forces further. And the fewer of us there were, the more chance Adams had of winning. Most of the guards at the side of the building were watching the Meds entrance, not expecting anyone to approach from elsewhere. There was no change in the direction of fire, which meant that Baker had not managed to reach Rogers with the message yet. Swallowing hard, and trying desperately not to think about what might have happened to my mother, I made my decision.

Holding my newly loaded gun in shaking hands, I checked that the nearest guard's attention was distracted, before standing up and starting to run. Head down, I sprinted as fast as I possibly could in the direction of the trees, where I knew the Resistance were hiding, aiming to tell the first person I found, even if it wasn't Rogers. The message could be passed along the line of citizens, and I knew I'd be safest if I managed to get back under the cover of the trees rapidly.

Before I reached the trees again, I heard the rattle of bullets in the air increase and knew they had seen me. Praying I could reach shelter without being hit, I surged forward, diving under cover as fast as I could. As my body slammed into the ground, I felt the impact jarring me, and lay still for a moment, catching my breath.

"Quin!" I heard a voice hissing to my left, and turned my head to see Will, crouching low and casting a concerned glance at me. "You alright?"

Crawling on my stomach, I inched my way towards her, noting that the gunfire had abated, presumably because their target had now disappeared. Closing the final gap between myself and Will, I grasped her arm and leaned close to her ear.

"Meds is –" I found that my voice had almost deserted me and tried again, "...clear. The women are out. Do you –?"

But Will was already raising a walkie-talkie to her lips. "Rogers. It's Will. Come in."

My heart soared with relief as the immediate reply came through. "Go ahead."

"I have Quin with me. Meds is clear. I repeat. Meds is *clear*."

There was a brief pause, as we waited for a response. The silence hung thick around us, and I glanced at the line of Shadow Patrol, my hands shaking. For a moment, I wondered if Rogers had understood, but then the walkie-talkie burst into life again.

"Resistance. It's time. We have the 'all clear'. Proceed with attack as planned."

On cue, there was a volley of shots from the trees around me. Startled at the sudden action from an enemy who had previously been silent, the Shadow guards reacted slowly. As I watched, several of the guards in the line fell, and those beside them took a step back. The hours of training at The Ridge had paid off, and as I watched, many of the Resistance bullets hit their mark, taking out a good number of the guards closest to us without them having to leave the cover of the trees.

I watched as Will took aim and pulled the trigger. Her first shot went wide, but she steadied her arm and tried again. I watched, as the Shadow closest to us took the hit. His body jolted and he looked stunned as he collapsed to the ground and lay still. We exchanged a glance of relief, and I began to take aim at the next guard, but found Will's hand on my arm.

"They're retreating. We've taken out those we can from this position." She nodded at the rest of the guards who were still standing. Most of them had moved several steps closer to the building. "It'll be a waste of bullets if we continue to fire from here."

I sighed. "We're going to have to move closer, right?"

The question didn't need a response. As I watched, various Resistance citizens were emerging from the trees, racing forward, guns blazing. The circle of Shadow guards reacted more quickly now, crouching low and returning fire.

The battle had begun.

"You ready?" Will's eyes pierced mine, and she jerked her head at the buildings.

I nodded, and straightened up. Together, we moved out of our cover and began to run across the field. My hands sweating, I attempted to keep my gun focused on its target whilst making progress towards the guards, preparing to fire it as soon as I felt confident I was within range. Although their numbers had been reduced by our initial volley of shots, there were still plenty of them in the formation, which had dropped back and held steady around the Meds buildings.

To either side of me, I was aware of my fellow Resistance fighters forming their own circle which closed in on the enemy, but as it did, the shots being fired at our now-vulnerable forces kept coming. Screams filled the air, and I knew that many of the bullets were finding homes in the people around me, even as we made headway across the field.

But the direction of the fight was changing. My heart thundered as I saw more of the enemy fall, their circle reducing further. As Will and I passed a number of dead Shadow guards, I dared to hope that we might make it.

Refusing to look sideways where I knew I would be confronted by the sight of the Resistance citizens we had lost, I moved on. I forced my thoughts away from the unknown fate of Cam, of Jackson and Cass, of Mason and Baker, concentrating only on making progress towards my target. Beside me, Will did the same.

We continued to encroach on the ring of Shadow guards, and eventually I knew we were close enough to hit them.

Attempting to steady my finger on the trigger, I pulled it, my eyes resting on the Shadow guard who was dead ahead. His gaze met mine and I knew he was about to fire. Before he could though, his face crumpled in pain and he clutched at his arm. My bullet had found its target, and although he wasn't dead, I had managed to injure him.

As I took aim again, there was a burst of sound which was not gunfire. In the distance, I could hear the crackle of the enemy's radio and a moment later, one of the guards raised a hand high and gave an order. While we couldn't hear the words he shouted, his meaning was clear. Without hesitation, the guards backed away further, retreating up the steps to the building and one by one, disappearing inside.

Taking advantage of their sudden withdrawal, our own forces surged forward, heading for the buildings and aiming to trap the guards inside with their leader. We were all aware of the protection the building would lend them and, while we were all still stranded on open ground, we would be easy to pick off once they regrouped inside and began firing from the windows.

I allowed myself a brief glance to my right, and spotted Rogers, his hand aloft, waving us forward. With no target to aim at, Will and I focused on moving forward more quickly, and reaching the relative safety of the building's walls before the guards inside managed to regroup.

We were only metres from the building when it began. From the window closest to us, a Shadow guard began to fire. Ahead of me, Will bent her head and forged onwards. I attempted to follow in her wake, my legs like jelly. We had almost reached our goal when I heard her cry out. She stumbled forward, falling to her knees. When I reached her seconds later, blood was pouring from a wound in her shoulder.

"Go!" she screamed, waving me past.

Ignoring the gesture, I grasped hold of her uninjured arm. For now, there was a pause in the flow of bullets coming from the window. I wondered if the guard was reloading. Taking advantage of the brief respite, I attempted to help Will up.

She shook me off. "Go!"

"No." I bent down and hauled on her again, determined to bring her with me.

She was clearly in pain, but seeing that I wasn't prepared to leave her, she attempted to clamber to her feet. Ahead of us, I could see some of the other Resistance fighters had made it. A small group of them were crouched low under the windows of the building, calling out to us, urging us on. I knew that time was not on our side. Offering Will my hand, I dragged her into a standing position and, my hand firmly in hers, we began to move ahead.

We had almost made it when the guard resumed his fire. My heart sank. Making a desperate attempt to reach the wall of the building ahead, I pulled hard on Will's hand, but it slipped from my grasp. As I turned to try and catch her, one of the bullets from the window found its target, ripping into her chest.

Again, she fell. Only this time, she didn't get up.

Chapter Forty One

As I stumbled away, I felt the tears stinging my eyes. Ahead, the Resistance citizens continued to beckon, and without the burden of a second person, I closed the distance between us quickly. My friends were still crouching low, to avoid the bullets coming from the building above. But the volley had slowed, the guards inside perhaps conserving their ammunition now there were no easy targets. As my body slammed against the side of the building, I collapsed sobbing against the first familiar body, feeling a pair of arms hesitantly tighten around me.

"I'm sorry..." a gruff voice murmured.

Through the fog of my tears, I realised who the voice belonged to. I shifted away from the figure who held me awkwardly and looked up into my mother's eyes. Whilst not exactly comfortable, she didn't look horrified at my closeness. For now, there didn't seem to be any activity inside the building. A glance across the field revealed a number of bodies, both Resistance and Shadow Patrol. All of them lay still, clearly no threat to anyone. I didn't look too closely at the bodies which were not uniformed.

The Shadows knew where we were. Unless they leaned out of the windows and put themselves in harm's way, their bullets couldn't reach us for now. But I knew it wouldn't be too long before they regrouped. I allowed myself to relax against my mother for a moment longer, forcing myself to take slow, deep lungfuls of air. Once I started to feel a little better, I backed away, shooting her a grateful look. Taking stock of the others around me, I was relieved to see Mason among the survivors, as well as Roberts, Hughes, and Rogers, who were also discussing our next steps.

"Whatever's left of his Shadow Patrol are inside," Hughes said. "He's running scared. Now all we have to do is get in there."

Rogers grimaced. "That's easier said than done."

"We got this far, didn't we?" Hughes' tone remained positive, his determination to avenge his community after Reed's attack clear.

Rogers seemed to rally. "Alright then. One last push?"

"Let's do it." Hughes balled his hands into fists. "We can't let it go, not now."

"Think he was telling the truth about the second wave of Shadows?" Tyler asked. "We've done well here, but there aren't enough of us to keep going indefinitely."

"Heard from Walker while we were waiting for your signal." Rogers countered. "He and Howard've been scouting The Beck, looking for other patrols. He hadn't come across any when I spoke to him."

I managed to find my voice. "We didn't see any when we came up from Dev, either."

"You can be certain that Adams' main goal is protecting himself." Baker's voice was scathing. "He'll have had the majority of his forces up here from the start."

"The Beck's not small though." Rogers warned. "It's

possible that he has other guards elsewhere, waiting on his command."

"All the more reason to get in there now." Hughes gestured to the building behind us. "Get rid of Adams, before any potential back up arrives."

"If they came from behind, we'd be trapped." Mason added unnecessarily. "And—"

He stopped as a new noise startled us all. In alarm, we turned towards it, watching, as two figures crept around the side of the building and came towards us. When they got closer, there were several sighs of relief as we recognised Tyler and Jackson.

"How did you—?" I gasped, glancing up at the windows.

"You didn't think we'd leave you to fend for yourselves, did you?" Jackson exchanged a grin with Mason, who was beaming.

Tyler shrugged. "By the time we got down the tunnel with the last few citizens, Anders was waiting. He's going to see that the mothers and babies get to Minors safely. Green and Thomas are with him. We figured you could use our help."

"And look," Jackson leaned towards us, tipping something out of the pack on her back and holding it out. "Anders brought these. Said he thought we might need them."

In her palm lay several small grenades, similar to those we had used earlier. Hughes picked one up and examined it.

"They're explosives, but not quite like the ones we used before." Tyler pointed at the windows above us.

Rogers followed her gaze. "How do they work?"

"They let out some kind of substance," Jackson hissed. "Should knock out anyone who comes into contact with it."

"And drive others out of the building," Tyler added.

"Sounds like this might be one of Montgomery's inventions," I offered, wondering for the first time where the scientist was hiding, and whether Cam was still with her.

Jackson was reaching inside her pack again. She retrieved a bundle of cloth and began to separate it into different sections.

"Need to protect ourselves though," Tyler muttered. "Make sure *we* don't breathe it in."

"How long does it last?" Rogers' voice was muffled as he fixed the cloth over his face.

"A few minutes at least," Tyler confirmed. "We should probably give it a little while if we're going in; let it disperse. And don't remove these if we're inside the building."

Rogers was still looking at the building above us. "Ok, does anyone know specifically where Adams is?"

I pointed to one of the windows not far from where we stood. "We think he was in there earlier. Although he may have moved by now."

"Alright. Divide up. In pairs, take one of these and assign yourselves a window. We should be able to cover all the ones on this side of the building. On my command, one of you breaks the window; the other throws the primed explosive through it."

"When they go off, just cover the exits." Hughes was staring at the closed door of the building. "The explosives will cause confusion and hopefully knock out a good number of the guards inside."

"If we're lucky, one of them will take Adams out," Jackson muttered.

"Ok, cover the entrances, catch the ones who try to run."

Rogers glanced at the group around him. "Hughes, Baker, Cass, Mason. You take the back. The rest of us will cover the front and possibly the side. Some of them might try to exit through the windows. Everyone ok with that?"

Nobody objected, and Rogers nodded to Jackson, who began handing out the explosives carefully. There were nine citizens in the group around me, and between us we could cover the three front-facing windows and one of the ones around the side. I hoped it would be enough.

Once we were all armed with the explosives, Rogers glanced around at our group. "Ready?"

We all nodded.

"Best of luck."

Hughes slid along the side of the building with Cass, until they rounded the corner and were out of sight. Mason and Baker followed suit positioning themselves under the farthest window on the front of the building; Roberts and I were the third to move. We waited nervously while Rogers, Jackson, and Tyler manoeuvered into position behind us.

"Alright?" Roberts whispered to me.

"Not really."

"I know." He sighed. "I just keep wishing I was back at home with Ross and Fenn."

I took in the fear in his eyes, which I knew reflected my own. "You'll be back with them soon," I whispered.

"Will I?" But he managed a small smile as we watched for Rogers' signal.

Seconds later, it came. As I pulled the pin from the bomb, Roberts raised the butt of his gun and smashed it against the window, which shattered into hundreds of pieces and cascaded down over our heads. We ducked, and once the waterfall of glittering shards had ceased, I stretched up and flung the small explosive as far as I could into the space beyond.

We stayed low, making sure that the protective material shielded the whole of our faces. Within seconds, a satisfying series of explosions ripped through the air. Inside, I could hear an ominous hissing sound, followed by shouts, and the sounds of confusion, muffled through the wall we crouched behind. The door banged open and numerous Shadow guards erupted from the building, fighting desperately to escape from the gas. Behind us, Rogers and Tyler fired over and over, incapacitating a good number of the fleeing guards.

I knew that any who made it out of the back entrance would suffer the same fate. After the initial burst of guards flung themselves down the front steps of the building, the doorway remained empty for a while. We sat, hoping that the gas had knocked the rest of them out and there would be no need for the fight to continue.

After a few minutes had passed, Rogers crept forward to investigate. As he approached the steps to the front of the building, there was movement in the doorway. Acting quickly, he leapt to one side of the steps and crouched low. Our guns trained on the entrance, we waited.

Slowly, three figures materialized out of the smoke. At the front stood two burly Shadow guards, side by side. They were coughing and spluttering, their uncertain steps confirming how badly the gas had affected them. They were still armed, but didn't seem able to focus properly, and began firing shots randomly into the open air. Concealed close to the side of the building, we were safe.

Behind them, an even wilder figure emerged. Bleeding

from a wound on his forehead, gasping for breath as he reached the safer outside air, was an almost unrecognisable Adams. He bent low behind his protectors, edging forward as they did. From his position on the other side of the steps, Rogers waved a hand at Tyler. As one, they aimed their guns at the Shadow guards' lower bodies, and fired.

Both men let out horrible screams of pain and dropped to the ground, clutching their legs. Roberts and I sprang forward and removed the guns from their hands with relative ease. Stationing ourselves either side of the guards, we trained their own weapons on them, though neither seemed able to fight back.

When I glanced back at Rogers, he, Tyler and Jackson had formed a semi- circle around Adams, their guns raised, blocking his exit. He glanced back into the shadowy space behind him, seeming surprised that he had run out of guards to shield him. Twisting back around, the mighty Governor stared at his captors in turn, his expression bewildered.

"It's over, Adams." Rogers fixed our ex-leader with a stare. "Give up."

As we watched, Adams drew in a deep breath and his gaze, which had been hazy and unfocused, seemed to sharpen. He reached around behind him and clutched at his belt. When he brought his hand back around the front, it held a gun.

I felt Jackson and Tyler stiffen, but Rogers continued to speak calmly.

"I said it's over. There's nowhere to go." Checking briefly that the Shadow guards were still incapacitated, Rogers continued, keeping his voice low and controlled. "Give yourself up, and you won't be killed."

Adams took a shaky step forward, a cough wrenching from

his chest. I could see the fury on Jackson's face as Adams moved closer to Rogers, who continued to wait for a response.

"Never." Adams glanced down at his weapon, turning it this way and that in his hands.

All three of the citizens standing around him raised their guns a fraction.

"Adams, you can't hope to kill all of us before we return fire." Tyler's voice sounded reasonable, but I could hear the tension in her usually calm tone.

"You don't have to die." I heard the pain in Rogers' voice as he went on. "No one else has to die."

"Ah, if only that were true." Adams continued to raise the gun, inching it slowly closer to a level where he could use it.

For a second, we were still, the air around us thick with the dissipating smoke and the scent of fear. And then, as though someone had accelerated time, Adams' hand shot upwards. But he didn't aim at Rogers, or Tyler, or Jackson. His hand moved higher than necessary to hit any of my friends, moving in a completely alien direction.

I heard a scream as he turned the barrel of the gun backwards, and placed it underneath his own chin. And then, before anyone could react, he pulled the trigger. I squeezed my eyes shut as the shot echoed around the empty field. When I opened them, Adams lay prostrate at the foot of the steps, the bottom part of his face destroyed. I looked away with a shudder, as blood began to stain the wood beneath his body

There was a silence, broken only by the heavy breathing of my fellow Resistance citizens. Tyler was the first to find her voice.

"Are you alright, Rogers?"

Our leader took a faltering step forward, his face devastated.

Tyler was quick to follow, grasping his arm and steering him away from the steps where Adams lay. She guided him to an empty patch of grass a few metres away, where he sat down on the ground and buried his head in his hands.

"Not your fault." Tyler bent down next to Rogers and slid an arm around his shoulder. "You hear me? This was *not* your fault."

"Lower your guns." She turned to Roberts and I, gesturing to the two Shadow guards who still writhed beneath us. "Look at them. They're harmless."

I glanced at the man on the ground at my feet. "Are we going to help them?"

Tyler nodded. "Try and stop the bleeding."

I stared down into the eyes of the guard. His face was twisted in pain, but he was biting his lip and attempting to remain calm. Motioning to Roberts to keep his gun handy, I holstered my gun and removed the cloth from my face. Bending to the man before me, I avoided his eyes while securing the material tightly around his leg.

"That should stop the bleeding," I pointed at the makeshift bandage, "for now, at least."

I moved across to repeat the process on the other guard, using Roberts' mask this time. Neither guard gave me any trouble, the second one even muttering a word of thanks as I tied off his wound. As I climbed to my feet, we heard a single set of footsteps approaching from the side of the building.

We all froze. Roberts raised his gun in readiness as a figure peered around the corner.

"Is it over?"

I had never been so relieved to hear my mother's voice.

Rogers looked up, his face pained. "Adams is dead, if that's what you mean. Anyone escape at your end?"

Baker shook her head. "There are a few injured Shadow guards though. Mason and Cass are just securing them... trying to attend to their wounds."

Rogers frowned. "They give you much trouble?"

She shook her head. "None at all. Most of them seem to have been badly affected by the gas. I figure if we can take them prisoner now, we won't have any issues. Hughes is just checking the building."

On cue, a figure appeared in the doorway, a look of intense relief on his face as he spotted Adams. Stepping over his body, Hughes pulled the thick material away from his face.

"It's all clear in there. Most of them got out. And those who didn't, well, I'm afraid..." he heaved a sigh, "there's not much we can do for them now."

Rogers hauled himself into a standing position, wiping a tired hand across his face. "You and I had better walk the perimeter, Hughes. Need to check there aren't any more Shadows lurking anywhere in the vicinity. And take care of any citizens who're wounded. Our own first, mind."

Hughes looked at Rogers' face. "Leave that to Roberts and I. You look exhausted, man."

Rogers looked like he might argue, but Tyler stepped forward and placed a hand on his arm. "We need you to message the others. There's still the threat of that second wave of Shadows."

The rest of us nodded our agreement, and Rogers gave in. "Alright. I'll contact Anders and Walker." He turned to Tyler as he pulled out his walkie-talkie. "Can you−?"

"Already on it." She smiled as he turned to walk away, raising the radio to his lips as he did so.

Tyler took over, practical as ever. "Right. Hughes and Roberts, walk around the edge of the sector, as Rogers said. Alert us to anyone who is still alive and can be helped."

The two men set off immediately as Tyler continued. "Baker, can you stay here and help to treat the injured? Get the others to assist as you see fit."

Tyler moved to the injured guards who now lay fairly still. Frowning, she bent to check the bandages on their legs. "Seems to be stopping the bleeding for now. But we'll need to take out the bullets at some point." She looked across at my mother. "Should we create some kind of system, assess how severe the injuries are?"

Baker nodded. "Yes. Bring them all here. Lay them out on the grass." She indicated the space where the two Shadow guards already lay. "Shadow Patrol here, and Resistance over there. That way, we can assess how serious their injuries are, try and prioritise."

As Baker spoke, I felt a surge of affection for her, and it hit me that I was no longer willing to let her keep me at arms' length. I hoped, from her behaviour over the past few hours, that she was beginning to feel the same way.

I was jerked from my reverie by a shriek from my right as Jackson spotted Mason returning from the other side of the building. Launching herself in his direction, she flung herself into his arms, her relief palpable. He responded with the same enthusiasm.

It was only then that I thought of Cam again. I glanced around, panicked, as Mason pushed Jackson gently away and turned to Baker.

"There are quite a few injured guards on the other side." He pointed at the area behind the building, and I wondered for a second whether Cam might be round the other side. "Cass is with them. We bound their hands, so they won't be escaping, but some of them need fairly urgent attention."

"As do these." Baker gestured at a number of people who had managed to haul themselves to their feet and make their way towards us, despite their injuries. I studied every face closely, but didn't see anyone familiar.

"Look, we're in Meds." Tyler interjected. "There are lots of supplies here: drugs, bandages and so on. Honestly, it's the best place we could be."

"Better go get them." Baker raised an eyebrow. "We're going to need as many as we can get our hands on."

"There should be plenty in the other building. I know where they're kept." Tyler called over her shoulder as she walked away. "Mason, get back round to Cass. Start bringing across the injured from that side, alright?"

As he set off, I swept my eyes across the field once more. There was still no sign of Cam. Panicked now, I turned back to Baker and Jackson.

"Have you seen Cam? I mean... since the start of the fight?" I fought to keep my voice steady. "Or Montgomery?"

Realisation dawning, the two women began sweeping their eyes over the field.

"It's just that... they don't appear to be among the..." I gestured to the bodies lying on the ground around us. "But they weren't with those of us attacking Adams' building just now. In fact, I haven't seen them at all since I got over to this side of the Sector."

Baker's sharp eyes darted across the field as she listened. I could see her taking everything in: the almost-empty field stretching out to our left; the dense trees which fringed the edges of the sector where Rogers stood, still speaking into the walkie-talkie; the still-smoking building beside us; and, finally, Hughes and Roberts, who were working their way methodically around the Meds border. I followed her gaze, but there wasn't a single person who looked remotely like Cam.

Eventually, my eyes returned to Tyler. She had just reached the building we had rescued the Meds women from earlier. Making quick work of the steps which led to it, she disappeared inside. As the door swung shut behind her, I scanned the windows of the building and froze.

"There!"

Baker spun to face me. "What?"

I hesitated for a second, unsure of myself. "I thought I saw... thought there was..." I gestured at the window, which now looked as empty as all the others.

"What did you see?" Jackson's voice was breathless.

I looked back at her hopelessly. "Maybe nothing. I'm not sure."

"We cleared that building before, Quin." Baker sounded irritated. "You were *there*. I don't see how..."

Despite her doubt, she shielded her eyes with a hand and peered at the building. And then, as I watched, her face changed.

"Baker?"

"I think you're right."

I glanced back at the window, but could see nothing. "About what?"

"There *is* someone in there."

I went cold. "And Tyler has just gone inside."

Chapter Forty Two

Abruptly, Baker dropped to her knees at the side of the Shadow guard. She bent over him, leaning close to his ear. "Who's in that building?"

He grunted, shifting slightly, but otherwise didn't respond.

I joined her on the ground, hissing in her ear. "Do you think it's Cam?"

Ignoring me, she leaned even closer to the guard on the ground. "I said, who's in there?"

"Don't know," he muttered.

"Look," Baker had lost her patience. "We can treat you. Get that bullet out of your leg. Or we can leave it in and let you die."

The guard's face blanched. "I don't know who's in there. But I do know that a couple of Shadows disappeared."

Baker stared at him. "They're not just lying dead inside that building?"

He shook his head. "No. Earlier. Before the fighting started. Adams couldn't find them."

"Alright." Baker stood up.

The guard lifted a hand towards us. "You said you'd–"

But Baker had gone, striding away without a backwards glance. I stood to hurry after her. Beside me, Jackson was removing the gun from the shoulder of the other Shadow guard, who was out cold.

"Ammo," she muttered, her teeth gritted. "Need more ammo."

I reached down and took the gun from the man who lay at my feet. He gestured to a pouch at his hip.

"There's your ammo. Take it." He grimaced. "Just come back and help us."

"We will." I promised, standing to leave.

"Come on!" Jackson had already set off after Baker, and I cast a glance of apology back at the guard as we ran.

It took us a few seconds to catch the older woman, who was making her way round the side of the building. When she reached the rear, she stepped out cautiously, peering across at the other door. In the distance, Mason and Cass were bent over one of the fallen Shadow Patrol guards, but Baker ignored them. Beckoning me to follow her, she raced across the grass and up the steps on the opposite side. Putting an ear to the door, she satisfied herself that there was no one lurking behind it and eased it open.

Inside, all was silent. The three of us crept through the space, holding our breath. Many of the doors were still standing open, the rooms behind them uninhabited. The canteen, though it showed signs of recent occupation, was similarly abandoned. As we drew nearer to the front, though, four of the doors were closed firmly, daring us to make a choice which one concealed the interloper.

As we reached the end, Baker indicated the room on the left, where the Meds citizens had been hiding earlier. She gestured to Jackson and I to take the ones on the right. My heart was in my mouth as we eased open the doors.

All three rooms were empty.

We closed in on the final door, which I knew led to a small office which the Meds Super on duty usually inhabited. I reached it first, and cautiously placed my ear to the door. To begin with I could hear nothing, but then, from inside, came the low murmur of voices. Nodding at Baker, I positioned myself at one side of the door, while she took the other. Jackson moved to join me, but Baker jabbed a finger in the direction of the abandoned canteen. For a moment, Jackson resisted.

"Wait," Baker mouthed at her, gesturing furiously at my friend.

Understanding that Baker wanted her to stay out of sight until the situation was clear, Jackson reluctantly stepped back into the canteen. The strategy was a good one: she could provide concealed back up if we needed it. But I hoped that we wouldn't have to call on her.

Guns ready, Baker and I thrust the door open and stared at what lay beyond.

The sight terrified me. On a chair at one side of the room, was Cam. He was bound and gagged, but didn't look like he was fighting his imprisonment at all. On the contrary, his expression was completely blank, and he stared directly ahead, as though he did not know us. His left arm had a tube inserted into it, through which was flowing some kind of clear liquid. To one side of him stood one of the missing Shadow Patrol guards, the gun which had been at his side, now pointing directly at us.

On the other side of the space, beside the only window in the room, stood another guard. His gun, however, was not pointing in our direction. It was aimed instead at a familiar figure whose hands were bound behind her back. One look at the furious expression on her face was enough to tell me that Tyler was not reacting well to being taken prisoner. At the rear of the room was a large upright screen, effectively dividing the area.

"It's getting pretty crowded in here."

The voice came from behind the screen. Hiding, out of sight and unreachable, was Montgomery. We kept our guns focused on the two guards as the scientist continued to speak, her voice totally calm.

"I started with a single hostage. Just good old Cam." I imagined her smiling behind the screen. "But then Tyler burst in here and, well... you're almost making it easy for me."

"The two guards were on her side, not Adams'." Tyler burst out. "They freed her from Cam, took him prisoner. She's in here looking for insurance... something valuable to bargain with... the meds—"

Tyler stopped abruptly as the guard at her side slammed the butt of his gun into her head. Baker and I winced as she fell to the ground, but we held our position. Behind us, in the hallway, I could hear faint sounds.

"You didn't need to do that!" Baker cried out, louder than was necessary.

Unfazed, Montgomery continued. "Foolish girl... I'm after more than just meds."

"What do you want?" Baker's voice dropped a tone, sounding alien in the confined space.

Montgomery's reply was immediate. "I want you gone. And you will be. Soon. That second wave of Shadows Adams mentioned? They're coming. It's only a matter of time."

CHAPTER FORTY TWO

"But he's dead," I blurted out. "They'll have no one to give them orders."

"Won't they?" She was, as always, mocking me.

There was silence for a moment, broken only by a sharp intake of breath from Cam.

"What have you done to him?" I couldn't keep the catch from my voice. "Is he in pain?"

From behind the screen, Montgomery gave a soft, menacing laugh.

I stared at Cam's face. He was expressionless, immobile, helpless. Looking at him brought to mind visions of Montgomery's enjoyment when she had experimented on Lewis, a citizen who had suffered a terrible chemical burn from a substance she had created. By the time she had finished with him, he had been beyond saving.

Gazing at Cam now, I felt sick.

Montgomery's voice came from behind him, emotionless as ever. "I've drugged him, of course. A new creation of mine, to keep him calm. I was going to give him a larger dose of the one I've been giving to the Shadows lately. Adams' instructions, of course. To toughen them up, make them more dependent, more malleable, less..." she paused, as though searching for the right word, "troublesome."

For the first time, Baker spoke. "So, they've been fighting with less and less idea of what they're doing?"

"Clever woman!" Montgomery exclaimed. "You're right. Adams was fed up with them second guessing his orders, thinking for *themselves*." I could almost hear her rolling her eyes. "Of course, it worked better on some than others. And I controlled the dosages carefully."

The two guards exchanged an amused glance.

"As for Cam here," Montgomery continued, "well, he's part of my insurance policy. As long as I have him, it stops you from attacking me. Until the backup arrives."

"So, you're hiding?" I spat out.

She laughed again. "Not hiding, as such. Just waiting in a safe place until the cavalry arrives."

My hands on the gun were shaking and I couldn't prevent a grunt of frustration from escaping my mouth. At my side, Baker stepped forward very slightly, placing a foot slightly in front of mine. I knew she was warning me to keep my cool, not to jump forward and act rashly.

"What if I told you they weren't coming?" Baker edged forward slowly, her voice as calm as Montgomery's.

"Not possible." Behind the screen, we heard the scientist shift slightly.

"I assure you it's entirely possible." Baker continued walking, stepping into the room a little further. The Shadow guards tensed. "We've just put in a radio call to our associates in the Lower Beck. They've been instructed to cut off the access to Meds and eliminate any remaining guards." She laughed cruelly, a sound put on for effect. "No one's coming to rescue you."

Taking advantage of the distraction, I shot a brief glance over my shoulder. There was no sign of Jackson, but the door at the far end of the building stood slightly ajar. I knew for a fact that we had closed it on our way in. I turned my attention back to the guards, who were still regarding Baker with mistrust. Behind the screen, Montgomery continued.

"You're lying." Her voice had risen a tone. It was only a slight alteration, but enough to suggest that Baker was getting to her.

"Am I though?" Baker continued, her own voice mocking now. "Are you willing to take the risk?"

"Are *you*?" Montgomery sneered. "Soldiers, prepare to execute the prisoners."

The Shadow guards immediately thrust their guns at Cam and Tyler. Cam's head lolled to one side, and the guard had to lean over slightly to ensure he would have a direct hit. On the ground at the other side of the room, Tyler moaned as the muzzle of the gun pressed against her temple.

"I have two people you care about in my power," Montgomery snarled. "You want to lose them? Go ahead."

"Alright, alright." Baker held up a hand. "I'll stay where I am."

Montgomery continued, "The rest of the Shadows are coming. And when they do, *I'm* the one who will control them. *I'm* the one they'll listen to."

"And if you're wrong?" Baker might have stopped advancing, but she kept on needling the scientist. "What if they're not coming?"

A hand appeared from behind the screen. In it, was a vial of pale pink liquid.

"Know what this is?" Montgomery sounded calm once more. "The fertility serum. And I have the entire stock of it in boxes back here. Every. Last. Drop. Without this, you Beck escapees will struggle to keep your brave new world going. Because, right now, there are very few of you capable of reproducing."

The hand disappeared. Baker glanced back at me, her eyes wide. Very slowly, she tapped a finger on the top of her gun, and inclined her head towards the man guarding Tyler.

"Trust me," Montgomery continued. "I always have a

backup plan. Try and defeat me, go on. I'm ready for you. Without me, and my knowledge, your people won't survive beyond this generation."

"Really? You think you're *that* powerful." Baker's voice dripped with sarcasm. "That there's not a single soul here who could do what you do? What makes you so sure?"

"Because I'm brilliant," Montgomery scoffed. "There is no one... *no one* here who's on a par with me. Adams knew it. He believed in science, with his beloved programme for the *gifted* kids. But I was always... always the most gifted of all. He knew it. Used it to his full advantage. But I outwitted him. He had no concept of what his guards were being given in the end."

I knew Baker was trying to keep Montgomery talking. Because, while she was talking, she couldn't give the order for Cam and Tyler to die. Ahead of us, the guards awaited Montgomery's command, their guns pressed firmly against the heads of their prisoners. My heart pounding, I wondered how the standoff would end.

And then, the window behind Tyler's guard shattered, scattering fragments of glass across the room. Taking full advantage of the momentary distraction, Baker swung her gun around and fired rapidly at Tyler's guard. I followed suit a second later, taking aim at the man who stood over Cam, who had momentarily relaxed his hold on the prisoner as he spun to face the window. My first shot caught him in the shoulder, and he fell sideways, clutching it.

"Put him out of action! Now!" Baker hollered.

I glanced over to see that she had fired a second time, and the guard she had attacked was lying flat out on the ground next to Tyler, blood pouring from his head.

Moving a step closer, I took aim again. The man lay on the ground, a pained expression on his face and an arm clutching his wound. His gun lay useless on the floor beside him. Deciding he wasn't much of a threat as it stood, I spun the gun around and slammed the end of it across the side of his head. He collapsed and lay still.

"Alright in there?" Jackson's voice floated through the now empty window. "Help is coming."

Outside, there were more shouts and the sound of pounding feet, and my heart soared, knowing that Rogers and the others were on their way. I turned to Baker, aware that the only remaining threat was Montgomery herself. My mother pointed at the screen, which remained in position. Montgomery had made no noise at all since the window had broken.

Together, Baker and I stared at it.

"It's over, Montgomery." Baker began, "You have no hostages. Your guards can't help you. You're totally out-numbered."

"Alright!" The quavering voice from behind the screen did not sound like the woman I knew. "I'm coming out. Stand back."

Baker and I took a small step away. Our guns aimed at the screen, we waited for Montgomery to appear. For a moment, there was silence. And then, for the second time in as many minutes, we heard glass shattering. This time though, the sound was of a higher pitch, and I knew instantly what Montgomery had done.

"No!" Baker leapt forward, hauling the screen out of the way.

The floor beneath Montgomery's feet was covered with

a pale pink liquid. It flowed freely from the mess of glass shards which were all that remained of the vials that had held the fertility serum. Behind it stood Montgomery, a single vial held aloft in one hand.

"Oops." She managed a tight smile, though when it faded, she looked almost ill. "This is it, I'm afraid. The last sample."

A strangled scream came from my mother's mouth. She closed the gap between herself and Montgomery, her gun pressing against the woman's temple.

Montgomery didn't flinch. "Kill me and I'll drop it. Come on Baker, you're not stupid."

We heard footsteps at the end of the hallway.

"Proceed with caution..." Behind us, Rogers was giving commands. "...several citizens in there... not sure..." His voice grew louder as he approached and we all heard the final order. "Do *not* fire until I signal."

"You're almost out of time Montgomery," I said quietly, trying to stop my voice from shaking. "Give us the serum, and we'll let you live."

From the sounds of their footsteps, I could tell that the citizens in the hallway were almost at the door. I held out a hand to indicate that Rogers should wait. Next to the woman who held the future of The Beck in her hand, my mother tensed. I held her gaze for a moment, willing her to stay in control. Then I looked back at Montgomery.

Taking a small step towards her, I held out my hand for the vial. "Give it to me."

"Call off your pitbull." The scientist shot a pointed look at Baker. "I'll hand it over when there isn't a loaded gun to my head."

"Baker," I waved a hand, hoping she would obey, "move

442

away."

Reluctantly, my mother stepped back, keeping her gun trained on the other woman. When she was occupying the space in between Montgomery and I, she stopped, clearly not prepared to retreat any further.

"Alright, Montgomery. That's as good as it gets." Taking a deep breath, I extended my open palm once more. "Pass it over."

Holding out the hand that contained the serum, the scientist took the final step towards me. As the vial made contact with my hand, I closed my fingers around it, my heart thundering. At the same time Montgomery twisted sharply, reaching her other hand behind her. Seconds later, her hand was between us again.

In it, there was a gun.

I felt myself being propelled backwards, and collapsed into the arms of someone behind me as a shot rang out in the small space. At the same time, those who had been paused at the door surged into the room, filling it with even more noise and confusion. I heard additional shots, some piercing screams, and clutched the person who had caught me tightly, praying that it would soon be over.

Eventually, the room went quiet. I looked up to find Cass' arms around me, her expression stricken. Running my hands over my body, I checked for a bullet wound which wasn't there. Remembering the serum, my gaze darted to my hand, which to my relief still contained the tiny vial.

A few feet away, Montgomery lay on the floor, blood staining the front of her usually-pristine white coat. Her eyes were closed, but her face was twisted with a pain which told me she wasn't dead. Not yet, anyway.

My eyes were drawn to a group of figures just in front of me. Rogers, Mason, and Hughes were crouched in a tight circle around someone, their voices murmuring, low and intense. My gaze travelled left and right. Cam was in the same position: fastened to the chair, the tube still feeding drugs into his neck. On the other side of the room, Tyler sat upright, tears streaming down her face as she nursed the wound on her head.

A sudden panic seized me. Struggling to my feet, I stepped over Montgomery and stumbled towards the three men, placing a hand on Mason's shoulder to steady myself. He slid backwards slightly to allow me access to the circle.

"She pushed you..." he stuttered, "threw you out of the way and... the shot hit her instead... but she's..."

My heart stopped as I saw what he had been leaning over. Baker.

I looked down at her, sprawled on the ground before me, frightening amounts of blood gushing from a wound in the side of her neck despite Rogers' efforts to stop it.

Suddenly I understood. The pressure I had felt was not Montgomery's bullet, but the force of my mother's hand. The scientist's shot had missed its target, finding its home in my mother's body instead.

Collapsing to my knees by her side, I took her hand gently in my own. Her expression had been one of pain and anguish, but as she became aware of my presence, it changed. A more serene look settled on her features, and she grasped my hand slightly.

"Thank you," I managed to whisper.

My mother gave a slight nod, and I knew she had heard me. Cradling her hand in mine, I watched as the light faded from her eyes.

Chapter Forty Three

As I exited the room clinging to Cass' arm, I felt some kind of autopilot take over. I was told much later that I sat holding my mother's hand until my friend had pried me away. During that time, Montgomery had lain a few feet away, still and silent. With all our focus on Baker, none of us had paid her much attention, and by the time anyone was willing or able to check on her, it was too late.

No one mourned her passing.

Rogers had spoken to various others via the walkie-talkie and established that there was nothing more for us to fear. The threatened 'second wave' of guards had never arrived. On their scouting mission, Walker and Howard had come across a large number of Shadow Patrol in the Assessment buildings, gathering additional ammunition and waiting for orders.

Between them, the two men had managed to barricade the gates to the compound, preventing the guards from escaping. Enlisting the help of the more able citizens from Minors, they had kept a constant guard on the entrance until they received word from Rogers that it was over. When the remaining Shadows were told that all their leaders were dead, very few of them had resisted capture. We had won the battle, but at a cost.

Around me, the long process of recovery began.

Now that the second Meds building was clear, Hughes instructed a small team to bring the injured inside, where they were placed into beds and given the best care we could manage. Cam had been detached from the tube which Montgomery had hooked into his system and transferred to the treatment room. Slowly, he had begun to regain consciousness. Despite Mason's injury being fairly minor, Jackson had made sure that he took a full dose of the anti-infection meds which were being handed out, and Rogers insisted that Hughes take some too.

Tyler had been brought to the makeshift care centre, but refused to spend more than a few minutes there. Once her wound had been bandaged, she was straight back outside, helping to collect and bring in the bodies of those who had not survived. Another Meds room had been dedicated to the dead, and those working to bring them in had the hardest job. I knew that Baker and Will were lying in there, alongside a number of others who had perished in Meds.

Thomas, Anders, and Green had managed to successfully transfer all of the women and babies to Minors, where they had taken shelter with the rest of the community. Anders had kept a nonstop watch on the perimeter to fend off any further attack, but only encountered a few stray Shadow Patrol guards most of whom surrendered quickly. The majority of the survivors were now being put to work: caring for the injured, providing meals, clearing and repairing the areas devastated by the fighting; but we all knew there was a long way to go.

Unable to stay in Meds any longer, I joined a group of

citizens who were taking medical supplies to the Lower Beck. We walked slowly, supporting one another as the adrenaline wore off and exhaustion enveloped us. When we arrived, we were directed to the canteen, where they were attempting to give help and support to those who had suffered in the earlier battle.

As we entered, I was struck by how quiet it was. The room had been divided in half, one section for the wounded, the other for the dead. I gave the box of bandages I had been carrying to an Agric citizen, who shot me a grateful smile before hurrying off to the closest patient. As I turned to leave, I noticed two male citizens transferring a body from one side of the room to the other. I watched them carrying the citizen with respect, and wondered how many more people we might still lose.

When they reached the far side, the men lay the body down gently. I ran my eyes along the bodies already resting on the cold canteen floor. I knew that McGrath was there, alongside an alarming number of others from the Beck Resistance who had been killed. I thought, too, of all the Ridge citizens who would now have to be buried as a result of a fight that wasn't theirs. Roberts had told me that this included Simpson, whose own injuries had been too severe for her to recover from.

We had lost so many people. Fighting back tears, I made my way to a bench at the side of the canteen and sat down. Moments later I was joined by Cass, who placed a blanket around my shoulders and sat down beside me. Her eyes reflected the horror I felt. Without speaking, I knew that she understood. Holding her hand in mine, I rested my head on her shoulder and closed my eyes.

Sometime later, I became aware of approaching footsteps. They stopped in front of the bench where Cass and I were sitting.

"Quin?"

I looked up, startled, to see Cam, who looked much recovered. "Cam? Are you–?"

"I'm fine. They've worn off, I promise." He even managed a weak smile. "Are you ok?"

Managing to stand, I took a small step towards him. He caught me as I stumbled into him, and held me close, wrapping his arms around me.

"Want to get some fresh air?"

I nodded, and was vaguely aware of Cass' smile as we exited the room together.

We walked away from the canteen in silence, taking the path which led to the wall. We passed a few citizens on the way, people I did not know well, each one greeting us with the same bewildered smile.

Cam kept a protective arm around me and nodded in response to the various people, understanding that I wasn't ready to speak to people just yet. Our closeness attracted a few curious glances, but we ignored them. When we reached the wall, we climbed the ladder, arriving at the top which was, for now, totally unguarded. We wandered along, hand in hand until we reached a familiar alcove, which jutted out and gave a view from which the waters could be carefully watched.

Pausing there, we leaned on the wall and looked out to the horizon.

"I hear you were responsible for saving me." Cam's tone was gentle. "Amongst others."

I shrugged.

"Thank you."

Blinking rapidly, I tried and failed to find the words to explain what had happened.

"I'm so sorry about Baker," he tried again. "Were the two of you very close?"

Tears filled my eyes as I finally found my voice. "Something like that." I turned to him. "Can I tell you about it later? I don't think I can manage it right now."

Nodding slowly, he placed his arms around me once more. Laying my head on his chest, I looked out over the water. The sound of it lapping gently against the base of the wall was hypnotic, and as I listened, I found the chaos of my thoughts begin to calm. Too much had happened over the last few hours. I wanted Cam to know about Baker, about The Ridge, about the life I'd experienced away from The Beck. But not at the moment.

I would tell him soon. We had time.

Epilogue

"See you soon." Tyler hugged me tightly as I stood up to leave.

The canteen was filled with Ridge citizens, all noisily chattering as they readied themselves for the day ahead. I missed living here, in some ways. The atmosphere here had always been positive, but things had only improved in the time since our final battle on The Beck.

I returned Tyler's embrace and turned to Hughes. "Take good care of her 'til then, won't you?"

"Sure thing." He winked at me and slung his arm around Tyler, who blushed furiously as I backed away. Heading for a table in the centre of the room, I crept up and closed my hands over a small boy's eyes. He shrieked with laughter and twisted round until he faced me.

"Quin!" he squealed with delight, allowing me to capture his cheeks and deliver a kiss.

"Hey, Rico. Sorry I missed you last night, but it was late by the time we got here."

I reached over his head and helped myself to a hunk of bread from his plate.

"Oy!" He tried to swat my hand out of the way.

"Too late." I winked at him.

Frowning, he shielded the rest of the contents of his plate

with his hands. "You were here last night?"

"I was. I looked in on you, but you were fast asleep."

Rico glared at Howard, who shrugged helplessly. "You were tired, little man. I didn't want to wake you."

"No fair!" Rico slumped in his chair, sulking.

I tapped him lightly on the head. "Hey, promise I'll come earlier next time. Come see you specially. How about that?"

Rico beamed at me, but he turned to frown at his father, refusing to forgive until Howard slid him an extra piece of bread. Glancing around at the rest of the table, I grinned at Ross, who was attempting to wrestle a spoon into Fenn's mouth as she squirmed on Roberts' knee.

"Does it get any easier?" I quipped.

"Nope." She laughed, and shook her head. "In fact, you'd think Coleman and Howard would've learned, but..."

She shot a sideways glance at her friend, who slapped her playfully on the arm. Her stomach was gently rounded beneath her overalls, and she looked adoringly at Howard who was still playing with his young son. Now there was a regular trade between the three islands, food was fairly plentiful and Hughes had lifted the single child rule, as he had always wanted to. Coleman and Howard had been among the first to take advantage, and now Rico was looking forward to the arrival of a baby brother or sister.

A sudden shriek from the other side of the table brought my attention back to Roberts, who was now sporting a large blob of mashed fruit on the side of his face. I smothered a giggle as he mock-frowned at me.

"You'd better be on your way if you're going to laugh at me like that Quin," he warned.

I held up my hands in submission. "Alright, alright! I'm

going."

"Back next month though, right?"

"Should be. I'm scheduled to bring over some more supplies. I'll stop by the apartment again, ok?" I smiled.

"You'd better." He wagged a finger at me as I turned to leave, but the effect of his threat was ruined by the spoon which Fenn had just poked into his eye.

I left the canteen and headed into the courtyard, where a number of people had now gathered. Rogers, Green, Walker, and Collins were there, readying themselves for their return to The Crags. Beside them stood Harris, Anders, and Jackson, who were waiting for me.

We were here for a number of reasons. Myself, Anders, Walker, and Collins were responsible for the transportation and exchange of the various supplies which were shared between the islands. Lead, bullets, crops: all were traded on a regular basis, and it meant that the three communities were thriving. A perfect job for me, it meant I got to travel between the three places I had previously called home and visit all the people I cared about on a regular basis.

The others, together with Hughes and Tyler, were representatives of our collective council. A male and a female from each community, elected by the citizens who dwelled on the different islands. Their monthly meetings involved coming together to discuss common issues and take feedback for our citizens to vote on. Since Adams' demise, it was the way we had run things. And it worked.

One of their first assignments had been to develop a justice system where we agreed on the punishments which would be doled out to the Shadow Patrol guards who had survived the battle. The council had ensured the construction of larger imprisonment units, where many of them were held until their trials, where each of them were able to give an account of their level of involvement with Adams' plan.

Following the hearings, the council had set up a system which allowed the accused to prove they had changed and were ready to reintegrate with society. After our success with Thomas, who now lived a quiet life on The Ridge where he worked as hard as any other citizen in the smelting plant, our leaders felt it was important to rehabilitate citizens whenever possible.

It was done on a gradual basis, and they were monitored all the time. Since the trials, more than thirty Shadow Patrol guards had successfully re-entered Beck society, or transferred to one of the other islands. It was a far better system, offering rewards for effective performance and contributions to society, rather than punishments for failing to do so.

"Ready to go?" Anders asked.

"Sure."

Waving good-bye to the Ridge citizens, I followed the others into the woods where we headed for the small harbour where our respective boats waited. I fell into step alongside Green, who I hadn't had much chance to talk privately with the previous night.

"How are you, Quin?" she began. "You look well."

"Thanks." I smiled. "I'm good. Sounds like things are going well at The Crags."

"They are." She slowed to allow me past a particularly narrow gap in the trees ahead of her. "It's been a challenge, but I'm pleased at the number of citizens who've chosen to move across to us recently. It's made a huge difference to the work in the mines, and we've even been able to create larger areas for crop-growing."

"How's the family?" I grinned at her.

"Great." She laughed. "We have our hands full, of course."

"Who has them right now?" I nodded at Rogers, who was deep in conversation with Walker just ahead of us.

"Harper. I miss them when I'm away, but she's great with them." She chuckled. "I guess it's nice to have a day off, just occasionally." She reached down and squeezed my hand tightly. "And maybe one day, Rogers and I will be able to have one of our own."

After the battle, one of our main priorities had been the reversal of the infertility meds administered to all female Beck citizens. In the end, it had turned out that Montgomery wasn't as unique in her brilliance as she had believed. Anders had used the single vial we had protected, plus some of the information in Montgomery's files, to replicate the serum. Much to everyone's relief, the council had instructed him to focus on making a large enough batch for every female who wanted it. It had taken months, but he had managed it.

Another issue had been the number of babies in need of good homes when The Beck infrastructure collapsed. Some of them were returned to their mothers, but with others it hadn't been so simple. The damage in the Meds building we had bombed meant that some records were destroyed and it had been impossible to trace the babies' parentage. Some of the mothers had been killed fighting for the Resistance in the battle, and there were also women who had been selected for Beck Birthing but never wanted a child.

Rogers and Green had been among the first to come forward and volunteer to take in some of the orphans, bringing two babies, a boy and a girl, back to The Crags with them. Anyone who witnessed their little family could see that they were extremely happy, but I knew that they were still hoping for a baby of their own. So far, it hadn't happened.

I returned the squeeze, before letting go of Green's hand. "You have plenty of time."

"I know." She tried to smile, but her eyes misted over as she let go of my hand.

I watched as she hurried ahead and joined Rogers, who slid an affectionate arm around her and held her close. Walker's laughter boomed from over his shoulder in front of us at something Rogers had said. Green made a face at him and turned to speak to her partner. As the harbour came into sight, Walker shortened his stride so he could walk next to me.

"Send Harper my best, won't you?" I asked, as always.

"Of course." He smiled affectionately. "She misses you."

"Green says you've had quite an influx of new people over there recently."

"Yes." We headed on to the small shelf of beach which led to our boats. "There seem to be a lot of Beck citizens who want to escape somewhere that's smaller, quieter. Allows them to forget."

"You can hardly blame them." I sighed.

"No. Not after so many of them lost people to the sickness or the battle. I'm only glad we've got rid of the sickness. For a few months there..." he broke off, frowning.

I thought about the citizens we had lost following the battle, to both injury and the lingering sickness. It had been a difficult time.

"Well, at least we seem to be free of it now." He scratched

his head. "Anyway, the newbies are only helping us to build on what we already have. Rogers and I oversee things, Harper runs the fields, Nelson and Shaw train the hunters and fishing folk, and Collins has taken over the kitchen since–" He paused awkwardly.

I nudged him gently. "Since Baker died, right? You can mention her name."

"Well, yes. Since Baker." He cleared his throat. "Sorry, Quin."

"It's alright." It had taken a while, but now I was able to hear my mother's name without feeling the guilt and sadness that had threatened to overwhelm me in the days following the battle.

Walker changed the subject. "And Green is busy setting up her education programme with Blythe, modelled on the one at The Ridge. It's going really well so far."

I smiled at his awkward segue.

The beach was empty as we approached, aside from our canoes. We bid good-bye to The Crags citizens and got on our way swiftly, not wanting to waste any more time. When we boarded the larger craft, Anders took the wheel while Jackson and I secured the canoe and Harris hauled up the anchor.

A pale sunlight reflected off the water as the boat moved away from the shore. It had rained heavily overnight, but it was warmer now and the journey promised to be smooth and trouble free. I leaned on the rail which ran around the stern and watched the shores of The Ridge retreat into the distance. We would reach the Beck before nightfall, if the weather was kind. I closed my eyes as the wind whipped through my hair, worn longer now. I could never bear to cut it these days.

A noise at my side alerted me to Jackson's presence and I

turned to smile at her.

"Hey, Jac."

"Hey yourself." She stretched her arms and leaned on the railing next to me. "Can't wait to get back. Who knows what Mason's been up to without me there to rein him in!"

I burst out laughing. Since Mason's lead mine discovery, he had become something of an inventor. He had begged Anders to let him into Dev, and was never happier than when he was experimenting with things which might improve our lives. Some of them worked out, others did not. But Anders was glad to have him on board, keen to encourage others to learn and create. It was one of the nicest parts of our lives on The Beck, post-Adams.

Jackson turned to glance at Anders, who was absorbed in a conversation with Harris and completely oblivious to us. He didn't like to be away from The Beck for long periods of time and I knew he was as anxious as Jackson and I to return home.

Beside me, my friend slid down the side of the boat, coming to rest against the wooden side and closing her eyes. "Anders said we could grab some rest."

I sank down onto the deck next to her, settling my back against the wood and leaning against her. "I won't turn that offer down."

"Quin?"

"Huh?"

"I'm glad you decided to settle back at The Beck." Jackson grasped tight hold of my hand. "Not sure I could've been happy with a large stretch of water separating us."

I smiled to myself, letting my eyes flutter closed as I returned the squeeze and relaxed.

I must have drifted off, because the next thing I knew, Jackson was shaking me awake and we were only metres from the Beck shoreline. I stood up and stretched, as we cruised closer to the harbour, where a familiar figure was waiting to greet us. Tapping her foot impatiently, Cass stood on the wooden jetty with a rope in her hands. Once we were close enough, I hopped out, grabbing a second rope and helping her to secure the boat. When we were done, she turned to me.

"Thought you were never going to get back!" She flung her arms around me for a brief second, before letting go just as abruptly.

"Well, I'm here now."

"About time!" I knew she missed me whenever I was gone, and liked to hear all of the news as soon as I returned. "How'd the trip go? D'you see Harper?"

"No. But Walker was there. He says she's just fine."

"How was Tyler?" Cass waved a hand at Jackson and Anders, who were still on the boat, before continuing breathlessly. "She still happy with Hughes?"

"Seems to be." I yawned, gesturing a hand up the hillside. "Mind if we catch up more tomorrow? I'm beat, and there's something I'd like to do before I head home."

"Sure." She slapped a hand on my back. "Have to get back anyway. Marley's waiting."

I watched as she sprinted off towards her pod, her hair flying madly behind her.

Turning back to the others, I smiled tiredly. "Mind if I head back?"

Anders waved a hand as he sorted through some of the resources we had brought back from The Ridge. "You go ahead. Jackson and Harris are going to help me out with something, but it won't take four of us."

Jackson looked up and smiled warmly. "See you at breakfast, Quin?"

I returned the smile. "Definitely."

It didn't take me long to make the now-familiar journey back up the Clearance hill to the rest of The Beck. The dense section of trees which had divided the Sector from the main population had now been thinned out, and there was a proper path leading between the two.

I reached the other side quickly, and headed through the trees, hoping not to meet anyone on the way. Before I reached the old entrance to Patrol, I took a fork in the path which led me to another area where the trees had been cleared, this time to make room for a number of different cairns, like those I had first encountered in The Crags.

We had designated the area for the burial of all the citizens lost in the battle. There were more cairns than anyone would have liked, but it provided a place of peace and solitude for anyone wanting to visit those they had lost. I often came here when I needed to escape.

I headed for a small cairn made of pure-white stones which rested under a particularly beautiful old tree. Placing my pack on the floor, I lowered myself to the ground in front of it. To one side of the stones, which I had selected and put together myself, rested a small wooden plaque, engraved with a single word in beautiful script. I reached out to trace the letters of my mother's name.

Closing my eyes, I listened to the wind whispering in the trees around me, until I heard a single set of footsteps approaching the clearing.

"Thought I might find you here." His voice still made my

heart race. Even after two years, when he spoke to me, his tone affectionate, I felt like the most important person on earth.

Emerging from the trees on the other side of the clearing, Cam smiled as he made his way towards me. Once he was within reach, he eased his tall frame down to the ground and sat behind me, encircling me with his arms.

"Everything alright?" he whispered.

"It is now." I twisted round in his arms, resting my forehead against his.

"Happy to see me?"

I grinned. "Always."

Leaning closer, he pressed his lips to mine softly. "Shall we go home, Quin?"

I took in a slow breath, wondering at the way we could now use the word to refer to a place that had imprisoned us for so long. But The Beck was no longer a place of desperation and fear. In a decade, there would be teenagers here who didn't even recall Adams and his methods. We were free of him forever.

I thought of Finn, of Miller, of the multiple people eliminated by Adams and his cruel ethos. Of Davies and Barnes, who had lost their lives in a desperate attempt at escape. Of Simpson, McGrath, Will, and Baker, all victims of the final fight for freedom. Their struggle had not been in vain. We had made it.

Placing an arm around Cam, I gazed up into his face. A familiar warmth filled his chestnut eyes as he jerked his head towards our Patrol-based apartment just the other side of the woods.

I returned his smile. "Let's go home."

Other Books by Clare Littlemore

If you loved The Flow Series, why not try **The Bellator Chronicles**, my thrilling dystopian romance trilogy?

Book 1: Compliance

A gender experiment. An exiled community. A forbidden love.

Sixteen-year-old Faith is proud to attend Danforth Academy, a cutting-edge school in the all-female province of Bellator. But when tragedy strikes a fellow student, she suspects there is a darker side to the prestigious institution. Determined to protect herself and her friends, she goes looking for answers.

Her investigation brings her face-to-face with Noah, a boy from Eremus: a community the Bellator authorities claim they destroyed years ago.

Faith has been taught that all men are monsters. She knows she should turn Noah in. But she is drawn to the intriguing stranger and his unfamiliar way of life. As she learns more about him, she begins to question everything she's ever known.

When a vicious attack involving both communities rocks the city, Faith finds herself at the centre of a web of lies.

Can she count on Noah for help? Or will he turn out to be the monster she's always feared?

Read Compliance for intense drama, gripping action, and a pair of star-crossed lovers you'll be rooting for long after lights out. Perfect for fans of The Selection, Noughts and Crosses and The Handmaid's Tale.

Book 2: Dependence (coming May 2022)

Book 3: Defiance (coming September 2022)

Author's Note

Thank you for reading *Quell*. I hope that you enjoyed reading the conclusion to Quin's journey. I love building relationships with my readers. If you enjoyed *The Flow Series* and want to hear about my next series, sign up for my readers' club:

Clare Littlemore Reader's Club

If you do, you'll receive a regular newsletter with giveaways, book recommendations, special offers, the occasional free short story, and (of course) details of all my new releases. I promise there will be no spam. ***I hate spam.***

And while you're here...

You can make a **big** difference. Being an indie author, it can be difficult to get my books noticed. And reviews are really powerful. If you liked reading *Quell*, please consider spending a couple of minutes leaving an **honest review** (it can be as brief as you like) on the book's Amazon page, on Goodreads, or similar. It genuinely doesn't have to be long - often just a single sentence is enough to convince someone to give a new author or series a try. I'd be eternally grateful.

Thank you *very* much.

About the Author

Clare Littlemore is a young adult dystopian and sci-fi author who thrives on fictionally destroying the world with a cup of tea by her side. The tea will often be cold, because her characters have a way of grabbing hold of her and not letting go until the final page of their story is finished. They regularly have the same effect on her readers. Clare lives in the North West of England with her husband and two children.

Come say hello:

- on Twitter at twitter.com/Clarelittlemore
- on Facebook at facebook.com/clarelittlemoreauthor
- Instagram: https://www.instagram.com/clarelittlemore
- in the Last Book Cafe on Earth Facebook group: https://www.facebook.com/groups/lastbookcafeonearth/
- or send her an email at clare@clarelittlemore.com

Acknowledgements

I can't tell you how amazing it feels to be writing an acknowledgements page for the fourth and final book in The Flow Series. It means that I have created and completed an entire series: a dream which would have seemed impossible a few years ago. But I would never have reached this point without the support of a number of people.

Firstly, Beth Dorward, my editor, who is always prepared to have 'another look' at the manuscript, providing extremely useful feedback which has proved invaluable in shaping The Flow Series finale. Similarly, my cover designer, Jessica Bell, managed to create just the right kind of mood with Quell's cover, its hopeful yellow tones suggesting that maybe, just maybe, Quin might get the ending she deserves.

My lovely team of beta readers have been amazing. Alison, Annabel, Freya, Lyn and Maria all took the time to read an early version of Quell and give detailed, supportive feedback. This allowed me to see the places where the book was well written and compelling, and places where it... well... wasn't. I hope the changes I made during the editing process did your comments justice, and that you're happy with the finished result.

Always supportive, Mum, Dad and Linda read my manuscript at various different stages (some of them more than once!) and can always be relied upon to provide kind and encouraging words about my writing. Another committed supporter is Lucy, a very good friend who is often the first person to see my stories, just a few chapters at a time. She points out early errors in my continuity and grammar which help to strengthen my work, and I hugely appreciate her support.

Last but not least: my family. My husband Marc never fails to encourage and support me, providing a cup of tea and a hot meal after a hard day's writing, offering to pick up the children to save me a job, or simply telling me I can do it on the days I don't believe I can. And I mustn't forget my children, Daniel and Amy, to whom this book is dedicated. Now they're a little older, they're proud to tell people that their mum's a writer, and I hope that my books encourage them to be brave and dream big.

Finally, to you: my readers. Whether you've been with me since the beginning, or only found The Flow Series recently, I hope you feel that Quell concludes Quin's journey in a fitting way, and that you will continue to read my books in the future. Thank you.

CPSIA information can be obtained
at www.ICGtesting.com
Printed in the USA
LVHW040737070423
743689LV00024B/464